Take me Home

Hearts of the Children
Volume 1: The Writing on the Wall
Volume 2: Troubled Waters
Volume 3: How Many Roads?
Volume 4: Take Me Home

TAKE ME HOME

A NOVEL BY

DEAN HUGHES

BOOKCRAFT
SALT LAKE CITY, UTAH

Visit us at deseretbook.com

Library of Congress Cataloging-in-Publication Data

Hughes, Dean, 1943-
Take me home / Dean Hughes.
p. cm. — (Hearts of the children ; v. 4)
ISBN 1-59038-332-X (alk. paper)
1. Mormon families—Fiction. 2. Salt Lake City (Utah)— Fiction.
I. Title. II. Series.
PS3558.U36T35 2004
813'.54—dc22
2004008727

Printed in the United States of America 54459
Malloy Lithographing Inc., Ann Arbor, MI

10 9 8 7 6 5 4 3 2 1

For Sheri Dew

D. Alexander and Beatrice (Bea) Thomas Family (1968)

Alexander (Alex) [b. 1916] [m. Anna Stoltz, 1944]
  Eugene (Gene) [b. 1945] [m. Emily Osborne, 1968]
  Joseph (Joey) [b. 1947]
  Sharon [b. 1949]
  Kurt [b. 1951]
  Kenneth (Kenny) [b. 1956]
  Pamela (Pammy) [b. 1958]

Barbara (Bobbi) [b. 1919] [m. Richard Hammond, 1946]
  Diane [b. 1948] [m. Greg Lyman, 1968]
  Margaret (Maggie) [b. 1953]
  Richard, Jr. (Ricky) [b. 1963]

Walter (Wally) [b. 1921] [m. Lorraine Gardner, 1946]
  Kathleen (Kathy) [b. 1946]
  Wayne [b. 1948]
  Douglas [b. 1951]
  Glenda [b. 1955]
  Shauna [b. 1959]

Eugene (Gene) [1925–1944]

LaRue [b. 1929]

Beverly [b. 1931] [m. Roger Larsen, 1953]
  Victoria (Vickie) [b. 1954]
  Julia [b. 1955]
  Alexander (Zan) [b. 1957]
  Suzanne [b. 1959]
  Beatrice [b. 1966]

Chapter 1

Gene Thomas was waiting and watching, concealed in dense undergrowth. He was part of a reconnaissance patrol made up of only five men, led by Staff Sergeant "Pop" Winston. For four hours now the soldiers had been observing a wide "high-speed" trail under a triple canopy of mahogany and teak trees. There was plenty of "sign" on the trail—fresh footprints made by Ho Chi Minh sandals—to indicate recent troop movement. Gene's team, called Spartan, was assigned to locate and report the position of a North Vietnamese Army unit, thought to be at least company-sized.

It was December 1969, but not a December like any Gene had experienced. The heat had been rising all morning, the air like steam from a boiling pot of soup. It was the monsoon season now, and rains came often, but that didn't cool the air much, and the humidity was worse than usual, if that was possible. Gene's fatigues were already soaked through, and drops of sweat were trickling down his sides. But the mosquitoes bothered him more than the heat. In such thick vegetation, insects didn't wait for night. That morning, when Gene had repainted his face with green and black camouflage, he had also applied repellent, but the mosquitoes were swarming around him anyway, the whining sound incessant. He had wanted to replenish the repellent, but Sergeant Winston had shaken his head no, and Gene knew why. He had been told by the men on his team that North Vietnamese soldiers had a nose for the smelly stuff. Gene was wearing gloves with the fingers cut out. He wrapped his fingers into fists to cover the exposed skin, hunched his neck into his cammo fatigues, and pulled his boonie hat down as far as he could, but mosquitoes found their way to his face and ears, even up his nose. The worst was not being able to slap at them, though he tried to rub his cheeks against his shoulder or to duck his forehead against his knees from time to time. What he couldn't do was move fast or make a noise and attract the attention of some sniper or NVA recon man who might be searching for the Americans after hearing the helicopter that had inserted them the night before.

Gene had been in Vietnam almost a month now. He remembered when he had thought he would be overjoyed to have those first thirty days behind him. But the month had ticked by one slow second at a time, and the tedious passage of those days only told him how excruciatingly slow eleven more months would be. After his first reconnaissance mission, he had told himself that he couldn't return to the terror, that he needed to transfer to a regular unit. The trouble was, most combat soldiers in Vietnam were facing these same jungles and the same fear, and so long as he stayed with a Ranger unit, he knew he was surrounded by the very best of fighting men. His company had been called "Lurps" at one time, a nickname derived from LRRP, or Long Range Reconnaissance Patrol. The unit had served under the command of the army's 101st Airborne Division, but only shortly before Gene's arrival in Vietnam, it had been transferred to the Rangers, a Special Forces unit with a reputation of being among the best trained of American forces.

Gene didn't think of himself as "bad," the way a lot of recon guys did. He would never go native, as some of the soldiers called it, would never take on the cocky manner of some of the "born to kill" types. All he wanted was to survive this place and get home to his wife and son. Still, there were times when he felt some of that Lurp mentality rubbing off on him. He rather liked the way other soldiers looked at him when he walked into the Enlisted Men's Club. They knew not to mess with him—or at least they did if he stayed with Melnick and Kovach and some of the other Rangers.

At the moment, however, he felt none of that. He knew he had some spooky times ahead—three days, if the schedule held, of little sleep and ceaseless fear. What he hoped was that his team could avoid contact, only observe the enemy and call in a report—and then get out. And he hoped that could happen before the day was over. Then he would have a few days before the next order came, and one nice thing about a reconnaissance assignment was that there were few, if any, duties expected of the men between missions. Lurps didn't pull KP, and rarely did they receive guard duty. After their days of intense strain, the relief came, the reward: a man knew he could relax for a few days. It was true that Camp Eagle took some fire from time to time, but it was usually only from distant artillery that did little damage and seemed nothing more than fireworks compared to the close encounters out in the bush.

When noon came the men didn't eat. It was common for them to eat only twice a day—and then to mix canteen water with their freeze-dried Lurp rations. This was to avoid cooking, since a fire would give away their position. But Gene was now glancing at Pop from time to time and wondering whether the team would sit by this trail all day. He had actually started the day hoping that would happen, since he hadn't been eager to hike the jungle and face the danger of an ambush. But his back was aching now, and the mosquitoes were making him crazy. He wanted to move, to do anything other than sit in this same awkward position.

There had been no indication of troop movement all day; it seemed unlikely that the enemy was nearby. But Pop knew what he was doing. He was on his second tour in 'Nam and had been wounded twice. He knew the backcountry as well as anyone. On Gene's first mission, Sergeant Caruthers had been the team leader, but he had tried to defend his men as they were running for an extraction helicopter. Caruthers had taken a bullet in the chest. Gene had carried him to the dust-off helicopter, and Caruthers had been flown to a hospital. Word had come back that he was alive, but no one knew much more than that. So far, since then, no one had been added to the team. Recruits were getting hard to come by. The war was supposed to be winding down, with troops being sent home and the number of Americans in the country dropping. Very few new men wanted to take on hazardous duty for the cause of a war that seemed already conceded to the North Vietnamese.

On this mission big Rick Kovach was walking point and serving as assistant team leader. Phil "Ears" Dearden was following him—walking "slack" for the point man—and Giles Melnick was carrying a backup radio, walking third. Gene operated the primary radio and walked fourth, with Pop handling rear security. Or at least that was the order, if they ever moved out.

By the middle of the afternoon Gene was struggling to stay awake. He hadn't slept at all the night before, and now the mosquitoes were finally leaving him alone as the sun penetrated the jungle. It was hard to sit and watch when nothing happened and the only sound was the occasional call of a few birds or some chattering monkeys. At night the jungle was sometimes wild with noise, but this time of day, even the bugs seemed to sleep. What Gene hoped was that rain wouldn't come. Monsoons could hit with fury, but more common were afternoon deluges that would strike with little warning and drench the men so they couldn't dry out before night—and the nights could be cold. Right now, though, a drenching rain seemed welcome.

Gene realized he had been hearing a noise for a time before it registered in his mind, but when it did register, he was suddenly fully alert. Something was moving, maybe on the trail. It was a subtle sound. There was no footfall in the damp earth; there was only the quiet swish, perhaps of legs moving, fabric rubbing, and now and then a click, maybe the sound of a canteen on a belt. Gene looked toward Pop, who glanced back at Gene and nodded. Gene checked Melnick, who was sitting about fifteen feet away to Gene's right. Melnick looked like a man who had lost a fight—with a beaten-down nose. His expression rarely changed. But he looked toward Gene now, his eyes alive for the first time all day. He had heard it too.

The surge inside Gene was familiar now, but he hated the feeling. His heart was suddenly pumping, the sound rushing in his ears, and he felt his throat constrict, his shoulders hunch. He wasn't more than ten or twelve feet off the trail, and he always wondered how effective his camouflage was. The sound was clearly coming closer. In another minute or so the enemy would be walking past, seemingly close enough to touch.

Gene felt as though his breathing was too hard, rasping, announcing his presence, so he tried to take shallow, panting breaths. It was something Pop had taught him, but it seemed instinctive, too, like the way his muscles were preparing to leap and run. He had thought a lot about bravery after his first couple of missions, and he had told himself that he needed to learn to deal with the tension out here in the jungle, but nothing he could say to himself made a difference. He wanted to duck down, hide his face, or crawl off deeper into the cover, but his best protection was to hold perfectly still.

He moved his eyes, not his head, as he watched the trail to his left, and maybe two minutes passed before he saw the first movement in the shadows of the trail. Gradually he could see a small man, dressed in the tan uniform of the regular North Vietnamese Army, not the black pajamas of the Viet Cong. He was carrying an AK-47 over his shoulder, and he was walking briskly, clearly not worried that anyone might be observing him. He tramped on by, his sandals making little sucking noises with each step. He glanced toward Gene as he walked by, and Gene didn't so much as blink his eyes. It seemed impossible that the soldier didn't see him, shadowed and camouflaged or not, but the man kept going, and Gene thought he heard a humming noise, as though the soldier were making a little music for himself as he walked. It was a surprisingly human thing to do. "Charlie" had always lurked in the jungle and sniped or set booby traps, and had seemed almost monstrous to Gene, but this was just a young man, much younger than Gene, and he seemed to be strolling along—what the men called "half-stepping"—rather satisfied and unconcerned. He was a kid, really, like the guys Gene had gone to high school with.

Gene let his eyes follow the figure until it was out of range, and then his eyes switched back to the left. He had expected others to follow, but the sound of the young soldier was fading and no one else seemed to be coming.

Pop snapped his fingers, softly. When Gene looked, Pop was pointing to the trail, nodding. He wanted the men to follow the soldier. The signal went from man to man, and all five pulled on their rucksacks and moved carefully onto the trail. But out on the trail, Pop held up his hand to stop Kovach.

Then Pop held his fist to his ear, and Gene knew to get the relay team on the radio. The relay man would pass information on to the Tactical Operations Center, back at camp. Once Gene had "commo," he passed the handset over to Pop, who whispered, "We're following a gook to his camp. We may need gunships."

Pop got his reply, then pointed forward. Kovach moved out. The others allowed some space but followed. Gene knew the goal wasn't to keep the North Vietnamese soldier in view; it was only to track his footprints while they remained fresh.

Kovach moved slowly, and he stopped often to listen and watch. The NVA knew how to set up ambushes. It seemed unlikely that a single soldier would walk along as a decoy to lead the team into a trap, but Gene wasn't sure. He only knew that Pop understood these situations, and Melnick did too. The idea was to let the soldier lead them to his unit, but the approach had to be flawless. The men couldn't make as much noise as the young soldier had. His company probably wasn't very close, since the recon team had heard nothing in the area, but still, they couldn't just bumble into a camp somewhere. They had to move like jungle animals:

hunting, sniffing, watching. The only difference was, once the prey was found, the idea was to pull back and call in Cobra gunships—or even F-4 fighters in certain cases—to make the kill.

That was the theory. But Gene felt as though he were walking into the maw of the beast. Every step was taking him closer to a fighting unit with AK-47s and ChiComs—Chinese Communist grenades. And these NVA units posted sentries outside their camps, the same as Americans did. If Kovach took one more step than he should, the team could bring hellfire down upon themselves.

For over an hour the men kept going, always slowly, stopping often, but moving up the valley under the eerie, green light of triple-canopy jungle. The weight of Gene's radio seemed to increase with time, but his cotton-mouth fear took his attention away from other concerns. There was hardly a sound under the trees, as even the birds held still with these five dark figures creeping into their territory. The men on Gene's team had shown him how to tape the links and buckles on his equipment to stop any rattles. They had taught him to "place" his foot, not drop it to the ground; to breathe smoothly, to say nothing. All communication was done with hand signals.

Gene didn't look far ahead but watched each step and then scanned the area around him in quick glances. He felt as much as saw Melnick stop at times, and then he stood still and listened. But there was a timing to all this, and on one of those stops, just when Gene sensed that it was time to move on, he noticed that Kovach, up ahead, had cupped his hand around his ear. Kovach listened longer than usual, and then Gene saw "Ears" step closer to him and tap him on the shoulder. Gene couldn't read their nods or gestures, but clearly they were conferring. Gene glanced back at Pop, who nodded confidently, as if to say, "They know what they're doing; just wait."

Kovach finally moved ahead, but this time he walked only a few careful paces before listening again. For another quarter of an hour they inched ahead this way, and by then, Gene was fighting his instincts. His muscles were tense, prepared; he wanted to bust out and run for all he was worth. He had heard sounds by then, too. He had heard voices a couple of times, and he thought he detected the smell of cook fires. What more did Kovach want? Why couldn't they retreat now and call in the wrath of gunships? Gene found himself allowing a little more space to stretch between him and Melnick, until Pop finally stepped forward and signaled for him to close the gap.

Gene knew what Pop would say if he complained about drawing too close to the enemy. Sounds were tricky, and if Pop called in an attack that wasn't dead-on accurate, the team would not only miss the chance to knock out this NVA unit; it could also bring down the enemy upon itself. When gunships suddenly attacked, the North Vietnamese understood what had happened. Lurps were in the area, locating them for air attack. If the attack wasn't effective, the hunt for the recon team would begin instantly.

So Kovach kept working his way forward, but the light was beginning to angle as the afternoon was getting away. The last thing Gene wanted was to pull up and make a night halt, this close to Charlie.

Then Kovach spun around. He pointed across his body to the jungle on the right. It was the signal to take cover. Gene's impulse was to leap into the brush, crash into the shadows and throw himself onto his face, but he knew better. He had practiced this move. He moved quickly but carefully, stepped into the shadows and then ducked down. He felt safer for a moment. The only trouble was, now he could see no one from his team, and he had no idea what to expect. But he knew one thing—knew it without thinking about it. If NVA soldiers were coming down the trail, they would see the team's tracks. Pop had taken an enormous gamble sending his men along the trail this way. Clearly, he had hoped to get close, quickly, and then fall back. But now the team was in trouble.

Gene waited. He breathed. He hardly realized that he was praying.

Maybe the words had never stopped going through his head: "Help us, Lord. Help us."

A minute went by. Two. What was the plan? Gene had no idea what he should do in a situation like this. His team was spread out, not ready to fight together, and there was no way to pull into a tight perimeter without making noise.

Automatic rifle fire suddenly crackled up ahead. Gene heard a shout, couldn't think what to do, and then heard Kovach. "Fall back," he was saying, his voice quiet but intense. Gene jumped from the cover and glanced up the trail. There were two men down on their faces, both in those tan uniforms. Gene saw blood, and he saw Melnick and Dearden and Kovach all coming toward him, running. He turned to run and bumped into Pop, who said, with amazing calmness, "Report the contact. Tell 'em I'm popping smoke where it happened. Call in the Cobras."

By then, all the men were together. Pop stepped in front and threw a smoke grenade up the trail. It popped, and a plume of purple smoke began to rise. As soon as Gene reached the relay operator and made his situation report, Pop said, "All right. Let's go. We've got to break contact."

And so Pop ran, and Gene ran right behind him, but there was no panic in Pop's pace. He was under control. Gene gradually accepted the cadence, but he wanted to run faster. He felt the weight of the radio, but he didn't care. He wanted to get as far from that NVA camp as he could. Still, he felt the confidence around him, heard how the men were running in a rhythm, their feet seeming to strike the earth in unison. He fell into the beat, ran hard but steady, feeling more assured as they moved in sync and put some distance between them and the enemy.

They covered maybe two hundred meters, Gene thought, and then Pop stopped. "Call the relay team again," he said softly.

Gene made the call while Pop studied his map. Once he had the relay man, Gene handed the handset to Pop. He gave his map coordinates and then said, "We'll pop smoke again at our present position. We've got a gook camp maybe fifty meters west of that first smoke, and gooks on the trail."

Pop pointed off the trail, and this time the team moved deeper into the brush than before, then hunkered down together. Gene felt the time stretch, wondered why he wasn't hearing choppers, and yet he knew that not more than five minutes had passed. He wished the team could call in artillery and get it going immediately, but this valley was too deep into the jungle. There was no artillery that could reach it.

Gene was expecting an enemy patrol at any second, moving down the trail, searching. He finally heard the big Cobras racing in, their rotors thumping the air. Pop heard them too, and he tossed a yellow smoke grenade out onto the trail. In a moment, a pilot called, confirming the color of the smoke. When the barrage of fire opened up, it was brutal. It began with mini-gun fire, starting close and then moving up the trail. Then rockets smashed through the jungle and pounded the earth, and the mini-gun fire continued in a deluge so constant that it was a roar, a waterfall of bullets, the red tracers lighting the sky.

Gene could hear the talk on the radio. "The gooks are heading up the mountain," a Cobra pilot was yelling. "We're ripping them up."

Pop's team was collected around Gene and the radio. They didn't cheer, not out loud, but they whispered, "Yes, yes."

"Get some, get some," Melnick was saying, hissing like Satan.

Gene felt the same emotion. *Get 'em. Get 'em all.* He was letting himself breathe now, finally drawing in the air his lungs had been needing.

The fire continued for maybe twenty minutes, gradually becoming sporadic. And then the chopper pilots announced they were moving out. Captain Battaglia was immediately on the radio from the LOH—an observation helicopter. He had apparently taken off after hearing that Spartan had contact. "Get your team in there, Spartan One," he said. "Get me a body count and take out any stragglers. Grab a prisoner, if you can."

"That's dangerous," Pop answered. "We could—"

"No. Get in there, Spartan One. We need to know what's going on while we have them on the run. If a lot of 'em got out, we need to know it."

"Roger that. Spartan, out." Pop looked around at the others. Gene knew that Pop hated the idea of putting his men in danger, just to get a body count. But Gene also knew how much Pop respected Battaglia, who always put his men first. There were some things that just had to be done. To get a solid count, the men needed to get to the camp quickly. But of course, that could give Charlie a chance to come up with a body count of his own.

"Let's go," Pop said. "Let's get in there, get a count, and then get ourselves extracted. If we don't get out tonight, they're going to be back looking for us."

So this time the men moved carefully but much faster. And they found the site where the jungle had been torn to pieces. The camp was there—shelters and fire pits and random equipment—but there were surprisingly few bodies. A quick look around produced only four.

"There have to be some more bodies up on the hillside, where the gunships chased them," Kovach said. "But it's crazy to go up there."

"Check for blood trails," Pop said. "But don't follow them far. We'll give the brass a good number, but we're not going to get wasted doing it." He was walking by the other men toward the upper side of the camp, where the soldiers had obviously run into the trees. He pointed off to his right and said, "Okay, we've got blood right there. Melnick and Thomas, follow it, but be careful, and if it runs more than thirty or forty meters, let it go."

Melnick walked ahead, watching for the blood. It was not a difficult trail. The vegetation was pressed almost flat, and the blood had obviously been flowing fast. Melnick had moved only fifteen meters or so into the tree line, with Gene behind him, when he stopped. Gene stepped up next to him and saw the body lying face down. It wasn't moving. Melnick stepped closer and kicked at the man's feet, and then he stepped around the soldier, with his rifle ready. He kicked the body in the side this time, waited, then finally reached down and rolled the man over.

Gene had seen the exit wound in the man's back, bigger than a fist. His uniform was ripped open and soaked with a dark blood stain. But as the body dropped onto its back, there was little sign of damage. Just two little holes. Gene felt nothing, didn't think much about what he was looking at, until he looked at the man's face. He wasn't a man, really. He was a boy—younger than the one Gene had seen on the trail. He might have been sixteen, but in truth, he didn't look more than thirteen or fourteen. His eyelids were slightly open, but his face was serene, like a sleeping baby.

Gene glanced away. He knew he couldn't make too much of this. This is what soldiers did. They killed the enemy. He had been telling himself that since basic training. He would see bodies, sooner or later; he would just have to accept that.

"Check his pockets," Melnick said.

"What?"

"Check for papers, maps—anything."

"He's just a—"

"That's what we do, Thomas. Check his pockets."

Gene knelt next to the boy, but that brought the face closer. He could smell the smoke from cook fires on the boy's uniform. But it was a new uniform; the boy had come down the Ho Chi Minh trail recently. He was a replacement, or maybe his whole unit was new. The uniforms at the camp had looked in good shape, too. Gene patted the boy's outside pockets, located nothing, and began to stand up.

"Try the inside pockets. That's where they keep things."

Gene hesitated, but then he slid his hand inside the boy's uniform, felt the warmth of his chest, just above the place where the bullets had emptied out his soul. Gene's fingers touched something inside the pocket, so he grabbed it and pulled it out. It was a kind of pouch, maybe a billfold. He handed it to Melnick and then tried the other inside pocket, which was empty. "Okay, let's go," Gene said to Melnick.

"Look at this."

Gene stood up. He looked at what Melnick was holding out: a black and white photograph, a picture of a pretty young woman holding a baby—a little boy, Gene thought, maybe six or eight months old. "This must be his sister," Gene said. "He's not old enough to be married."

"Naw. He's older than you think. And they get married young." Melnick laughed. "I hope she's got something going on the side. This little gook ain't going to be jumping back into her sack."

Gene started walking, fast. Melnick didn't have to say a thing like that. He remembered what he had been thinking when the gunfire had started. *Get 'em. Get 'em all.* But he hadn't known the men in the gunships were shooting boys.

Melnick caught up, back at the camp. "Hey, don't let it bother you," he whispered. "At first you think about it a little, but after that you just say, 'Better him than me.'"

Gene didn't say anything. He was tired. He wanted to get away from this camp. What he didn't know was that he was about to vomit. It happened before he could do anything more than spin to one side. And then it happened again in another gush. After that he remained bent, with his hands on his knees, and he spit on the ground, over and over.

Kovach was walking back by then. Melnick told him, "We found us a wasted gook. But I don't think Thomas enjoyed the experience. Look what he did."

Kovach laughed. "Hey, don't worry about it, Thomas," he said. "We've all coughed up a few cookies in our time. You won't do it next time."

Gene didn't say anything. He was embarrassed, but he was angry about their laughter. There was nothing funny about the experience.

Dearden and Pop had come out of the trees by then. "Thomas, call in a sitrep," Pop whispered. "Did you guys verify that kill?"

"Yeah, Sarge," Melnick said.

"Call in nine kills," Pop told Gene. "That ought to be enough to keep the big boys happy."

Gene didn't know where the number nine had come from. He had seen only four here at the camp, and the one on the trail, but he wasn't about to question the number. He swallowed hard, and then he grabbed the handset and called in the situation report. He told the CO that the team had nine confirmed kills.

Pop took the handset then and said, "Spartan One here. Request an extraction. There's a clearing at the camp. Get a slick on the way, and we'll pop smoke to bring him in." Gene thought the words sounded more like a command than a request, but Gene had seen it before. Captain Battaglia let Sergeant Winston make most of the decisions on the ground.

Pop gave the handset back to Gene. "There's a slick on its way," he said. "The captain liked the nine kills."

To Gene nine seemed a strangely inadequate number, given all the ordnance that had been fired. But Gene was still trying to get used to the idea that he had been involved in killing *people*. He had always known that, of course, or thought he had. But he had never seen the bodies up close.

Melnick passed the picture around. Dearden and Kovach took a look at it, but when it came to Pop, he closed the wallet without looking at the picture, then stuck it into his pocket. Dearden was watching Gene by then. He stepped closer and stood in front of him. "Look, Thomas, you don't have to worry about what we done here," he whispered in his heavy southern accent. "These gooks infiltrated this country, and it's our job to kill 'em. It ain't our fault someone gave us that job."

"I know, but—"

"Just let go of it." Dearden had a way of bobbing his head as he talked, his big ears seeming to wave with the motion. "It's not our job to think. We just do what we gotta do."

"Okay."

Kovach spat on the ground, and then he cursed in a whisper. "I don't bat an eye when I look at 'em anymore. It was gooks just like these ones that wasted a lot of my good friends. And don't think they cry for any of us." He swore again, used the army word for everything. "Just forget all that stuff. Like Dearden said, it ain't our job to think."

But Gene did think. He thought about the ears cut off enemy soldiers that some Americans collected from Vietnamese bodies and hung around their necks. He hadn't seen that, but he had heard about it. But he didn't argue. He just felt the evil of it all.

"To me, they're not humans the same way we are," Melnick whispered. "They sneak around like snakes or lizards or something, and they kill just to kill. I don't think they're Communists. They don't believe nothing. They just want to fight the big white boys and kill 'em. Makes 'em feel like they ain't four feet high—and smelly little rodents."

"Shut up, Melnick." Pop stepped up close to Kovach. "The North Vietnamese are as brave as any soldier you'll ever fight. If we didn't have our air power, they could take us on, toe to toe, and we'd have all we could handle." He cursed. "Don't give me any more of your 'big white boy' talk either. Or this little black man will tear your throat out."

"Hey, I was just—"

"I know what you were doing. Don't start it again. Thomas is doing what he has to do, but it doesn't bother me one bit if he doesn't like it. What scares me is any man who does. Now come on, let's secure the landing zone before the slick gets here."

Melnick was a foot taller than Pop and twice as thick. But he looked like a boy facing his principal, his eyes cast down. "Sure. All right."

Ten minutes later a slick was descending, and before it touched the ground all five men were on board and it was veering off and away. Some rifle fire from the ground proved that plenty of NVA were still alive out there, but the helicopter got out quickly, and Gene was relieved to be heading back to camp. He had gotten his wish. They were out in a day.

He leaned back, letting the vibration and noise of the chopper fill his head. He didn't want to think anymore—Dearden was right about that. This was war. This was exactly what he should have expected. His father had told him he would never really understand war until he was in the middle of the fight, but Gene had figured he *did* understand. War, obviously, was about killing and being killed. But those had just been words, sounds in his mouth that had never really made it to his brain or his body. Reality was that boy down there—the pulp that had been left after his spirit had been torn away by a couple of bullets.

Reality was also that young woman—sister or wife—and the little boy up in the north somewhere. Gene didn't want to think of Emily, or Danny, but he had been thinking of them in flashes ever since he had seen the picture. He wondered what that Vietnamese boy would have done had he reached into Gene's pocket and found a similar picture. Emily was real, and she cared about him. Would the young soldier have accepted that, or would he have talked like Melnick? Gene didn't know. He only knew that a young man, a real one, was dead, and maybe a young woman was a widow; a child, fatherless.

Gene had begun to shake. He was glad for the vibration in the helicopter, glad that no one could see he was upset. But he felt as though he were going to shake apart. He and America had killed a young man, and he couldn't remember what the reason was. He tried to think, tried to remember what he had believed at home, how he had explained the war, but nothing came—not a single thought that explained why he was here and what he was doing. He wondered what God thought of all this—what he thought of war.

But Dearden grasped Gene's arm—hard—until Gene looked at him. Then he yelled into his face, above the roar of the helicopter, "You gotta stop it, Gene. I told you—just don't think."

Gene nodded. He knew Dearden was right.

Chapter 2

Kathy Thomas had been assured by the mayor, José Dias, that the barrio council meeting would start promptly at seven o'clock. But it was almost seven-thirty now, and the mayor had only just arrived. Four other men had come in ahead of him, but Kathy wasn't sure whether they were members of the council. They hadn't sat up front even though there were chairs that seemed arranged for that purpose. But if they weren't members, maybe no one from the council was there. As far as that went, Mayor Dias had told Kathy earlier that he couldn't remember how many members were on the council. How would he know when he had a quorum? It was all very confusing and, to Kathy, frustrating. There were things that needed to be done, problems that could easily be solved, but how could the Peace Corps teach the people anything if the barrio leaders couldn't get themselves organized? Her Peace Corps director kept telling her to work through the local government, not to supersede established authorities, but that was like asking to let the inmates run the asylum. The mayor was a dear man, in his way, but he had no idea how to get anything done.

"Just stay calm," Martha Sommers, Kathy's roommate, kept saying. Kathy and Martha were sitting on the back row in a little room upstairs in a *sari-sari* store—one of the crowded little general markets in town. There were several rows of wooden folding chairs crammed in, wall to wall, and Kathy had wanted to sit in front, but Martha kept advising her not to come on too strong, to be patient and wait her turn, and then only to make suggestions, not to seem demanding or superior. Kathy understood every word of that. She knew how she appeared to people sometimes—as some sort of know-it-all—but changes were badly needed in San Juan, the little barrio where she and Martha were working, and the local people hardly seemed to notice.

Kathy had lived in the barrio all fall, and it would soon be Christmas. She had come to the Philippines dedicated to the idea that she could make a difference, but she had been assigned as a teacher's aide at a high school, and though she had worked very hard at the job, she could never get over the idea that if she were suddenly to pack her bags and go home, few people would even notice. She taught two classes herself and supported a teacher, Mrs. Sanchez, the other hours, but even in her own classes, Mrs. Sanchez supervised, and the students often turned to her rather than Kathy for their answers. Kathy's ability with Tagalog had improved—the students were understanding her better all the time—but even that was frustrating. The classes were supposed to be taught in English, and yet the students' command of English was really not adequate to understand the kinds of concepts that excited Kathy. All discussion seemed limited by the filter the language created, and when she made an effort in Tagalog, however improved she was, she hardly felt that she was reaching more than the surface of what she wanted to say.

The only encouraging thing was that Kathy had seemed to break through personally to most of the students. She could tell they liked her, and she liked them—but then, that was part of what frustrated her. She wanted things to get better for these young people. They all came from little barrios in the area, and they all lived in similar conditions. There were things in their towns that had to be changed at a fundamental level or Filipinos would never make much progress. It was that idea that had been pushing her lately. She could do some teaching, and she would have some nice memories of the students, but what she feared more than anything was that she would leave the Philippines after two years and her presence there would have meant nothing. If she couldn't push through some basic changes, she saw no reason for her government to have sent her. And that's why she was sitting in this humid little room tonight. She had to take her first steps. Dear Martha, sweet girl that she was, was cursed with too much patience—or plain passivity. There were times when a person had to pressure a little or change never would occur.

Gradually, more people were arriving—all men—and some even sat in the circle of chairs up front. When the mayor finally started the meeting, Kathy checked her watch. It was 7:48, almost an hour late. That was the kind of thing the Filipinos needed to learn—to operate on more of a schedule. Martha kept telling Kathy that Filipinos weren't as uptight as Americans about time, and Martha actually found that rather pleasant. Kathy tried to accept the idea, but it seemed part of the overall problem in the barrio. People said things to be pleasant, or to satisfy one another, but no one ever seemed to take a promise very seriously. To Kathy, "We'll start at seven" was a promise. Things could change only when people began to mean what they said.

"Do you think he put my item on the agenda?" Kathy whispered to Martha.

Martha smiled. "I've never seen anything I'd call an agenda at these meetings," she said. "But he sees you sitting back here. He knows you want to say something."

"If he doesn't call on me, should I—"

"Just wait, Kathy. And don't push them. If you do, you're dead before you start."

Kathy had heard that advice all day—all week. In fact, she had practically heard nothing else since she had arrived in San Juan. Maybe Martha was right to warn her, but Kathy also knew that Martha's attitude was part of why Peace Corps volunteers sat around and talked about their failure to make a difference in the Philippines. Here was all this American know-how, and volunteers were failing to teach it to the people out of fear of overstepping some sort of cultural barrier. The problem was, some things about the culture were the heart of the problem. If those things couldn't change, life would never get better for the people.

But Kathy kept still. Mayor Dias spoke in Tagalog, and Kathy wasn't getting all of what he said, but he was using lofty language, and more than anything, praising all the men of the council and extolling the greatness of the Filipino people. It was pretty to listen to, but there seemed no real point to it all. He continually repeated certain phrases, then doubled back and started all over. "What's this all about?" Kathy finally asked Martha.

"He says things like this every time," Martha said. "It's like a political speech."

"State of the Union address?"

Martha laughed, softly. "Yeah. Something like that."

After a while there seemed to be no air in the room, and men kept coming in. There were now nine up front, besides the mayor. Body heat was pushing the temperature higher all the time, and the odor was rising, too. At least Mayor Dias finally introduced a discussion about a complaint he had received. People who lived near a little bar in town were concerned that men sat outside too late at night, drinking beer and tuba—a beverage made from coconut milk. They made too much noise, and there had been some fistfights. Something had to be done—or so said Mayor Dias. But the discussion went on and on, with everyone having something to say but no one offering a solution. Kathy had the impression that some of the men in the room frequented the bar and didn't want to see it forced into an earlier closing. The discussion gradually wandered away from the bar itself and touched on drunkenness and a sermon a priest had given on the subject, and beyond that, if Kathy understood correctly, the idea that certain celebrations made drinking, even drunkenness, acceptable at times—with weeknight drunkenness remaining disgraceful.

Kathy wanted to scream. Was this only the first agenda item? Were there lots of other things to talk about? How late would the meeting go?

But suddenly the mayor was saying that the group was honored to have two good friends with them—young teachers from America, members of the Peace Corps. He wanted to be certain that they had a chance to speak before the meeting went on any longer. She loved the kindness in his voice, but there was also something condescending in his manner, as though he were saying, "Let's tolerate these *girls*. Let's allow them to say something and get it over with." Kathy couldn't help wondering why no motion had been offered or whether someone at least needed to table the discussion about the bar before they moved to her item. But she found herself walking to the front of the group, suddenly aware, as she often was in this society, that she was by far the tallest person in the room. With the men all sitting, they seemed to be gaping up at her like children. She was not new to the barrio now; everyone knew her. But she still felt like a circus sideshow "giant lady" when she stood before these men, who were all smiling. Maybe they were being pleasant and accepting, but it was hard not to feel that they were laughing a little, just to see such a curiosity.

Kathy didn't know what to do with her hands. She finally gripped them together at her waist. The heat of the room was worse now that she was standing up, and she felt a trickle of sweat descend along her ear. She was cutting her hair short these days, because of the humidity and heat, but she felt her bangs sticking to her forehead and she brushed through the hair with her fingers. "I will speak in English," she said. "I believe you will all understand me. My Tagalog is not very good."

They all nodded, still smiling. Mayor Dias, who had taken a seat behind Kathy, said, "Yes, yes. We understand bery good."

But most of the men spoke a kind of pidgin English, at best. She had often realized that when she said anything beyond basic pleasantries, people sometimes pretended to understand when they didn't. She had thought all day how she could make her point simply. "The Peace Corps comes to the Philippines to learn. We want to understand the good things here, and take those ideas back to America." The men were nodding again, but she felt the heat rising in her face, and she knew her color was rising too. She was lying to them and she knew it; she suspected they knew it, too. The truth was, she liked Filipinos, but she really didn't expect to learn much from them. "We also hope to share with you ideas from America that might help you."

They nodded again. "Yes, yes," the mayor said for all of them.

"You may know, in the United States, very few children die. Here, it is not uncommon for your children to die in their first years. I'm sure you would like to see more children grow up strong and healthy."

"Yes, yes," Mayor Dias was saying again, but she wasn't certain that all the men had understood.

"In America, we are very careful about germs." She looked to the mayor. "Do you know this word? Germs? Bacteria?" From the back, Martha spoke a word, and everyone nodded, and they looked more serious.

"In America, we wash our hands before we cook. We wash our hands after we go to the toilet"—she had learned not to say "bathroom"—"and we give our children many baths, to keep them clean."

Kathy saw that a solemnness had come over the group, and she didn't know how to interpret it. Were they concerned or were they resentful? She didn't want to imply that anything was wrong with them. She merely wanted to suggest some things that would help. "Martha Sommers and I would like to visit families in the barrio. We would like to teach the children about washing their hands, and teach women about keeping food clean. We would like to teach about taking more baths."

"Yes, yes," the mayor said, and the men nodded.

So what did that mean? Did she have approval that easily? "There are also other things we can do. Sometimes the children do not go home to use the toilet. Sometimes they use the streets or the alleys. I have even seen men do this."

A couple of the men smiled, but most stayed as solemn as before. But she couldn't read from their faces what they were thinking. All this might be insulting, and she didn't mean it that way. "When people use the streets this way, germs spread. Bacteria. It's very bad. This may be one reason your children become sick. It's one reason some children die. It also causes adults to become sick."

"Yes, yes," the mayor was saying again, but his tone didn't imply that he saw any importance in the subject.

Kathy looked around at him. "We could lower the death rate," she said. "We could save lives if we had public toilets."

He nodded, looking serious. He was a tiny man, shorter than most of the men in the barrio and slightly built. And yet, he had a way of stretching and raising his chin high, like a little rooster. He smiled when he talked, almost as a mannerism more than an emotion, so that when he took on a serious look, he always seemed to be faking. He had been nothing but respectful to Kathy and Martha, but he never seemed to pay much attention to what they said to him. Sometimes Kathy wondered whether he fully understood her.

"If we had a public toilet in the barrio—close to the school, perhaps—the children wouldn't have to run home. We could teach them to use the toilet and then to wash their hands. This, alone, could save many lives. We could also drain away some of the water that stands in low places in the barrio." She felt her passion rising, took a breath, and tried to continue in a calmer voice. "Standing pools can breed germs, and mosquitoes hatch in the water. Mosquitoes are another cause of illness. Sidewalks would be nice too—or boardwalks. That way people wouldn't have to walk in the mud during the rainy season. The toilets are most important, but there is so much we could do to make the barrio look nicer, and maybe be a little more . . . healthy."

Somewhere along the way, she had lost them. She had gotten too excited, talked a little too fast, probably used words they didn't know. Or maybe she had implied too much that was negative about the way they lived. But no one was reacting. They were all watching her, looking less focused, as though they hoped she was finished.

Kathy looked around at the mayor. "Thank you," he said. "This bery good."

What did that mean?

"Do you think it's possible to do these things? We can teach the people about bacteria, and I think we could help raise some money to buy building materials for the toilet. Miss Sommers and I would help in every way we could."

"Yes. This bery good."

"Do you need to call for a vote, or—"

He looked mystified, as though he didn't understand the word. Kathy looked back to Martha. "How do you say 'vote' in Tagalog?" she asked.

Martha stood, but she didn't address the question. Instead, she said, in Tagalog, "Senorita Thomas and I love your children. We feel bad when they are sick. A toilet in the city would be healthy for them. And we can teach them about washing their hands—if this is what you want. We don't want to do anything that you, Mr. Mayor, or your council, would wish us not to do. We are only here to help where we can."

The mayor stood. "Thank you, Miss Sommers, Miss Thomas. It bery good that you come to us."

"Should we plan to go forward then, and teach the children?" Kathy asked. She turned toward him just as he stepped forward. She felt as though she were twice his size, as though she were an immense presence, almost on top of him.

"Yes, yes. Teach the children," he said quietly, and he stepped back a little.

Did he understand what she meant? "May we visit the families?"

"Yes. Bisit the families. Teach the children."

"What about the toilets?"

"This bery good."

"Should we—"

But from the back of the room, Kathy heard Martha say, "Thank you, Mayor. Thanks to everyone. We were honored to meet with you tonight."

Martha was moving toward the door, and she motioned for Kathy to follow. All the men stood. "Tank you, tank you," they were saying.

The mayor walked to the door and shook hands with Martha and then with Kathy, "Thank you bery much," he kept saying.

But Kathy felt somehow that she was being ushered out the door, pulled by Martha and pushed by Mayor Dias. She walked down the steep flight of stairs, through the store, and on outside. It was only there that she dared to say, "Martha, we didn't get a commitment. You know how these guys are. They won't do a thing unless you get everything nailed down. We didn't get *anywhere* with them. I don't think they even understood what we were trying to tell them."

Martha stopped and turned toward Kathy. She reached up and took hold of her shoulders, and then she waited for Kathy to look into her eyes—those quiet, gray-blue eyes that were lovely for their gentleness but annoying now for their calmness. "Kathy, the harder you push them, the less you'll see happen. I keep telling you that."

"That doesn't make sense. I just told them that their children are dying and we can do something about it."

"I know. But people do things certain ways, and it's very difficult to ask them to change."

Kathy stepped back a little, enough to break Martha's hold on her. "That's stupid, Martha. There's nothing precious about the right to use the streets as a bathroom. Why would anyone want to walk around in that stuff?"

"It's not that. It's just that they have to feel the importance of what you're talking about. You can't force something like that."

"What do you mean? Don't they believe us? Don't they believe in germs?"

"I don't know, Kathy. But we Americans aren't very healthy about the way we live either. Look at all the sugar and fatty foods we cram into ourselves. We know it's not good for us, but if someone from another country came in and tried to get us to stop, do you think we'd thank them and then give up our potato chips and Coke?"

Kathy nodded. "Okay, okay. That's a good point. But human waste in the street? How can anyone want that?"

"I'm just saying, take it easy. We'll visit the families. We'll teach them about germs and hand washing, and we can teach about using toilets. But it will take time. Those toilets may not get built while you're here, but we can gradually raise the children's consciousness, and maybe it will be the next generation that finally makes some of these changes."

"And in the meantime, think how many kids are going to die."

"And think how many Americans are going to die from obesity and diabetes before we get it into our heads that we can't eat the way we do."

"Okay. But I'm going to check back with the mayor. I can get some of our Peace Corps volunteers over here, and we could build the toilet ourselves, but I need his permission and support."

"Don't get him angry, Kathy."

"*Angry?* How would we ever know if he was angry? These people just smile and nod. They don't ever tell you what they really think."

"Kathy, they're nice. And the last I heard, that's not such a bad thing."

"It is when it's dishonest."

Martha was shaking her head again, the way she had done so many times the past few months. And Kathy knew the speech. Filipinos didn't like to offend people; they cared more about getting along than about being right. They were not competitive; they were cooperative. That all sounded good, but Kathy wasn't sure. They were nice people, but they seemed sort of sneaky, too. Mrs. Sanchez resented Kathy, and Kathy knew it, but she never said a word to indicate how she really felt. She *pretended* to be Kathy's friend, and yet she seemed to be thinking only of outlasting Kathy, not truly supporting her.

~

The next day, Kathy and Martha decided to start their visits, or at least Kathy did, and Martha agreed to go along. They picked the family of one of Kathy's students, since Kathy was still trying to keep up with her parental visits required by the school. That way she could make her required visit, and since the family had lots of younger children, they could try at the same time to start their lessons on hygiene.

But the visit turned out to be more complicated than Kathy had ever imagined. Rain was pouring in the afternoon, so hard that it sprayed through their umbrellas, soaking them, and there was no avoiding the puddles or the ubiquitous mud. By the time they arrived, pretty Martha looked like a drowned little mouse, and Kathy could only imagine what she looked like herself. The rainy season was supposed to be over, and this was supposed to be the "cool" time of the year, but it rained hard at times during the "dry" season, and even though the heat had backed off a bit, the humidity never went away.

All the same, Mrs. Roces was happy to welcome Kathy and Martha into her home. Martha and Kathy took off their shoes and left their umbrellas outside, but they still dripped water on the floors. Mrs. Roces kept saying, "Only water, only water," and had them sit on rattan chairs in the living room, seemingly unconcerned. Kathy was touched by her kindness. Leonara, Kathy's student, sat next to her mother on a chair brought in from the kitchen, and Leonara, without saying so, seemed thrilled to have her teacher in her house.

Kathy complimented both Leonara and her mother for Leonara's success at school. She was a shy girl who rarely said anything in class, but she turned in all her work, and she wrote English better than many of the students. Eventually, Martha asked Mrs. Roces if she and Kathy could speak to the other children in the family, and Mrs. Roces called them all into the little living room—five children from twelve to two. The oldest and youngest were boys, and the three little girls in between all looked amazingly near the same age to Kathy. They seemed delighted to meet Leonara's teacher, but when Martha spoke to them in Tagalog, they all laughed. Kathy didn't know whether they found the pronunciation funny, or whether it was merely strange for them to hear a foreigner speak their language. "They speak good English," Mrs. Roces said in Tagalog, so Martha tried that, and Kathy tried to join in, but everything still seemed comical to them. Kathy supposed the mere visit of a blonde American and probably the tallest woman they had ever seen was such a novelty that it was all they could think about. But she wanted to get past that. She tried to explain about the little "bugs" that lived on their skin, and Martha made an attempt in Tagalog again when the English wasn't all that effective, but the children kept looking at their hands, trying to spot the insects on them, and this, for some reason, remained the source of constant laughter.

Finally Martha said, "Let's just show them what to do."

Kathy wasn't sure what that meant. She had always assumed that kids *knew* how to wash their hands; they just didn't do it very often. But Martha took the children to the kitchen and asked Mrs. Roces for a basin and soap. Mrs. Roces had a hard time coming up with either one. When she finally did, the water wasn't warm, and Martha had to heat it on the stove.

By then, Kathy was beginning to see the problem. Soap helped, but hot water was important, and she had a hard time picturing this poor mother heating water for the kids to wash before every meal.

When the kids did take turns washing, they delighted in rubbing their hands together until they made suds, but they seemed to see it all as a game, and Kathy had no idea whether they understood what they were supposed to be learning. "Do this before you eat, every time," Kathy kept telling them, "and after you use the toilet."

"Yes, yes," they would say, like the mayor, but she held out little hope that it would happen. Kathy glanced at Leonara, hoping for some sign that she understood and would give her mother help with this.

Finally, Martha let the children return to their play, and then she said to Mrs. Roces, "I'm sure you understand how important this is. You know about bacteria. No?"

"Yes. Certainly."

"If the children eat with dirty hands, they can get sick."

"I understand."

"Can you have them wash this way before they eat?"

"Yes. Certainly."

"Good."

"It's *very* important," Kathy said. "Too many children die from disease. They should come home to use the toilet, too. It's not good to go out-of-doors."

"Yes. I understand."

"Mrs. Roces," Martha said, "when you kill a chicken and bring it into the house, there is bacteria on the chicken. And the same with the fruits and vegetables that you buy at the market. It's important to wash everything well, and it's important to wash the chicken, and then heat the meat until it's cooked all the way through. Do you know what I mean?"

"Yes. It's what I do."

"Very good. You're a good mother."

Kathy could feel that Martha was going to leave now, and yet she didn't believe for a second that anything was going to change. "Leonara," she said, "we have you wash your hands at school, always before lunch. You've learned this, haven't you?"

"Yes, ma'am," she said in English.

"Can you help your little sisters and brothers wash their hands and remember to use the toilet—not go outside?"

"Yes, ma'am."

"It's very important, Leonara. It could save their lives."

"Yes, ma'am."

"And if you help your mother cook your food, be sure to wash your hands before you do. That way, your brothers and sisters won't get sick."

"Yes, ma'am."

"It may not seem like—"

"Miss Thomas, she understands," Martha said. "I know she'll do it."

Kathy nodded and smiled. "Yes. I'm sure she will."

And then they left. But Kathy felt like screaming. It was as though she had spent an hour punching a giant marshmallow. It accepted every blow, never fought back, but it hadn't moved an inch.

Kathy felt something inside her shrinking away—some enthusiasm or hope, even some goodwill. She liked Mrs. Roces, loved sweet Leonara, but she could do nothing for them. What she wished more than anything was that she could go home. It was cold at home, probably snowy. She wanted to deal with that kind of world: one she understood. She wanted to be home for Christmas, wanted to get mad about the war, or argue with her dad—do anything that worked in some way she understood. She wanted to hear someone say, "You don't know what you're talking about," or "If you don't love America, why don't you get out." She could shout at someone like that. Here, there was no one to shout at, not even anyone to dislike.

Something else was bothering Kathy, although she didn't want to admit it to herself. She had received a letter from Marshall Childs that week. It was a response to a letter she had sent him, although he had taken a long time to write back. It was a nice letter, in a way, but polite, not personal, and even though Kathy read the letter several times, there was not so much as a hint that he was interested in her any longer. He didn't even ask her to write again.

Kathy had heard from her grandmother that Marshall was going with someone. Kathy suspected he must be getting serious and was only being courteous by responding to her letter. It was silly for her to worry about that. She had known for years that nothing would come of their brief romance, but lately Kathy had felt lonely, and she had begun to worry whether she would ever marry. Maybe her choice to enter the Peace Corps would only delay her opportunities to meet someone. Maybe she would miss her chance—just as her father had warned her she might. For a long time she had been telling herself she didn't want to get married any time soon, but she was feeling an emptiness in her life lately, and she wasn't sure what it would take to give her life more meaning.

Outside, the rain had stopped, but the sun had come out, and that was raising the temperature. Kathy wished she could spend just one full day without her skin feeling sticky. She thought of being wrapped up in a coat and gloves and muffler, shivering in the Utah cold. The idea was wonderful.

"Kathy, don't give up," Martha said as they walked along in the mud that was called a street. "Things happen slowly, but things do happen."

"Okay," Kathy said. But she didn't believe it.

Chapter 3

Diane and Greg Lyman had arrived late in the night at Diane's home in Ogden, but this morning Diane had had to get up early anyway. Jennifer had slept a lot in the car the night before, so now she was wide awake and wanting Diane's attention. She was almost three months old now, and she was becoming much more aware of what was going on around her. Diane loved to play with her when she was so willing to coo and smile, but at the moment Diane felt too dragged out to do anything more than hold her. It was only five-thirty, and another couple of hours of sleep would have been wonderful.

So Diane was relieved when Bobbi came walking out in her robe. "I thought I heard you out here," she said. "Let me have her. You go back to bed."

But Diane's mother looked tired. Diane could see more lines around her eyes than she remembered, and the skin of her neck was showing signs of age. Bobbi had turned fifty this year, but she had always looked young for her age. Diane didn't like to think that she could ever get old. "Are you sure you want her?" Diane asked. "Don't you want to sleep a while longer?"

"Not when I can play with my little Jenny. How often am I going to get that chance?"

"She's all yours, then. I changed her diaper and nursed her. She should be all right for a while."

Bobbi laughed. "I think I can manage. Go get some sleep. You look really tired, honey."

"I am."

Diane handed the baby over and started to walk from the kitchen, but before she reached the door, Bobbi asked, "Is everything all right, Di? I know you're tired, but you looked upset last night when you got here."

"It was a long ride, that's all, and we got off to a late start. I wanted to stop for the night in Boise or somewhere, but Greg thought we needed to push on through and get it over with." Diane leaned against the door frame and let her burning eyes go shut for a moment. Her parents had remodeled the kitchen since Diane had been away. The new Formica cabinet tops, in a color too close to orange, were a little bright for Diane's taste, and so was the new fluorescent lighting. "I guess, all in all, it was the right thing to do. Now we're here, and we don't have to face another day in the car."

"But you sound discouraged."

"No. Not really. I'll be glad when Jenny starts to sleep through the night, though. I thought I knew how much work it was to take care of a baby, but I guess there's no way to understand until you have one of your own."

"The first months are the hardest, but you're right. Raising a child is the biggest job you'll ever do." Mom stepped closer to Diane, held the baby in one arm, and put her other hand on Diane's cheek. "It never gets easy, either. I worry more about you now than I ever have—just because you're away and I can't do anything to help."

There were things Diane wanted to say, things she wanted to discuss, but not now—she needed to sleep. Besides, if she said anything, Mom would only worry all the more, and the fact was, there was nothing her mother *could* do to help.

"But everything is okay, isn't it?" Bobbi asked.

"Sure. Greg and I were both really tired last night, and we got into an argument—you know, when I wanted to stop for the night and he didn't. It was a stupid thing to fight about."

"Sure. But it happens."

"But you and Dad never fight, do you?"

"I do," Bobbi said, and she laughed, "but your dad doesn't. It's really hard to have a good fight when your husband won't join you."

"He's a sweet man, isn't he? I don't think I realized that until now."

"He thinks before he speaks, Di. It's what I ought to do. It's what all people ought to do. It's not that he doesn't get upset with me sometimes, but he thinks things over and then he takes his stand when he feels he needs to—but he doesn't get mad. Sometimes it's frustrating. When I get mad, I try to needle him into fighting back, but I'm glad he doesn't take the bait. We've never had a really terrible fight, and it's all because of him."

"I guess I'm going to have to be the one in our marriage who's more like Dad. I usually am. But I was so tired last night, and Greg kept saying he wanted to get to Utah in time to do his Christmas shopping. I just didn't see what difference it made. He's still got three days."

Bobbi walked back and sat down at the kitchen table, all the while smiling and nodding at Jennifer. Jennifer was watching Bobbi's every move with those huge blue eyes of hers, and she was smiling back at times. "Arguments are usually not about anything very important. They're almost always about pitting one partner's will against the other's. It's just so hard to meld your purposes every minute of every day. We're all little babies, after all is said and done. We want what we want, and I think we get weary of all the compromises and adjustments marriage forces on us."

Now Mom was saying things Diane did want to talk about, and suddenly sleep didn't seem quite as important as it had a few minutes before. Diane walked back to the table and sat down across from Bobbi. The old chrome table was gone, and a pretty maple one had taken its place. "So what do you do about that?"

"Resist acting like a baby, I guess. Richard and I have gotten so we're more and more alike. We don't clash over very many things. But it's like you said—you get tired and cranky, and you let something silly become important. Marriage, if you ask me, is all about muddling through the best you can—but it's never perfect. You have perfect moments and lots of wonderful days, but you never get to the point where you don't have to make an effort to keep things working. Or at least that's how it is for us."

"What about the man being the patriarch? How does that work?"

Diane saw her mother's head come up, but Diane looked away. She didn't want to hint that this was an important issue. Above all, she didn't want to tell her mother some of the things Greg had told her. Mom would think the worst of Greg if she did.

"I'm not sure I understand the role of patriarch, Diane. But I understand that marriage is a partnership, and the priesthood doesn't make the man the boss. Your dad has never once told me that he had the right answer for us—*because* he was the man. The Doctrine and Covenants makes it very clear how wrong unrighteous dominion is, and if you ask me, when a man starts trying to run the show, that's exactly what's going on."

The fact was, Diane hadn't had to ask. She knew what her mother thought about this, and she knew her own feelings, too. Even Greg liked to talk about being "partners" in marriage, but he also liked to invoke his own "final word," through inspiration, when the two disagreed. Diane didn't want to deny his right to the Lord's guidance, but when she had a different opinion, she was suddenly up against not only Greg but God. She resented that Greg would put her in that position. She said her own prayers, and she tried to get her own answers. But challenging Greg only perturbed him and brought on hints at best—accusations, at worst—that she wasn't listening to the Spirit.

Still, what was Diane supposed to say to her mother? She never should have started down this road. If she quoted her mom to Greg, he would only guess that Diane had brought up the subject. So Diane tried to keep the conversation generic. "I agree," she said. "But sometimes, in the

Church, people seem to think that a woman is supposed to tag along behind her husband and just let him do all the thinking."

"I guess. But you look at the good marriages and they don't work that way. Just read some of President McKay's talks. He's always treated Sister McKay with respect. You don't hear him saying that the man makes all the decisions for his wife."

President McKay had been sick lately. He was ninety-six, and failing. It didn't seem that he could live much longer. Diane had known him as the prophet all her life, and she had often thought about the way he talked about families. It was part of what had convinced her, for such a long time, that there was nothing more she wanted in life than to be a good wife and mother. She had never expected to feel the unease she had experienced lately, like an unremitting stomachache. She wondered every day what to expect when Greg came home from school. He had been sweet lately, almost to excess, bringing her flowers and professing his love more often, but there were still awful days when he was moody, even hostile, and in spite of his promises, Diane wondered whether he would lash out at her again sometime, maybe throw her against a wall, as he had once done. He had promised that "his mistake" was a one-time thing, and he had spent some sessions with Bishop Hunt. For a time, the bishop had taken Greg's temple recommend away, but he had returned it now so that Greg and Diane could go to the temple while they were in Utah, and both the bishop and Greg believed that all the soul-searching had been good for Greg. He had committed himself never to touch her in anger again.

But the argument in the car the night before had turned bitter, and Greg's wild anger had frightened Jennifer, made her scream. Diane had wondered the rest of the way to Utah whether Greg might have gotten violent had he not been driving the car. He had apologized all the way from Burley to Ogden, and he had told Diane he was wrong. They really should have stopped back in Boise, but the tender expressions were hard to believe after the tirade of insults she had had to hear.

Diane could almost predict flowers today, or a special invitation to dinner—something of that sort—but she didn't want to be bought off. She had disagreed with him—expressed a different opinion—but the truth was, she hadn't been cranky. She hadn't demanded or even been forceful. Her mistake was that she had brought up the idea of stopping a second time, and he had already told her he didn't want to. That's all it took, and what Diane had thought about in the night when she had held Jennifer and nursed her was that she didn't want a life of being careful, always waiting for the next explosion.

Bobbi was now playing with the baby, covering her face with the blanket and then pulling it back and saying, "Boo!" Jenny was kicking and smiling, looking bright and happy. It was the first time the two had been together since right after Jennifer had been born. Diane thought how nice it would be to live closer, where Mom could help once in a while, and where Jenny could know her grandparents.

"Diane, Greg doesn't feel that way, does he?"

"You mean, like he's the boss?"

"Yes."

Diane had only a second to make a choice, but she just couldn't talk to her mother about this. "No, of course not," she said. "I just hear things like that at church sometimes." She got up. "Well, if you don't care, I *am* going to sleep just a little more."

"No. Of course I don't mind. It's what you need, honey."

So Diane went off to bed. But she couldn't sleep. She was wide awake. She lay next to Greg and listened to his deep breathing, like growls, and she wondered what life had in store for her. She stayed in bed the better part of an hour, but she only found herself increasingly worried. So she got up and made herself some toast and drank some milk to stop the hurt in her stomach. Greg was still asleep.

On Christmas afternoon, after spending the morning with the Lymans, Diane and Greg went to Grandma and Grandpa Thomas's house for the annual family gathering. Most everyone was there, and the house was noisy, but Diane sensed some reserve, especially in Alex and Anna, and in Emily, Gene's wife. Gene was in Vietnam, and Aunt Anna admitted to Diane that she was worried. "He's ended up in a dangerous job, going on reconnaissance missions," she said, "and we don't understand how that happened. Alex says he must have volunteered for it, and we didn't think he would do something like that."

But Diane wasn't surprised. "He's always wanted to be like his dad," she told Anna.

Anna was washing pots and pans even though the cooking was still going on and dinner hadn't yet been put on the table. She turned toward Diane and brushed a strand of her blonde hair away from her eyes. Her hair had streaks of gray now, but she was a beautiful woman. Diane had always hoped to hold onto her own looks as long as Anna had. "I think you're right," Anna said, "but don't say that to Alex. He told Gene not to take chances. He talked to him a long time about that. I just don't understand why Gene would put all that aside and volunteer for something that puts his life in such jeopardy."

The idea frightened Diane. Gene had always been her favorite cousin. He was older, and handsome, and he treated her so well. She missed him, and she missed Kathy, who was in the Philippines, in the Peace Corps. What Diane longed for was to turn time back, to be there as a high school girl, or a college student, and to bring back those days when she and Gene and Kathy had used this time to talk things over and compare their hopes for the future.

What was best about the day was that everyone wanted a turn with Jennifer. She was the newest baby, the second great-grandchild, and the first girl of the generation. She was passed all around, but she seemed not to mind at all. She had slept again, later in the morning, but she was wide awake and happy now, and Grandma Thomas couldn't get enough of her. She kept taking her back after the various uncles and aunts and cousins had their turns. But Aunt Lorraine wanted her all she could, too. She admitted to Diane that she and Wally wondered whether Kathy would ever marry, and they wanted so much to have a grandchild themselves.

Grandpa Thomas had been having some health problems lately. Both his knees were giving him trouble, and he was walking rather slowly. He had always looked so big and strong, and his hair had stayed mostly dark. It was hard for Diane to see the lines in his face folding into deep creases, but what worried her most was what Grandma Bea told her: his heart had been acting up. It had gone out of rhythm a couple of times. He had been dealing with high blood pressure for quite some time, she said, and now he seemed to be in the early stages of congestive heart failure. It was something that his medicine could handle for now, but according to Grandma, it was the kind of condition that would only get worse.

"But don't worry too much," Grandma told Diane. She was bending over her oven, checking the turkey and speaking more loudly than she really needed to. "He's a tough old buzzard. He'll be around for a long time. The only thing that concerns me is that he goes out back and works in the yard and in the garden when it's way too hot. This time of year he isn't so bad, but he gets out there and shovels the walks when I tell him to pay one of the grandkids to come over. But he doesn't like to wait. When the first flakes hit the ground, he's out there pushing them off the front walk—bad knees and all. He just hates the idea that he can't do everything he did when he was forty."

"Can't you convince him to take it just a little easier?"

"No. But I never could." She shut the oven door and straightened up. She smiled, showing her dimples. She looked remarkably young for her age. "The doctor says it's good for him to get out and do some things, but not to overdo. If he'd take a walk or something, the way I do, that would be better, but he can't understand that. He sees people out jogging, the way some do now, and he thinks that's the craziest thing he's ever heard of." Grandma made her voice as deep as she could and imitated Grandpa: "People don't *work* enough these days. If they'd work harder, they wouldn't have to get out there in the street in those little short pants, looking like fools."

Diane heard a big bear's voice behind her, like the one Grandma was impersonating. She realized that Grandpa had stepped into the kitchen. "Well, it's true, isn't it?" he said. "I can't believe anyone has to get out in the traffic and run around, just for exercise, with all the work there is to do in the world."

Diane turned around and hugged her grandpa. "But don't shovel too much snow and give yourself a heart attack."

"I don't. Bea just fusses about everything. I figure, if I'm going to die I'd rather do it while I'm doing something worthwhile, not out there prancing around without my garments on."

Grandma Bea rolled her eyes. "Your grandpa was born old," she said. "Nothing scares him more than change. I think it's great that people are trying to keep in good shape. I just might buy me some running shoes and some cute little shorts and go out jogging."

"You could do it, Grandma. You're in great shape."

But Grandma was laughing. "Not that good. And what I don't want to do is show off my varicose veins."

Diane had lost track of Jennifer; she decided to look around for her. She walked from the kitchen into the dining area and found Joey and Sharon, Gene's brother and sister, talking with Wayne, Wally and Lorraine's son. Joey was engaged now, planning to get married in the spring, and Wayne, from what Diane was hearing, had a "serious" girlfriend. They were back at the University of Utah, after their missions. Sharon was a junior now, at BYU. The three were deep in discussion, the way Diane and Kathy and Gene had always been. Someone had said that

Kurt, Gene's other brother, was supposed to be coming over, but he hadn't arrived yet. Bobbi had told Diane that Kurt's life was still not on track. He would soon be old enough for a mission, but it didn't seem likely that he would end up going. The teenaged girls—Diane's sister Maggie; Beverly's older girls, Vickie and Julia; and Kathy's sister, Glenda—were in a huddle in the living room. Diane loved that, seeing them together, talking about school and boys and the new clothes they'd gotten for Christmas. The boys had gone upstairs, Douglas with them, even though he was the cousin who would always be a child. Pammy and Shauna and Suzanne, the preteen girls, who were suddenly looking like teenagers themselves, had wandered off somewhere too. Diane wondered how this had happened, that all the cousins were such good friends. Diane wanted something like that for Jennifer. She wanted her to know Danny, Gene's son, and be his lifelong friend. Greg sometimes talked of living somewhere else after law school, and Diane had never said she was opposed to that, but today she felt she wanted to come back here.

Diane found Jennifer with Aunt Beverly, sitting in Grandpa's big chair. Beverly's husband, Roger, was with the other uncles, sitting around the dining room table, talking about something important—probably football. But Aunt Beverly was alone nearby with Jenny, talking to her out loud, laughing at her. She didn't notice Diane until she stepped close and said, "Jenny's never had so much fun in her life. She loves having so many people play with her."

"She's such a sweetheart, Diane. She's going to be as beautiful as you."

"Just don't ever tell her that she's pretty. I don't want her even to think about that."

Aunt Beverly smiled as though she understood what Diane was saying, but she didn't comment. It was the quality Diane loved about Beverly. There was something so serene and satisfied about her. She was pretty herself, in her way, but she never worked at it. She had soft, long hair and pretty eyes, but she hardly bothered with makeup.

"Can you believe I'm going to get me another one of these, at thirty-eight?" Beverly asked. "Here Suzie is, eleven. I didn't think we'd ever have another baby."

Diane had only heard since she got home that Aunt Bev was pregnant; she wasn't showing yet. "Do you think you're up for it?" Diane asked.

"I think so. I can't say it wasn't a surprise, but I've missed having a little one around. I know it's going to feel like twice as much work this time, but with the kids all in school, it'll be nice to have someone home with me again."

"How does Uncle Roger feel about it?" Diane knelt down next to Beverly and held out her finger to Jennifer, and then she talked to her. Diane saw a look of recognition come over her face—or at least wanted to think so.

"Roger rolls with the punches. I think he worries about the expense as much as anything. We're going to have four kids going off to college and on missions, one right after the other here in a few years. He liked to think that we'd have that one expensive time and then things would get easier. Now we'll have a little caboose to follow along behind. But that won't be so bad, by then." She laughed. "Or at least that's what I tell him."

"What if you had told him you wanted a baby and he hadn't wanted one? What would you have done?"

Beverly, for the first time, looked directly at Diane, as though she picked up the seriousness of Diane's question. "I don't know," she said. "Roger usually lets me have my way. Sometimes I have to stay after him for a while—like when we bought our house a couple of years ago. He liked the ward we were in, and the neighborhood, and he didn't really want to move. But the kids were getting bigger and our little house was really crowded. And then it just seemed that if we were going to move someday, we needed to do it before the kids were in high school."

"So did you just talk it out and make a decision together?"

Beverly smiled, then looked back at the baby. She obviously sensed that Diane was looking for some direction, but she didn't say so. "I don't think that ever happened, exactly. We're not the type to sit down and write all the pros and cons on a sheet of paper. Maybe we should be. But mostly, I kept bringing it up, and the next thing I knew we were driving around looking at new homes—or building lots. He got excited about building and doing some of the work himself. It was just one of those decisions that evolved. We always sort of knew we would get another house, sooner or later."

"Did you pray about it?"

Beverly thought about that, and her face showed her curiosity, perhaps about herself. "I don't remember. We might have. We probably brought it up in our prayers, once we had figured out, more or less, what we wanted to do. But we never worried ourselves too much about it. It just seemed the next step in our lives, I guess."

It all sounded so easy. Diane could hardly imagine such a process. And there was one thing she had to know. "Didn't he ever get mad when you kept bringing it up?"

Beverly took a long look at Diane, and Diane saw her concern. "Roger gets mad if the Utes lose to BYU," she said, "or if a garbage sack tears open halfway out to the garbage can—you know what I mean?—and then he growls a little. But I can tell him what I'm thinking anytime. That's really how it has to be."

Diane knew what Aunt Beverly was saying: "Diane, you can expect that from Greg. You *should* expect it."

"But if you bring it up over and over, can't it seem like nagging?"

"I guess. But that's not what I would do. I'd just tell him, 'Roger, we need to start thinking about another house'—and I'd give him my reasons. How could that upset him?"

"You probably know how to say things," Diane said, but that implied things Diane knew she didn't dare talk about. "So when is your baby due exactly?" she asked, and that was the end of that.

Diane realized she had to stop asking such questions. She'd soon have the whole family talking and wondering about her. But it was helpful to have some idea how her mother operated, and Beverly. She told herself she had to move Greg gradually, break him away from patterns he might have learned from his own family. Diane's uncles and aunts all seemed to have perfect marriages, but it couldn't be that easy. Certainly they had had to work out differences in their first years together.

Diane left Jennifer with Aunt Beverly, since the two were so happy together, and she went back to the kitchen. She whipped the potatoes that Grandma had boiled, and she watched Grandma prepare the turkey gravy—something she didn't really know how to do. She loved the smell of the baking rolls and the pies set out on the counter. This was how Christmas was supposed to be. This is what she wanted for her own family.

Diane told her aunts about Seattle, about the antiwar demonstrations on campus and all the hippies in the U-district. She liked being the one who had been away from Utah and "seen some things," but she loved more than anything just being in the middle of the talk as a grown-up. She loved these aunts and Grandma Thomas more than any women in the world, and she had always longed for what they had. She wanted to believe that she was in the early stages of creating their kinds of lives for herself and for her own family.

After dinner at Grandma's house, Greg and Diane stopped back at the Lymans' to see some of Greg's family who were coming over for pie late in the afternoon. Everything was much more formal there, with nice china and linen napkins—and softer conversations. Diane tried to imagine growing up in this house; she told herself it was no wonder she and Greg were different. And once again, she lectured herself: We can work things out. We started in different places, but we can grow together.

Later, as Greg and Diane drove back to Ogden, Jennifer fell asleep in

Diane's arms. Diane tried to calculate the feedings she could expect during the night. That was the worst thing about coming home—throwing Jennifer off schedule. "I'm going to try to sleep a little longer in the morning," she told Greg. "That first morning we were home, Mom wanted to take Jenny after I nursed her, so I could sleep, but I must have talked to her too long. By the time I got back to bed, I couldn't go back to sleep. She hasn't offered again since then, but I think I'm going to ask her tonight if she can do that in the morning."

"Boy, I've slept since I've been here," Greg said. "I think I'm worn out from the semester I've been through."

"I think so, too. You've been snoring—the way you do sometimes when you're really tired."

"I'm sorry. Why don't you punch me when I do that?"

"It's okay. I like to hear you next to me."

He reached over and took hold of her hand. Diane loved that. "Maybe we can stay in bed *together* for a while in the morning," he said.

Diane was a little uncomfortable about that at home, but she didn't want to say so. Instead, she said, "Okay. But I do want to sleep for a while. It's been so long since I've done that."

A few seconds passed, and she thought she felt him tense a little. She gave his hand a squeeze. "But we will. Okay?"

He didn't say anything. They were past Bountiful now, on the freeway. "Remember to take the mountain road," she said. He knew that. But she wanted to say something to keep their conversation going. She didn't want him to be upset.

"What were you and your mom talking about that morning?" Greg asked.

"When? The first morning we were home?"

"Yes. You said you talked to your mother a long time."

"Oh, you know. Just this and that. Jennifer, mostly."

"Did you tell her anything about the argument we had coming down?"

Diane hesitated. She was tempted to lie, but she didn't think she should have to do that. "Well, sort of. She told me I had looked upset when we got home. I just told her we'd both been really tired and we had had a little spat."

"Why did you bring that up?"

"I don't know. She understands. Every couple has arguments."

"You haven't told her anything about what happened in Seattle, have you?"

"*No*. I promised you I wouldn't say anything, and I won't."

He drove on past Lagoon, an amusement park, and took the cutoff to the mountain road. The silence worried Diane. "It was so fun to see everyone today," Diane said. "But I miss Kathy and Gene. It's not quite the same when they're not home."

"You hardly talk to my family."

Diane took a breath. She could hear it in his voice—the tension she feared. "I thought I did. Your mom and I talked for a long time."

"You don't say a thing to my dad or my brothers." He let go of her hand and put both hands on the steering wheel.

"They all talk to each other. And they don't take much interest in Jennifer, the way my family does." But that had definitely been the wrong thing to say. She waited. She feared what might be coming next, and she knew it was important not to react, to think of a way to smooth things out.

"I think you'll have to admit, most men don't pay a lot of attention to babies. I don't think there's anything strange about that at all."

This was better. He had softened his tone. He was trying. "I know. That's true. It just means that your mom and I have more to talk about. But I like everyone in your family. Your dad's always been wonderful to me." She touched Greg's arm.

He drove for a time again, staring straight ahead. She wondered what he was thinking. She wanted to say something about staying in bed together in the morning. She needed to please him in some way.

"What were you talking to your Aunt Beverly about?" he asked.

"She's pregnant. You heard about that, didn't you?"

"Yeah. That strikes me as rather bizarre, if you want to know the truth."

"I guess it wasn't something they planned."

"Did you say anything to her about us?"

"What do you mean?"

"Did you blab to her about the fight we had?"

"No. Of course not."

"Are you sure?"

"Yes, Greg."

"I came into the room and I heard her saying something to you about Roger not getting mad at her. How did that subject come up?"

Diane didn't make a decision—not exactly—but she knew the truth wouldn't work this time. "She was telling me about their building a new house. She said she had to nag Roger for a long time about getting started, but he didn't get mad about it."

"I'll bet you told her that I have a terrible temper—that you wouldn't dare nag at me."

"No, Greg. I didn't say anything like that. I don't talk about things like that with other people."

"But it's what you think."

"Greg, we've talked a million times about this. You're the one who says you have a temper and need to control it. I can get pretty mad, too. Everyone can."

"I just don't want you spreading the word through your family that you married some loser who can't hold his temper."

"I won't."

"Not even your mother."

"Not even Mom."

"Is that a promise?"

"Yes. I told you that before. We'll work out our own problems."

And that was the end. He had nothing more to say for miles. So Diane finally took hold of his arm and pulled it away from the steering wheel, and then she held his hand. "I love you," she said, and when he didn't answer, she added, "In the morning, I don't need to sleep in."

He gave her hand a squeeze, and the tension was gone. But Diane had wanted that sleep. She was the one who was silent the rest of the way back to Ogden.

Chapter 4

Gene was lying on his cot, staring at the metal roof of the hooch he lived in. The room was dark and damp, and he wanted to get up and do something, but he didn't know what—and he didn't have the energy anyway. It was January, 1970—and still the rainy season in the central coast area of Vietnam—but no rain had fallen for a few days, and the temperature was in the high eighties. For three days the Spartan team had been prepared, ready to insert into the mountains west of Camp Eagle, but heavy fog had socked in the terrain so tight that helicopters couldn't get anyone in. That should have been a relief—another day in camp, another day without danger—but the waiting was torture. Gene thought he would rather get out there, face the three or four days of terror, and get it over with, but he knew very well there was no logic in that. When the mission ended, he would come back to wait and then go out again. All his life now was either waiting for the terror or facing it. He honestly didn't know which was worse.

That morning Gene had tried to find something to do. He had reread some of Emily's recent letters, and then he had written a letter to her, and one to his parents. But he had hardly known what to say. He always told his family as little as possible about the work he was doing. The army didn't allow him to say much about the missions, and any general descriptions would only worry everyone. So he told them that he had found a strong LDS group in the camp, and he attended church when he wasn't away on Sundays. If he said much more than that, he only had the weather and his living conditions to complain about, and he knew that no one wanted to hear him talk about that in every letter. Above all, he couldn't tell them how frightened he was about death: that he might be killed, or that he might have to kill. He did tell a little about Pop Winston and his friend Phil Dearden, but he kept his comments light, didn't describe the darker side to the moods most of the men experienced.

After he had posted the letters, he read his Book of Mormon for a time. But the men in his hooch were as uptight as he was, and their talk was anything but conducive to feeling the Spirit. Kovach and Melnick were not such bad guys, really, but they were profane, cynical men, who hated the army, hated Vietnam, hated the rain and the mud and life in a hooch. They drank a lot of beer and never seemed to tire of vile things to discuss. Dearden, who bunked next to Gene, was actually quite religious, although he also spoke army language with great fluency. But he wasn't loud, and he liked Gene. He was constantly teaching Gene the ropes, advising him about keeping himself alive in the boonies.

Pop Winston was a quiet man, sometimes silent all day, but Gene didn't feel the tension in him that he saw in other men. This was his second tour, and he had served about half of that now. Gene had noticed something he didn't quite understand: new guys were nervous, but the ones who had been around for a few months seemed to settle into a kind of fatalism. They had nothing to look forward to but more of the same, and their year looked like forever. But most soldiers, once they could count their remaining days in double digits, began hoping for an end, and they were horrified at the idea of going through so much misery only to be shot up so close to going home. Gene had heard similar comments from lots of men: they said they could deal with death if it came, but they didn't want their legs blown off in a land mine, and they didn't want their guts torn up with a belly wound. They didn't want to deal with all that pain, and they didn't want to go home "messed up." But Pop wasn't like the others. He didn't say much about his own feelings, and he didn't complain. Still, Gene was pretty sure that Pop felt plenty and thought plenty; he just kept it all to himself.

Most of the men slept a lot. They got little rest while out on patrol, so when they returned to camp, they sometimes slept most of the day. It was an escape, and there was so little to do otherwise. The other men on Gene's team spent lots of time in the evenings drinking, and they stayed up late, but then they would sleep until it was time to get up and go drink again. Still, once a mission was announced, most of the drinking stopped. The men knew their work, and they weren't about to put themselves or their team in danger by going on patrol hungover.

Kovach and Melnick had gotten into an angry argument earlier in the day, had almost come to blows, and Gene had never really understood what it was all about. It had started with Melnick telling Kovach that he carried too much gear on patrols, that it slowed him down. Then it had moved on to insults about who had guts and who could be depended on. Pop had finally told them to shut up or get out of the hooch, and they had left.

So Gene lay on his cot feeling very much alone, soaked in his own sweat. Dearden and Lattimer were sleeping, and Pop left for a time. Gene wanted to think about home; he tried to. He wanted to see Emily in his mind, and Danny. He had their pictures in his footlocker, but he wanted to envision them in his mind and feel a sense of them. The problem was not just that he couldn't bring them into focus; it was as though his mind couldn't do the work.

He was drifting into some cloudiness, some kind of stupor, like the fog that was lying over the mountains. He couldn't feel. He knew the heat had something to do with that, but there was also some blankness that had gotten inside him, as though his soul had left him. He tried to console himself. Seven weeks had passed; before long he would be down to three hundred days left on his tour. That was something. In that first week after he had arrived, he had expected to be overjoyed to have a couple of months behind him. The only problem was, those weeks now seemed like a vast expanse of time, as though he had always been here. What would happen to him over the next three hundred days? How could he go back and pick up where he had left off? He had lost all sense of who he had been, what he had wanted and expected. Emily was now an idea, not a person. Danny was growing and changing, and Gene was always behind in his thinking about him. Each picture he received was surprising. His baby was turning into a little boy. It was all happening a day at a time, and Gene couldn't get those days back. Danny was nine months old now, and Gene hadn't been there when he first crawled, first said a word. Before long he would be walking, and Gene would miss that, too.

Emily wrote loving letters, full of bravery and encouragement, but Gene sensed they weren't real. She didn't want to be honest with him any more than he was with her. He knew this was a hard time for her, and he felt . . . but that was just it, he didn't feel. And part of that had come from a conscious effort. He had come back from the mission when he had looked at the dead boy—the one with the picture in his pocket—and he had known that he couldn't allow himself to feel that much reaction to what he had seen and to what he would certainly see again. Dearden had told him not to think, and he knew that was the only answer.

Right now, all he wanted was for this day to end. He wanted to mark one more day off his calendar, and then he wanted to sleep. He wished he could sleep away the entire year and then wake up one morning ready to catch his "freedom bird," as the men called the airplane that took them home.

He was drifting, half asleep, when he heard Pop say, "Thomas, we're going today, at last light. The fog has cleared enough that they think they can get us in."

Gene sat up. Kovach and Melnick were back, with Pop. They sat down on their cots and began checking their gear. Melnick murmured something about being glad to get going, and Gene understood that. Suddenly his heart was beating again, and his stomach was uneasy, which felt better in a way, but he also felt the semi-sick sensation he had felt before high school football or basketball games. No one ever said it, but a thought was in Gene's mind, and he knew it was in the other men's heads too: I'm going out to face death again. And killing. He felt the dread in his stomach, and he noticed it in his hands, which were trembling ever so slightly. Kovach and Melnick celebrated their kills, laughed about them, told the stories when they returned to camp, but Gene wondered—did they really like it, or was it easier to deal with if they told themselves they did?

The Huey made two fake insertions low in a valley and then actually inserted the men onto a high ridge, using a bomb crater as a landing zone, but Gene could see fog still lying in the valley below. He didn't like the idea of moving around in that stuff, just one more impediment to deal with, and one more danger. In the beginning he had told himself the brass wouldn't mess with men's lives, wouldn't put them in harm's way needlessly, but he had heard too many stories by now, seen too much. It was almost as though the "higher ups" got bored, or they needed to report that they were doing something. A lot of men felt that Lurp patrols were inserted with no clear necessity at times and under conditions that didn't make sense. The rainy season was especially miserable for the patrols, and fog was one of the greatest threats. If a team needed to be extracted in an emergency situation, there was often no way to get helicopters in. This afternoon the fog had cleared a little, but it was likely to build again with the night, and then there was no saying how long it might last.

But the men hunkered down and waited. Then, satisfied that the insertion was "cold," they moved into the valley toward a trail and a "blue line," as the men called rivers, since rivers were marked in blue on their maps. This was strictly a reconnaissance mission. The team was to take up a position and watch and wait for enemy movement. There was always worry that NVA units would work their way close to camps and then send sappers, with explosives, through camp wires, or fire mortars and rockets from close range. The goal on this mission was to spot that kind of movement and head off any possible attack, but not to engage the enemy.

The team moved slowly and carefully into place and set out claymore mines that could blast enemy infiltrators with a hail of flying balls of steel. Then they formed a circle-shaped perimeter—and they waited again. Pop had all the men stay on alert for a couple of hours and then assigned hour-and-a-half shifts to each team member for the rest of the night. Gene was glad to take an early watch. He hoped that after he was finished he would be able to sleep. But the night cold gradually settled in, and Gene was soaked from both inside and out—from his own sweat, and from the watery air. There was no drying, so the cold penetrated slowly through his poncho liner and through his clothes, and then into his core. There was no way to carry enough bedding to stay warm at night. The idea was merely to survive until morning and then let the rising heat reverse the misery.

Gene eventually fell into a sleep-like state, but he never lost consciousness of the cold, and what brought him back to full wakefulness was a shivering that he couldn't control. He feared that he was rattling, his body shook so hard, but he couldn't stop himself. He waited and longed for light and was sure it would soon come two hours before it did. When the men finally stirred and opened their Lurp rations, Gene was just happy to move. He mixed water with a chicken and rice meal and waited for it to soften, but he ate only a little. He was still too uneasy to feel much hunger.

No one said a word, but Gene could see the look in each man's face; they expected nothing but torment. Boredom and misery were actually the best things to hope for, but contact with the enemy—the adrenaline rush, the movement, the pumping of blood—could take on a certain attraction at times like this. Most of the men claimed that's what they hoped for, and maybe they meant it. After a firefight, he had seen how enlivened the men were.

After eating, the men pulled in the claymores and moved into a position close to the trail and river they were supposed to watch, and then they sat—all day. It was not exactly clear when the rain began to fall. Under the cover of a double or triple canopy of jungle growth, the dripping never stopped this time of year, but rain increased the pace, and by midmorning water was not just dripping but running off trees in little rivulets. Gene sat next to Dearden, with the other men posted in pairs just a few yards away. The team had a new guy along, only on his second mission. He was a nineteen-year-old kid from Tennessee named Ben Lattimer. He had come in sounding rather brash but had lost some of that on his first patrol. There hadn't been any enemy contact, but he had found out what fear was all about. Pop was keeping him close for now.

The men wrapped themselves in poncho liners but didn't dare use ponchos. The plastic surface made too much noise when raindrops hit it. So they kept their heads ducked a little and simply let the rain soak them. But the cold gradually turned to oppressive heat, and the rainwater was almost as hot as the air. Gene shed the poncho liner, but he was soaked through, and the temperature kept going up. Eventually, sweat was running down his face and into his eyes. He drank all the water he had, and then he held his canteen under a dribble falling from the vegetation around him. But all this had to be done with utmost care, with as little motion as possible. Stillness was protection for the men, and they practiced it with a discipline that Gene had been forced to learn.

The day was even more tedious than the night, and eventually Gene began looking forward to the temperature drop that would start as the sun went down. But he feared the night. He dreaded the cold, but worse was to be drowned not only in water but also in darkness. The North Vietnamese knew the jungle. Charlie could disappear in the day, hide in tunnels or caves or dense jungle, but just when it seemed he wasn't there at all, he could come creeping through the dark. Gene had heard so many stories by now, he never lay down at night without wondering how close someone was, out there looking for him.

Gene tried to play mind games to occupy his daylight hours. He would do little math tricks: start with a number and double it, and then keep doubling as long as his brain could do the math and hold the answer. He would watch a subtle shadow, judging the movement of the sun by the change. He would tell himself that when the shadow touched a certain point, perhaps another hour had passed, or that the day was half gone. Sometimes he would take a mental drive around Salt Lake, but his favorite trick was to replay his high school games. He would try to think of a scoring drive in football, remember the plays he had called, the passes he had thrown. Over and over he replayed his team's loss in the state semifinals. He could remember every mistake he had made in the game, and he could picture how the game should have gone, how it would have gone had he cut to the left instead of right, or had thrown the ball an instant sooner.

But these were the mind games that caused him trouble. They all brought back the sense of himself he had had in high school—and what he had thought life was. He had known his own potentialities then, had believed unequivocally that life was going to be good to him, that great things were going to happen. He had been good at so many things then—not just sports, but almost everything. And he had lived in an atmosphere in which everyone thought well of him, in which everyone knew he was the star, the guy who was going somewhere. He had sometimes thought about war, about proving himself as his father had done, but he had never once imagined anything like this: sitting in heat and cold and water, feeling the leeches on his skin, under his fatigues, knowing he had to live with them for the moment, knowing there was nothing to look forward to, nothing to hope for except the end of the day—and knowing it was a useless hope anyway, since another day like it would follow.

But the day did finally end, and after another night of pain and shivering, the sun didn't rise. The fog had moved in again, thick, and the air only glowed a little. At least the rain had stopped, although that didn't make all that much difference, since the dripping continued. Pop moved the men that morning even though that wasn't the plan. Certainly he knew that everyone wanted to get up and walk, stir their bodies a little, kill a bit of time. But by midmorning, Pop signaled for a stop at another site along the river, and again the wait lasted all day. No one was moving, nothing was happening. Another bitter night followed.

On the third day the new reality was forming. The team was supposed to be extracted that afternoon, but with the fog, there was little hope of that happening. Gene had felt very little hunger up until now, but the thought of being stuck in the jungle for an extra day or two—or maybe much longer—turned the food he was carrying into precious stuff. He ate sparingly that day, hoping to stretch his supplies, if necessary, but now feeling the want of the food, wishing he had some of the food back that he had buried with the packaging the first two days.

He also longed to complain a little—tell the other men what he was feeling. It was infuriating that Captain Battaglia or some higher officer had sent them out here on this worthless mission when this fog was obviously a danger. Still, he knew he couldn't talk. Pop sometimes whispered instructions, but there was no idle chat, not even idle grousing. During the first day or two that usually didn't matter much, but as fears decreased and missions stretched, the silence became one of the major tests of mental strength.

Gene called in a situation report late in the day and heard what he expected: Captain Battaglia said there was no getting the team out that night, but another storm was moving in, and that should stir the fog enough for an extraction the next day—but only later on, at best. Pop whispered to the men to conserve their food, but everyone had clearly begun to do that.

Back in "the world," as the soldiers called the States, people were going about their lives; college students were acting important, putting on their antiwar rallies; and everything was business as usual. People back there talked about "the war" as though it involved expansive battles and victories; no one stateside knew what this war really was: men in jungles searching for a phantom enemy, killing a few and counting them, as though somehow the count would finally mount up so high that North Vietnam would cry uncle. But out in the jungle, none of that was possible to believe. It was an endless game, with a never-ending supply of bodies to count. What was obvious was that there was no way to win the war this way. A soldier knew that instinctively. And so there was only one thing to achieve: another day alive, and the distant hope that your own days would actually add up to 365.

Gene had never heard a single soldier express the hope that the war would end before a year had passed. A gradual withdrawal had begun, but that only made the men's presence trivial, and it angered soldiers who were not likely to get out until their own year had been completed—perhaps not long before the war was conceded. Somehow, Gene felt, someone ought to answer for that—for putting men through this misery, now with no talk of victory. But, ironically, the ones who were often disparaged, especially by the antiwar freaks, were the soldiers themselves. Every time an actual battle had been engaged in Vietnam, the American forces had won. They had fought just as bravely as American men had ever fought, and yet the withdrawal had begun, and few soldiers really believed that the ARVN troops could take over and hold off the armies of the North.

Gene often thought of his cousin Kathy. In some ways she had been right about this war. She had understood some of the politics long before he had. But he felt anger toward her, too. In reality, she knew nothing at all about Vietnam. She didn't know what men—a lot of them still teenagers—were going through "for their country." She needed to go out with him on one of these patrols. Then she could talk about the war. It wasn't being "right" about the politics that counted; it was knowing what the war had turned into, and then doing what you had to do anyway—because your country asked you to. That was one thing she would never have to experience.

The night passed one more time, and then another day. Gene did not spend the day hoping for an extraction that afternoon, even though the rain had started again. He simply assumed that anything bad that could happen, would happen. Dearden and Melnick were both having trouble with "immersion foot" by then, an ailment that plagued soldiers in the wet season. Once boots got soaked, they never dried, and the flesh on a soldier's feet would begin to rot. The men didn't wear anything inside their boots because socks only held more moisture against the skin. Gene watched Dearden remove his boots and saw a lot of skin pull off. He let his feet dry for a time, but then he had to put the boots back on. Dearden was in serious pain, and walking had become an ordeal.

But the fog lifted, at least in patches that afternoon, and a slick made it into the same crater where this mission had begun. The best part of the mission was the hike back up the muddy hillside, simply because Gene finally felt a sense of purpose: to get to the top of the ridge and get out. He also liked helping Dearden up the mountain and feeling that he was doing something of worth.

On the slick, flying back to camp, he tried to be happy that the ordeal was over, but he was still too angry and too miserable. His only hope was that there would be a longer break between missions this time, but that meant going back to the waiting—and the nothingness.

As the men walked back to their hooches, Melnick said, "I'm going to get myself *wasted* tonight. I want to set a *record* for drunkenness. I want to find out just how blind and numb a man can make himself."

Dearden wasn't much of a drinker, but he said, "I want my own six-pack tonight." He was walking with an arm around Gene's shoulders and another around Lattimer's. Gene would have thought he would want to rest and heal, not limp off to the Enlisted Men's Club. He couldn't imagine any satisfaction in getting drunk, but he did envy the guys that they had something they could look forward to. He wanted a shower, more than anything, and a chance to burn the leeches off his legs and groin, but he knew better than to expect much from a shower. By the time he dressed again, he would be sweating through his fatigues.

He was almost to the hooch when Pop stepped closer to him and said, "You ought to go over to the club with the team tonight."

"And watch everyone get drunk?"

"You gotta stop saying that kind of stuff. A couple of the guys don't feel like you're one of us."

"Hey, they can trust me. They ought to know that by now. But I don't see what that has to do with getting drunk."

"You don't have to drink. Just go with us. You need to unwind some way or another."

Gene nodded, but he didn't like the idea. He had been with Melnick and Kovach one night when they got drunk. They had become obscene and abusive—more than usual—and they had tried the whole time to shame him into "being a man" by drinking with them.

But Gene did go to the club and sit around a table with the other men, at first actually enjoying himself more than he expected to. Kovach, after a couple of beers, was—to be honest—at his best. He dropped some of his hostility and joked around, and everyone seemed to laugh more than seemed called for. Gene laughed too, even though some of the humor was not the sort of thing he felt comfortable with. The truth was, vulgarity was so much a part of his world now, he hardly noticed it. At least there was a little cleverness thrown in, and the chance to feel halfway human was refreshing.

What Gene found hard to take was the smoke in the room, along with the blaring music. It was so loud that it was hard to hear what people were saying. "Can't they turn that awful music down?" Gene finally said, and the other men laughed.

"Hey, that's *soul* music, Daddy," Melnick said. "Watch what you say about that stuff. You're gonna make the Sarge mad."

Gene looked at Pop. "Do you like that kind of music?" he asked.

Pop laughed. "What do you want to listen to? Neil Diamond?"

The men laughed again, and Melnick said, "I think he's more of a Sonny and Cher man."

Gene didn't know what to say. He had always been so involved in sports when he was growing up and had never listened to the radio much. He had liked the Everly Brothers in junior high, and like everyone else, started listening to the Beach Boys and the Beatles during his high school and college years. But while he had been on his mission, music seemed to change; he could hardly make sense of it now. He liked Aretha Franklin songs, and he liked the Supremes, but a lot of what people called "soul" or "Motown" was just too loud and suggestive for Gene's taste. Jimi Hendrix was supposed to be great, but his music hurt Gene's ears. The British groups were the same way. All they knew how to do was scream.

"I grew up on James Brown," Pop said. "Otis Redding. Marvin Gaye. That's my music. The louder the better."

Pop always seemed aware that he and Gene had come from different worlds, but it didn't seem to matter much to him. It was Melnick who could never let up on Gene. "Drink a little beer and this music sounds a lot better," he said. And when Gene didn't answer, he started in again.

"Hey, what's it going to hurt to have a beer? I don't get that. What does that have to do with religion?"

Gene was not about to get into a detailed discussion of the Word of Wisdom. He knew that was pointless. "We just don't drink," he said. "We don't think it's good for you."

Lattimer was looking at Gene. "Who's *we?*" he asked.

"Mormons. I'm a Mormon. We don't drink." Gene hated that he had to raise his voice so much to be heard. He didn't feel the need to announce to the whole room what he was.

"I hear it's more than the music you don't like," Lattimer said. "You don't like black people, period." He looked at Pop and grinned. Maybe Lattimer hadn't lost his cockiness after all. Gene and he hadn't gotten to know each other very well. He had taken the cot at the far end of the hooch from Gene, and that's where he tended to stay. Gene did know that Lattimer had been to college for a year. He was a tall, lean guy who spoke with a subtle Southern accent and had the style of a moneyed family. Gene had a hard time imagining why he had volunteered for a Lurp unit.

"That's not true," Gene said, and he hoped that was the end of it.

"Hey, I know some Mormons in Memphis. They told me that 'colored boys' can't be preachers in their church. That's how they said it, too, and they were happy about it."

Gene looked at Pop, the only black man on their team. He had hoped this subject would never come up. "Maybe you know about this, Sergeant Winston. Black men aren't given the priesthood in our church. But it's not like it seems. It's not a racist thing."

Pop smiled, but he said nothing.

"What are you talking about?" Lattimer asked. "That's like saying you belong to a country club that doesn't let Jews in, but you're not anti-Semitic."

"I'm not a racist, Sergeant," Gene said. "It's hard to explain, but Mormons aren't prejudiced. I mean, maybe some are. I'm not saying that no one is. But no more than other people, in other religions. And if they really live their religion, they're not racist at all."

But Lattimer wouldn't let the matter go. "Look, Thomas, believe whatever you want, but don't start telling me you have a separate church for white people, and that's okay. I've seen that all my life in the South. At least things are starting to change down there. Some people are saying that that stuff isn't right."

"We have black members," Gene said. But he knew there weren't many, and he really wanted to stop this before it went any further.

"Oh, sure," Lattimer said, "they can sit in the congregation. They just can't get up and preach. They—"

"Lay off of him," Dearden said. "Thomas is a better man than you'll *ever* be."

"Yeah, right, Dearden. You Louisiana boys don't care how a white man treats blacks. You'd just as soon see them all—"

"Hey!" Pop yelled. Gene turned back toward Pop. "Thomas, I don't even know what a Mormon is. And I don't really care. I have no plans to join your church, and I certainly don't want to be a preacher. So let's drop this whole thing."

"That's fine with me, Sergeant," Gene said. "But I want you to know, at basic, my best friend was a black guy from California."

"Ooooh. Don't try that one," Lattimer said. "Don't give us the old, 'Some of my best friends are colored folks.' Right, Sarge?"

Pop gave Lattimer a long, harsh look that stopped him. And then Pop looked at Gene again. "Listen, Thomas, do your job. That's all I care about. I came over here a religious man. My mother took me to church every Sunday when I was growing up. But I don't believe in nothin' now. I believe Charlie wants to kill me and I want to kill him first. And that's more or less what this whole world is about. There's no one I fear more than some guy who tells me he don't mind if I'm black. I figure he's a liar or he wouldn't even bring it up."

"I didn't bring it up. I never would have. I just wanted you to know I don't feel the way Lattimer says I do."

Pop didn't speak for a long time, but he was smiling a little, and Gene saw the cynicism in his stare. "I'll tell you what. Let's try to stay alive. If I go down, you help me if you can—without getting yourself killed. And if you go down, I'll do the same. But if it's a choice between you and me, take you. And I'll take me. That's how things are. Let's not act like it's any different from that."

"Pop, I have a cousin who was on that march to Selma. She was born and raised in our church, and she did everything she could for black people. She was down in Mississippi during freedom summer, and—"

"Thomas, what does this have to do with anything?" Lattimer asked.

"I'm just saying, she's a Mormon, and she fought for civil rights. I wasn't like that, but now, I know she was right. I feel the same as she does."

"I'll tell you what civil right I want," Pop said. "I want a piece of the action. I used to think the white man had to give it to me. Now, I know that I gotta take it. And that's what I plan to do. I'm smarter than most of the white guys I know, and I'm tougher. But the best thing I got going for me, I came to 'Nam, and now I know how things are. Every man in this world has a knife hidden behind his back. He pretends he won't use it, but he will. He will if that's the only way he can get what he wants. Now I know that, I know how to operate. This place has taught me how to stay alive. It's given me an edge. And I'm going to take advantage of it."

"I don't believe that, Pop. I really don't. Some people will stick you if they get the chance, but most of them won't."

"Oh, is that right? Well, finish out your year, if you can keep yourself alive that long—which I doubt—and then talk to me again."

"You came back for a second go-around."

"Yeah, that's right. And maybe that's because I like the way things are over here. There aren't any hypocrites in the jungle. You know what to expect."

"I don't believe that's why you came back. You're not as bitter as you claim."

Pop shrugged and didn't answer, but Gene saw something a little softer in his look.

"I think you still believe some of what your mother taught you."

"Let's just let it drop. All right?" Pop said, and then he looked away.

It was Dearden who said, with his Louisiana drawl, "Pop saved my life a couple of times—put his own life on the line." He looked at Lattimer, not at Pop, when he added, "I'd do the same for him. So don't talk to me about what color he is. None of that matters out here."

Lattimer let it go, and Gene watched Pop, who took a big drink of his beer. But he did give Dearden a quick glance, and when he did, Dearden gave him a nod. Then Dearden, without making eye contact with anyone, said, "I'll put my life on the line for any of you guys." A big smile stretched his mouth out wide, and then he added, "Even Lattimer."

Chapter 5

Hans Stoltz was leaning over a drawing, but his mind wasn't really engaged. He was producing another blueprint for a small apartment building, but he was merely making a few changes to a basic plan that had been used many times before, and it was an architect, not he, who had designed the changes. The housing shortage in the German Democratic Republic was still a problem, and the government really had no hope of catching up, so construction never stopped, but the buildings were little more than boxes—unimaginative, bare-bones structures. Hans liked the people he worked with, especially his boss, and he liked his new freedom to walk outside, sit in a park, or shop at a market, but his life was actually not very different from the one he had led in prison. There was little to hope for and little to do other than work. He couldn't afford anything more than his rent and food, and a limit had been placed on his chance for advancement.

Still, Hans had learned not to feel sorry for himself. He had lived a monastic life for more than two years now, including his time in prison, and he had accepted the simplicity. He watched for chances to learn what he could on his job, always requesting challenging projects, and he also used his evenings for learning. He still studied his scriptures, and he had borrowed reading materials from his branch president. Church-related books were rare in the GDR, but it was occasionally possible to borrow a copy of an old Sunday School manual or an early edition of *A Marvelous Work and a Wonder,* by LeGrand Richards, brought in before the wall had gone up in 1961. What had thrilled him more than anything lately, however, was that his branch president, President Schräder, had lent him a copy of Talmage's *Jesus the Christ*. No such material could be brought into the country now, or ordered from outside, but this copy had been handed down through the family, and President Schräder guarded it carefully. He only lent it to Hans because he knew how much Hans would value it.

Hans had spent many evenings lately not only reading the book but writing out long passages that were especially interesting—or in Hans's mind, beautiful. The book was in English, and Hans's English was not as strong as he would have liked, but he had bought a used German/English dictionary, and he didn't mind working his way through, translating as he went, and improving his English at the same time. In some ways, he liked the slowness of the process, since it gave him time to savor the ideas, and time was one thing he had. He liked to fill his evenings with something that inspired him and kept his mind off things he couldn't do anything about.

So he had been putting in late nights, but there was an excitement about finding the amazing nuggets of insight and inspiration. He had spoken in sacrament meeting recently, too, actually given one of the talks he had created in prison—with a few changes—and had received a remarkable response. He was suddenly considered a scholar, even an orator, and branch members were according him a special respect during discussions in their meetings. President Schräder had since asked him to teach a youth class in Sunday School—the same kind of position he had once held in Magdeburg—and he loved the preparation that went into the class. He liked the young people, and he realized as never before that he had grown a great deal since the last time he had been a teacher.

But he had wonderful memories of that time in Magdeburg, when he had been working toward a future, full of hope. He hadn't known then that young Elli Dürden would take such an important place in his recollections, but he found, now, that she represented a brighter time. He liked to think of her humor, her playfulness. It was something that had been missing from his life for such a long time now. He found that he could laugh with his friends at church, and he surprised himself at being perhaps the most congenial of the men in his office, but still, he spent many hours alone, and in his little apartment some of the somberness of prison seemed to return.

He was putting the final touches on his drawing when *Herr* Meier, his supervisor, approached his desk. Hans worked in a room with three other draftsmen, all of whom had occupied this same room for many years. But *Herr* Meier had taken to giving Hans some of the harder projects lately, and he seemed to consult with Hans more than with the others. Hans believed in himself, knew he had some talent and actually more education than the others, but he also sensed that Meier liked him.

"Hans," *Herr* Meier said as he stopped next to him and glanced at the drawing, "could I speak with you for a moment?" He motioned toward his office. This was unusual. Most often Meier spoke to Hans in front of the other men.

"Certainly," Hans said, and he slid from his chair. He was happy for a break in his routine.

Hans followed Meier into his office and was surprised when he shut the door. He motioned for Hans to sit down, and then he slipped behind his desk. He was a gentle man, and friendly in his way, but formal, and always measured in the way he spoke. He wore white shirts with starched collars, and always dark ties, and he seemed to take special care of his grooming: his fingernails, his hair, his polished shoes. Hans supposed that he was not more than fifty, but he seemed older, with his thinning gray hair, and Hans thought of him as a sort of grandfather. "Hans, you have asked me about the possibility of travel away from Leipzig. When I've asked government officials about that possibility, I've been told that it wasn't approved."

"Yes. I understand." Hans had first asked in December, with the thought of traveling home for Christmas. He hadn't had the money to make the trip, but his parents had offered to pay for his train ticket if the travel were allowed. Hans didn't know whether it was a *Stasi* agent or some party official who had denied the trip, but it was certainly what he had expected. Meier had told him at the time that a way might be opened later, perhaps for the following Christmas, but he couldn't promise anything.

"I spoke to a higher authority recently. I told him what fine work you are doing and what a well-behaved young man you are. I suggested that it might be right to reward you for your work by granting you a little more freedom."

"That's very kind of you." What Hans expected now was a little speech about continuing to work hard so that travel rights might be granted at some later time.

"I received word this morning that if you wish to travel home during a holiday, there would be no objection."

"Is that so? You mean, even now?"

"When the opportunity arises. There will be no vacation time for you at this point, but on a government holiday, it would be possible."

Hans quickly saw that he had actually been granted almost nothing. Without time off, he hardly saw an opportunity. He worked half a day on Saturday. If he took a train to Schwerin on a Saturday afternoon, he would have to start back on Sunday afternoon. Only if a holiday fell on a Monday would he have the time to make the trip worthwhile. But he told *Herr* Meier, "I appreciate this very much. I will try to save a little money for a train ticket, if I can, and watch for a time when I might be able to get away."

"Hans, I could let you take a Saturday off—unofficially—some time. That would give you more time."

"Yes. That would help a great deal. I'll still need to do some saving, of course, but I'll speak to you about it when it seems possible."

"Could your parents help you with the cost?"

"Yes. They have offered. But if I can manage it myself, that would be better."

"Hans, I think it's shameful what you are paid for your work. I promise I will continue to make the case that you deserve a better wage."

"Thank you, *Herr* Meier. I appreciate your concern for me."

Herr Meier straightened a little. "I certainly don't mean to imply a criticism of our government. Party officials always look for signs of contrition and recommitment to socialist ideals. When a man has made a mistake, it is only right that he pay a price. But the goal is more than punishment. Ultimately, the purpose is rehabilitation, and trust can only be regained with time and effort. This offer to make travel available to you is the first step in showing goodwill to you—in response to your own good efforts. I don't know all the details about what you did to lose trust at one point in your life, but you have impressed me as a fine young man, willing to work hard and eager to improve your skills."

"Thank you, *Herr* Meier." Hans slid to the edge of his seat. He knew that Meier was not one to chat. Hans had worked for him for three months now, but he knew nothing of his personal life. Meier's office was small and plain—a square, with four white walls—but there was a family picture on the wall behind his desk, an old one, showing a young Meier with a wife and two young sons. Next to the photograph was a plaque with a government seal on it. Hans couldn't read the words from that distance, but he knew it was a commendation for superior work or production, a reward for *Herr* Meier's service to his country. The man clearly understood his role in the system.

"I wanted to mention one other matter, Hans."

"Yes. Please."

"The official I spoke with expressed a concern that I will pass along to you. He said that you have demonstrated your ability to work, but you have shown little enthusiasm for the ideals of a socialist state. He believes your first loyalty is to your religion, and he suggested that this impression only adds to your predicament. It would be easier to believe in your rehabilitation if you showed an interest in joining the Party."

"Thank you for telling me, *Herr* Meier."

Hans hadn't said what he was supposed to say, and Meier hesitated long enough to give him a second opportunity, but Hans wouldn't—couldn't—say it. They both knew what Hans's silence meant, but *Herr* Meier didn't comment. Hans knew he had probably managed, in a moment, to lose what he had gained with Meier. Maybe the man wouldn't report his unwillingness to join the Party, but Hans knew, as he had always known, that being active in any church, but especially one that wasn't considered mainstream, was a hindering factor in a career. Hans felt the pang, after the note of encouragement, but he didn't dwell on it when he went back to his office. Maybe, in time, he could receive some small raises, but his life was never likely to change very much. He would have to find his joy where he had learned to find it in prison: inside himself and in the Lord.

Hans did leave Meier's office with a thought, however—one that built in his mind all afternoon. He wanted to find a good time to travel home. He would prefer to have more than two days, if possible, since the trip was fairly long, but a trip to Magdeburg was another possibility. The train connection to Magdeburg was direct and the distance much shorter. Even without a Saturday morning off, he could leave Leipzig after work and be there in two or three hours. That would give him a chance to visit friends Saturday evening, attend church, and still have some visiting time on Sunday afternoon before catching a train back in the evening. He was sure President Neumeyer would let him stay in his home if he wrote to him ahead of time. It was the brightest thing he had thought of for a long time, and he began to calculate the possible expense. He normally used almost all his money just to get by, but he had eaten less during his time in prison than he did now, and he had been all right. He was probably a little too self-indulgent these days. If he could save a few marks a week from his food budget for a while, he could make the trip. So that afternoon he walked a little out of his way to the downtown train station, determined the price of the trip, and began to calculate how many weeks before he could have his money. By the time he got back to his apartment, he was so excited he wrote to President Neumeyer. He gave himself four weeks, which would put him into March, but committing to a date would force him to hold down his expenses.

What Hans didn't say to himself was that he was going to see Elli. In fact, he fought back the impulse to dwell on that aspect of the trip. He had written to her before Christmas and let her know that he was out of prison, and she had written back, but both letters had been cordial, not particularly personal, and Elli hadn't said anything about her plans—or about Rainer. Hans knew that his old college friend Rainer Kuntze had shown an interest in Elli and in the Church, but Hans had no idea what had come of that. It seemed likely that if plans were set, or Elli had been engaged, she would have said something about it, so her silence on the subject was mysterious. Was she implying that she no longer thought of Hans as anything more than an old friend? Or was she demanding with her silence that Hans show the first sign of interest? The only thing Hans knew for certain was that he couldn't show that interest. Any man who had to starve himself to take a short train ride was in no position to think about marriage.

Still, he was excited, and his sparse meals didn't bother him. He decided he should eat that way all the time and begin to build up some savings so he really could travel all the way to Schwerin without asking for help from his father.

Hans did receive an invitation from the Neumeyers to stay with them, and he made the trip on the day planned. He spent a wonderful evening with the family, and then on the following morning he went to the branch priesthood and Sunday School meetings. He knew almost everyone, and he appreciated the great happiness people felt for him, everyone knowing about his time in prison. Most of them knew the charges against him—that he had helped a friend who had tried to escape the country—but virtually no one seemed to see that as a crime. They didn't say that, of course, but they spoke of the tragedy that he had lost his chance to finish his education, and they wanted to know what his future held. When he described his work and his likely future, they shook their heads. What they didn't do was denounce the government. In the GDR people knew better than to say everything they thought.

Before Sunday School began Hans was standing near the front doors to the branch house talking to Roland Dillenbeck, one of the young men who had been in his Sunday School class when he had lived in Magdeburg. While he talked, Hans kept watching for the Dürdens to come in. He had thought of writing to tell Elli he was coming, but he had decided that would send the wrong message. All the same, when he finally saw her step through the door, he found himself unable to concentrate on what he was saying to Roland. And he couldn't believe what he was seeing. Elli was a woman. She had always been pretty, but she was changed in some way he hardly knew how to define. She was taller, and she had grown beyond her "little girl" shape, but something in her manner, even her motion, had mellowed. When he had known her, she had been excitable, even silly at times, but now she was looking at him calmly, and she walked toward him with her hand out, but she wasn't bouncing, wasn't giggling. "I heard you were going to be here today," she said, and she seemed pleased, not thrilled.

Hans shook Elli's hand, and then he greeted her parents and her little sister Helga. Then he was approached by another family he had also been friends with. By the time he got inside the little chapel, he was separated from Elli, so he sat next to Sister Neumeyer. He couldn't see Elli from where he sat, but he kept thinking about her. She had been so enamored with him as a sixteen-year-old, and she was only nineteen now, but she seemed to have grown past him. She was like her mother, with those wonderful deep dimples and pretty blonde hair—longer now—but also with a composure he never would have predicted. He had not expected her to charge him and hug him, but he was disappointed that she could greet him with such neutrality.

Hans couldn't concentrate at all during Sunday School class, and that worried him. He was doing exactly what he told himself not to do, filling his head with this pretty girl. He just couldn't do that. He decided not to talk to her after church—and then changed his mind several times. He finally told himself he couldn't leave Magdeburg without at least knowing what was happening with her and Rainer. All these years he had wondered whether Rainer had actually been the one to report on him and bring about his imprisonment. He didn't want to believe that, but he felt enough doubt that it worried him that Rainer might be a deceiver, that he might not be good for Elli. He told himself it was all right to care enough about her to learn her plans.

So when the class ended, he made certain that he moved rather quickly to the hallway before the Dürdens got out ahead of him, and even though he spoke to some other members, when Elli came out, he made a rather brusque break. He stepped to Elli and said, "I hope you know how much it meant to me that you wrote while I was in prison. Letters were very important to me then."

She was smiling with a little more spark now, as though some of the old Elli hadn't disappeared after all. But she only said, "I didn't write very often. I'm sorry about that."

"I never knew how often you wrote. Sometimes, for no reason at all, they wouldn't give me my letters—or they would hold them for a long time before they gave them to me."

She nodded. And she was smiling even more. He realized he was smiling too, and it was embarrassing because they weren't saying anything that should cause them to react that way. "Where are you having dinner?" she asked.

"With the Neumeyers."

"Can you come to see us?"

"I could walk with you now. Sister Neumeyer said she won't serve dinner until later, when President Neumeyer comes home. I told her I might do some visiting before then."

"Then walk with me."

"It's cold."

"I like the cold."

She wasn't pretty anymore, he decided. She was beautiful. And she was still smiling. He knew already that he was making a mistake. He needed to wish her well, tell her good-bye, and then not think about her anymore. But he helped her put her coat on, and then he walked outside with her. The coat was plain black, not fancy, but she wrapped a bright red muffler around her neck, and the color was striking against her fair hair and her round blue eyes. The two hadn't walked far when she said, "Don't you want to ask me about Rainer?"

What did that mean? Was she about to make an announcement? "Yes. How is he doing?"

"He finished his studies. He lives in Berlin now. He wants to marry me."

"Have you set a date?"

"I didn't say I wanted to marry him."

She glanced at him. He saw the quickness in her eyes, the hint of laughter. This was something else he remembered from the younger Elli. "Do you?" he asked.

Hans and Elli had walked along this same street one Sunday afternoon long ago, and everything seemed familiar, as though time were looping back on itself. But the trees were not yet budding, and there were piles of dirty snow on the sidewalk. What crossed Hans's mind was that things couldn't repeat themselves; they changed. What he wished was that he had been allowed to stay, to finish his schooling, to watch Elli grow.

Maybe then Rainer never would have been an issue, and Hans would have been able to offer something.

"He hasn't joined the Church. He tells me he wants to, but he worries about his career. He thinks he should wait and join after he has achieved a better position."

"I can understand why he would feel that way."

"But it's wrong, isn't it?"

"I wouldn't want to make that judgment. We all find our way to deal with the realities of living in this country."

"I don't know whether he believes in the Church. I think he wants to believe. He tries. But maybe it's only for my sake."

"He must love you very much."

She didn't answer. She pulled her muffler up around her ears, under her hair, but she didn't look at him. He had no idea what she was thinking. What she finally said was, "I never know what to think about Rainer. I can never trust his sincerity. I like him, and for a time I thought I wanted to marry him. Maybe I will after all. But I have doubts about him, and I won't marry him until all my doubts are gone."

Hans waited, hoping she would look at him. When she finally did, he saw that she wasn't smiling now. She was watching him, too, and he knew what he was supposed to do. He was supposed to tell her where he stood, tell her that he wanted her to consider him as another suitor. His impulse was to compete for her, but he couldn't forget what he had told himself hundreds of times. It wasn't fair to her to pretend he could give her a life.

"I like Rainer," Hans said. "I consider him a good friend. I've had reason to wonder about his loyalty to me, but I've chosen to think the best of him. I think you're right not to marry him if you have doubts, but my own opinion is that he is a good man."

"Hans, I'm too young to get married. It's not what I want now. That upsets Rainer. He tells me that he accepts the teachings of the Church, but he hasn't lived the way we do, and I don't think he's comfortable with my attitude. He says he likes to know that I'm pure, but I'm not sure it's what he really believes. Maybe it's just what he feels he has to say to me."

"It's possible. I really don't know." There was plenty more to say. Hans knew that Rainer had spent weekends with his former girlfriend, and he had laughed at Hans for being so inexperienced with women. But Hans had no idea how truly Rainer had changed. What he didn't want to do was say anything negative about him. That wouldn't be fair.

"I want to wait to get married. I think Rainer will show who he really is, in time. By then, maybe someone else will take an interest in me." She stopped. Hans stopped too and turned toward her. She looked at Hans intently, and then the smile came back. "I'm trying very hard to act grown up today, Hans, but you need to know, I'm not."

He saw the Elli he remembered, still holding back but seeming ready to giggle. Hans had no idea what to say.

"You always thought I was a little girl when you lived here. Maybe I still am. But you've become much older in a very short time. The Spirit has changed you. Before I get married, I'd like to be more like you."

"I don't know. I still—"

"I think I can do it, Hans. I'm trying."

He knew what she was saying, but he couldn't talk about that. "You've grown up a lot, I'm sure," he said.

"Hans, I'm *very* happy to see you, if you know what I mean. For two weeks, since I heard you were coming—from the Neumeyers, since *you* didn't write to tell me—I've been telling myself not to get excited. But I *am* excited. And I don't want to talk about Rainer anymore. So there. That's everything I promised myself not to say to you—almost everything—and now you know the truth. I haven't changed very much—even though I wanted you to think that I have."

Hans tried to think what he should do, but again he avoided her actual meaning. "We don't change very much. No one does. I went through some hard times, and I guess I do feel older, but I'm still much the same."

"You were always mature, Hans—always ahead of other people your age."

Hans didn't know whether that was true. But it wasn't the point anyway. There was so much openness in her pretty eyes, and she had taken such a chance to say what she had. He wanted to respond. He wanted to plead with her to forget about Rainer, to wait for *him* until he could find a way to provide a life for her. But he couldn't do that. "You say that you want to wait to get married, Elli, and I do think that makes sense. But my case is different. I may never marry. I might not ever be able to give a wife and family a decent life. I'm hardly making enough to pay my rent and feed myself, and I have almost no hope for much improvement."

"I know. I've thought about that. But in this country, it almost always takes two to live. People manage. Lots of members in our branch have meager earnings, but they're very happy together."

Hans felt a surge of joy and an equal stab of panic. He absolutely couldn't encourage this girl to think that way. She had no idea how limited his future was. No one in the branch was getting by on so little. "I'm considered an enemy of the state, Elli. That will never go away."

"Sometimes things change. You're so good, God is going to open a door for you. I'm sure of that."

"It doesn't always work that way. Lots of good people suffer terribly in this life—better people than me."

"I don't know anyone better than you, Hans."

He couldn't think what to say. He could hardly believe what he was seeing in her face.

"Now I've said *everything* I wasn't going to say," she said. "You know exactly what I think of you."

Hans looked down at the pavement. "I think you're a wonderful young woman, Elli. It's been very nice to see you again. I hope everything turns out just right for you."

"Things might change, Hans."

"No. My boss spoke to me not long ago. If I want to make some headway, I need to join the Party and disassociate myself from the Church."

"And you won't do either one."

"Of course not."

"Still, doors open sometimes, just when we think they never will."

"And other times, they never do, Elli. That's something I have to accept."

She stood for a long time, now looking away from him. When she finally looked back, tears were in her eyes. "Hans, I've told you how I feel about you. Can't you give me some idea what you're feeling?"

"Elli, you're a good friend. I appreciate that. I've always liked you."

He saw the hurt in her eyes, maybe even a little anger. But he didn't know what else to do. She turned and began to walk, and he walked alongside her. But they didn't talk. When he reached her apartment, he went in and chatted with her family for a while, and then he left. She didn't walk him to the door, and he was glad she didn't.

That night the ride back to Leipzig was drearier than he ever could have imagined. He had known, instinctively, that he was setting himself up for misery by going to Magdeburg, and yet he hadn't been able to resist. But he wouldn't go back. He had to move ahead with reality, not allow fantasies to trick him into ruining Elli's life. She *was* young, and other young men would catch her interest. She would find someone who would make her much happier.

Hans kept talking to himself, trying to embrace the simplicity he would return to in Leipzig, telling himself that he had to accept what the Lord wanted him to learn and to view his life as a blessing, no matter how it appeared at the moment.

Hans's preoccupation with his thoughts kept him from noticing much of what was happening around him, but gradually, as the train continued south, he began to feel uneasy. A man in a dark suit was sitting in the same car, and it seemed as though he glanced Hans's way a little too often. Hans tried to tell himself not to be so suspicious, but when he got off the train in Leipzig, the man did too, and then he walked across the big open area of the train station in the same direction. Hans was more than leery by then. He walked out the doors, then doubled back and returned to the station. The man, who was just coming through the doors, looked confused for a moment but then walked on out.

Hans waited for a time and then walked outside again. There was the man, pretending to read a map, but waiting. So Hans walked on home and let the man follow, and he finally gave way to the despair he had been fighting. When would his life ever take a better turn?

When Kathy walked into the Makati chapel, near the center of Manila, she was surprised that everything felt so familiar. The building looked very much like the churches she had attended in the States, and boys were preparing the sacrament, hurrying at the last minute, and the members, some seated, some gathered in clusters, were chatting, laughing, shaking hands. Since Kathy had been a little girl, her bishops and Sunday School teachers had been telling her it was important to be reverent in church—and reverent actually meant "quiet"—but Mormons never were. Maybe they were ashamed of themselves for talking in the chapel, for not sitting down for a few minutes of contemplation and spiritual preparation, but if they were, they showed little sign of it. It was a strange delight to Kathy this morning, just to see something that seemed transported from Salt Lake. Some of the men, especially the older ones, were wearing their embroidered *berong Tagalog* shirts, but most had on white shirts and ties, and the women, other than choosing a little more color, looked like the sisters back home.

"Good morning, Sister," a little man said. Most members were too busy talking to friends to worry about a visitor, but this man was extending his hand, smiling—with a tooth missing in front—and then grasping her hand strongly. "How are you?"

"I'm fine, thank you," Kathy told him. "How are you?"

"Oh, bery fine. Where you from, Sister?"

All his words seemed to blend into a kind of waterfall of sound. It took her a moment to realize what he had asked. "I'm from Salt Lake City, but I live in a little barrio now—just outside Manila. I'm in the Peace Corps."

"Ah, bery good. You come now to us, ebery week?"

"As often as I can."

A gray-haired woman was stepping up next to the man now. "This my wife," he said. "Silverio is our name."

Kathy reached her hand out, but she was taken by surprise when the short sister reached with both hands, took Kathy's arms, and pulled her down so she could look her in the face. "You are so beautiful," Sister Silverio said. "So tall and beautiful. You member of the Church?"

"Yes." But Kathy felt her answer more deeply than Sister Silverio ever could have imagined. Tears had come to her eyes, and she wasn't sure why. But others were coming, and everyone wanted to say hello. Most of the women embraced her. Kathy kept glancing toward the branch presidency and the Sunday School leaders, now on the stand. She was sure it was time for the meeting to start, and she seemed to be creating too much of a fuss. She knew that in the barrio nothing ever started on time, but maybe here, where Mormonism had taken hold, the branch president would be bothered by such a delay—so much "irreverence."

But it all happened rather quickly, and then the Silverios took Kathy to a pew and invited her to sit next to them. A man walked to the podium. Kathy assumed he was the superintendent of the Sunday School. The men she supposed to be the branch presidency were sitting on the other side of the stand. The man at the podium was wearing a rather dazzling red tie. "Good morning. We are very happy to welcome you to Sunday School. We especially welcome visitors," he said in English a bit clearer than the Silverios'. He was looking straight at Kathy. Kathy nodded and smiled. Sister Silverio was patting Kathy's hand.

Two young men—obviously Americans, and obviously missionaries—had just come in. Even though they were a little late, they walked to the stand and took seats behind the branch presidency. Kathy watched them during the announcements. One was tall, with neatly trimmed hair and strong facial bones. He looked like an athlete, American through and through. She watched him scan the audience. When his eyes landed on her, they held, and gradually he began to smile. She pretended not to notice, but the smile had seemed a little more than a greeting. Did he know her? Did she know him? He did seem familiar, and the smile had softened her first impression. There was something playful in it.

Kathy sang the opening song with the Silverios: "The Lord Is My Light." It was a hymn she had sung many times without thinking much about it, but again she felt the tug inside her, the sense of the familiar, of good memories. "He is my joy and my song; by day and by night, he leads, he leads me along."

She thought of the idea. The Lord is my song. What a lovely metaphor, and it felt true. A man with a chirping sort of voice said the prayer in English that was barely understandable, but she heard the pattern she knew: the gratefulness followed by requests for the Lord's Spirit, his blessings, and then, "In the name of Jesus Christ, amen." And the entire congregation joined in, voicing the "amen."

It was silly, but she was fighting back tears again. All this was just so comfortable, so much who she was—or at least who she once had been. She had thought her homesickness was more or less gone by now, but the discouragement of the past few months had left her feeling deadened much of the time. This was a trip home.

What followed was the "practice song," with a spirited woman beating out the rhythm emphatically, urging with the other hand for the singers to keep up. She stopped a couple of times, explained that a certain note needed to be held longer or that it wasn't right to breathe in a certain place. Did every ward have a woman like this, everywhere in the world?

And then came the sacrament, with young men—some as sleepy looking as Salt Lake boys—moving according to a preset plan, passing the trays back and forth to each other in the center pews, covering the side pews from front and back, working toward the middle, and then lining up to march to the sacrament table when the young priests stood up. Kathy thought of her brother Wayne. At twelve he had passed the sacrament for the first time. Kathy had been fourteen by then, and a little jealous that boys got to serve the sacrament when they didn't take it nearly so seriously as she would have. Wayne had been the one to walk to the stand that day and hold out the tray to the bishop. But the bishop was his dad, and Kathy remembered how happy, probably proud, her father had looked. Wayne had served all those on the stand, and then, as he walked down the steps, he had glanced at Mom and Kathy—looking serious but very pleased with himself. That had hardly seemed important to Kathy then; she never would have expected to retain the memory. But it was there in her head now: the sense of her mother sitting next to her, and Douglas holding her hand. She had known things then—clear and sure—without actually having thought much about them. She wished she knew the same things now. It seemed at the moment that all those assurances were still with her, however dormant they had long been.

She ate the bread, rich and brown like the handsome boy who presented it to her, and a realization struck her. This boy didn't look like the barrio boys, not even like her students. It wasn't just the white shirt and polished face, either. He looked as though *he* knew something. It was as though he had a grasp of bigger things, nobler possibilities in life. Maybe she only assumed that he did, since he had been taught what she had been taught as a girl, but there was also something in his face that said, "I know who I am."

She had tried so hard to provide her students with a larger vision of life, to make a case for education, for caring about their community, for seeing the possibilities in life. The students were polite, and they claimed to understand, but they never seemed to show it in their faces. Not one of her students had the look of this young man, with a subtle confidence in his eyes. She glanced toward the missionaries in their white shirts and ties. Had they managed this? If not this pair, the ones before them, or the ones before that?

The adult Sunday School class was rather comic, like a pidgin version of a Salt Lake ward discussion. The clichés were even the same. "The Lord answer ebery prayer," a jolly older man said. And then with a smile he added, "Sometime he say no!" Everyone laughed. But the teacher was a wise man, well-spoken, and he asked the class to think more about that. "We try to *tell* the Lord what we need," he said. "We should trust that he is the one who understands our needs better than we do."

It wasn't a new idea for Kathy, but it struck her with more meaning than it had before. She wondered whether she hadn't been telling the Lord, all her life, what it was she wanted, and then blaming him for not agreeing. It seemed a possibility. And yet, she told herself to be careful. She had prided herself for a long time in using her brain, not her emotions, to sort out her beliefs. She didn't want to rush to conclusions on the basis of emotions that were natural, given how homesick she had been all winter. Emotions were important, but they didn't prove anything.

When the meeting was over, she had a chance to chat with the branch president, whose name was Luna. He was a young man—too young to be a branch president, it seemed—but smart, and good, she could tell. His hair was neatly combed, like a little boy's, and he had innocent eyes, dark and friendly, open. "Will you be with us all the time now?" he asked. He sounded almost American.

"I'm not sure," she said. "I'll try."

"We need you, Sister Thomas. So many of our members are new. They need the example of young people like you."

"Actually, I'm not the best example, President Luna. I'm really not. I have my struggles with the Church."

He smiled. "This happens sometimes to young people who grow up as members. But there comes a time when we are needed and we step forward. Perhaps it's time for you to do that."

Kathy didn't know what to say. It sounded true, and he had that same confidence about him that she had seen in the boy passing the sacrament—a look she had almost never seen in the Philippines. "I may not be able to get away every Sunday, but I'll try."

"Could we call you to serve in some way?"

"I'm not sure. Probably not."

"Do you play the piano?"

"Yes."

"Lead music?"

"Yes."

"Oh, Sister, that would help us so much. Sister Torres is wonderful, but she can't do everything herself."

"I can't promise, President. I'm not sure that the Peace Corps would want me to put in all my Sundays here in Manila. There are things to do in the villages."

"I understand. Let me know what you *can* do." He took her hand. "But remember, we need you. Maybe you need us even more."

Kathy shook his hand, and she thought she would come back again next week—if at all possible.

The Silverios were standing nearby, waiting. They wanted to take Kathy home for Sunday dinner. She could spend the afternoon in their home and return for sacrament meeting. But Kathy had told Martha she would be back early in the afternoon. She had to travel by jeepney, with a series of transfers, and it was unpredictable how long it might take to travel across the city and out to the barrio. She decided she'd better go back now and think whether she could stay the whole day on future Sundays. So she thanked the Silverios and was about to leave, but the elders were waiting at the door. "Hey, how are you?" the tall missionary said. "Someone told me you're from Salt Lake."

"Yes, I am. Is that where you're from?" Kathy moved a little so some of the members could get by. She could feel the heat from outside. The building wasn't air-conditioned, but it was holding some of the morning coolness.

"I'm from Murray, actually. But I went to the U of U for a year before I came on my mission. I'm Elder Wimmer. Dale Wimmer. This here is Elder Moffat. He's from down in Fillmore."

Elder Moffat said, "Hi," but nothing more. He was shorter than Elder Wimmer, and he had the look of a new missionary—his shirt still bright, his trousers shiny. But his face didn't show any of that self-assurance that was shooting off Wimmer's teeth and eyes like the hero in a cartoon.

It was fun to hear the ring of a Utah dialect, one she always noticed and yet never knew how to define. "I live in Salt Lake, but I didn't go to the U," Kathy said.

"Were you down at the Y?" He was holding his scriptures, but he tucked them under one arm, then tucked both hands into his pants pockets. He had big arms, thick at the biceps.

"No. I went to a school in the East. Smith College."

"Joseph Smith?" Elder Wimmer asked, and he laughed.

Kathy always found it irritating that Smith was such a prestigious college and yet so many Utahns had never heard of it. Elder Wimmer, in spite of his good smile, wasn't seeming quite so charming now. "Well, good luck," Kathy told him. "I'll come to church as often as I can."

"Do you get any news from home? We don't hear much."

Kathy could tell that Elder Wimmer liked the idea of talking to someone from home, but she wasn't sure she wanted to stay around to chat. "I don't hear much either," Kathy said. "My parents write, but they just give me family news."

"I guess you heard that President McKay passed away."

"Yes. My mom wrote me about that. I guess it's good, since he was so weak. But I'll miss him."

"We all will. But I'm sure Joseph Fielding Smith will be a great leader. We always receive the prophet who is perfect for our time."

Kathy smiled. "I guess," she said. "He seems like kind of a grouch to me."

Elder Wimmer was clearly surprised. He stared at her as if he weren't quite sure he had heard her right.

Kathy was embarrassed, but President Smith did seem to be "all business"—not at all like sweet President McKay. "I'm sure he'll be very good," she said, the words sounding unconvincing now.

"What are you actually doing here?" Elder Wimmer asked, as though not quite sure of her loyalty now.

"I'm in the Peace Corps."

He flinched, his head actually jerking backward. "*Peace Corps?*"

"Yes. You sound surprised."

"I've never heard of a Mormon in the Peace Corps."

"There are quite a few, actually." Kathy wasn't really sure that was true, but she did know of some.

"That's good to hear. I thought you had to be a hippie or a drug addict to get in."

Kathy felt a little surge of temper, but she wasn't going to argue. "Apparently not," she said, giving the words all the ice she could. "Have a good day, Elders."

"Hey, wait a sec. I wasn't trying to insult you." He reached for her but stopped short of taking hold of her arm. "We've just had some bad experiences with the Peace Corps guys we've met up with. We tracted a pair out, and they were pretty much atheists. Then they started saying that America was wrong to be in Vietnam—and all this other anti-American stuff. The one guy said he joined the Peace Corps mainly to stay out of the war."

Kathy gave Elder Wimmer one of her long, cold stares. "Well," she said, "I suppose some people could say that if you weren't serving a mission, that's where you would be."

"Hey, I did my six months in the Reserves. I could still get called up when I get home."

"But you did the six months, hoping to avoid being drafted. Right?"

"Sure. I'm not saying I was all hot to get to the war. But I don't tear down my country. If I get called up, I'm not going to run off to Canada or something like that."

"Maybe it takes more courage to *refuse* to go to war than it does to fight one that's immoral." It was not the kind of thing Kathy said anymore. She had long since decided that things were much more complicated than she had once believed, but she couldn't help letting this know-it-all realize that his opinion wasn't the only one. She had gone too far, however, and she regretted it. She didn't want to start one of her old quarrels, not here at church, not with a missionary. "Well, anyway, I'll see you." She stepped toward the door.

"So you're against the war, huh?"

Kathy turned back and took another long look at Elder Wimmer. She controlled her voice and said, as flatly as she could, "Elder, I didn't think anyone was in favor of it anymore. Nixon promises us every day that he's going to get us out of there. That's all any of us who opposed the war ever asked for."

"But he stands for peace with honor."

She smiled. "I think you should spend the afternoon reading your Book of Mormon a little more closely. I don't think God sees a lot of honor in what we've done in Vietnam."

Elder Wimmer took hold of his scriptures in one hand—a Bible and a triple combination, in zipped-up covers—and he held them up and looked at them. "You must read a different Book of Mormon than I do, Sister. Maybe the Peace Corps has its own version." His tone was suddenly harsh.

"Is this how you talk to the people you teach if they happen to disagree with you?"

"Hey, you started it."

This was a young boy. He had only looked mature. But worse, Kathy was reverting to her own childish habits. "I really do wish you well," Kathy said.

Elder Wimmer stepped a little closer and said in a whisper, as though he didn't want anyone else to hear, "Well . . . I don't wish you well. I've seen what the Peace Corps does. They come over here and say they're going to make the Philippines better, but they don't accomplish a single thing. People who don't believe anything have nothing to teach."

"Maybe we're not here to teach."

"Then what in the world are you here for? These people need help."

Kathy put her hand on his chest and pushed him away. "You know what? I probably *won't* see you next week. You've helped me make up my mind. You've done some good work today, Elder. You've driven an evil Peace Corps worker away from the members."

"Hey, don't put that on me. If you don't fit here, that's *your* problem."

Kathy nodded. She looked at those self-assured eyes. Maybe confidence was overrated, she decided. "You're probably right about that," she said. She turned once again toward the door.

It was Elder Moffat who said, "Sister Thomas."

She looked back.

"Come back, okay? We don't all have to agree about *everything*. I don't agree with some of the stuff Elder Wimmer just said."

Kathy smiled. "That's good to hear," she said. She looked back at Wimmer, and she took a big breath. Then she tried to smile. "I'm sorry," she said. "I do appreciate what you guys are trying to do."

"Hey, I didn't mean to smart off," Wimmer said. He shrugged. "You really should come back."

"We'll see," Kathy said, and she left. She caught a jeepney just down the street and had to crowd onto one of the parallel benches that faced each other in the back of all these extended jeeps. She hated the press of bodies against her on both sides, even though the one on her left was a cute little girl. The air was heavy, too. This was still the dry season in the Philippines, but lately thundershowers had been hitting hard in the afternoons. The hottest time of the year was coming in April and May, and the rainy season would follow. Kathy dreaded that, but she was getting used to feeling sticky. What she wasn't used to was the chaos on the streets of Manila, with all the jeepneys, bicycles, taxis, buses, and motorcycles. No one seemed to pay any attention to the stoplights or stop signs, so pedestrians crowded in among the vehicles, just to find a way across the streets. Kathy couldn't stand to look sometimes as the driver took crazy chances to change lanes or beat a car to an intersection. And all the while people were making hissing sounds or shouting "*Para!*" for the driver to stop, which he did suddenly, in crazy places. People piled off then, and the driver's assistant, a woman, would stand at the back and hold up her fingers to indicate available space on the benches, always claiming more than it seemed possible to bring on board.

It took four changes, from one jeepney to another, to reach the spot where Kathy could board a crowded, stinking bus full of at least as many rabbits, chickens, and ducks as people. Kathy was still disheartened by her conversation with the missionaries, and the dreadful trip back to San Juan didn't increase her enthusiasm to go back to church again. She had liked the people so much, and President Luna. She had even liked the idea that she was needed. But Wimmer was probably right; she didn't fit. Sooner or later that always became clear.

By the time Kathy finally reached her little house in the barrio, the rain had opened up and drenched her. She really didn't mind. It was the closest thing she had experienced to a real shower in a long time. She had grown used to the dip-and-pour showers she took every day, but she sometimes longed for just one hot shower and the chance to stand in it for a few golden minutes. She went straight to her room and got a towel, which she used to dry her hair a little, and then she walked back to the living room, where Martha was sitting on the floor.

"So how was church?" Martha asked.

"It was okay."

"But not great?"

"I liked it, actually." Kathy didn't want to make the missionaries look bad, so she decided not to relate all of Elder Wimmer's sarcasm about the Peace Corps, but she told Martha, "I talked to a guy from Salt Lake. He's over here as a missionary. He told me the Peace Corps isn't doing much good in the Philippines."

"And *he* is?"

It was an interesting question. Martha was painting her toenails—although Kathy couldn't imagine why. The rain was pelting the metal roof, roaring, rattling, seeming to shake the whole house. Inside, the heat was powerful, and the air wasn't moving at all. Kathy's wet blouse was clinging to her, and her sandals were soaked. She wasn't sure why she had started this conversation, and Martha's response made her think maybe she should go change her clothes, but Martha had asked, and so she said, "When you see the people who go to our church, you do have to say that something good is happening to them. They looked so sharp and well dressed, and—"

"Well dressed? That's your measure of progress? Making them into middle-class Americans?" The words were sarcastic, but Martha's tone, as always, was gentle.

"No. But you could see something in them. They looked like people who have goals and are doing something with their lives. Isn't that what we want to see happen with the kids in our school?"

"Maybe it's what *we* want. I'm not sure it's the right answer. We try to teach them the great American way, but maybe they understand what's really important. They know how to treat each other, for one thing."

That was true, to a certain extent, but the people were more complicated than Martha was making them sound, and Martha had to know that. Filipinos could make nasty comments about one another, and gossip seemed a national pastime. They did believe in something Peace Corps trainers had called "smooth interpersonal relationships." It was terribly important in the Philippines not to embarrass anyone, or even to openly disagree. People could be amazingly evasive and indirect so as not to contradict or affront anyone. Filipinos also believed in a code that no American could quite understand. It was called, in Tagalog, *utang na loob*. This was a system of reciprocating, of paying back favors, of looking out for relatives and friends. To defy it was to disgrace oneself. It all seemed a little too obligatory to Kathy, and yet, Filipinos were a kind people, and congenial, as Martha said. But that still left a question in Kathy's mind. "Why are we here, then? Aren't we supposed to help them?"

Martha extended her leg and looked at her toes. Then she pulled the other foot close, ready to start the second set of nails. Her hair was down, blonde and pretty, and it fell forward, covering her face, when she bent over. "Say I'm building a house," she said, "and someone comes by and offers to help me cut boards and drive nails. He doesn't have to tell me I'm doing it wrong. He's helping me, and together we get the job done."

"What if you know a better way? Or you have some better tools? Can't you make things easier for the other guy that way?"

"It depends on how you look at it. Maybe your way is faster. Is that better? To Americans it is. But not to everyone. Maybe enjoying the work is more important than doing it a certain way. I don't think Americans know much about enjoying life. We only know about being more efficient, pushing harder, and collecting more stuff to cram inside the house once it's built."

Kathy had said things like that herself, and for the most part she agreed, but something had looked different at church today. She was still trying to clarify the idea in her mind. "My point is that certain things are right and good—like love, for instance—and it's okay to teach it, or show it, or do whatever it takes to promote it."

"Certainly."

A giant cockroach was working its way along the base of the wall. Kathy watched, without emotion, hardly thinking what it was. She had long since stopped trying to kill them. They were part of the house now, like the lizards that chattered at night and the big green frogs that found their way into the house, even the rats. "What if a person believes in God, and that belief has made him happy? Isn't it okay to teach that?"

"I don't know. So many people are pushing their own road to happiness. It becomes a kind of gimmick. Guys sell vitamins with the same pitch."

"But what I'm saying is, I saw happiness today. I saw people who have been lifted up by what they believe. And I don't see us doing that in the barrio."

"I don't think these people are unhappy."

"But there's something missing. They don't know what life means. They just trudge along. The people I saw today have glimpsed something, and it's changed them inside."

"Kathy, I don't know how to say this, but you grew up with the same beliefs those people have, and yet you're as confused about this world as I am. I don't see the big payoff. Some of the happiest people in this world are misguided by some religious nut, or some charlatan. The question is, what makes *you* happy? I've watched you ever since you told me you were a Mormon, and you're a very good person, but you're not happy. I'd say I'm happier than you are, and I just accept life without really believing a whole lot."

Kathy was stopped. It was true. And yet, she had felt some happiness that morning.

Kathy let the conversation go, but it plagued her. When she went to bed that night, she asked herself, wasn't she happy, and if she wasn't, why not? Maybe Elder Wimmer was right. If she didn't fit with the members, it was because of her, not them. She worried that things would always be the same for her. If she went to church, sooner or later she would be arguing in Sunday School, or getting into little spats like the one with Elder Wimmer today. She wanted to go sometimes. She wanted to experience the Church in another culture and really find out whether it made lives better. She wanted the feeling that had touched her that morning—the sense of coming home. But if she went every week, the branch president would ask her to accept a calling, and she wasn't ready for that. What she feared more than anything was that if she went all the time, she would soon feel what she had felt in Utah, and in Massachusetts, that she really was out of place with people of her own faith.

Something else was bothering her. All her life she had been taught that she should be an example, that she should show the fruits of the gospel in the way she lived. But Martha had lived with her the better part of a year, and she saw in Kathy little sign of happiness. Kathy had wondered what was missing in the people of the barrio. Maybe she should have been asking what was missing in herself.

Chapter 7

It was March, 1970, and Gene had been in Vietnam almost four months. His days remaining had dropped below 250—with well over a hundred behind him—but that didn't help. He found that his sense of self, of being Gene, was slipping away. He pleaded with the Lord for help, for the Spirit to be with him, but the repetition of missions, the almost constant discomfort, were not the biggest problems anymore. The numbness he had been feeling for a long time had only deepened. It was probably what he needed to survive the patrols and the days of waiting in between, but he wondered sometimes whether he was human anymore. It was so hard to care about anything. He desperately needed a sense of connection to Emily and Danny, but thinking about them only brought back the worry, the dread of the next mission, and so it was easier to vegetate, to sleep all he could, and to mark off another day. The other men found release in their drinking, their camaraderie, but it was the drinking as much as anything that kept him separate from them. On patrols, he felt an attachment that went beyond anything he had ever known. The men needed each other, and every one of them had to do things right. He was amazed, over and over, at the commitment of the men to silence, to caution, to keeping each other alive. No one wanted to be the guy who made the mistake that got them shot up. But back from the patrols, the men partied together, sharing that, too, and Gene usually didn't go. Pop still thought he should, but Gene ended up feeling out of place, even resentful, as the men got drunk.

At least Dearden, who didn't like to drink much either, gave Gene someone he could talk to on some of those long, empty days. Dearden had been raised a Baptist, and his family was busy with church work at home. They sent him newsletters from their congregation and reported to him what the local members were doing in his hometown of Tallulah, not far from the Mississippi border. "Ears," as the men called Dearden, was a simple guy, with little to say about politics or even about the war, but he had great stories about hunting and playing ball in high school. Gene had told him plenty of his own sports stories. He liked recalling those glory days. He tried to play down his own heroics, but it hadn't taken long for Dearden to figure out that Gene had been captain of every team, obviously a star player. He loved to pump Gene for more and more details about that, and about girlfriends, life in Salt Lake, and even life for Mormons. Gene was equally curious about a kind of life he had never known. Dearden had lived on a farm, outside town, and he told stories about his childhood days out in the woods with his hunting dog. He wasn't really a loner—he liked people—but he understood being alone, and Gene liked the fact that he didn't feel the need to talk every second when the two were together.

Sunday was Gene's chance to meet with men who understood him and looked at the world the same way he did. He depended on that, but he was often on patrols on Sundays and had little chance to get close to the LDS soldiers. Most of them were in the 101st Airborne, but in this war they were basically ground troops; they spent a lot of time out in the field. Each time Gene got to church services, different men were there.

One Sunday, when he entered the tent that was used for church meetings, he didn't recognize the man who was greeting everyone. "Chaplain McFarlane," the man said, and he stuck out his hand.

A major named Collings had been leading the services the last time Gene had been there. He wasn't a chaplain, but he was a career soldier in his late thirties, and a high priest. He had been a rather formal man who really didn't say any more than he had to. The chaplain seemed like the bishops Gene had known growing up—smiling, greeting everyone, shaking hands.

"I see that you're a Ranger, Corporal Thomas," the chaplain said.

Gene had received his corporal stripes just the week before. "Yeah. But I didn't train for Special Forces. I ended up in a Lurp unit that got transferred over to the Rangers."

"What's a Lurp unit?"

The chaplain was short, with rounded cheeks and an overall kind of softness to him. He wasn't heavy, but his muscles hadn't been hardened, and there was no hardness in his face, either. Gene knew by instinct that he had never been in combat. "It's reconnaissance work," Gene said, but he decided not to explain beyond that.

"Well, nice to meet you. I hope I'll be getting to know you better. Are you going to be around for a while?"

"Yeah. Forever."

Gene hadn't meant to sound cynical, but it had come out that way. Chaplain McFarlane gave him a pat on the back and said, "I'm sure it seems that way," and then he turned to the next man coming in.

Gene looked around the tent. He had seen some of the men before, but most were either young guys, eighteen or nineteen, or they were officers, some of them quite a bit older. Today there were fifteen or so sitting on wooden folding chairs, Major Collings among them, and after Gene sat down, several more came in. Some of the men shook Gene's hand. Sometimes Gene wished that he could find a friend here among the LDS soldiers, but his life was such that he probably wouldn't be able to spend any time with a guy who was in a regular unit. So he didn't say much, just waited. The air was hot already, worse than outside, even though the side flaps of the tent were rolled up. It would only get worse as the hour went by. He hated the smell of the tent. It was the smell he associated with the army, some chemical treatment probably, or some packing material that rubbed off, but it was the smell of so much of the equipment he used, even the smell of a new uniform.

The chaplain eventually walked up front and, looking rather unmilitary with his weight mostly on one leg and a hand in his pocket, said, "Brothers, it's great to be here with you. All this is pretty new to me, but I understand you've been having just one meeting on Sunday mornings."

Major Collings, who was sitting on the front row, said, "That's right, Chaplain. We've always passed the sacrament, and sometimes we've taken turns giving talks, but since we never knew for sure who would be here, more often than not I would try to lead some sort of discussion."

"That sounds good. I've prepared a few things I want to say, but I hoped we could have a discussion, a sort of priesthood meeting, after we pass the sacrament." A little table was sitting at the front of the tent, covered with a cloth. That much had apparently been organized ahead of time. "Maybe I can call on these two men here to help us out. Your name was Pederson, wasn't it?"

"Yes, sir."

"And what was *your* name again?" He looked at the second young man.

"Beck, sir."

"Would you two bless and then pass the sacrament for us this morning?"

Pederson said he would, but Beck said, "I could if you've got it written out somewheres. I don't think I could just say the prayers off by heart."

The chaplain smiled. "The prayers are in the scriptures," he said. "I'll show you where."

Then he led the singing himself: "Redeemer of Israel." There were no hymnbooks, but Chaplain McFarlane sang the words out loudly, and most of the men knew them well enough to follow along. They sang with some vigor, too, with the chaplain's upbeat tempo, and that felt good to Gene.

He felt something stir in him, as though he were coming awake after a long sleep.

Chaplain McFarlane called on a young soldier named Pierce to say the opening prayer. Gene liked the words of the prayer—the things the soldier prayed for but also the familiar sound of the language. Pierce sounded like a Utah boy, and maybe that was part of it, but Gene liked to hear "we call upon thee" and "watch over us at all times." It was language he had grown up with, language he used himself when he sat on his cot or lay on it at night and said his own prayers. Pierce said, in closing, "Help us to accept thy will, Father, and to learn from the challenges we are facing." It was an understatement, and it touched Gene. Here they were, all of them in situations of peril, and there was nothing to do but accept that the outcome might not be what they wanted. Gene wanted to believe that he was learning something from his "challenges," but right now, he had no idea what it was. Still, the words were a good reminder. Maybe this time in Vietnam could be put to good use if he went about it right and kept a good attitude. He tried to tell himself that all the time, but when he was in the jungle he found it difficult to see anything positive in the experience.

After the prayer, the sacrament was blessed and passed, and Gene took the chance to bow his head and try, harder than usual, to pray for the Spirit. He needed this lift, needed to come away feeling better than he had all week. He concentrated on the words of the second prayer, and then he made some promises of his own. He was going to read his scriptures more consistently this week, pray with more sincerity. He was going to write a good letter to Emily today and reassure her that he was clinging to the Lord, just as he knew she was.

Gene also asked the Lord to let him live. He never knew whether it was right to ask, when so many were dying, so he told the Lord he could accept His will—but if it was God's will, he wanted to get back to his wife and have the chance to raise his son.

After the sacrament had been passed and the cover placed over the trays, Chaplain McFarlane stood again. "Brothers, I've been in the army for a while, but I'm new to Vietnam. Every one of you knows what's going on here better than I do. But I hope you know that not everyone back in the States is putting you men down. The ones who yell and scream and burn the flag get all the headlines, but a whole lot of Americans appreciate what you're doing. Throughout the history of our country, men like you have been called upon to leave their families and go off to fight for our freedoms. Many have paid the ultimate price, and such men will always be our heroes. America's good name is being battered by a lot of people these days, but let's never forget, we don't fight wars of aggression. We've come all the way to the other side of the world, with nothing to gain but the knowledge that another people will be able to retain the same freedoms we enjoy. So don't listen to the critics who put you down; rely on the knowledge that some things are worth fighting for."

Chaplain McFarlane hesitated, and then he asked, "Brothers, I'd like to know how you feel about that. Would anyone like to comment?"

Some time passed, obviously more than the chaplain was comfortable with. He was about to say something else when a man in the back, not far from Gene, raised his hand. He was a buck sergeant, a young guy not more than twenty. "Some people are talking now like wars are always evil, and they even want to say that God doesn't want us over here. But in the Book of Mormon you see how God isn't against war if men are standing up for what's right."

And then an older man, a captain, added, "I have to laugh when these college students talk like they think they can just pick and choose their wars. They don't happen to like this one, so it's all right to turn traitor and refuse to serve. But you just can't do that. I'm not saying everything about this war satisfies me, and I don't know why our country is trying to back out before the job is done, but the way I look at it, that's not my decision. I serve my country, and when my president asks me to fight, that's what I'm going to do."

Some other men picked up on that theme, and some more comparisons to the Book of Mormon came up: war being acceptable when it was fought in defense of family and country. Gene was uneasy with some of that, although he never would have said so. It wasn't that he disagreed; it just seemed a little too simplistic, given some of the things he had seen. Still, it was good to hear men who were patriots. He hadn't heard much of that lately.

Eventually, Pederson, the young man who had blessed the sacrament, raised his hand. Gene had noticed that he was a corporal, and from the look of his boots and fatigues, he had been in-country quite a while. "There's something I'd like to ask you men about," he said. "I don't want to sound negative, but I've seen some things lately that I don't really understand."

Gene felt the atmosphere change. The men grew quiet, even seemed to tense, as though they feared what he might bring up. Gene felt uncomfortable himself. There were realities in war—in this war—that most men wouldn't want to carry with them into church. The temperature in the tent, even that smell, seemed to be getting worse.

"I got in a situation here a while back," Pederson said. "Our platoon was making a push, trying to clear out some VC we had reports on. We checked out a village, searched all the huts and everything, and we didn't find anything, so we were moving out. But then we started taking sniper fire from the ville we had just walked out of. My squad leader got hit in the back. He dropped dead right next to me. A couple of other men were shot up too. So our platoon leader got on the radio and called in an air strike. Some F-4s swooped in and fired up the place with rockets. Then they came back with napalm and set everything on fire.

"We gave it some time, and then we went in to mop up. Some people ran off, and we didn't shoot at them or nothing like that, but in the ville, everyone was dead. Women and kids. Old men. I found this dead woman in a burned-down hut, and she was holding her dead baby. Both of them were burned black. All our guys were glad about getting back at the ville—you know, since someone shot at us from there—and I know somebody there had to be VC. But my platoon leader had us count everyone—all the kids and women and everyone, and he put down on his report that it was a VC village, and we killed a bunch of the enemy. That's not the first time I've seen something like that, and I don't know how I'm supposed to feel about it. I didn't think I'd ever be killing women and children—then counting them as enemy kills. I've tried really hard not to think much about it, but when I shut my eyes, sometimes I see that lady and her baby, all black and burned up, and I don't know . . . I just . . . don't feel good about it."

"That stuff is not our fault," someone said. "That's just the way this war is."

The tent was like a hothouse. Chaplain McFarlane was clearly nervous. "I suppose in any war, there are—"

"Chaplain McFarlane," a Pfc Gene had met—a guy named Hutchings—said, "I had something like that happen too. My platoon killed a bunch of farm animals—water buffalo and cows. The word came down from the CO to do it. He said the people in the village were feeding the VC, so we had to punish them for it. But without their animals these people can't survive."

"Have you ever seen those refugee camps down in Saigon?" another boy asked. "When the people lose their villages, or get their rice patties destroyed, they end up in refugee camps, and those places look like the concentration camps you read about in World War II. The conditions are just sickening. People die in those places all the time."

The chaplain was looking around, obviously hoping for help from the officers. "No one wants to claim that war is a good thing," he finally said himself. "That's not what I was saying." He looked at Major Collings.

Collings stood up and turned around. He looked down at Corporal Pederson, standing almost over him. "War isn't pretty," he said. "And officers have to make hard choices. In World War II, millions of civilians died. That's something we try hard not to do in this war. But it happens. You can't get around it."

"But sir, we keep saying we're here to make things better for these people," Pederson said. "I don't think the people in the villages know anything about Communism. They just want to farm their rice paddies. I thought I was over here to help them out, but they're scared to death of me—and anyone else in an American uniform. It just doesn't seem like anything is working out right. One guy, maybe a VC soldier, shoots at us from a village, and all the people in the village end up dead. What did that accomplish?"

"If they want to stay alive, they should see to it that the VC stay out," a sergeant said.

Pederson turned in his seat and looked back at the sergeant. "But they can't keep the VC out any more than they can keep us out," he said. He didn't sound argumentative, just confused. "One side or the other just keeps coming through, and either one will kill them if they do the wrong thing. What are they supposed to do?"

The sergeant started to respond, but Major Collings held up his hand and stopped him. "This is a church meeting, men. We don't want to start debating this war, the way everyone is doing back in the States. The important thing is, we have to answer for ourselves. In all my years in the army, I've never acted toward civilians in a way that I'm ashamed of. I've never had to do anything that keeps me awake at night."

He was about to continue when Private Hutchings said, "I got an order to kill that water buffalo. I didn't have a choice."

The tension was back. Major Collings looked at the young man for a long time. "I understand what you're saying. You did what you were told, and that's what you have to do. An officer had to make a hard choice, and maybe you didn't like it, but he's the one who has to answer for it. Just leave it at that."

Gene knew the discussion was over, but he also knew that the major's answer didn't satisfy him. Weren't there times to say, "No, I won't do that"?

Gene had heard entirely too much of this kind of talk lately. Back in "the world," he had heard antiwar types talk about wiping out villages and napalming babies, and it had all seemed an exaggeration by people who didn't really know what they were talking about. But Gene had heard firsthand accounts from Lurps about interrogating captives by threatening to push them out of helicopters—and then doing it. Another technique was to ask a man a question and then shoot him when he didn't give a proper response. The assumption was that the next guy in line—who had watched all that—would be more "responsive." Melnick had told Gene a story about five guys taking bullets in the head, and chances were, they actually didn't have the answer the Americans wanted.

It was all immensely dirtier than Gene had expected. When people had talked about "fighting for freedom" back home, he had pictured an enemy—a bad guy who had to be stopped. But he hadn't imagined the complications. Everyone told stories about innocent-looking teenaged girls who were actually Viet Cong, hiding AK-47s in their skirts, or about children throwing grenades. Some of the stories must have been true. But the effect was to put fear into everyone. The enemy and the friends looked alike, and American soldiers, after being in the country for a time, suspected everyone. They wanted to stay alive, and so it was easy to pull the trigger and ask questions later. Somewhere in all that, it was hard for Gene to see where the "fighting for freedom" happened.

The chaplain had obviously learned a quick lesson. He changed the subject from the war to the spiritual resources the men could call upon to deal with their fears. But the damage had been done. Gene left the meeting wondering, more than before, what kind of war he was fighting.

Two days later Gene and his team were inserted into the nearby mountains at first light. The Huey dropped into a clearing near a river at the bottom of a valley. Gene was off second to last and was running for cover when he saw Lattimer drop. He had been going hard, and then he just crumpled. Gene hadn't heard any shooting, the sound of the props making so much noise. His thought was that Lattimer had stumbled and would be up and going, fast.

But it didn't happen. Lattimer lay sprawled, one arm and his rifle under him, the other flung out wide. And then Gene saw the red, the bloody hole, the size of an apple, in the back of his camouflaged uniform. At the same moment, he saw Kovach fire his weapon. Gene stopped, unclear what he was supposed to do, but Pop grabbed him and pulled him back toward the helicopter. Gene spun back, but the slick was lifting. The men were in the middle of a hot landing zone, fire coming from somewhere, and nowhere to go.

Then the rush of the blades was back, and he knew the helicopter pilot had seen what was happening. He was dropping back into the zone, putting his own life in danger. Gene was firing his CAR-15 by then, but not at anything he could see. Melnick and Dearden had Lattimer, and they were pulling him, running for the slick. Gene jumped on first. He grabbed Lattimer by one arm and pulled him on board. And then everyone was piling on and the Huey was lifting while the men were still on the skids. The pilot got up only thirty feet or so and then dropped the nose and angled away, barely clearing the trees.

Gene still didn't know what had happened. Had there only been that one bullet fired—the one that took out Lattimer? Maybe a sniper? But Lattimer was facedown on the floor, and the bullet had had to come straight through his chest. Pop was ripping at Lattimer's jungle utilities. He slapped a bandage against his back and then he and Melnick rolled the boy over.

Gene saw Lattimer's face, the pallid blue skin. He was gasping, his lips purple, and his tongue was reaching, as though he were gagging. Pop tore open his shirt, but there was only a little bullet hole, almost no blood. Pop clapped on another compress, and then he yelled into Lattimer's face, "You're all right. We've stopped the bleeding. We'll have you back to camp in a few minutes. Just hang on." He gave Lattimer's face a little slap. "Do you hear me? Hang on. Keep fighting. We'll get you out of here."

But Lattimer wasn't hearing anything. His body was convulsing as he gulped for air. His eyes looked wild, but he wasn't seeing, wasn't hearing.

Pop kept after him, yelling into his face, but Melnick had given up. Gene saw him turn from Lattimer and rest his head on his arms, across his knees. Melnick already knew what Gene was just starting to realize. The bullet was through a lung, and who knew what else? He had to be bleeding inside. But it was his face that told the story. His body was fighting for air, but he was already gone.

Gradually, the struggle ended. The breaths became shorter, shallower, and quivering replaced the convulsions. Pop tried one last time to call him back, but the blue was not only in his face but also in his hands and chest. Then the breathing stopped.

Pop stared at Lattimer for a long time, and then to Gene's surprise, he lay down next to him and held the boy in his arms. And now it was Pop who was quivering. Gene couldn't see his face, but he knew the man was crying. Pop had always been proud that he brought his team members back alive, that he had never lost anyone. Gene had always thought it was a matter for Pop of doing his duty, being able to tell himself that he had done his job well. He didn't think that the man would cry. Lattimer was cocky, hard to get close to, not someone Pop would seem to care so much about. But that wasn't it. Lattimer was a boy, and he was dead. That's all a guy had to know.

Gene wanted to stop looking at Lattimer's face, but he couldn't look away. He saw the way the flesh had lost its shape, the cheeks sagging. His jaw was hanging open, the fillings in his teeth showing. Gene thought about some mother in Tennessee who had taken her son to the dentist for his checkups, had probably gone with her husband to his Little League games, had sat at his high school graduation ceremony and hoped for her big, handsome boy to marry well, have a good career, produce some pretty grandchildren for her. She would get the news later today, he supposed. She would come to the door, and someone would be standing there in a uniform, and she would know what that meant. In his mind, she looked exactly like his own mother.

Gene was crying now too, and, as always, he thought of Emily. And Danny.

Gene had known about Americans dying, of course, but he hadn't seen it happen until now. And this was one of his own team, a guy who had been waiting with him that morning at the helipad, joking about getting some good "contact" for once.

But it wasn't until Gene was off the slick, and a medevac helicopter had taken the body away, that Gene thought about the discussion at church. He wanted to believe that he was fighting—that Lattimer was fighting—for freedom. He wanted Lattimer's mother to believe that that's what he had done. But whose freedom? How? Where? Young guys were dying on both sides, but who was gaining any freedom? The politicians were planning to pull out. And the soldiers in 'Nam didn't believe for a minute that the South Vietnamese troops could hold off the NVA. Most of the people Gene talked to seemed to think that a year or two after the Americans pulled out, the South would be overrun. So what had Lattimer died for?

Gene felt sick. He hadn't known how dead a guy could be, lying there in a helicopter, his flesh turned to rubber. Gene didn't want that to happen to him. He believed in an afterlife, and he believed in America, and he believed in freedom. But he didn't want to die in Vietnam for reasons that were no longer clear to him.

Chapter 8

Diane had baked some chicken breasts, but now she didn't know how to keep them warm without drying them out. She had expected Greg to be home for the past half hour, and she had wanted the dinner to be nice. The editors for the law review at the University of Washington were going to be announced that day, so the dinner was a celebration, since Greg was sure he would make the staff. He was actually holding onto some hope that he might be appointed as the head editor, although he admitted that wasn't likely. What Diane knew, of course, was that he would be disappointed if he didn't get it. It was one of those delicate times when she would have to build him up a little but not say anything that might irritate him. She thought it best to make it a romantic evening, with a nice little dinner and a promise to put Jennifer down early. But Diane was nervous about that. She had tried to keep Jenny up, not let her have a second nap, so she would be ready for bed early, but Jenny had been playing on the living room floor and had fallen asleep. She hadn't slept long, but she was wide awake now, and it was hard to say when she would feel like going to bed.

Diane had spent some time that afternoon talking to Mary Innis on the telephone. Preston, her husband, was taking forever to finish his Ph.D., and it was frustrating to Mary. Mary appreciated his love of learning, but he was so meticulous about his research that he couldn't seem to move ahead on the actual writing of his dissertation. Finding a college teaching job without a completed Ph.D. was tough these days, and Mary had spent way too many years waiting to escape her status as "student wife." But Mary was patient with Preston and could even laugh at his being the absentminded intellectual. "I don't know how he goes to the library and works right now," Mary said. "The campus is practically on fire, and he sits in the middle of all that chaos and reads his books."

Spring, 1970, at the University of Washington had been crazy. All the usual antiwar demonstrations were going on, but in March the Black Student Union had protested the university's involvement with BYU in sports. Similar protests had been going on at Stanford and quite a few other universities. Some students felt that BYU was supported by a racist church—because of its practice of not granting priesthood to blacks—and they argued that their universities should withdraw all contact with BYU. When the University of Washington had not responded to the protests, black students had occupied Thomson Hall, a classroom building. Seattle police had never before been called on for help, but Tactical Squad men in blue visors and carrying nightsticks were brought in this time, and the protestors were dragged out of the building. This only brought on more demonstrations. The university administration eventually agreed not to schedule any new events with BYU but argued that it had to carry out its current contracts. For a time things got crazier, and Greg came home every night with stories of students denouncing him and other Mormons. Diane knew it was a tough situation for Greg, but some of the guys in the ward seemed to know better than to argue with people. Greg had never learned that.

The BYU issue seemed to die down after a while, but then, recently, Nixon had announced that he was invading Cambodia. Campuses had gone crazy, everywhere, and "The Weathermen," a violent offshoot of Students for a Democratic Society, marched into the ROTC building at the University of Washington and trashed the place. At Kent State University, where the protests were considered out of hand, the National Guard was called in, and in an atmosphere of chaos, some of the guardsmen fired into a group of protestors, killing four of the students. The next morning Greg had gone to campus and found the entrances barricaded.

Protestors had staged what amounted to a takeover. Students, in a mass rally in the quad, voted to strike, and a large percentage of students had stopped going to classes. Greg, of course, was not about to do that, but normal procedures were disrupted, with many of the more radical professors agreeing with the students and closing their classes. The university had finally had to announce that grades for the term would all be pass/fail.

Through all this, protests continued daily. Students had taken over the I-5 freeway one day and been beaten by police. Some of the more excessive reactions from the police—pushing several students off an overpass, in one case—were caught on local television news. Most students saw that as brutality, but Greg placed the fault with the students, and that made him less than popular at the law school. Since then, there had been a lot more craziness, with more buildings attacked and even a group of local "vigilantes" beating up students in the U-District. When the chief of police admitted that the vigilantes had actually been off-duty police, that had only made students angrier.

Diane heard Greg's version of things, but she also watched the news on television and sometimes read the student newspaper that Greg brought home. All of it seemed horrible to her. She preferred BYU, where people didn't act so crazy, where students didn't resort to protests. Still, she read enough of the student point of view to feel dubious about the war in Vietnam, and she wondered whether the police didn't make things worse on campus instead of better. Of course, she never told Greg what she thought. He got angry every time he talked about the radical students who were taking control of the university, and the weak, liberal administration that kept bowing to their demands.

Diane wished sometimes that she could warn Greg to be more careful, but he had no patience when she hinted that he might be wrong about the way he handled things at the law school. When she talked to Mary, Diane wondered what it would be like to be married to someone who listened to her opinions and didn't overreact when she disagreed.

Mary had become a kind of lifeline for Diane. They talked on the phone almost every day, and Mary had a way of drawing Diane into the real world by making sure she knew what was going on. Diane had come to feel a need to read newspapers or watch the news on television, just so she wouldn't seem stupid to Mary. In April Mary had called, almost breathless, worried about the three astronauts on board the crippled Apollo 13 spacecraft. Diane hadn't known what she was talking about, but because of Mary, Diane had followed the story on TV and radio, and the two had rejoiced together when the men had splashed down safely. They often talked about the war, too, and about women's liberation. Mary was a solid member of the Church, but she saw things very differently from Greg. She seemed almost as liberal as Diane's cousin Kathy, but not so argumentative about it. Diane had never been certain about her own opinions on political matters, and she still wasn't, but she did suspect that Greg didn't have the last word on everything.

Mary never seemed to be afraid to tell Preston exactly what she thought. In fact, Mary had told Diane that afternoon, as they had talked on the telephone, "You act like you're scared of Greg. I don't think that's healthy. If you don't start talking more honestly with him, you're never going to have the kind of relationship you want."

Diane appreciated Mary and her "big sister" kind of advice, but upsetting Greg wasn't worth it. "Sometimes, in a relationship, maybe one has to give a little more than the other," she told Mary. "Greg is always going to be a wonderful provider, and he really does love me. It's okay, I think, if I pamper him just a little."

Mary hadn't responded for a few seconds, and Diane knew what she was thinking, but then she had only said, "Greg's lucky to have you, Di."

Diane liked that thought. It had bolstered her the rest of the day. But now she had to deal with her almost daily problem. Greg liked to come home to a hot dinner, but he could never say for sure when he would get there. She turned the heat down to "low" on the oven, and she hoped he would come in soon. She had some frozen corn in a saucepan, ready to heat, and she had prepared a green salad. She had baked some rolls, too, and covered them with a cloth. She hoped they would stay fresh.

Diane knelt by Jennifer. "Should we pick up your blocks before Daddy gets home?" she asked. Jennifer could crawl now, and she had managed to scatter her toys all over the little living room.

Jennifer, of course, didn't understand the content of the question, but she saw her mother begin to gather in the blocks, and she didn't like the idea. She squealed in protest and grabbed a couple of blocks, which she pulled against her chest and held tight.

"Okay. You can play with the blocks, but let's keep them over here."

Diane was on her hands and knees, gathering in the scattered blocks—so they wouldn't look quite so messy to Greg—when the door opened. She looked up, saw Greg, and knew immediately that something was wrong. He gave her a hard look that seemed to say, "Don't ask," and then he walked into the bedroom. She heard him changing his clothes, but she didn't approach him. It would probably be a mistake to ask him what was wrong—better to let him tell her when he was ready—but he might also be annoyed that she didn't come to him. She got up, tried to think what to do, and then finally walked to the door of the bedroom. "Are you okay?" she asked.

"No, I'm not okay."

"What happened?"

"They got me. The people who hate me got their way."

"What do you mean?"

"I didn't make law review."

"Not at all?"

"What did I say, Diane? I didn't make law review. There aren't any *levels* of not making it. I should have been the lead editor, and I'm not even on the staff."

"How could they do that?"

"The bleeding hearts have control of everything right now, Diane. All rational thought has been proclaimed out-of-date. I had the nerve to say that I didn't think students should be shutting down our university; that's all it took."

Diane didn't know what to say, or what to do. She did feel he had been cheated. He was ranked near the top of his class. But she had worried that this might happen. It was what she had tried to hint, that he couldn't discuss things with people without getting into angry, sarcastic arguments. He didn't have to become a radical, but he also didn't have to refuse to hear other people's points of view.

"You know you deserved a position," she finally said. "That's what counts."

Greg had pulled on an old pair of khaki pants. He was buckling his belt, but he stopped and looked at Diane. He stared at her for several seconds. He sounded dispassionate, not angry, when he said, "Diane, I don't know whether you're merely stupid, or whether you say things like that to make me crazy. I want to think the best of you right now, so I'll conclude the former. You really are that dumb."

Diane couldn't breathe. She knew that everything could explode at any moment. She said nothing. She slowly turned and walked away, back to the kitchen. She added a bit of water to the corn, and then she turned on the burner. She was trying not to say things to herself that she would regret, but she couldn't fight the feeling that she *hated* Greg—that she had finally come to that. She walked to Jennifer, who had started to fuss. Jennifer had a sense for this tension, seemed to know as well as Diane that a fuse had been lit and a detonation was likely to follow.

Diane carried the baby to her high chair and then got some baby food from the refrigerator. She was going to give Greg some time, and give herself some time too, and then deal with her feelings later. But Greg came into the kitchen. "Look, I'm sorry I said that. I think what you are is naïve, Diane, and that's not such a bad thing. But it's hard to deal with sometimes. Think about what you just said. No one is going to look at my résumé and say, 'You *deserved* to be on the law review. That's what counts.' Some of those ultra-liberal law professors obviously blocked my appointment, and my career is stunted right from the beginning. The worst thing is, there's not one thing I can do about it. I could protest and make a big fuss, and that would only be looked at as more proof that I'm not one of them."

Diane was sitting on a kitchen chair next to Jennifer, feeding her some strained peaches. She decided it might be best, for now, to continue to do that and still not say anything.

"Look, Diane, I'm sorry I hurt your feelings. But you'll have to admit, this is a tough thing to deal with. Maybe you could cut me just a little slack."

"I know it's hard, Greg. I feel really bad for you. But I don't know what to say."

"I wouldn't mind if you got mad, a little, and told me you thought I got a raw deal. It would be nice to know that you're on my side. Because right now, I don't feel that."

"I *am* mad. I do think you got cheated."

"But?"

"Nothing."

"Well, then, tell me this. Why do you sit there and feed the baby? Couldn't you give me a moment of your attention? Couldn't you *sound* a little angry, if that's what you are?"

Diane turned around. "Greg, it makes me sick that they didn't give you what you deserve. You worked so hard for it. But it's hard to know what to say. That's all."

Greg took a couple of steps toward Diane. "Why? Because I might call you *stupid?*" His voice was rising now, shaking.

"No. It's just very upsetting to you."

"Oh, brother. You're a piece of work, Diane—do you know that?" He spun around, walked across the kitchen, then turned, suddenly, and walked back, this time coming closer. He stood over the top of her, his hands on his hips. "You don't really care about anything outside this little apartment. I get knocked flat on my back, and the only thing you're worried about is whether I might come home upset. Wouldn't that be awful if I let off a little steam? Wouldn't it be terrible if your tranquil life were upset for half an hour?"

"That's not what I mean."

She could hear him breathe with a kind of fury. She looked at his chest, not his face, when she said, "Let's not do this, Greg. I really am sorry about what happened. I don't know what else to say."

"It's not what you *say*, Diane. It's what you feel. It's what you *don't* feel. If someone did something to you, I'd be ready to go after him. I'd punch him out. But this happens to me and you don't even react."

She wasn't going to do this anymore. She didn't answer. But that seemed to raise the temperature.

"I'm getting out of here," he said. "I can't stand to be around you right now."

He walked to the closet by the front door and was looking for a jacket when Diane caught up with him. "Please don't leave, Greg. I'm sorry I haven't said the right thing, but I do know how wrong this is." She touched his arm. "Stay home. I've got a nice dinner almost ready. Maybe we can put Jennifer down early tonight and talk this out. I don't know how things work over at the law school, so it's hard for me to say what I think, but you can let off steam here with me. I want you to."

He was smiling, but he was giving her that perplexed stare he often used with her. "I don't want to *talk* it out. And if you think a little loving, Diane-style, will lift my spirits, you're wrong. Boredom is not what I need right now. What I want, and you've *never* given me, is support—genuine, heartfelt support. You spend your life worrying about *your* needs, and I'm doing everything I can to supply those, but all I see ahead of me is a long life with a girl who doesn't possess the power to think beyond her own nose—the little beauty queen who doesn't know how to grow up. But let me tell you, cutie pie, you're losing your college-girl good looks, and that leaves you with *nothing*."

She did hate him. It was not hard to admit that now. But the implications were going to change her life. She didn't know what she was going to do, exactly, but she had taken all she was going to take.

"Don't give me that *pained* look. Just once, let's think about *me* for five minutes."

Suddenly Diane didn't care how Greg would react. She wasn't going to be careful any longer. "Okay, let's think about you, Greg. You have high grades. You'll get a good job. Or you can go back to Utah and join your dad's firm. I do think the law school cheated you, but it's not the tragedy you're making it out to be. And now, let's think about *us*. You just told me that you can't stand me, and you see no worth whatsoever in me. So where do we go from there?"

"That's just the trouble. There's nowhere to go. You don't try to change. You've learned to cook about five dishes, and you keep the house clean. That's about the extent of what you have to offer. I spend my days talking about important ideas, and I come home to a girl who hasn't had a thought enter her head in her entire life. About the best I get is a quote from Mary Innis once in while. The woman may be homely, but at least she can carry on a conversation with her husband."

Always before, when Greg blasted her with his big guns, Diane had cried, but that was not her response this time. She looked him in the face and hoped he could feel her hatred. "You make me *sick*," she said.

"Well, what do you know?" He leaned toward her, his face close to hers. "You *can* get mad. But only for yourself, not for me."

Diane was on the edge of a decision, but she was scared. She didn't know whether she could do it. She held her gaze, matched his, but she didn't respond.

"I should have known what I was getting when I married you, Diane, but I didn't know you'd stay a child forever. I guess that's what I have to settle for."

She suddenly knew. "No, Greg. You don't have to settle for me. I'll let you off the hook." She walked back to Jennifer, who was crying again. She gave her a piece of banana, lifted her from her high chair, then carried her into the bedroom and set her on the bed. She opened her closet and reached into the back for her suitcase, which she set on the bed and opened.

Greg had watched all this and now was standing in the doorway of the bedroom. "Don't bluff, Diane. You've tried this act before."

Diane didn't say a word. She got out underwear first, packed it carefully, and then got a couple of blouses from her closet. She was thinking, all the while, about how she would do this, but she wasn't in a panic. She would go to Mary and Preston's apartment and ask to stay the night, and she would call her mother, who could make flight arrangements for her. She had thought about this moment a good deal lately, had considered all the implications—and she was scared—but she also felt surprisingly calm. Now that the reality had come, she knew she had to take the steps one at a time, just do what was necessary. Greg had said things that couldn't be taken back, and even though she had only known for a few minutes that she hated him, she couldn't imagine how that could ever change.

"Don't forget to take all your shoes. You can't live without a pair of shoes for every little *outfit*. And by the way, I sure hope you can find someone who'll be able to buy all the *stuff* it will take to keep you happy. You've been spoiled all your life, Diane. Some guy's going to have to learn to live with that—if you can *find* such a guy. You're a little heavy for a beauty queen these days, you know."

She looked up at him for a moment, but she didn't say anything. In fact, she took his advice and got a couple of pair of shoes to put in the suitcase.

"Okay, enough. You think I'm going to beg you to stay at this point, but I'm not going to do it. Just put that stuff back in the drawer and let's go have dinner. Deep down, you know you're not going to give up the *free ride* you're getting from me."

She looked at him again. "I hate you, Greg," she said. She tried to say the words without emotion, but she couldn't do it. She began to cry.

Greg was coming toward Diane by then, and she cringed as he grabbed hold of her arm. "You hate *me?* This is the lowest moment of my life, Diane. I got kicked in the teeth today, and I came home desperately in need of support. And what do I get? A tantrum. Don't talk to me about hate. I'll *show you* what hatred looks like."

Jennifer had sat like a little statue through all this, but suddenly she began to howl. "Let me pack," Diane said, and she tried to pull away from him.

"You're not leaving," he shouted, and suddenly he shoved her, sent her stumbling toward the wall.

She caught her balance and then turned toward him. "I hate you," she said again, but now her crying had stopped.

She stepped toward the suitcase, but he rushed her and threw her back again. This time she hit the wall, hard, and then he was on her. He lashed at her with the back of his hand, struck her across her cheek and ear. She slumped to the floor, grasping her face, but he grabbed her by her arms and pulled her up. "You're not leaving me," he said. "You can't walk out on me now, when everything else has gone wrong. You know that will destroy everything I've tried to do."

She knew his logic. He had an image to keep. If she left him, it wouldn't look good for his career. The thought of that infuriated her. "Let go of me," she screamed at him, and she tried to pull away.

He was grasping both her arms just below the shoulder, hurting her, trying to keep her from breaking loose. When she wouldn't stop struggling, he suddenly shoved her against the wall again, hard. Her head hit the wall and lights whirled in her brain. She would have slumped to the floor, but he was still holding her. For the first time she really was afraid how far he might go, but she whispered, "My, my. What a tough guy."

"Diane, don't do that. Don't make me any angrier. Just put your things away and then we can talk. This doesn't have to be as bad as it seems."

That made her laugh, and the laughter seemed to fire his temper again. He pulled one hand away, deliberately, and then he slammed her in the side of her head with his open hand. She dropped this time, and he let go of her. But Jennifer was screaming, terrified, and Diane could only think that she needed to get out of the apartment, and she needed to get Jenny away so she wouldn't see any more of this.

Greg had stepped back by then, and when she looked up, she saw that look in his face, as though he had finally realized what he had done. She managed to get to her feet, even though she was dizzy. She stepped to the bed and reached for Jenny, who had crawled to the edge and was reaching for her. "It's okay, honey. We're okay."

"Diane, I shouldn't have done that. But this time it was mostly your fault. You have to admit that much. You did everything you could to make me furious."

Diane knew better than to enter into that discussion. She held Jenny tight, and she began to edge around the bed, past Greg. She decided not to worry about the suitcase. The important thing was to get out. She hoped his anger was over now, and he wouldn't hit her again, especially with Jenny in her arms.

"Where are you going?"

"Don't follow me or I'll call the police." She didn't take a coat. She didn't even take a key to the door. For now, she simply had to get out and get to Mary's house. All the other decisions would come later.

But now the other Greg was returning. "Di, don't leave, okay? I'm sorry. I'm really sorry. I went crazy. I didn't know what I was doing."

But she had made it to the door, and she got out. As she hurried down the stairs, she heard him at the top, still pleading, but at least he didn't chase after her.

It was a long way to Mary's—eight or nine blocks—and a Seattle drizzle was falling, but she didn't have so much as a dime to use a pay phone, so she walked. She grasped Jenny close to her, kept telling her that everything was all right, but Jenny never really stopped crying, and Diane's own voice was full of tears. Still, she walked hard, and she told herself that she could deal with this whole thing if she just kept doing whatever came next, and right now, she simply needed to get to Mary's house. That was something clear to think about. The other thoughts tried to penetrate: the embarrassment, the troubles ahead, life alone, a future for Jenny. But she didn't let any of that sink very far into her consciousness.

"This is for you, honey," she told Jenny. "I know it's cold, and I know you're scared, but we're going to be okay. You won't remember any of this someday. That's the best part. If we had stayed, there would be all kinds of things in your head that you won't have to face now."

When she reached Mary's she was out of breath, and the pain had made its way into her face and head, but she was relieved when Mary opened the door. And she was even more relieved when Mary seemed to size up the situation in only a second or two. "Come in, come in," she said. "You can stay with us."

Diane had never told Mary about Greg's hurting her the time before, but she had the feeling that Mary had figured that out for herself. She certainly knew what had happened now.

"You're freezing," Mary said, and she took Jenny from her arms. Then she wrapped another arm around Diane, and Diane finally let go. Mary was much taller, much bigger than Diane, and she pressed her head against Mary's shoulder and felt safe. She cried hard, and now it was Mary who was saying, "It's okay now. We'll help you. You'll be all right. I'm glad you came here."

But Jennifer was crying hard again, so Diane pulled herself together, took Jenny back in her arms, and walked to the couch. It was the first time she realized Preston was in the room. He was standing by the opening to the kitchen, looking quite amazed. "Do you need to go to a hospital?" he asked.

Diane knew that her eye had been closing as she had walked, and she assumed that the bruise must look bad. "No, I don't think so," she said.

"It might be good to have a doctor document this, Diane," Mary said.

Diane didn't know why. She didn't want to call the police. She didn't want Greg to go to jail. She just wanted to be free of him. "No. I'll be all right. I just need to use your phone if I can. I'm going to call my mother. She'll pay for me to fly home."

"Is that what you're going to do?"

"I guess so. I don't know what else to do." And now some of the thoughts she had been fighting off did register. Everything would change. She would have to live at home for a while. She would need to figure out a way to support herself. Her life was going to be hard; she might never be happy again. She had always imagined a perfect life, a perfect family, and now it was gone. Maybe it had been coming for quite some time, but she had tried not to believe that, and now she had a whole new kind of existence to face.

"I was afraid this would happen," Mary said. She sat down next to Diane and put her arm around her shoulder. "I've known people like Greg. They have to have control. If anything or anyone tries to take it away, they lash out."

"He didn't make law review. He was really upset."

"That doesn't excuse him."

"I know." And it didn't. But Diane wondered now. Why hadn't she shown him a little more support? She had been afraid to say the wrong thing, but she really should have shown some disgust with the professors who had cheated him. If she had done just that much, he never would have taken out his anger on her.

"Diane, if it hadn't been this disappointment, it would have been another one. Every man has bad things happen to him, but most of them don't hit their wives."

"I know." But Diane wasn't finding the hatred in her now. She didn't have Jenny's diapers, her food, her bottles. What would she do about all of that? "Jenny hasn't eaten very much. And I don't have her stuff."

"Hey, baby stuff is one thing we've got around this place." Diane could hear the kids in the next room, a little TV area. One of them was getting angry with another over something, but Mary didn't seem to worry about it. "Have you eaten?"

Diane tried to smile. "I didn't get a chance," she said. "But I left something for Greg."

"Okay. We've eaten, but I've got some casserole left over. If you eat some of it, that will be some that Preston won't have to eat tomorrow. He'll appreciate it." She stood. "I'll heat that up again, but do you want to call your mother first?"

"Not for a minute."

"Okay. But you need to call her. You can stay here as long as you want, but you probably do have to go home, don't you think?"

"Yes." But the thought of it made her stomach sick. She was starting to wonder whether there wasn't some other possibility. "I'm not really hungry, Mary."

"I know. But eat a little, and let's get something for Jenny. I can see how scared she is."

Diane followed Mary into the kitchen, and she held Jenny while Mary found a bottle she could sterilize. She put it on to boil, and then she found some rice cereal that she mixed with milk. She gave that to Diane, and Diane had just started to feed Mary when the phone rang. Mary picked up the phone on the kitchen wall, said, "Hello," and then, "Oh, hi, Bishop."

Diane guessed what this was, and in truth, she felt a little relief. But she told herself she had to be strong.

"Yes, she is here. But Bishop, you need to know, she looks bad. Her eye is swollen, and she has big red bruises on her face." She listened for a time, and then she said, "Okay. But we're taking care of her for now. She can stay with us tonight."

Mary handed the phone, with its long extension cord, to Diane, who was sitting at the kitchen table. "Bishop Hunt wants to talk to you," she said. But she held the phone for a moment with her hand over the mouthpiece. "Diane, be careful, okay?" she said. "Greg will say anything right now, but sooner or later he'll do the same thing. I have a sister who's been through all this. She stuck it out for nine years and the guy never changed."

Diane nodded, and then she took the phone. "Hi, Bishop," she said, and she felt her voice break a little.

"Sister Lyman, I'm so sorry about what's happened to you. Do you need any medical attention?"

"No. It's just bruises."

"But maybe you ought to be looked at, just to be sure."

"I'm fine."

"I've got Greg here at my house, and Diane, he's a broken man. He's wondering whether there isn't some way to salvage your marriage."

"I don't think so, Bishop. This wasn't the first time. You know that." She glanced at Mary, who nodded. "And you know all the promises he made last time."

"Yes. And I'm not about to tell you what to do next. Have you had a chance to think that through?"

"I'm going home. I'll call my parents tonight. They can get me on a plane tomorrow. I'll have to get a key from Greg so I can get into the apartment and get my things. Maybe you could ask him to give you one, and I could get it from you in the morning—something like that."

"We can work that out, I'm sure. But let me ask you something else. Greg wants to talk to you. He wants to sit down with you, with me there, and look for an answer—something other than ending your temple marriage. Do you think that's possible?"

Diane was surprised by her reaction—especially to the words he had used. She found herself wishing there were an answer. But that's not what she said. "Bishop, it wasn't just that he hit me. He said terrible things to me. He's done that over and over. And I don't love him anymore. I told him that."

"He told me about that. You told him that you hated him. That's part of what made him so mad. But it's also part of what's tearing him up so much now."

"I don't know if I hate him. What I hate is the way he treats me."

"Well, now, just saying that seems like a step in the right direction. Maybe there are ways for him—maybe for both of you—to make some changes."

"Bishop, he lies. He'll say anything when he wants to get me back. And then it starts all over again."

"I understand. That would be the danger. On the other hand, he tells me that he loves you and Jennifer more than anything in the world. He knows he's in danger of losing his eternal happiness right now, and I've got to say that I believe him—he really is sorry."

"He's always sorry."

"I know. But before you leave, would it be worth one conversation? Couldn't we just get together tomorrow and explore the ways you might approach this? Greg says that he's willing to get professional help."

"I don't know. I need to think."

Mary was saying, "Stick to your guns, Diane."

"Should I call you back in a little while then?" the bishop asked. "Or do you want to go home and take some time to consider what's best?"

But that was the worst: going home, facing the life she didn't want.

For several seconds Diane held her breath and told herself not to say it, but then she did. "I guess we could talk. I'm willing to do that much."

Mary was shaking her head, sadly, but the bishop was saying, "Good. I just don't see how it can hurt to spend some time looking for answers and giving all this some prayer."

"I'll stay here tonight, Bishop."

"Fine. Can you meet us at the Institute building in the morning?"

"I guess so," Diane said. She was almost sure she was making a mistake, but she wanted desperately to believe that her life wasn't in ruins.

Chapter 9

Hans got home from work a little later than usual, not because he worked overtime, but because the May weather was so beautiful he took his time, sat for a while in the grand park by the opera house, and then stopped at a dairy store to buy a little cheese. He liked to talk to old *Herr* Hartmann who owned the store. Hartmann had an opinion about everything and wasn't afraid to say what he thought. "I'm old," he would say. "What's the government going to do to me?" Hans wondered at times whether it was wise to talk to a man who was so open in his disgust with the Communist regime, but Hans didn't really say much in response, and *Herr* Hartmann talked the same way to everyone. Hans merely wanted someone to chat with for a little while before climbing the steps to his apartment and settling in for the evening. He thought often these days how much he would like to be married, to have someone to come home to, to have a family. He was still saving for a trip to Schwerin, even though his parents had recently come to see him again. That had been wonderful, but since they had left he had felt the emptiness in his little apartment more than ever. At first, after getting out of prison, the freedom to look out a window, to walk outside, even to go to work, had been enough for him, but as days had run into months, the quiet of his life had come to feel more weighty. The men he worked with all had their own families, and they weren't ones to invite him over or ask him to go with them anywhere. He thought at times of going to a movie or eating out, but the fact was, he couldn't afford to do anything of that sort—not unless he gave up the idea of traveling home from time to time.

But he could sit in the park and watch the kids play, watch the swans on the lake, and maybe talk a little with someone who came by. He could chat with old *Herr* Hartmann. These were small pleasures, but pleasures all the same. Hans was not yet twenty-two, but he lived an old man's kind of life, he realized, not so different from the older fellows who sat in the park every afternoon on sunny days. Some of the old men played chess, and he had thought of doing that, but the game could take hours, and in truth, he still valued the time he had each evening to prepare his Sunday School lesson, and to read—not only the scriptures but also other books that interested him. He had always loved to think about his world, about geology, history, philosophy, anything that helped him understand a little more. So he borrowed books from the library—sad and old as its collection was—and he liked the idea that he was growing by learning, even if his job offered less challenge than he would have liked.

Hans told himself every day that he shouldn't think about Elli, and that was because he *did* think of her every day. During his years in prison he had pictured a sixteen-year-old girl, cute and funny, and someone willing to write to him. Now he knew that she was growing up, was prettier than ever, and along with her lovely lightness, had developed more substance. And she cared for him. After all this time she had kept an interest in him. "I don't know anyone better than you," she had said, and he had known what she was trying to tell him. "People manage," she had also told him. There were people in her branch who were married and didn't have much, but they were still happy. He knew the problem with all that, knew that he was making far less than the people she was talking about, but she had talked about doors opening—just when it didn't seem possible—and it was hard not to let his thoughts dwell on that possibility. He wanted to pray for that, for such doors to open, but in prison he had asked for what he had now: this freedom, this chance to live. It seemed wrong to get what he had asked for and then to raise the stakes.

For now, at least, what he needed was to live in such a way that he deserved what he had already received. He was trying to be more than a

Sunday School teacher to the young people in the branch. He was trying to be a mentor. He spent time after church with the ones who were interested and had questions. These young people went to school every day, where religion was laughed at. It helped for them to talk to someone who had been through the same system fairly recently, and who understood. He could answer some of their questions—the ones that had answers—and he could tell them the process he had been through, the steps he had taken to gain a testimony. The fact that he had been such a skeptic at one point in his life was helpful now. One young man in the branch, Rudolf Greiner, was brilliant, a top student in his *Gymnasium*, and capable of becoming a major scientist in the GDR. He was wrestling with so many of the same issues Hans had faced. At times he saw contradictions between the principles he learned in science and what he understood from the scriptures. Those matters Hans could help him with, and Rudolf had been touched enough by the Spirit that he wanted to find answers. But the practical issue was harder. What if Rudolf was held back from achieving his potential greatness because of his membership in the Church? Hans didn't offer him easy answers, but he described his own experience, what he had thought about in prison, his feelings about the scriptures. Brother and Sister Greiner, Rudolf's parents, thanked Hans every time they saw him. "You're saving his life," they kept saying, and that seemed an exaggeration, but Hans did feel satisfied that he was making a difference.

As Hans climbed the stairs to his apartment, he was thinking how he would spend his time. He would eat his cheese with some nice bread and a little wurst, and then he would put in an hour on his Sunday School lesson. He was coming up the last flight of stairs, asking himself which of his books he wanted to read, when he realized that someone, a man, was standing by his door. He stopped, then saw the smile.

"Hello, Hans. What's wrong? You didn't expect me?"

"Rainer. What a surprise." Hans hurried on up the stairs and held out his hand. "It's good to see you." They shook hands and laughed, and then Hans said, "Come in. Come in."

Hans unlocked the door and the two stepped inside. "You see what a fine apartment I have," Hans said. "A palace for a king, don't you think?"

"A very small king, I would say. It's like our old college room, cut in half."

"And so it should be. There's only one of me, you know."

"Yes, of course."

Hans's words had rung with sadness—more than he had intended—and he saw in Rainer's eyes that he pitied Hans. "Sit down, Rainer. My chair or my bed. Those are your choices."

Rainer stepped toward the chair that Hans had pulled out, but he didn't sit down. Rainer had always been tall, but he seemed bigger now, more filled out. And he looked older. The shock of dark hair that had always drooped toward his eyes was more under control now, shorter. "Hans, I want you to know, I didn't tell them. *Stasi* agents interrogated me many times, but I told them nothing. I told them over and over that I had no idea about Berndt, that you had never discussed the subject."

"That's good, Rainer. It's what I always believed about you." And Hans did feel some trust, but he said nothing more. He knew how the *Stasi* worked. Rainer could be lying. He could have been sent by an agent to learn what he could about Hans's loyalty. A bad report could send Hans directly back to prison.

Rainer sat down. Hans walked to the window and hoisted it, then perched himself on the windowsill, where he could feel the air from outside—and where he could watch the street. The evening would be cool, but the room had been closed up all day and was still warm. It even smelled musty. "I'm sorry for the messiness," he told Rainer. Hans had pulled his bed covers up that morning, but he hadn't really tucked things in properly. And he had left an unwashed dish and bowl in the sink.

"What mess? You've lived in a room with me. You know what a real mess is."

Hans laughed, but he felt uneasy. He wondered what Rainer could possibly want. "What brings you to Leipzig?" he asked.

"I came to talk to you. I talked to Elli, and she gave me your address."

"Were you in Magdeburg?"

"Yes. I go as often as I can. I suppose you know about Elli and me."

Hans hesitated. He wasn't sure what Rainer meant. Had something new developed? Were they engaged now?

"I want to marry her. I'm sure she told you that. And I can't tell you how much I've changed, Hans. It started with you, and then grew as I got to know the members of the Church in Magdeburg. They were all happy in a way I had never known. I didn't think I could believe in God, but everything has changed for me. I pray every day. I want to join the Church. I want to raise my family as Mormons."

Hans nodded. Rainer sounded sincere, but Hans remembered Elli's doubts. Even more, he felt a surge of jealousy. He didn't want to feel that way after telling Elli they could never think of marrying, but here was Rainer wanting to take away the woman Hans thought about every day. "When are you going to be baptized?" he asked, understanding the implication of his question.

"I'm not certain. You know the problems this would cause me. I'm developing a fine future, and all that could be cut off the instant it's known."

"Not always. You've built up some trust by now. There are Mormons who have done quite well."

"You don't know my boss. He's a Party man, completely. He would stop me instantly."

Hans didn't like what he was hearing. Rainer had said "Party man" as though he now held the Party in contempt, but Hans remembered his enthusiasm for Communism when the two had lived together. Had religion really changed his opinion about all that, or was he acting, trying to gain Hans's confidence? Hans looked outside again, scanned the area, noticed the people on the sidewalk across the street. Then he tried to say something that would sound as neutral as possible: "It's the choice we all have to make."

"Yes. But there's one other. It's what I want to ask you about."

"What's that?"

Rainer stood and walked to Hans. He leaned against the wall, by the window frame. And then he spoke quietly. "I want to get out of the GDR, and I don't know how to do it. You're the only man I know who has experience with an escape. I thought maybe you could help me—maybe put me in touch with someone who might know what to do."

Hans was frightened. This was just the sort of thing the *Stasi* would do. Hans had told *Herr* Felscher over and over that he didn't know the people who had been involved in Berndt's escape, but the *Stasi* would not necessarily believe that. If Rainer was working with them, this was a way to get Hans to say the wrong thing. But the truth hadn't changed. "Rainer, I knew Berndt. I knew no one else. Berndt purposely didn't tell me the names of anyone involved. I have no contacts and no knowledge of such matters."

"But you told me that you considered escape for a long time. You tried to get out by way of the North Sea."

Hans tried to remember what he had told Rainer. He was certain that he hadn't said anything about the attempt he had made with his parents, by ship, and there was no way he would say anything now. He could put his family in jeopardy, and he could reveal a part of his past that Felscher had never learned. But Felscher knew about the first attempt Hans and Berndt had made. "Rainer, we were nothing more than children. We tried something that didn't work. We took air mattresses and tried to paddle out to the shipping lanes. It was crazy."

"It could have worked. You told me that."

"Yes. But it would have taken perfect timing, and there was no controlling that. It was all luck." He thought of Elli out on that water in the night. Was that what Rainer wanted to do? "Are you thinking that you would try to take Elli with you?"

"Of course."

"No. It's far too dangerous. The coasts are probably patrolled better now, and we failed back then."

Rainer turned and stepped to the bed, then sat down. "Hans, I need some help with this," he said. "I have to find a way out of this country. Don't you have any ideas? Don't you still think of getting out yourself?"

"No, Rainer, I don't. And it's not just that it's difficult. In prison, I was offered the chance to leave. My uncle, in Utah, had arranged for me to emigrate—had paid our government money so I could—but I decided to stay. I think the Lord wants me here to help the Church survive and grow. I don't think of our government as my enemy now. The Church teaches us to honor the country we live in. We have the liberty to practice our religion in the GDR, and that's what I want to do."

"Is this what they taught you to say in prison? You can't possibly believe what you're saying. I'll never be happy until I get out of this place. I want to join the Church, but I want to do it in a land where I can live the way I want—not with a government that restricts my choices."

Hans walked to the chair and sat down in front of Rainer. Rainer was leaning forward, looking down, so Hans waited for him to look up. "Read about Christ's apostles, Rainer. They were frightened at times when he was with them, but once he ascended and they received the Holy Ghost, they were like lions. They preached the gospel in spite of the Jewish leadership that opposed them, and in spite of the Romans. They taught the people what Christ had taught them—and they baptized thousands. They built the kingdom. Maybe we have to use more care, but we can do a great deal. I know I have to do more."

This was touching on the dangerous, but it was what Hans believed.

Rainer was shaking his head. He sat up straight. "Hans, you say that, but what can we actually do? We can talk to people, but we take a chance, just doing that. And if people join the Church, they have to wonder how much of a problem it will be for their families. Very few dare to do it. I want to go somewhere that gives me the right to live as I please. Most countries are that way, Hans. This must be the most oppressive nation in the world—unless it's the Soviet Union."

Hans said nothing. But he thought he heard some exaggeration in Rainer's voice. Was he trying to draw Hans in, get him to say something he shouldn't? Had Rainer made a deal with a *Stasi* agent? If Rainer was under suspicion, he could possibly make things better for himself by reporting on Hans.

Rainer continued to wait for Hans to respond. Finally, he said, "You know what I'm saying is true. Don't you?"

"I told you, the Church teaches us to honor our government. I haven't always done that, but I do now."

Rainer nodded. Was he saying something? Was he letting Hans know that he had said the right words? Was all this being recorded? Rainer waited for a time before he asked, "How do you feel about my marrying Elli?"

"How does *she* feel about it?"

"I think she told you, she wants to wait. She thinks she's too young. And she wants me to join the Church first. I want to do that, but I want to get out of this country first."

"Rainer, if Elli loves you, and you can give her a good life, I wish you the best. But she's right. You have to be willing to stand up for what you believe—here and now. I don't blame her for expecting that."

"That sounds pretty to say, Hans, but if I join the Church, I'm not sure I can give her a good life. That's just the problem."

"She wants a good man more than anything."

"Yes. I think she wants you."

Hans had looked away, toward the window, but his head jerked back toward Rainer now. "Excuse me?" he said.

"You heard me. She's stalling me while she waits to see what you will do." For once, Hans had no question that Rainer was saying what he really felt.

"Rainer, you have a future. It could be limited if you join the Church, but it won't be ruined. I have *no* future. I can offer Elli nothing."

"But you wish you could?"

Hans thought for a time before he told the truth. "Yes. It would be nice, if it were so."

"So we're competitors."

"No. I told Elli there's no chance for things to change enough for me to think of marrying her."

"You two must have discussed the possibility, or you wouldn't have told her that."

"Not really. Not directly."

Rainer smiled. "I understand. But we both know." He stood up. "I don't blame her, Hans. You're a better man than I am. I've come to religion late. It still scares me, this standing up for what's right. I doubt Elli will ever have me."

It was hard for Hans not to like hearing that, but the situation appeared tragic—a complicated triangle in which no one was likely to end up happy. "I hope things work out for you, Rainer, but I wouldn't try to escape. I don't think that's the answer."

"You might be right." Rainer walked to the door.

"Do you have to go already?"

"I do. I'm taking a night train back to Berlin. I didn't have much time for this trip."

"I'm sorry I couldn't help."

"I knew it wasn't likely. I'm grasping at anything right now." Rainer put his hand on the doorknob, but then he looked back. "Hans, *Stasi* agents have questioned me again recently. Twice. They are still suspicious about you. They think I knew about your involvement with Berndt, no matter how many times I deny it. So you must be very careful. I probably shouldn't have come here. I could have put you in danger by making the contact. If they know, they may question you. It's crazy living under such surveillance. I hope I haven't caused you any more trouble."

Hans believed all this, and now he wondered whether he hadn't been too doubting of Rainer, from the beginning. "We're good friends, Rainer," Hans said. "There's nothing wrong with our seeing each other."

"Yes. That's what we'll say. But they see conspiracy everywhere."

"As long as we stay true to each other, as we've always been, nothing will happen to us."

"Yes," Rainer said, and Hans studied his eyes carefully. He thought he detected a moment of disengagement, when Rainer avoided looking him straight on. He hoped that wasn't true. In any case, Hans walked to his friend. They shook hands, and Rainer said, "Thank you, Hans. You're a good man."

"And you are, too. But Rainer, whatever you do, don't put Elli in danger. Will you promise me that?"

"What if she wants to escape with me?"

"I don't know. But don't convince her to try it if she's hesitant. Don't tell her that it isn't dangerous, when you know it is."

"I'll be honest with her."

"Have you talked about this with her?"

"No."

"Rainer, you know my advice. Don't try it. And don't even mention to Elli that you've considered the possibility. Don't give her information she would have to deny."

"But if I decide to try, I want her to go too."

"I know. I simply say again, it isn't wise. Stay and support the Church. Elli would not be Elli if you took her away from her family."

Rainer was obviously perplexed. He was looking over Hans's shoulder, not at his eyes, when he said, "I have much to think about. But I wouldn't ever do anything to harm Elli."

"Is there anything you can promise me?"

Again Rainer thought for a time. "I don't know. I won't knowingly put her in danger, but if I can find a safe way to leave, I would like to do it."

"There is no safe way. Not anymore. There are only huge gambles."

Rainer nodded, but he added no promises. He stepped out the door. Hans watched as he walked down the first flight of stairs and then turned back and waved. But Hans was still worried. Suddenly he realized that he wanted to track Rainer outside. Would there be a contact out there somewhere? Hans had scanned the street from the window where he had chosen to sit, and he had known from the time that he sat down there that it was a little act of surveillance he wanted to make. He had seen no one suspicious looking, but it wasn't likely that an agent would wait that close or appear that obvious.

Hans stepped out, locked the door, and then walked carefully down the stairs. He heard the downstairs door open and close before he moved quickly down the front hall and reached the same point. When he stepped out, he stayed in the alcove in front of the doors, then looked out carefully. Rainer had walked to the nearby corner and was waiting to cross the street. Hans watched from the alcove until Rainer had crossed and then saw that he was continuing straight ahead.

Hans hurried now and crossed the same street, and then walked behind Rainer, well back. What he soon realized was that Rainer was watching for someone to follow. He stopped rather often, looking into shop windows and then up and down the street, on both sides. Hans had been wise to stay so far back. He was able to step into alleys or doorways when Rainer stopped, but he wondered whether Rainer hadn't spotted him.

Rainer also did what Hans would have done. He turned a couple of corners, obviously taking an indirect route to wherever he was going. Hans knew the technique. If he turned a corner too soon after Rainer had, Rainer might be standing there, waiting for him. But was it Hans he was trying to lose, or was he being careful about being followed by a *Stasi* agent?

In either case, Rainer's technique was successful. After the third turn, Hans walked around a corner and tried to act natural, just in case he did run into Rainer, but Rainer was nowhere in sight. Hans continued along the street, on the off chance that he would spot Rainer again, but he intended to start back toward his apartment at the next corner. What he was wondering now was what Rainer would do. Was he the kind of man who would make big promises to Elli and talk her into something dangerous? Hans feared that most, but he was also concerned about the other possibility, that all this talk was a ruse. Maybe Rainer had only been looking for information, using the escape story as an enticement. For that matter, he could report anything he chose, whether Hans had actually said it or not. If he was working for the *Stasi*, they would be happy to have a witness against Hans. They didn't need proof. What did they care about truth?

Hans reached the corner and decided to turn back toward his apartment, but he stopped at the big intersection and scanned the area. He was about to walk away when he thought he saw Rainer sitting on a bench at a bus stop on the opposite side of the intersection. Hans moved to a better vantage and assured himself that it was actually Rainer, but then he moved quickly around the corner and down a street away from Rainer's view.

It made sense that Rainer would be there. He could catch a bus to the train station from that corner. And his indirect route to arrive there made sense if he was worried about shaking anyone who might be following him. Of course, the bus stop could also be a place to meet someone. So

Hans walked all the way around the block to the left, hoping to reach a point where he could watch from a distance.

A bus could come while Hans was making the long walk, so he half expected Rainer to be gone by the time Hans could see him again, but when he reached the corner, Rainer was still there, and he was still watching, scanning the area, right and left. Hans waited until Rainer was looking another way, and then he moved around the corner and stepped inside a little hardware store. He could see out a window from there, but he felt certain Rainer couldn't see him inside the dimly lighted shop. Several buses stopped, then drove on. Rainer didn't get on. Were the buses on a route to the train station? Hans couldn't tell from where he was.

But then Hans saw something he hadn't noticed before. A man was standing in a door front across the street, not far from Rainer. The man was wearing a suit and hat. He looked a little out of place, and he wasn't going anywhere, just standing and watching. Was he watching Rainer? He seemed to look in that direction more often than not, although he was doing some scanning of his own.

Everyone held the same position for a time. Rainer let another bus go by, and the man didn't move on, which seemed strange. Hans stayed where he could continue to watch. And then, as another bus approached, Rainer stood. He got on the bus, but as he did, the man in the suit also hurried toward the bus. He waited behind a couple of other people, and then he, too, boarded and the bus pulled away.

What did it mean? Had the two scheduled themselves to meet this way? Or was Rainer being followed without his knowledge? Hans was almost sure that the man's boarding had not been a mere coincidence. But if they were meeting, why had they stayed separate from each other? Was it Hans they were worried about? Did they think he might follow? Or had Rainer spotted Hans and warned the man off? Whatever the case was, the situation looked bad. If Rainer was planning to meet the man, Hans could be in big trouble. If Rainer was being followed, that could be just as bad.

The *Stasi* could see some sort of conspiracy in Rainer's visit. If agents knew that Rainer was looking for a way out of the country, or if Rainer tried an escape, the *Stasi* would want to know why he had visited Hans first.

But as Hans walked back to his apartment, it was Elli who came back to mind. Her friendship with Rainer and—as far as that went—to Hans, could look bad for her. Or worse, the thought that struck him and would plague him constantly now, was that Rainer might convince her to try something stupid. She could end up in prison herself, and that, to Hans, was unthinkable.

Chapter 10

Diane and Greg were sitting in their kitchen, at the table. Diane had cooked spaghetti, and she had tried to make a sauce from scratch, but it hadn't turned out all that well. Or at least she didn't think so. But Greg was putting away plenty of it and claiming that it was "Fine, just fine." It was what he had been doing for two weeks. The term at the law school was over now, all but finals, and so he was busy studying, but he had studied more at home than usual, and he had treated Diane with constant care and tenderness. The little extras—bringing home Chinese takeout and telling her not to cook, vacuuming the living room for the first time ever, telling her how much he loved her—all that was nice, but everything seemed a little forced. Still, she knew how hard he was trying, and she appreciated that.

"Look at Jenny," Greg said. He had put a little dab of Diane's spaghetti sauce on her tongue, and she was making little sucking motions, looking rather pleased. "She likes it."

"I can't believe it. She's such a fussy eater."

"Hey, I told you, it's good stuff. You've come a long way with your cooking, Di. You've worked hard at it, haven't you?"

Diane had to laugh. "Not really. I just try to find good recipes, and then I follow them. My mom always says that some people are good cooks and others are just good readers. That's my mom, and I'm afraid that's going to be me, too."

"But the knack for it comes along. I see that happening to you."

Diane looked back at Jennifer. All these compliments were starting to get a little more than she wanted. She sensed too much of an act behind Greg's behavior, and that made her wonder when a rupture might come, and then the dam could break loose again.

Greg got up and carried his plate to the sink. He rinsed the plate and his utensils, and he put them in the dishwasher. Then he came back for his and Diane's salad plates and the salt and pepper shakers. "You know, I got thinking today, I want to do well on my finals, but I don't feel the pressure I've always felt before. I think maybe missing out on law review was a blessing in disguise. Next year I can relax and concentrate on my classes. I can still shoot to graduate high in my class, but I won't have all that extra work to do."

"Are you sure you feel okay about that?"

"Yeah. I really do. I'll be home a lot more, which is something I've been promising for a long time and haven't really done. I think that will relieve a lot of the tension between the two of us—and be good for Jenny, too."

"Greg, I don't want you to feel like you can't stay at the library when you have to. Jenny is a lot noisier now than when she was really little. By fall she'll be walking around, getting into everything."

"I know. But if I'm here more, it will give you some time for yourself once in a while. That's one of the things the bishop and I talked about. He said student wives with babies have the toughest jobs, but it's the students who seem to get all the special treatment."

"But I'm not working, and a lot of the women in the ward are."

"Well, anyway, it will be better if I come home more. It's funny, too—I had this interesting thought today. Modern Mormons don't have to suffer for their religion much at all, not the way the early Saints did. I don't have the slightest doubt I was held out of law review because I'm a Mormon, but I almost like that thought. I'm not about to turn my back on what I believe, just to please all those radicals on the faculty."

Diane had never been sure it had been Greg's religion that had hurt him. She suspected it was his intolerance for views other than his own.

But she didn't want to say things like that to herself anymore. She had told him she hated him just two weeks before, and those were words that couldn't easily be forgotten by either one of them. Since then, she had considered telling him she loved him, but she didn't want to sound insincere, let alone *be* insincere, and the words had never come. All she knew was that the bishop felt she should give Greg another chance, and Greg had pleaded for that. She respected Greg for how hard he worked at anything he set his mind to do, and she knew how hard he was trying now. Maybe he had learned his lesson, and maybe she could begin to feel love for him again. She certainly wanted a father for little Jenny.

Behind everything Diane did these days was the persistent fear that her life would be a mess forever if she had to raise her child alone. At the same time, she felt a certain tension whenever Greg was home, and she wondered if her life would always be like this. Would she always be thankful for his sweet behavior but a little untrusting of it, or would she always be waiting for the next outbreak of anger? Either possibility was terrible to think about, and it was unsettling to think those might be her options. She hadn't expected life to be like that.

But she was trying to give Greg lots of affection and to understand a little more of what he expected in that part of their lives. She could tell he appreciated her efforts, but there again, she wished she didn't feel it was an effort.

When Greg went off for his finals the next morning, she kissed him good-bye and wished him good luck, and she said a prayer for him. She felt good about that. Lots of people had told her that marriage wasn't just love; that a good relationship took work. Maybe that's what she and Greg were learning, and maybe life would look a whole lot better as they both tried harder to satisfy the other.

Diane's goal that day was to pack up things that had to be taken to Utah, since Greg had decided to return and work for his father again that summer. She also wanted to do some cleaning. They would be returning to their apartment again in the fall, and she had never done much "deep cleaning" since Jenny had been born. She needed to go through her closets and throw some things out, and wash woodwork and walls. That sort of thing was never easy with Jennifer wanting attention all the time, but Diane brought her into the bedroom, gave her some toys, and talked to her while she worked. She got a good deal done, and when Jenny went down for a nap, she decided that might be the time to begin the packing. Diane wanted to take home her summer clothes and then leave them home. They almost never got any use in Seattle. Greg had also set aside some books he wanted to keep but wouldn't need during his last year of law school.

Diane had turned on the radio. When Peter, Paul, and Mary sang "Leaving on a Jet Plane," she sang along, and she suddenly felt happier than she had in quite some time. She would be going home soon. That could be hard in some ways, but it changed the dynamic with Greg. Maybe she wouldn't feel that she had to be so careful all the time, with the stress of school absent for a while, and especially with others around. In the summer, Greg would come home and want to go to a movie or out to dinner. He never seemed to have time for that in Seattle. She still hadn't seen *Butch Cassidy and the Sundance Kid*, and it seemed like everyone else in the world had. Greg kept talking about going to see *Patton*, but they hadn't done that yet either.

Diane packed the summer clothes in a box, since she would need her suitcase for her dressier clothes and all the personal items she had to take home for such a long stay, but she ended up taking too much time making decisions about the things she wouldn't need in Seattle. She was working on borrowed time when she got to Greg's books, since Jennifer was likely to wake up soon. She was trying to make them fit into a box that wasn't really shaped right when she pulled a book back out and the cover flipped open. A slip of paper fell onto the bed. Diane paid no attention to it, for the moment, but once the books were packed and she had set it on the floor in the corner, she picked up the paper—a scrap torn from a yellow legal pad. She glanced at it to see whether it was something Greg would want to keep and was surprised to see a feminine-looking script that clearly wasn't Greg's. It was a note:

> Greggy,
>
> Are we going to be good little law students and stay for ol' Knockwurst's lecture, or are we going to cut class? I wouldn't mind an early start. Girls have needs too, you know.

Diane was stunned. What did it mean? The note wasn't signed, but Diane was sure it was something Sondra Gould must have written. But was it serious?

Diane sat down on the bed. She tried to think. She didn't want to assume the worst, but what else could it mean? Knockwurst was the name Greg used for one of his professors, a man actually named Nickman. Diane couldn't remember: Had Greg had that class last fall, or was it the year before? Since Diane had complained about Greg's friendship with Sondra—a relationship that some people had seen as too familiar—Greg had backed off. He claimed that he rarely saw her. She had dropped out of his study group, and Greg had told Diane he was glad, that he was weary of her arrogance.

Diane read the note again. It didn't have to mean an actual affair was going on. She might have been joking around, but there was no way a woman should write a note like that to a married man. And why would they cut classes together? Diane felt her throat closing off. Maybe now, this really was the end of everything.

Jennifer had begun to cry. Diane went to her. She held her tight, wondering whether the two of them would be on their own after all, and she tried to think what she should do. Her first thought was that she had to confront Greg, get everything out in the open, and then see where they stood. If he had had an affair, she wasn't going to sit still for that. She knew women who had forgiven their husbands for such things, but Diane had always told herself she couldn't do that. She slipped to her knees in the living room, still holding Jennifer. "Please, Lord, tell me what to do. Guide me through this. I don't want this to be true."

When she got up, the thought that was in her mind was that Greg had his faults, and he may have flirted with Sondra, but he wouldn't do anything really wrong. He had a temper and a cruel streak when he was mad, but an affair was premeditated, a deception, and she just couldn't imagine that Greg would go that far. But another thought kept pressing itself into her mind: his disappointment with Diane's lovemaking. Would he use something like that as an excuse?

No. She couldn't imagine it. He could rationalize, but he couldn't look the bishop in the eye and claim to be morally clean, if, in fact, he wasn't. Greg simply wasn't that kind of person.

It was that thought that kept building all day, and by afternoon, Diane had made a choice that hadn't seemed possible when she had first read the note. She was going to throw the note away and never mention it to Greg. Sondra was forward and a terrible flirt—people had told Diane that—but surely she was only being suggestive and playful in the note. Greg had backed away from her at some point, and maybe it was because he had finally seen her for what she was. Showing the note to Greg would only cause a huge scene and end all the good feelings that had built up over the past couple of weeks. It could bring out the worst in him, too, and she didn't want to think about that possibility. Maybe she was being a coward, but part of marriage was thinking the best of your partner, not jumping to the worst conclusions.

Still, it was an uneasy afternoon, and when Greg finally called, late in the day, she was surprised he hadn't already come home. "Hi, Sweet Potato," he said. "I'm in the library, cramming a little for tomorrow. But I think I did really well on the test I took today."

"Good." Diane was a lot more nervous than she wanted him to know, so she said nothing more.

"What have you been doing?"

"Cleaning. And packing some of our things."

"That's good. Did Jenny let you work?"

"Yes. She was really good today."

"Great. Well, listen, I need to look a few things up. I should be home in maybe an hour. Okay?"

"All right."

"Are you okay?"

"Sure. I'm fine."

"Don't start cooking anything, because I'm not exactly sure how long I'll be. When I get there, we can just open a can of soup—or we can make some grilled cheese sandwiches."

"Okay." But when Diane put down the phone, she realized that tears had come to her eyes. She was wondering, Could he be with her? Was something still going on? It was horrible to think so, but Diane remembered all the late nights when Greg had said he was with his study group or in the library. Diane was so naïve; she had never questioned any of that. But Greg could have been checking into hotels, for all she knew; he never told her anything about their money. She thought of looking at Greg's credit-card receipts, but she told herself he would be furious if he realized she had done something like that. But what was she supposed to do, just live with the suspicion? If he had been carrying on an affair all year, she was such a silly little fool.

Diane still hadn't torn the note up, as she had promised herself she would do. She had slipped it into a drawer with her socks and underwear, aware even then that she might need to pull it out in some circumstance. She got it back out now, read it again, and she made a decision. She would be nice to Greg. She would give him a chance to explain, but she would make it clear that he shouldn't have been this familiar with another woman. This was a chance to find out whether she and Greg could talk out a difficult problem and do it with some control. But she was terrified, and her nervousness only grew as the sixty minutes stretched to ninety.

Diane fed Jennifer and grew more anxious as Jennifer spit out all the strained peas she tried to feed her. So she switched to peaches, almost the only thing Jenny ate with pleasure. But all the while Diane was watching the clock. By the time she heard Greg at the door, almost two hours had passed, and she was wondering whether he had really been at the library.

"I'm home," he called out. "Sorry I took so long." She stayed in the kitchen and heard him go first to the bedroom, as always.

In a few minutes he came out. "Should we make those sandwiches? I'm a starving man."

"Sure. In just a minute." She took a breath and tried to calm herself. She took the note from her pocket, but before she handed it to him, she said, in a quiet voice, "Greg, I don't want to make a big deal out of this. I don't think it means what it seems to mean, but I need to know for sure. This fell out of one of your books that I was packing." She held out the note.

Greg looked curious, but when he unfolded the paper, she could see that he recognized it immediately. She thought she saw panic in his eyes for a moment, but he calmly took time to read the note carefully, nodded, and then smiled. "This is funny," he said. "I know how it looks, but it's typical Sondra Gould humor. We had that class from Nickman in the morning, and we used to get together with our group over lunch and then on into the afternoon." He smiled again, but Diane didn't like the look on his face. His ease seemed self-conscious, and his smile was forced. "She's just joking about wanting to eat—and being suggestive about it. That's one of the reasons I stopped studying with her, as you know. Sometimes it really did seem like she was hinting around that she wanted something to happen between us. I think it was just flirting, and she didn't really mean anything by it, but it still seemed wiser to stay away from her."

"Okay. That's kind of what I thought." But Diane's heart was still pounding. Did he seem so nervous just because she had put him in an awkward situation? Or did he have a good reason to be worried?

"Are we okay?" He stepped to her and put his arms around her.

She tried to hug him back, but she was still upset from the thoughts that had run around in her head all day. "Greg," she said, "I'm really a trusting person. All day I've been worried that I was *too* trusting. Maybe something was happening, and I just wasn't smart enough to catch on."

"I understand. I wouldn't want some guy to write a note like that to you. I should have told you about it. And I should have started avoiding her sooner than I did. It just didn't seem any big deal. You have to know how Sondra is. I don't think she has any morals."

"When you were gone so late all those times, that was really just to study, wasn't it?"

Greg pulled back. "Come on, Di. You say you trust me, and then you ask me something like that?"

"I just don't want any doubt between us. After I read that, I started thinking that I never questioned anything you did."

"Hey, I can play that game. You've been here alone all day. There are a lot of guys around this apartment building. Maybe you've had some of them in for a little fun. That could happen. It happens all the time, from what I hear. But I've never questioned you about the possibility."

"Okay. That's right. We do have to trust each other."

"Yes, I think we do. But you say you don't want any doubts. What does that mean? Are you going to wonder about this the rest of your life—and wonder where I am every time I have to stay at the office late?"

"No. I'm not saying that. But people said you were too familiar with her at school, and then I read this note, and it did put some questions in my mind. But what you said sounds right."

"It *sounds* right?"

"I'm just saying I believe you. But I had to ask—just to clear things up. You know—so I *wouldn't* have any doubts."

"I would think the Spirit should tell you that, Diane. You should know by now what I'll do and won't do. I've got to admit, it bothers me to think you would spend the day thinking things like that about me."

She saw the change in his stance, the rise in his shoulders as he leaned forward, seeming to press her backward. She had to be careful. "I'm sorry. I prayed today, and the Spirit did tell me that you wouldn't do anything like that."

"Then why didn't you tell me that? What were you trying to do, just make me squirm? Is that the plan for the rest of my life? I made a mistake a couple of weeks ago, and now I have to watch every move I make, just to prove myself?"

"No. I don't feel that way. It's over. You answered my questions. Let's tear the note up and forget it."

He did rip it up, and he walked to the cabinets and opened the door under the sink. He tossed the scraps into the garbage can, and then he looked up. She could see what was happening. His anger was building, not dissipating. It was what she had seen so many times before.

Diane heard Jennifer begin to whimper. "So you say it's over, but what are you going to be thinking about me when I'm in my profession and I have a late meeting or have to take a trip out of town? I just had no idea you were so suspicious."

"Greg, I'm not. But the note was just so inappropriate. There's no way she would have written that note if she hadn't expected you to think it was funny."

"It was funny. That's exactly what it was."

"But it was improper, too. You're a married man." Jennifer was crying harder now. Diane walked to her high chair and got her out, then held her.

"I know that. I told you that. But most of the world isn't quite so innocent as you pretend to be. People tell dirty jokes that would make you blush. I don't like that kind of stuff, but a guy has to live in the real world. I can't say, 'Don't tell stories like that around me. I'm a nice Mormon boy.' I could have told her I was offended, or something like that, but she would have thought that was all the funnier."

"Okay. I see what you're saying. I'm going to open a can of soup."

"You couldn't even cook, could you? You were that upset with me?"

"You told me not to."

"But it's not like you to wait until I get home. You never do. I know what you were doing—just building this thing into something huge in your mind."

"I was nervous about bringing it up to you. That's all. But I thought I should, just so we could clear the air."

"So it's clear now, isn't it?"

"Yes. I'll never bring it up again."

"You'll just think about it."

Diane wasn't going to keep this going. She carried Jennifer with her, and she bent to get a can of chicken noodle soup from a cabinet. "There's cheese in the refrigerator," she said. "If you could cut some slices and get out the bread, I'll get the soup going and then grill some sandwiches."

"I know how to make a cheese sandwich, Diane."

"Honey, I'm sorry. I shouldn't have made such a big thing out of this. Let's just let this go now. Do you feel like you're ready for your test in the morning?"

"No. I'll have to study most of the night. And now I can't think straight."

"Calm down. Let's just get some dinner together, and then I'll keep Jenny out here and you can study in the bedroom."

"You know what I hate?"

"What?" Diane turned away from the cabinet and looked at Greg.

She knew what was happening now. His anger was spiraling. He was looking for a fight.

"I hate it when you tell me to *calm down*. It's your other suspicion. I've tried so hard to treat you right these last two weeks, and yet you're always expecting me to mess up again."

"No, I'm not, Greg. But why do you want to keep this going? I've told you I believe you."

"Yeah. Right." He turned and walked to the bedroom. But Diane thought that was a good sign. He had gotten mad, but he hadn't touched her, and now he was walking away. She hoped, in a while, he would be calm, and everything would be okay. But as she opened the soup, with Jennifer still clinging to her, she wondered whether life would always be this way. He had done something wrong, or at least had something to answer for, and she had ended up apologizing. And the fact was, when she had seen his anger rise, she had been terrified that the clash was coming and he would come after her again.

Still, he hadn't done it. That was something to build on.

When she had the first sandwich grilled, and the soup heated, she called him. She had used a place mat, put some potato chips on the plate with the sandwich, and given him about two-thirds of the soup. She was waiting for the second sandwich to finish grilling when he sat down without speaking. She could see that he was working this thing up, that he was still furious. "So tell me about the test today. Did you feel like you did well?"

"I told you on the phone. It was fine. But don't you want to know why I didn't come directly home?"

"You told me. You were in the library."

"But how can you be sure? I might have been making out with one of the librarians, back in the stacks."

"Greg, don't, okay?"

"Don't what?"

"Don't keep it up. I told you, it's over."

"It'll never be over! You and the bishop have your minds made up about me." Suddenly he lashed out with his arm, flung the plate and bowl off the table. The soup bowl crashed against the wall and broke, and soup splattered in all directions.

Jennifer screamed, and Diane stepped back to the cabinets. She held the baby and waited. She hoped that was the whole show.

But he got up from the table and glared at her. "So what now? Do you want a divorce? I broke a bowl."

Diane was surprised by her answer. She hadn't thought of it until he asked, but she knew she had had enough. And it was Jenny she was thinking of. "Yes," she said, and then she began to work her way out of the kitchen, sidestepping so she was always facing Greg. She assumed—hoped—that he wouldn't lash out at her when she was holding Jennifer.

But he let her leave. She could see he was raging, but he didn't come toward her. It didn't matter. She couldn't live with these kinds of scenes all her life. She walked to the bedroom and got out her suitcase. When she set Jennifer down, her whimpering turned to screams, but Diane talked to her calmly, and she packed quickly. She had gone through her things that day, so everything was organized. She would only grab enough to get by for a while. She knew better what to do this time. She needed to get out, take a taxi to Mary's this time, call her parents immediately, and get to Utah. For two weeks she had been considering how all this would go if the same troubles started again, and so she actually found some calm about her decision. She feared the future, but she had also considered it, had thought through her choices. She would have to stay with her parents for a time, and find a job—and then she would make her way from there. She couldn't think too far into the future but just take one step at a time. "We have to do this, Jenny," she whispered, still trying to calm her. "It's for you."

Diane was able to grab enough things for herself and for the baby in only a minute or two, and then she shut the bag and picked up Jennifer. But as she did, the bedroom door came open. "This isn't right," Greg said. "I lost my temper, but I took it out on a bowl, not on you. I kept my promise to you."

Diane lifted her suitcase off the bed. She knew better than to say anything, or to approach him. She simply held Jennifer and waited. Jennifer was clinging, suddenly silent.

"I had a right to be offended. You accused me of something I didn't do. I threw a little tantrum, but I didn't hurt anyone. You said it was over. And I agree. So put the suitcase down, and let's go from there."

"I need to leave, Greg. I can't do this anymore."

"Can't do what?"

"Just let me go. I'm going to walk out that door. Please don't block it, and please don't hit me."

"Oh, man. You're something. The anger is always supposed to be my fault. How can I *not* get mad when you say something like that?"

She waited now. She saw he was losing it again.

"Put the suitcase down, Diane. You promised the bishop you would work with me to rebuild our marriage. I've done everything he asked me to do. Now you do your part." He stepped toward her and reached for the handle of the suitcase, but when he tried to pull it away, she clung to it. Suddenly he jerked hard, pulled it loose, and sent it flying into the wall. Jennifer screamed.

Diane bolted forward, trying to get to the now-open doorway, but he grabbed her arm and jerked her around. "You're not leaving, Diane. We're going to stick this out."

She spun hard, trying to pull her arm loose, but his grasp was firm, and her arm pulled away from Jennifer. She tried to hold her with the other arm, but Jenny was slipping down her body. Diane dropped to her knees to keep her from falling, got hold of her, and was trying to get up again when

Greg shoved her and sent her sprawling onto her back, still holding the baby, who was now in a wild panic.

"You're not leaving again. We're going to stay right here and talk this out. So don't try to get out that door."

"I'll call the police," Diane said. She rolled to her side and let go of Jenny for a moment as she tried to get to her feet. But this time it was a fist that caught her on the side of her head. It crushed her ear and sent wild flashes through her vision. For a moment she felt everything begin to spin. But she fought her way back to her knees, and she grabbed for Jennifer again. She would take whatever else he had to dish out now, but she would fight her way to the door, or to the phone. She would do whatever she had to do, but she would get Jenny away from him forever.

When Diane looked up, she saw the look of surprise on Greg's face, as though he was as stunned as she was. "I wasn't going to do that," he said. "I didn't mean to."

But he stepped back from her. She got up, hugged Jenny for a moment, and then got her suitcase. She even got her jacket from the closet and a little coat she had ready for Jennifer. And this time she took her wallet.

"I'm so sorry, Diane," Greg was pleading. "I love you. Please don't leave me."

Diane heard it, but it didn't reach her. She had a baby to think about.

It was cool when she got outside. She stopped long enough to put the coat on Jennifer, and then she walked toward the U-District and stopped at a little grocery store. She had thought this all out ahead of time. She had even put a card in her wallet, with the number for a taxi company she could call. She made the call, and she called Mary to warn her, and then she waited inside where it was warm. And she talked to Jennifer the whole time, even sang her some of her favorite songs. "You are my sunshine, my only sunshine," she sang, and she didn't cry. Then, when she got to Mary's, she called her parents. That was hard, because she had said so little to them before, but they didn't really seem surprised, and they reassured her, made her feel that everything would be okay.

Later that evening, Greg called. He cried; he begged; he asked for one more chance. Diane was moved more than she wanted to be, but she told him, "Greg, I'm going home. I have a key to the apartment with me. I'll stop by in the morning for the rest of the things I want to take. Don't be there. Don't try to stop me. I'll call the police if I even see you're there. Give some thought to what *that* would do to your career. You're just lucky I haven't called already."

Chapter 11

Kathy Thomas was stuffing a pile of papers into a little valise. She was about to face another evening of reading student essays, which she dreaded, but she knew it was important that her students continue to write. The school year was almost over, but she didn't want to let up. It was frustrating to realize how little progress they had made in their writing during the year, but the problem was, they didn't speak much English outside the school. It was hard for them to compose in the formal style expected in an English paper. Their parents—if they spoke English at all—used odd idioms and strange mispronunciations. The kids had a hard time breaking themselves of those habits.

But Kathy was feeling better than she had for a while. She had received some interesting news that morning. Mrs. Sanchez would be returning to college for the next school year, and Kathy would stay in San Juan. She would teach the classes Mrs. Sanchez normally taught. Kathy was excited to be a regular teacher, not an aide, and even more excited not to have Mrs. Sanchez looking over her shoulder all the time. Kathy had started to feel lately that however inexperienced she was, she could do as well as most of the faculty. She wasn't impressed with their teaching methods.

Kathy turned to get up from her chair and was startled to find Mrs. Sanchez standing near her. She had entered the room without Kathy's realizing it, walking in her quiet way, like a cat.

"Excuse me, please, Miss Thomas," Mrs. Sanchez said. "I didn't want to frighten you."

Kathy laughed. "It's okay. I just didn't know you were standing there."

Kathy longed for a relationship that was less formal. Mrs. Sanchez was always polite, but she was almost too respectful. Kathy was, after all, twenty years younger. Kathy would like to have worked with someone she could laugh with, or talk to personally. Some of the teachers seemed a little more open that way, but the atmosphere among the faculty members was, generally speaking, more proper than seemed necessary. "It's wonderful that you're going back to the university next year. Are you excited?"

Mrs. Sanchez nodded. She was dressed in a white blouse, as always. She was a nice-looking woman, trim, with pretty, clear skin. "Yes, it will be very nice."

"Is this something you've been wanting to do for a long time?"

Mrs. Sanchez's eyes wandered away from Kathy's, and she seemed to choose her words carefully when she said, "Dr. Retanda believes it will be good for me to receive another year of instruction."

"You mean you didn't want to?"

But this was the wrong thing to ask. Kathy saw it immediately. "I'm happy to go," Mrs. Sanchez said, and she walked to her desk.

Fine. At least that desk would be Kathy's next year, and she wouldn't have to carry her own things around with her all the time. Maybe she would buy some rat poison, too, and see if she couldn't kill off some of the rodents that came to school like Mary's little lamb each day. She was going to do some things her own way. The kids actually got fleas from their desk seats, and they would squirm and scratch themselves. Surely there had to be a way to solve a problem like that.

"I want to do some experimenting next year," Kathy said, and yet she knew her statement was actually a way of protesting Mrs. Sanchez's curt way of cutting her off. "I have the feeling that all those grammar and usage drills we've been doing don't really help that much. What teachers in the United States have found is that the best way to teach the mechanics of writing is to have the kids write every single day—and write a lot."

Mrs. Sanchez opened a drawer and looked in, as though she were seeking a way to avoid Kathy's eyes, and then she said, softly, "Consider how many papers you must read, if you have them write so much."

"That's just the thing. You don't always have to read them. You can have them write in journals, or do what's called "free writing." There's a guy named McCrory who has this new book out that's really changing the way people are teaching writing. You just have the kids write their thoughts—sort of like brainstorming. Fast and free. A lot of times they write better when they relax and just let their language flow. Then you can help them revise and correct the errors, but you don't have to spend so much time doing boring drills. Apparently, there's no evidence that teaching kids to diagram sentences, for instance, actually helps them write better."

Mrs. Sanchez raised her head and finally looked directly at Kathy. But she didn't say anything.

"I'm not saying that's all I'll do, but I think that kind of relaxed writing could help our students. A lot of teachers are having their students gather into small groups and then read each other's work and critique one another. That way the teacher doesn't have to mark up everything the kids write with a red pencil."

Kathy had no more than said the words when she realized they must sound like a direct reference to the red pencil on Mrs. Sanchez's desk and, of course, to the user. Again, however, Mrs. Sanchez said nothing. In fact, she looked away, back at the open drawer.

"Don't get me wrong. I won't throw the baby out with the bathwater. I'll still teach grammar. I know kids who don't speak much English at home need that. I'm just saying I want to try a few new techniques. I'll let you know how it turns out. You might want to try some things like that when you get back."

Mrs. Sanchez shut the drawer without having gotten anything from it. She stood, and in a gentle voice, said, "Miss Thomas, thank you. I appreciate any ideas you have for me. Simply remember, consistency is very important. If the students lose a year of grammar study, they won't be ready for the following year."

"Oh, I know. I'm just saying, maybe some of the drills don't help that much, and more writing will. When the kids revise, they still have to get the commas in the right place. When they do their formal papers, I'll mark the mistakes."

Mrs. Sanchez nodded, but she didn't look pleased. "Have a very nice evening," she said.

"Okay. I'll see you in the morning. And don't worry. I'm not going off the deep end with the kids. I just want to try a few things."

Again, Mrs. Sanchez nodded, and then she left.

Kathy watched her all the way out the door, and then she rolled her eyes. The students had been drilled to death. They understood sentence structure and punctuation, and they could get verb tenses right when they had time to sit and think, but when they spoke, or had to write with any speed, they either became halting and unsure, or they reverted to the pidgin English they had heard all their lives.

Still, Kathy told herself she had to be careful. If she did anything too different from the other teachers, she would surely hear about it. What she wanted was to let the kids learn to express themselves, learn that writing was saying something you actually meant, not just stringing words together in proper forms. Most of these kids were afraid to have an opinion. After all, an opinion might offend someone. Just once Kathy wanted to hear her students enter into a true discussion—an actual exchange of ideas. Back in the States, Congress had passed a bill to give eighteen-year-olds the right to vote. That meant young people needed to be thinking about their world while they were still teenagers—the way she always had. There was no reason, as far as she was concerned, that Filipino kids couldn't do the same.

Kathy finished the school week and then used the weekend to clean house—which Martha never seemed to worry much about—and read student papers. She decided not to go to church. She had been back only once since she had gone the first time. Bishop Luna had asked her again to become more involved, but Kathy didn't see how she could. Another set of missionaries was working with the ward now, and maybe not all of them had the point of view of Elder Wimmer, but she hadn't forgotten his opinion of her. She was one of those dangerous "liberals," as far as he was concerned, and he was probably right. She thought at times that she could be who she was and still be part of the Church, but she wasn't sure that could happen while she was in the Peace Corps. Mormon missionaries and Peace Corps volunteers surely saw a lot of the same problems, but they came at them from different directions, and Kathy didn't know how to make the two work together. Maybe during school vacation, when the pressure of her work let up, she would go to her meetings more often, but only if the bishop let her sit on the back row and enjoy the things she liked about being there—without having to serve in a calling.

On Monday afternoon, after school, Mrs. Sanchez disappeared immediately. Kathy finished up some recording of grades, and she was getting ready to leave when Dr. Retanda, the school principal, stepped to her door. "Miss Thomas, please, may I speak with you?"

"Sure. Come in."

He stepped through the door, stopped, and nodded, almost as though he were bowing, Asian style. He was wearing one of the embroidered *barong* shirts. She had noticed that he had two, which were both rather worn, but he wore one or the other every day. "I hope your school year is coming to a happy conclusion," he said.

"Well, yeah. Mostly." Something in Kathy wouldn't let her respond to his formality. She almost went out of her way to talk like an American, just to let him know that some people in the world didn't make quite such a big deal out of authority figures. "But I'm looking forward to next year now that I know I'll have a regular teaching load."

Dr. Retanda certainly knew what Kathy was saying—that being an aide had been frustrating to her—but he ignored that implication and said, "Yes. We are happy to have you teaching on a full schedule. We trust that you will do very well."

"I hope so. I'm sort of green as a teacher, but I'm going to give it everything I've got."

"It is most important that our students have consistency, Miss Thomas."

So that's what this visit was about.

But Kathy wasn't going to do this the hard way—the Philippine way. "Dr. Retanda, Mrs. Sanchez doesn't have to worry. I told her I wanted to do a little experimenting with some techniques I've read about—just to see if they might add some fluency to our students' writing. But I'll still have them do the grammar and usage drills."

"Yes. That is good, Miss Thomas. And please, maybe it is better not to experiment too much. Consistency is most important."

"All right. If that's what you prefer, but I really don't understand. Why are we even here if we can't bring some of our ideas with us? I thought the whole point was for us to learn from you and for you to learn from us. I don't know an awful lot about teaching English, or teaching writing, but I've been trying to learn. I've been studying some of the latest techniques. What can it hurt to see whether some of them aren't helpful to our kids?"

He nodded again, even bent slightly from the waist. "Yes, I understand how you feel. You must understand, however, Mrs. Sanchez will be teaching again the following year, and you will return to the United States. It is very important to us that we have consistency."

"Dr. Retanda, I don't even know what that means. You want to stick with the same old things, whether they work or not. And Mrs. Sanchez ran to you the minute I told her I wanted to try something new. Why couldn't she just talk it out with me? What's she so worried about? We can disagree without getting mad at each other."

But Kathy had done it again. She saw the sternness in Dr. Retanda's eyes, knew she had insulted him. "Miss Thomas, Mrs. Sanchez has taught here for many years. It's most important that you respect her, and do as she wishes during the time she is gone. She will perhaps learn new techniques. She will—"

"No, she won't. You know she won't. She has a certain way of doing things, and that's how she'll always do them. And even if she did come back with something new, you probably wouldn't let her try it. You have to have *consistency*, even if it's *consistently* wrong. What you really mean is, you don't like change."

Dr. Retanda met her eye-to-eye for just a moment, and she saw his real response, an anger that wanted to release itself. But then he looked past her and said, "Miss Thomas, please. It is unkind to speak this way of Mrs. Sanchez. And of me."

"Okay. I know. I'm sorry. I'll do whatever she wants me to do next year. And then I'll go home and wonder why I ever came here. But don't worry. I won't be a problem for you."

He certainly understood her sarcasm—her *disrespect*—but he didn't call her on any of that. He merely said, "Thank you, Miss Thomas. Have a good evening." And he walked from the room, his feet not making any more sound than Mrs. Sanchez's did.

Kathy didn't know when she would receive her next visit, but she knew most certainly that it would come. As it turned out, most of the week passed, and then on Thursday afternoon her Peace Corps Regional Representative, Bill Goldman, finally showed up. Kathy had thought about all the things she could say to explain, but she was tired, had another stack of papers to read, and was in no mood to justify herself. So she said, "Come on in, Bill. I thought you'd be here before now. I'm sure Dr. Retanda squealed on me at the beginning of the week."

Bill laughed, and then he did step in. He took a seat on one of the rattan chairs in Kathy's living room. He stretched his skinny, bare legs out in front of him, put his hands behind his head, and asked, "So Kathy, how are things going for you?"

"You know better than I do. How are things with you, Bill?"

"Better. We finally got our office repaired. It got hit pretty hard in the earthquake."

An earthquake had struck Manila early in April. San Juan had felt the jolt, too, and a couple of old buildings had received some damage, but Manila had been hurt a lot worse. Still, Kathy didn't want to make small talk about the state of Bill's office. "Just start chewing on me, okay?" she said. "Let's get it over with."

Bill was a dreadfully thin man with pale skin and a dark, trim beard. Back home, in Wisconsin, he had been even more into the antiwar movement than Kathy. He had served jail time for occupying a building at the university. Kathy knew he was as anti-establishment as she was, and it really wasn't in him to take on the role of a boss.

"*Well*," he said, "I did receive a call on Tuesday. It sounds like you already realized you upset a few people."

"Just give me the word, Bill. I'm sure you promised Dr. Retanda that you would. Then I'll promise to be a good girl from now on. But I have to tell you, I'm not sure right now why we ever came to the Philippines. They *love* us here—as long as we don't do anything."

This time Bill didn't laugh. He sat for a time and apparently considered his response. He was wearing a white shirt that was wet with sweat. Kathy could see the dark hair on his chest, through the fabric. It was not a good look. "I know how you feel," he finally said. "I think we all get frustrated at times. But I get to hear all the good news, too, and we do have our little triumphs. Lots of them, actually—even if some of them are fairly subtle. One thing I've heard is how much your students like you, for instance. You're a good model for them. They get to see a strong, smart young woman, and that's something these kids—the boys as much as the girls—need to experience."

"That's all very nice, Bill, but don't I remember, somewhere back in my training, that one of the reasons I was coming here was to bring some of our teaching methods?"

Bill smiled. "Yes, I suppose we did say something about that."

"But see, the problem is, I came here fresh out of school, and I felt inadequate. So I've been reading like crazy to figure out what these kids need—so I can fulfill our promise and give them some help. And now I've apparently created some sort of international incident. All I wanted to do was let the kids keep a journal, do a little free writing, and maybe try some critique groups."

"That's not what this is all about, Kathy. You know that. From Dr. Retanda's point of view, you showed disrespect both to him and to the woman you teach with. He said you raised your voice and told him he wasn't a good principal."

Kathy had her defense ready, and on Tuesday she would have used it. Maybe Bill had let her wait all week on purpose, and maybe he had been wise to do so, because Kathy was, by now, ashamed of some of things she had said to Dr. Retanda. "Actually, I did show him disrespect," she said. "It's the kind of disrespect we're accustomed to in the States—we'd call it being 'open' with each other, or some such thing—but I knew very well when I was talking to him that I was breaking all the rules of politeness. In my defense, I'll only say that after a year of bottling my feelings up, I did pretty well not to tell him what I *really* think of him. He's a little chauvinist pig, if you want to know the truth."

Bill rolled his eyes, but he couldn't stop himself from laughing. "Kathy, I know what you mean. But we've talked a lot about divesting ourselves of our own cultural biases. I won't give you a speech about that because I know you understand."

"Look, I didn't call him a chauvinist. I'm just telling you, that's what he is."

"But think about it, Kathy. When it comes to attitudes about women, a lot of things have changed in the United States in the last few years. You can't expect everyone in the world to make that same transition overnight."

"Hey, I don't. We haven't made all that much headway in America, as you know very well. But it doesn't change the fact that most of the men in this country treat women with condescension and *disrespect*. I haven't tried to change that. I'm just telling you that's how it is."

"But what about your problems with the mayor?"

"What?" Kathy had been sitting back, relaxed, but now she sat up. This one she hadn't expected.

"Dr. Retanda told me you've upset the whole barrio council, especially the mayor."

"Are we talking about the council meeting I went to, clear back before Christmas?"

"I guess so. Dr. Retanda said you spoke to all the barrio leaders and demanded that they build public toilets."

Kathy slapped her forehead with the palm of her hand. "Oh, brother!" she said. "Bill, this is a joke. Martha made me be so careful that I hardly made my point. All I did was explain how important hygiene was. I asked for permission to teach the kids to wash their hands, and the mayor said that was fine. Then I asked them to consider building public toilets. The kids around here think every alley is a bathroom. Dogs run through the stuff and track it all over town. Then the people wonder why their children get sick and die."

"What did the mayor say?"

"What these people always say. Thank you very much. We're so happy you came tonight. We'll do nothing at all, but we aren't going to admit that out loud."

"Have you pushed him on it since then?"

"I saw him a couple of times, and I brought it up. I just asked whether the council had thought more about it. He always says, 'Yes, yes. It's *bery* important. We do this. Bery soon.'"

"I think you're showing disrespect again."

"Only where it's deserved."

"Look, I know what you're talking about. But we've built toilets in some places, and the kids—plus a lot of the men—still go in the alleys. The thing you have to remember, though, is that we plant an idea, and it only gradually takes hold. We just have to live with that. You can't push these men too hard. To them, you're a young girl, and you're a foreigner. They may comprehend what you're telling them, but if they feel like you're trying to show them up, they'll never respond."

"Then why don't we go home? I can think of better things to do with my time. I could sit and bang my head against a wall all day and get just as much satisfaction."

"Kathy, come on. That's enough. You've got to soften your approach, but one day those men will build that public toilet and they'll think it was their own idea. Sooner or later, the idea you started in the council meeting will end up saving some lives. Don't tell me you've saved a lot of lives back home in Utah."

Kathy was nodding, just barely, not to him, but to herself. "Okay. Good point. Martha tells me all the same stuff."

"Kathy, she'll be going home in a month or so, and we'll be sending someone else to live with you. You're going to have to be the one who teaches some woman from the States how all this works. It's time for you to start acting like the veteran you are. You've got that first year almost behind you."

"I know. You're right. I did feel really bad after I said that stuff to Dr. Retanda. It won't happen again."

"All right. Good. But go ahead and do a little experimenting with your class. If something works for you, let some of the faculty know. Just do it without getting pushy."

"Me? Pushy? That's the old me—before you and I had this nice chat. I don't act like that anymore."

"Right." He stood up. "Well, good luck, my friend."

"Do you want to stay for dinner? We can probably scare up some rice and fish heads for you."

"Sounds delicious, but I think I'll pass. I'll pick up a dozen *balut* and eat them for snacks on the way back."

Kathy shuddered. *Balut* was something she still hadn't tried and didn't plan to. They were half-formed duck embryos, boiled in the shells. Kathy had seen them, with their little beaks and feathers. They crunched when people chewed them. "You do that," she said.

"You don't happen to have a cold beer I could wash them down with, do you?"

"Afraid not."

"How did you ever get into the Peace Corps? I couldn't survive in the Philippines without beer."

Kathy laughed and shrugged her shoulders, but she took the remark as a little insult. He was only joking, of course, but she was tired of those kinds of comments. She thought again how often people told her—no matter where she was or what she was doing—that she really didn't fit in.

Martha got home not long after Bill left. She went in and changed out of her school clothes, and then, as the two tried to figure out what they really were going to eat that night—rice and something probably, even if it wasn't fish heads—Kathy told Martha all about the conversation.

"It doesn't sound like he was too hard on you," Martha said.

"I think he's learning from the Filipinos. He chewed me out *nicely*."

"But was he upset?"

"No. Not exactly. He was pretty good about it. And I know he's right. I know you're right, too. But I'm not sure I'm ever going to get used to this place. When I see a problem, it just makes sense to me to do something about it. And I can never quite understand why most everyone thinks that's a strange way to deal with the world. But maybe it's time I start catching on. I've been driving people crazy all my life."

Martha sat at the little kitchen table. She had tied her hair up to keep it off her neck, and she was wearing short shorts and a cotton T-shirt. She looked comfortable but way too provocative to walk outside. She would shock everyone in the barrio if they saw her. But the heat in the house this afternoon was caught inside, as usual, with no air moving. Kathy wanted to dress the same way, but it wasn't in her to do it. "You can't get discouraged, Kathy. When I leave, you've got to keep up the fight."

"Hey, if I could fight, I'd be fine. But that's what gets me into trouble."

"Well . . . *fight* isn't the right word. I should say, 'Keep up the love.'"

Kathy laughed. "You can't ask a giraffe to be a kitten, Martha. I don't know how to do things your way."

But Martha said, "You're a lot softer than you know, Kathy. I didn't think so at first, but I've seen you with the kids this year. They know who you are, and they love you for it. You've done a lot of good, whether you know it or not."

Kathy liked to think that was true. But she also remembered Martha's other assessment of her: that she wasn't happy. Kathy had thought a great deal about that the past couple of months. She knew this drive of hers to fix things was part of what made her seem angry and unsatisfied, but she had never thought of herself as unhappy. She wondered what it took to feel more satisfied with life. Was it a matter of giving up and not trying to make changes? Did the Filipinos have the secret? The idea was almost impossible for Kathy to accept. But she did want to be happy—certainly happier than she had been lately—and she wasn't sure what it would take to get herself to that point.

During the final week of school, she did keep Martha's words in mind, and when she said farewell to her students, most of them embraced her, and some of the girls cried. Kathy cried too. She didn't know whether she had accomplished much with her students, but she did love them, and they seemed to love her. That did make her feel good about herself.

On the day after school let out, Kathy finished up her grades, turned them in, and then cleared out her things. She was carrying a box back to her house when it occurred to her, after all the busyness, she really didn't have much to do for a while. She was free to travel, and she did want to see more of Luzon, but she would also have some leisure time here in San Juan during the vacation. One thing she had thought about doing was recruiting a few of the male Peace Corps volunteers to come over and help build the public rest room that the mayor had never gotten around to. In some towns, volunteers had installed a septic system and built a little building with one or two flush toilets. Maybe the mayor wouldn't mind if Peace Corps volunteers did all the work and local workers didn't have to do anything. She just wasn't sure she had the nerve to bring it up with him. If she wasn't careful, she could get herself reported again.

That afternoon she walked into the little center of the barrio, and she looked around in a couple of the *sari-sari* stores. She wanted to find a new shower curtain, and she had a promise from the school that someone would come and work on the shower—try to get it operating so she and Martha didn't have to dip and pour. Of course, she had heard that promise all year, but the vacation seemed to be a good opportunity for one of the maintenance people to find time. The shower curtain was more of a wish than a genuine need, and besides, she could find no such thing in the stores, so she bought some crusty *pan-de-sal* rolls from the little bakery and some nice fruits next door—mango, papaya, and cooking bananas—and then she started her walk up the hill toward home. She was stepping carefully through a little muddy section of the street when she looked up to see the mayor smiling at her.

"Miss Thomas, bery nice to see you," he said.

Kathy, of course, didn't believe that, but she said, "Nice to see you, Mayor Dias. How are you today?"

"Bery good, tank you. It's hot. Bery hot." He wiped his face with a red handkerchief.

"Yes, it is."

"You are finished with school now. You like that?"

"Oh, yes. But I miss the students already."

"The families in our barrio—and in the other barrios—they tell me you bery fine teacher."

"Thank you. That's nice to hear. I love the kids."

"And you teach them to wash hands, yes?"

"We're trying. Maybe Miss Sommers and I can make more visits now that we're not so busy with school."

"Yes, yes. And our council, we build the toilet. This bery important."

Kathy couldn't believe it. He would always claim that and never do it. But why would he report that Kathy had been too pushy and then make this promise? It was some kind of game that Kathy didn't comprehend, no matter how many excuses Martha and Bill made for the people. But Kathy saw an opening, and she thought maybe she could make her request. "I have friends in the Peace Corps—some of the men—who would be happy to come here and help. We could dig the trenches and even build the building. We could do that for the barrio, as our gift."

"Yes, yes. We like this help. We choose a place to make this toilet. We make plans. After this, we bery happy for this help."

Kathy had to watch her step, and she knew it, but she said, "It's best if we do this during our vacation. Some of the other volunteers are also teachers. We have more time now while school is out."

"Yes, yes. I understand. We make these plans bery soon. But rain comes now. This not a good time for building."

"If you could just pick the spot and then tell us where you want the trenches dug, we could start right away. It should be near the school, I think. It wouldn't matter to us if it rained on us while we were digging."

"Yes, yes. First we must have council meeting."

"When is the next one?"

"Soon. Bery soon now."

Didn't the man know when the next meeting would be held? How could that be? Kathy absolutely had to stop, but she knew what would happen. The vacation time would pass and nothing would be decided. And that might be her last chance to get the job done. "Mayor, don't misunderstand. I know you must meet with your council. But couldn't you call a meeting next week? Now is the best time for our people to do some work for you."

"Yes, yes. We have meeting soon."

Did he mean they *would* meet next week? "Mayor, I'm sorry. I don't mean to be impolite to you. It's just that it's *so* important. It really is a matter of life and death. Human waste spreads terrible germs. People are getting sick who don't have to get sick. Children are dying. I hope you understand, that's the only reason I keep bringing this up. I only want the children to be healthy."

"Yes, I understand. But rains come soon. Not good now to build such a toilet."

"It rains *every* year, Mayor. Why didn't you try to do something during the dry season?"

She saw the change in the mayor's eyes; she saw the wall that was rising between them, and suddenly she was furious. All she was asking was that he do something to protect the children of *his* barrio. How could he resent her when her intentions were so pure?

But she held her tongue and took a breath. "Let us know when we can help you," she said.

"We can build this toilet," he said. "We have men."

She knew what he was saying, understood this was his quiet way of telling her, "We can look out for our children without the Peace Corps telling us what to do." Or in other words, our pride is more important than our children. Kathy exploded. "But you *won't* do it. You'll stall around forever, and while you're *planning*, more babies will die. I hope you can live with that, Mayor. You're not a leader. You would be a joke if there was anything funny about this."

He stared at her, but he didn't say a word. She didn't know whether he was insulted or disappointed or furious. How could she tell with people like this?

"Well, Mayor, now you have something to do. Go report me to my leaders. With any luck at all, they'll send me home, and we'll both be a lot happier."

Kathy had burned her bridges now. Maybe she would quit. Maybe she would be transferred. The only thing she was sure of was that she had lost her chance to do any good in this little town.

CHAPTER 12

As the helicopter descended, Gene felt that usual tightness in his throat, felt his heart jolting against his ribs. "Lock and load," Pop shouted above the sound of the rotors. Gene chambered a round, then gripped his rifle and waited. He hated those final feet of descent when everyone on the slick was vulnerable if the enemy was out there. He hated the noise of the engine, too, knowing how far into the jungle it could penetrate. If NVA troops were in the area, they would all be trying to spot the slick, or at least guess from the sound where the insertion was taking place.

Before the skids could even touch the ground in the deep elephant grass that was flattened by the blast from the rotors, all six men on the team were off and running. As Gene charged toward the brushy cover, up a hill, he was glad for the motion, but he wanted quiet, and he was relieved as the Huey nosed quickly away. In less than a minute the men were into the brush, down and frozen in place. There was not a sound; even the birds and insects were silent. The sun was angling low, making long shadows, with streaks of light through the brush, and all was calm except for the still-labored breathing of the men.

Gene watched Pop, who was staring, listening, concentrating hard. The routine was always more or less the same. They would "lay dog" and listen for maybe twenty minutes or so, and then get away from the landing zone, the spot the enemy would converge on if any of them had seen or heard the insertion. After that, it was time to set up a night perimeter and hunker down. Gene had been out on some uneventful patrols lately, in areas that had turned out to be quiet. Another team, however, had made contact in this same valley just a week before, and the soldiers had taken two casualties, both shot up pretty badly.

Sweat was running down Gene's face, even into his eyes, but he didn't wipe it away. He blinked hard, but that was the only movement he allowed himself. Silence was everything for these first few minutes, and experienced guys had no tolerance for a man who moved just because he was uncomfortable. Mosquitoes didn't matter, and neither did a numb leg or an aching muscle caused by a badly chosen first position. Discomfort had to be tolerated until Pop gave the nod. When he did, Melnick established communication with the company commander in his now-distant observation helicopter. He reported, in whispers, a cold insertion and thereby released the transport slick to return to base.

All remained quiet after the "commo check," and the insects began their evening chant—a sign that no one was moving toward the team. So Pop moved the men out rather more quickly than usual, and after a tedious movement to a better site lower on the mountain, the men set out their claymore mines and settled in for a silent night—no talk, just waiting, and as much sleep as possible. Gene knew how to do all this now, and he even dealt with the fear more efficiently, allowing it a proper place, like an extra organ in his body, sending off the right signals, keeping him alert and sharp, but creating little conscious awareness. What he couldn't do was sleep—never the first night, and usually little through the entire patrol. But it didn't matter. It was more important to stay alive than to sleep, and there was time for sleep between patrols.

A man named Saunders had been assigned to the Spartan team for this mission. Most of the teams were short of men these days, and some were going out "light," with five, sometimes even four men. Since Spartan had lost Lattimer, the men had gone out light themselves a few times. Not many new guys were coming into the unit to replace the casualties the unit was regularly taking on. At least Saunders was experienced. He had been an assistant team leader on some patrols. Kovach was ATL this time, but it was always good to have lots of men who knew the ropes. Saunders was a slight, little guy, like a kid—and he *was* only nineteen, but he had a reputation for being fearless.

Pop had assigned Gene an early watch. Afterward, he wrapped himself up against the coming cold. He shut his eyes and actually reached a state of relative insensibility; time passed a little faster than it might have in full wakefulness. At about the time his inner clock was telling him that dawn couldn't be far away, Gene heard a sound. All the men heard it at the same time, no one much deeper asleep, obviously, than Gene was. It was a sharp crack—a mistake—maybe someone slipping on the damp ground, in the dark, and striking his rifle stock against a tree, or maybe . . . Gene didn't know, but it wasn't anything normal out there in the jungle at night. No animal or insect made a sound like that.

Pop whispered for everyone to come to full alert, and the men sat up, got their weapons ready, and waited. The sun was bringing a hint of light to the sky when Gene heard the next sound. This was clearly someone moving through brush, carefully, but making a bit of a scrape. Gene could make out Pop's head now. He nodded, merely to say, "Yes, they're out there."

Gene had seen a couple of situations like this before. Sounds carried, and the enemy might not be all that close. The first thing to do was trust the cover, merely hope that a small patrol was searching, perhaps aware of the insertion the night before. Charlie could easily work through the area and never find the team. If he happened to get too close, the claymores could be fired, but if that happened and a larger unit was searching, the team would be in trouble. The claymores might take out the first wave, but the location would be revealed, and six guys would have their hands full.

Gene thought he heard a whisper at one point, and twice he heard movement again. What he couldn't tell was whether the sounds were getting closer. But eventually the noise disappeared, and that was a good sign that a patrol had missed them. Pop finally signaled for the men to pull in the mines and prepare to leave. He also had Melnick contact a firebase that was the relay station for communication with TOC. He took the handset and whispered, "We're compromised here and heading for our E and E extraction site. We're going to need a slick and possibly gunships."

Gene hadn't known whether escape and evasion would be necessary, but he was greatly relieved. The men worked their way up the mountain, under double canopy at first. The jungle was still dark except for a glow that made silhouettes of the trees and brush. The heat wasn't coming back yet, but now that the men were moving through the watery air, sweat was running down Gene's sides and along his ears and nose. He felt as though he were nothing but nerve endings, his whole body seeming to listen and watch. He knew his own motion, could hear the sound of the men in front and back of him, but he strained to hear what else was there. Kovach stopped much more often than usual, walking only five minutes or so before waiting that long. If a unit was still around, searching, it was crucial to get a read on it without giving away the team's own position.

Kovach was well ahead, and Gene knew he would soon be coming out from under the canopy into thick brush. It was a dangerous area, less covered and harder to get through. If the men were going to get to the ridge, this was where they would be most vulnerable. But they kept moving, and Pop made a tough decision. He signaled to Kovach to use a trail he had come across. That meant easier movement, less probability of noise, but the NVA might also be on the trail, or they might be watching it.

Gene was nervous about the decision. But he knew the thinking: the trail was a gamble, but it could get them quickly to the ridge, if that proved necessary.

They moved up the trail quickly for several minutes, and then gunfire opened up. It was paralyzing—the sudden explosions, the flashes. Kovach was firing on full automatic, and there was another sound—

probably AK-47 fire. Gene dropped onto his face, but by then the fire had stopped and Kovach broke sound discipline. "I got him, but now we gotta get to the ridge as fast as we can," he said. It was a whisper, but it was intense, and Gene saw Melnick, in front of him, take off hard. Gene was already up, running. This was going to be a hard climb, up a wet path, with the enemy trying to get to the trail to cut them off. Gene felt as though he were running with an animal in chase. But it was good to know that Pop was behind him, covering his back.

The run was exhausting, with the heavy radio weighing Gene down, but he didn't slow. No one did. They kept charging, holding their weapons ready, watching the sides of the trail. Gene could hear the pounding of boots, the rattle of equipment, the hard breathing—everything the men normally avoided. The idea of it was terrifying. It was like screaming down the mountain, "Here we are. Right here!" But they made the run in maybe eight or nine minutes, and as they broke onto the ridge, Pop grabbed Gene. "Call for the extraction," he said.

By then the LOH was in the air, and Gene was able to reach their new CO, Captain Shreeve. He had taken over for Battaglia just the week before. "We've had contact down here," Gene told him. "We need a slick, and we need Cobras. We're at the E and E, on the ridge."

"Roger that," Shreeve said. A few seconds ticked by, and then the CO's voice crackled over the radio again. "The slick just took off. He's fifteen mikes out."

Pop grabbed the handset. "Then give me gunships *now!*" he demanded, his voice in a rage. "We won't last fifteen minutes up here."

"Roger that."

"Set out claymores," Pop told his men, but he didn't have to. Kovach and Saunders were already working on that. And then Pop organized the men into a line, taking the chance that no one was behind them, coming up the opposite side of the ridge. "Stay down, now. Don't waste ammo shooting into the brush. Don't shoot unless you see somebody. Get your grenades ready."

He moved up and down the line, checking to see what the men had in the way of ammunition. By the time he got back to the end of the line, right of Gene, the CO was on the radio again. "The gunships are in the air, out of Firebase Sword. Ten mikes."

Pop cursed but then took the handset and said, "All right, tell 'em we're in deep trouble up here. They gotta come in hard." He returned the handset, then looked at Gene for a moment. "The captain just wished us good luck."

Good luck? To Gene, and obviously to Pop, it seemed as though an officer, high in the air, was playing with chess pieces, calculating that to get to checkmate, he might have to give up a few of his pawns. But there was no checkmate. There never was. The game never ended.

Gene watched the brush down the mountainside. It bothered him to think that if he died here today, he would die for nothing. The mission hadn't accomplished a thing. He felt a surge of anger, but at the same time he was praying: "Lord, get us through this one."

A couple of minutes must have passed, and Gene knew it wasn't more than that, but it seemed as though the ten should have gone by. He kept listening for the gunships, even though he knew they weren't close yet. Then he saw movement in the brush. The NVA had obviously followed the men up the trail, but now they were spreading out, preparing to make the assault. What Gene knew was that the soldiers would be shooting mortars up the hill before long, that they would do that before they came out into the open.

It was another couple of minutes before Gene heard the first thump of a mortar being launched. "Here it comes," Kovach said, and everyone ducked down. Gene heard the whistle, the suck of air, as the mortar passed over. It landed behind them, beyond the ridge, and exploded harmlessly. But that didn't matter. There would be more, and they would gain accuracy with each miss. Thump. Thump. Two more were on the way. One exploded in front of Gene and sent dirt and debris and spinning shrapnel flying over his head. He wanted to dig in, but there was no time for that.

Two more thumps followed, and dirt was exploding again, but as Gene looked up, he saw several men in NVA uniforms break from the brush. They ran up the mountain, muzzles flashing fire, bullets buzzing, cracking, kicking up dirt. But then the claymores blew, the backblast hitting Gene with a powerful concussion. When he looked up, most of the NVA soldiers were down, and the others were falling back. Only a few minutes passed, however, before another wave was charging up the hill. Gene fired, but not as carefully as he wanted to. He was too excited, too scared. Still, the enemy soldiers went down in a wave, one falling after the other. One man went over backward and rolled down the hill. The others were on their faces, and Gene watched them, waiting to see whether they would move. One tried to roll onto his side and he took another blast from up the line. Pop yelled, "Don't waste the ammo. He's down."

And then it was quiet again. But Gene could see men in the brush, glimpses of tan uniforms moving, spreading wider. This was it, a bigger attack, and Gene knew how it would start. He listened for the mortars. "I'm sorry, Emily," he said out loud, and he felt sadness replace the panic he had felt a moment before.

The thumping sound, two of them again, sounded, and this time one struck to the left of Gene, in the middle of the line. He heard someone cry out. Two more struck in front of the line, and dirt filled the air. Gene ducked, but then he looked to his left and saw that Kovach was hit. The man was lying on his side, curled up, gripping his shoulder, with blood running through his fingers. He was cursing and moaning, in terrible pain. Gene wondered what he should do, with another attack coming soon, but someone had to stop Kovach's bleeding. He started crawling toward him, but just as he did, he felt something grab his leg, turn it on fire. He looked down to see blood pumping through his fatigues from the side of his right thigh. He pulled loose the towel he kept tied around his neck and wrapped it around the wound. Then he tied it tight, all the while watching for the next wave of the attack. He listened for the gunships, too, knowing that he and his team couldn't last much longer. But he heard no choppers.

Now the North Vietnamese were coming again—lots of them this time. Gene twisted around and began to fire. Men were falling, but others kept coming, and only a couple of grenade blasts finally sent them back down the hill. Lots of the enemy were on the ground, but there were plenty left, gathering themselves again, down in the brush. It must have been a whole platoon the team was taking on.

"Pull in closer," Pop called. "They're moving around us. We gotta watch our backs now."

It was a horrifying thought, being surrounded. Gene dragged himself closer to Pop, but the movement took the pain in his leg to a new place. He looked back as Melnick and Saunders came crawling from their end of the line and took up a position behind Gene and Pop. They formed a kind of circle, but now Gene could see that Kovach wasn't moving in. He was still curled up, lying on his side, but Gene could see now that the shrapnel had torn a piece of flesh out of his upper chest. Blood was pooling under him. He wasn't dead, but Gene knew he soon would be.

"Someone help Kovach," Gene yelled.

Melnick cursed. "We can't. Not yet. Where are those gunships?"

"We're going to get it from every direction," Pop said. "Keep firing even if you take a hit. If we can hold them off once more, those ships should get here."

Another minute passed, and that had to be good, but Gene didn't bother to hope. "Take care of them. Please," he was saying, in his mind, over and over. "Help Danny grow up all right."

There were no mortars this time, not with NVA on all sides, but when the gunfire started, it was an unremitting rumble. Gene tried to fire at targets, tried to make sure he took someone out, but it was hard to see with so much dirt in the air, hard to concentrate. He heard screams and knew they were coming from nearby, that others in his team were being hit. But nothing registered clearly except the chaos of sound and movement and bright flashes of muzzles and tracers.

The NVA were still coming. Gene grabbed his grenades, started rolling them out, not far from himself, and ducking as they exploded. It was like throwing up a wall in front of himself, and he liked the sense of protection. He used three, and had only one more, but it didn't seem to matter what he did. He threw the last one, ducked, and then grabbed his rifle again. But through the dust he saw an enemy soldier running down hill, and then he saw him fall. It was only then that he realized that a terrific wind he had been feeling was from props, almost directly overhead, and two gunships were tearing up everything in sight. The noise was a frightening roar, but it was like the voice of God to Gene. "Thank you. Thank you," he began to mumble.

The gunships swung left and right but stayed very close. The brush down the hillside was exploding, limbs and leaves flipping about. After a couple of minutes, the Cobras began to work a wider area, opening up some space around the men who were down. Gene finally dared to look around him to check on his team. He saw that Saunders was torn up, his face covered with blood. Pop was already with him, and Gene tried to drag himself in that direction. But then he saw the wound. Saunders had taken a bullet under his eye, and the bone had been ripped away. There was blood and brain where his eye should have been. Pop shouted to Gene, words no one could have heard, but he must have been saying that Saunders was dead.

Gene looked for the others. Then he saw Dearden. He was on his chest, lying still, his face in the dirt, his eyes open. Gene pulled himself toward Dearden, frantically, then grabbed him and turned him over. But a huge chunk of Dearden's forehead was gone. Gene shook him, yelled to him, told him to hang on, but he knew that made no sense. And then Pop grabbed Gene by the shoulder and pulled him away. He pointed to Kovach, who was still on his side, gasping for breath. Melnick was with him.

Pop had blood on his face, but he seemed to be moving all right. He grabbed his rucksack and ran toward Kovach. Gene was in terrific pain, but he tried to crawl closer. By then Pop was pulling Kovach's shirt open. Gene saw lots of blood on his chest and didn't know for sure where he was hit, but Pop applied a bandage, and Melnick helped him secure it.

The roar of the helicopters continued, but Gene finally realized that a new sound was overhead. Another blast of air was striking them. It was a slick, descending, just slightly down the ridge. Pop and Melnick got up. They lifted Kovach between them, and as the slick hovered just above the ground, they set off toward it. But they had only gone a few steps when Melnick dropped, as though he had been struck over the head. Gene had been trying to get up, to make his own run for the slick. Now he pushed himself harder, made it to his feet, and hobbled to Melnick. Pop was pulling Kovach toward the slick, by himself. Gene had to help Melnick.

Blood was oozing through Melnick's fatigues in two spots on his back. He was big, and Gene struggled to stay on his feet, but he shifted around the man, then grasped him under the arms and struggled backward, pulling him. The gunfire was still loud from the Cobras, and Gene could hear the crack of bullets near him, too. He expected to be hit at any moment, but he kept pulling, and then Pop was there, taking one of Melnick's arms. They moved faster together, and then they lifted Melnick and shoved him onto the helicopter. Pop jumped on board and grabbed for Gene, who was still on the skids when the helicopter lifted. He could hear the metallic ring, a series of pings, and he knew the slick was being hit, but he also felt Pop's strong hands pulling him onto the floor of the helicopter.

Gene rolled onto his side and looked at Kovach, who was lying close to him. His bandages had pulled away, and Gene saw the gush of blood. He was almost lost in his own pain and confusion, but Gene knew there was some other reason why Pop was cursing. Gene could smell smoke and hear the sound of the engine, running rough. It had taken a hit. They were off the hill, but they weren't home. Maybe the helicopter was going to go down. Gene felt the inevitability of it all again. They weren't going to make it. They were still going to die.

But the slick kept hanging on, sounding like a tractor, not moving fast but making its way. Gene shut his eyes. He knew it was maybe twenty minutes or more back to camp at this rate. He didn't know if there was somewhere else to put down, or whether Kovach and Melnick could live if they did, but he dared to pray again now. "Don't let us crash," he pleaded. "Not now." He didn't know whether he was speaking out loud; he hardly knew the inside of himself from the outside at this point. The pain was filling him up, and the chaos seemed to have been dragged up from the ground, as though it were still flying with them. The noises kept slamming Gene, crashing inside his head: Kovach moaning, Pop swearing, shouting to Kovach that he had to live, and that busted engine clinging onto life, filling the slick with smoke.

Gene didn't think he had lost consciousness, but when the slick began to descend, he assumed it was in some spot far from the base. It was only after medics had gotten Kovach and Melnick off, and had come after Gene—really only when he was being carried to a medevac helicopter—that he recognized the Camp Eagle helipad. He was heading for another helicopter, on a stretcher, but something had happened. The pain was gone, and his head was in a fog. He couldn't think well enough to know what it meant.

At the next helicopter there was a delay. Gene rolled his head to see that Kovach was surrounded by men working on him. "How bad?" he said, not knowing whether anyone could hear him.

"You're going to be okay, Thomas," Pop said from somewhere.

"No, Kovach."

"I don't know. He lost a lot of blood."

"Melnick?"

"He'll make it."

But then Gene thought of Dearden, his friend. Dead. He thought of Saunders, the tough guy. Dead. Maybe Kovach. He didn't know what it meant yet. He couldn't think. He was floating, it seemed. He couldn't feel the stretcher anymore. He was lying in air.

"Can I go home?"

"What?"

"Is it bad? Will they send me home?"

"I don't know, Thomas. It's hard to say."

Gene slept through most of the next two days. Pain medicine kept him from hurting much, but he slept restlessly, dreaming in repetitive, confusing sequences, sometimes seeing all those NVA soldiers coming up the hill, sometimes the gunships, but mostly he saw Dearden on his chest with his face in the dirt. Gene would awake, startled, and hope for a moment that he had dreamed Dearden's death, but then he would know that however distorted the scene was in his mind, it had happened. No one could tell him anything about Melnick or Kovach; no one seemed to know.

But on the third day, in the early morning, Pop was standing over him when Gene awakened. Pop had on new jungle fatigues. "How're you feeling?" he asked.

"Not too bad, I guess."

"At least we got to sleep on some clean sheets for a while," Pop said.

Gene tried to think what that meant. He hadn't thought about sheets, hadn't exactly known that's what he was doing. And yet he remembered now, how he had thought he was home sometimes, how he had liked the pillow under his head. But it also meant he wasn't going home. That's what Pop was saying. "Did you get hit?" Gene asked.

"Sort of. A bullet sliced open the skin on my head, but it couldn't get through my thick skull. You know what they say about black guys. Hard heads."

"What about Kovach and Melnick?"

"They're alive. But not good. They'll both be messed up for a long time. Kovach is still day to day. He might not make it."

"Dearden and Saunders both got wasted, didn't they?"

"Yeah."

"Did someone go back for them?"

"I don't know. Probably."

"What are they going to do with you, Pop?"

"I'm heading back to Eagle this morning. I'm supposed to wait a couple of weeks before I go out on a patrol. But I've only got twenty-seven days and a wake-up now."

"Don't go out again. Just tell 'em you've got bad headaches or something like that."

Pop shrugged, and then he said, "I'd rather be out in the jungle than back at the camp thinking about all this."

Gene knew what he meant, knew it powerfully. Each time he had come to consciousness, he had feared the sleep that kept pulling him back. He didn't want to see those dreams again.

"You and me, they put us both in for Bronze Stars."

"What?"

"Shreeve says we're heroes. What do you think about that?"

Gene felt as though he were back in that half-awake state, when nothing made clear sense. When had he been a hero? "What are you talking about?"

"We pulled Kovach and Melnick onto the slick."

"That's what you do."

"Sure. We both know that. And Shreeve knows it, too. It's his way of glorifying the whole stupid mess. Probably makes him feel better about himself."

But Gene couldn't think about that. He didn't know how to put all this together. He hadn't had time to ask himself how he felt about being out there, about everyone being shot up. The only thing he knew for sure was that he had done nothing heroic.

"I'm not taking any medal for this mess," Pop said. "I'm going to shove it back in Shreeve's face. I'd like to ram the pin into his heart. Shreeve knew we were in a hot area. He should have had gunships on the way when we called the first time. There's no reason we had to take that many casualties. Battaglia would have gotten us out of there."

Gene had thought the same thing back on the ridge, but now the idea struck him much harder. "I don't want a medal," he said, and the words fired his anger. How could Shreeve foul things up so badly and then call his men heroes for trying to survive?

"You'll be here a while," Pop said. "I heard they did some surgery on you yesterday."

"Yeah, they did. But I don't know what they did, exactly."

"Well, if I were you, I'd take my time recovering. Tell them it hurts. Tell them you can't walk. If you can figure out a way to get home with this thing, do it."

"I don't think it's that bad, Pop."

"I know. But you've still got a long way to go, and this mess over here is getting worse every day."

After Pop was gone, those were the words that stuck in Gene's mind. He slept again for a time, but when he awakened, his head was clearer.

He realized now that he did like the clean sheets, even if the sleep scared him. He wondered how he could go back to the jungle and face everything again. If he did, he thought, he would get himself killed. He really should have died this last time. He'd only had seconds left in his life when the helicopters had arrived. The next time, they might be seconds late, and that would be that. He had always told himself he might die, but in truth he had believed that he wouldn't. Now it seemed only a matter of time.

Gene thought he understood some things about his father now. His dad had been shot in the leg in Normandy. He had recovered in England, and he had gotten married there. After his honeymoon, he had gone back to war. How could he experience that joy, that respite, and then go back? Maybe that war had made more sense, but Gene knew what scars it had left. His father still couldn't talk about the things he had seen there, and now Gene knew why.

But Alex had told Gene not to lose the Spirit, to keep praying. And that's what Gene did now. He told the Lord that he didn't understand why he, why anyone, had to do this. He told the Lord how much he hated war, how bad he felt about his friends, the ones dead and the ones defiled by bullets. He told the Lord that he was afraid of the meaninglessness of all this, that he had always thought there were reasons for things, but he couldn't see the justification for what was going on now. The war was not being won, couldn't be won, as far as he could tell, and yet men were staying and dying.

What Gene didn't do was pray to go home. His wound wasn't bad enough for that, and others had to stay. He had no right to ask. What he prayed for was some kind of peace within himself, but he felt no sense of that. When he slept, he saw the shooting and killing again.

After a week, a letter came from Emily. She had had a telegram telling her that Gene had been wounded. She didn't know how serious it was. She hoped he was all right. She hoped he would be home soon. Gene read the letter and tried to understand what she must be feeling, but she was writing from the world where things made sense, or seemed to, and he was in a place that had its own rules. He wanted to feel what she felt, think what she thought, but he hardly knew her now. And how could she ever know him again? She hadn't seen what he had seen.

Gene wondered, too, why he was alive and Dearden was dead. Dearden had been such an uncomplicated guy. He had joined the army for reasons he hardly understood. He had told Gene once that he had probably watched too many war movies. And now his family had gotten word that he was dead. Some young guy from North Vietnam—who had heard too many war stories himself—had shot Dearden, and then probably ended up dead himself.

Gene hated the smell of the hospital, the antiseptic that only masked the stench of all the wounds. There was a man in a bed next to him who had lost both legs to a land mine. He didn't want to talk to anyone. He slept most of the time and stared at the ceiling when he was awake. Another man on the ward had had his jaw blown away, and most of his face was bandaged. Gene had heard a nurse whisper that he would be flown to the States as soon as he was stable, but that he was in for a lot of surgery and "would never really look normal again." Gene wondered how many hospital wards were filled with more of the same. Earlier that day, when Gene was only partly awake, one of the men in the room had been playing his radio. Gene had heard Creedence Clearwater Revival singing, "And I wonder, still I wonder, Who'll stop the rain." Gene had never understood the song until today.

Chapter 13

Hans Stoltz was at his desk when his supervisor walked into the large workroom. "Hans," *Herr* Meier said, "could you step into my office for just a moment?" The invitation would not have surprised Hans so much if he hadn't seen a stranger enter the office a few minutes earlier. It was July now, and hot outside, and yet the man had been wearing a dark suit. He was certainly a government official of some sort.

As Hans got up from his desk, one of the other draftsmen, a man named Schramm, smiled at Hans. "Be careful," he said. "That fellow looked like a *Stasi* agent to me."

Schramm was only teasing, perhaps, but he had apparently noticed what Hans had seen: a certain arrogance in the man's bearing, a style of looking about, of taking everything in, that had caused Hans to reach the same conclusion. Hans was always amazed at the way Mormons were considered suspect by the government when, in fact, a healthy fear of officials, even cynicism, was shared by almost all the citizens of the GDR. Officially, a majority of the people were Party members and apparent enthusiasts of the socialist movement, but privately they often joked about government leaders, and in certain moods they even dared to denounce the loss of freedom most people felt. Schramm had told Hans one day, "If there were an earthquake, and the Berlin Wall fell down, I wouldn't want to be close by."

"Why is that?" Hans had asked.

"If a man didn't run fast, he could get trampled in the rush—*into* West Berlin."

Hans had shaken his head as if to express a little disapproval. He wasn't going to get pulled into a conversation of that sort or commit himself either way. Schramm might be discontented with life in East Germany, but it was always possible, too, that he had been asked to probe a little from time to time to find out what Hans's actual feelings were. One of the realities of life, and everyone in the GDR knew it, was that informants were everywhere, and the *Stasi* recruited almost everyone, sooner or later, to report on others. Many a person had made a casual joke or expressed an opinion, only to be dragged in to answer for it. Sometimes a reprimand or "slap on the hand" was all the careless speaker had to endure, but in far too many cases people had been jailed for nothing more than "dangerous" comments. Needless to say, most people were careful what they said, and those who weren't were exactly the ones suspected of baiting the others.

So Hans made no comment about the stranger who had entered the office earlier. He merely walked to *Herr* Meier's door. He stepped inside but waited, not sure what he was supposed to do.

"Come in. Come in," *Herr* Meier said. "Please, shut the door."

The man in the suit had gotten to his feet. He was a well-built young man. He looked as though he had taken a deep breath, inflated his chest, and was now hanging onto all that air. He didn't smile. He nodded, and a lock of hair fell to his forehead, but he pushed it back with his fingers and then stood stiff, his chest still expanded, apparently waiting for *Herr* Meier to introduce him.

"Hans, this is *Herr* Feist from *Staatssicherheitsdienst*. He wishes to speak to you for a few moments."

So Hans's instincts—and Schramm's—had been right. The guy was *Stasi*. Hans shook hands with the man, and then he sat down by the door. Feist was near *Herr* Meier's desk. He turned his chair so it was facing Hans, and then he sat down. He was actually smiling just a bit now. "*Herr* Stoltz, I have been following your case. And I am pleased to say that I have received many complimentary reports on your work and on your attitude. You should know that *Herr* Meier is a strong advocate on your behalf. He feels that your youthful indiscretions are behind you now, and you are committed to a life of service to our nation."

"I appreciate his confidence," Hans said, but he saw Feist's reaction. The man had certainly wanted Hans to make some sort of declaration, affirm what Meier had said about him. Hans had plenty of training in these games, and he rather enjoyed finding ways to stay true to his actual feelings without being stupid enough to reveal any thoughts that could get him sent back to prison.

But *Herr* Feist's smile was gone now. "Speak up for yourself, *Herr* Stoltz. Can you verify that what your supervisor says is true?"

"Yes. Certainly. I made mistakes as a young man. I now have no desire to leave my country. I do the very best work I can do, and I don't believe it has been found inadequate. I think I am, in every way, a good citizen."

All that was true, but there had been none of the usual socialist rhetoric. "You've expressed nothing of your loyalty, your pride in our system of government, your commitment to the cause of socialist reform."

Hans knew it was important to look at Feist directly, to speak firmly. But he chose his words carefully. "I love this land," he said. "I love the good people of this country and what we are trying to do, together, to make it an even better place to live."

Feist continued to stare at Hans, as if to say, "That wasn't the right speech, and you know it," but he let it go. "You know, of course, that your government has reason to continue to observe your behavior. Perhaps you were young, and perhaps you were misled when you made your mistakes, but naturally there will always be reason to measure your performance with care. Certain limitations of travel and employment will always exist for you. You understand that, I believe."

"I understand it fully," Hans said, and maybe, this time, with too much conviction. Feist was watching carefully now, as though measuring the tone of Hans's words. Hans glanced at *Herr* Meier, who was staring at his hands, which were gripped tightly together on his desk. Hans sensed his nervousness; he told himself it was time to be careful. He didn't want to anger Feist, or to raise unnecessary questions, but as much as anything, he didn't want to disappoint *Herr* Meier, who had supported Hans when he hadn't had to. "*Herr* Feist," Hans said, "I was instructed as I left prison in Berlin that I must spend my life proving myself, that advancements in my place of work would be limited and would come only after I had demonstrated my good intentions and trustworthiness. I have accepted those conditions, and I am very pleased to be released from prison and able to work. I'm thankful that I can walk outside, come here to work, and do something worthwhile."

That was better—even though Hans had left out the socialist language. Feist nodded and then again whisked his hair out of his eyes. "Very good. I am here to inform you that your government appreciates your hard work and is willing now to grant you new freedoms—much sooner than you may have expected. Our prison system is not founded on a desire for retribution. It is intended to reform. When a man behaves as an enemy of the state, he must be corrected, but if he's willing to accept that correction, he will, in fact, receive encouragement and reward. Socialism seeks to embrace every worker who joins the cause of justice and reform, even one who comes to that cause late."

"I appreciate such fairness."

Now Feist was smiling again, just a hint—a kind of rounding in his upper lip. "You will be happy to know that you are no longer in a probationary state. You are a free citizen of the German Democratic Republic. You may travel, as time allows, and participate fully in all aspects of our government."

"Thank you very much."

"You will be paid at a normal salary for first-level government office work." Now a genuine smile appeared. The man clearly understood his own irony. "Of course, with a full paycheck comes a full payment of rent. You may find that life is slightly more difficult without the government support you have received in providing for your living quarters."

Feist seemed to see some humor in that, but Hans didn't. "Will I be allowed to stay in the same apartment?"

"Yes, of course. Or you can seek another place, if you think something else is more to your liking."

"Not likely," *Herr* Meier said. "Leipzig is no easy place to find an apartment these days."

This seemed merely Meier's way of entering the conversation, perhaps with the hope of introducing a friendlier tone. But the comment was not without controversy. The GDR had never been able to produce enough apartments, had never caught up since the end of World War II, twenty-five years before. Newlyweds often had to apply for apartments and wait many months, even years, for a place to live—all the while making do by living with parents or subletting rooms that were much too small. It was one of the most common complaints people expressed, and they spoke of it more openly than they did their other living conditions. Inadequate living space and an inadequate supply of food—at least in terms of variety—were never-ending issues, and *Herr* Meier had perhaps strayed into an area a super loyalist might not like to hear mentioned.

Strangely, however, Feist didn't seem to mind. "It's true. Since you have a small place to live, you probably ought to find some satisfaction in that. Subletting is awkward, in my experience, and that, I suspect, is the only way you would find a less-expensive room."

Hans nodded. He was quite sure that was true. But he wondered how much money he would earn and whether he would be able to pay for his apartment and his food and still be able to take a trip home from time to time. "Excuse me, *Herr* Feist," Hans said. "I'm wondering whether it would be allowed for me to seek work in Schwerin, so I could live closer to my family."

"No. I wouldn't pursue that. You are being given this opportunity precisely because you have served so well in your position in this office. It's where your government needs you, and it's where you have a strong advocate in *Herr* Meier. Perhaps, at some time in the future, something of that sort could occur, but not at the present."

Hans had to suppress a smile. It was a nice irony that Feist could praise the state in such glowing terms, telling Hans he was a free citizen, only to tell him, immediately, where he could and could not work. But Hans wasn't about to say that. "Yes, I see," he told Feist. "I understand completely."

"Do you have any other questions, Hans?" *Herr* Meier asked. Feist waited, watched Hans, and he looked accommodating.

"No. Thank you. I appreciate your coming here to let me know, *Herr* Feist." Hans stood. "I'll try to make the most of my opportunity." Hans, of course, now intended a little irony of his own, but Feist didn't seem to notice.

"But there is something else," Feist said. "Please, sit down again for a moment, Hans."

Hans glanced at *Herr* Meier, who appeared surprised. "Yes. Of course," Hans said, and he took his seat. He wondered why the man had used his first name for the first time.

In the same relaxed voice that Feist had gradually taken on, he said, "Hans, you received a visit not long ago from . . ." He stopped and pulled a notebook from the pocket inside his suit coat. He turned a few pages, then studied one closely. "Rainer Kuntze."

"Yes. He visited me."

"What can you tell me about this visit?"

Had all this been a setup? Why had the man offered the new freedoms first? Was it an incentive? If Hans didn't say what the *Stasi* wanted to hear, would he lose the very freedoms he had just gained? Hans had thought a great deal about the situation that was now before him, knowing that it might come up, sooner or later. He understood the complexities, knew that there were no right answers. If Rainer was actually working for the *Stasi*, then Feist knew what Hans and Rainer had talked about. Hans had clearly done the right thing in not offering Rainer any help in escaping the country, but now, if he didn't admit Rainer's intentions, he could be in trouble for not informing on a disloyal citizen. On the other hand, if Rainer was only suspected, and Feist had no proof of what Rainer had wanted, Hans could be sending Rainer away to prison. The fact was, Rainer might have been setting Hans up—and Hans could lose everything for the sake of a false friend. But how could Hans inform on him? He would rather go back to prison than break his promise.

"Rainer was my roommate at the university. We are friends. He came to pay me a visit."

"He was only in your apartment a short time, and yet he traveled all the way from Berlin. That seems strange. Did he come to Leipzig for any other reason?" Feist was still trying to sound friendly, as though he were merely curious.

"I don't know. He only told me that he wanted to stop by and greet me."

Feist looked toward *Herr* Meier. "What's your opinion?" he asked. "Does that sound reasonable? Would a man travel so far to see a friend, and then stay only a few minutes?"

"I don't know. As you say, perhaps he had other reasons for being here." Hans saw alarm in Meier's eyes.

"It would seem normal to me that a visitor would say, 'I'm here in Leipzig for this or that reason; I thought I would come by.' Isn't that the usual way people converse?"

Meier looked at Hans and seemed to be saying, "Go ahead, Hans, clear this up."

"Rainer told me he only had a few minutes, but he wanted to see me.

I assumed he must have other purposes in being here, but we didn't bother to talk about them—since there was so little time."

"But that isn't what you said before."

"I said that he wanted to greet me, but he didn't tell me why he was in Leipzig."

"Could this be a lie?" Feist asked, again looking at Meier, not Hans. "Could it be that Hans is hiding something from me?"

"I wouldn't think so," Meier said. "I don't know why he would lie about this."

Feist took his time. He turned back toward Hans and looked at him for several seconds. Then he looked back at Meier, more or less over his shoulder. "I can think of reasons. I have plenty of experience in these matters. I can imagine that Hans and Rainer talked about something neither wants to admit. I can imagine that their conversation was in some way dangerous to our state. That would be an example of why our good friend Hans, who tells us he is true to our government, would not want to admit to the things he and his friend talked about. So I think it would be wise for him now, considering that he has just gained his freedom, to be truthful and forthcoming. I am almost certain he doesn't want to lose these newfound pleasures." He twisted forward again, looked at Hans, and waited. His chest was still held high.

"We talked about the things Rainer has done during the time I was away. We talked about my work here. Things of that sort."

"Did you talk about his visiting your church, in Magdeburg?"

"Yes." Hans felt his heart thumping harder all the time. This man knew plenty about Rainer.

"What did he say about that?"

"During the time we shared a room at the university, he became acquainted with some of my friends in my church. They were friendly toward him, and he liked them. So sometimes, while I was gone, he visited those families. They have become his friends, too, so he has returned to see them."

"Is he a member of this little cult?"

"No. He is merely friends with some of the members."

"What about a young woman named Elli Dürden?"

"Yes. He's friends with her and her family."

"Does he sleep with her?"

"No."

Feist laughed. "What? You know this? Did he talk to you about such private matters?"

"No. But Elli has strong beliefs. She doesn't believe in sleeping with a man until she's married."

This struck Feist as powerfully funny. He laughed with a force that sounded almost like anger. Hans knew how these things went. Feist was coming after him now. He had started casually, but he would gradually turn up the heat. "You know very little about your young Mormon friend, Hans. She and Rainer have plans. I suppose they read the Bible together, but I think he knows her the way men know women in the Bible. Do you understand what I mean?"

Hans didn't answer.

"I'm going to give you another chance, Hans," Feist said. "I know things about your friend Rainer. I know what his plans are. I want you to tell me the truth. Otherwise, I will assume that you are part of his plans. I'll assume that you and he and Elli have made these plans together."

Hans had thought of all this before, every angle of it, but never about Elli's loyalty being questioned. If the *Stasi* knew that Rainer was trying to get out of the country, would they accuse Elli of planning to go with him? What would they do to her? If he tried to protect Rainer, could he actually make things worse for her? Maybe he needed to admit what Rainer had said—just come clean that Rainer had asked for help in escaping and Hans had offered no help. This would get himself in trouble for not reporting the conversation, but he could separate himself from Rainer as much as possible. If Hans put Rainer on his own, would that reduce the chance of Feist seeing this as a conspiracy of friends—and would that help Elli?

Hans had no idea what to do, but he had learned not to admit anything that could be used against him—and he still didn't want to break his promise to Rainer—so he let his former statement stand. "I have no plans with Rainer. He visited me. We greeted one another as friends. There is nothing more to tell you."

"Rainer has been arrested, Hans. He was caught trying to purchase false identity papers. People only seek such papers when they plan to leave our country illegally. This was not his first attempt, either. He had made inquiries for such papers earlier, so we watched him for a time. He visited you, only briefly, then sneaked away, watching suspiciously as he made a circuitous trip to a streetcar. You were also observed leaving your home shortly after he left, following mostly the same path. We are pleased with your progress, Hans, but you can see why we are uneasy about this visit. You are a young man who once tried to leave our country, who later helped a friend in a similar attempt. Now, you are seen with a man who has the same intent. What are we to believe? You have an opportunity, this instant, to tell us what you know. You can advance your cause by showing your loyalty, or you can persist with your claim and put yourself under deep suspicion once again. Do you want to keep your new status, or would you prefer to throw everything away for a man who has proven himself to be a traitor?"

"I know nothing about Rainer obtaining false papers."

"You are avoiding the real issue. Whether you know anything about obtaining the papers doesn't matter. You must tell me exactly what you know. Are you two planning an escape together?"

"No. You know that can't be true. I was offered the chance to leave when I was in prison. Everything was ready. My uncle had paid the money. I chose to stay. You must know that."

"Yes. That is true. So I'm willing to believe that you have no plans to leave with Rainer. But I think he came to ask you for help, since he was surely aware of your past experiences."

"How would he know that?"

"You were roommates. You talked of these things. Surely he knew why you were imprisoned." Feist had now returned to his friendlier voice, a voice of reason, as though he were on Hans's side and only wanted to help him.

"Not from me. I've said that many times."

"Yes. You have *said* it." A little heat returned to Feist's voice, but he calmed again and added, "But what if it's not what Rainer has said? If Rainer has told us the truth, and you refuse, do you see what a problem you have created for yourself?"

"Yes, I do."

"Good. Then tell me the truth. It will be better for you."

"I have told you the truth. Rainer visited me. We talked for a short time, and then he left. That is all there is to say."

"Explain to me your behavior after he left. Where were you going?"

Hans knew he had a problem. He wasn't going to inform on Rainer, but he decided to tell the truth about this. "I followed Rainer. But I lost him. I continued to look around, and I spotted him again. I watched him until he got on the streetcar, and then I returned to my apartment."

"Yes, I know all this. I'm asking you *why* you followed him."

Hans took a breath. "When I was in prison, *Herr* Felscher asked me many times about Rainer. He made claims about things Rainer had said about me. I doubted those things, but I have worried that perhaps Rainer was trying to help the government build a case against me. When he visited me and left quickly, I wondered whether he was planning to make some sort of report on me. I followed him to see whether he would meet someone."

"And did he?"

"I don't know. I only know that someone was following him—someone besides me. Maybe the two were meeting. I have no way of knowing."

Feist seemed encouraged. He leaned forward and said, "Finally, a little honesty. Now tell the whole truth. What did he come to your apartment to talk to you about? If he had illegal plans, and you refused to help him, tell us that. That will clearly be much better for you. If you try to protect him, we know you are not yet committed to your government."

There was no way out. Hans could not win. But he was not going to say anything that would harm Rainer. If he turned his conscience over to the GDR, he gave up everything—his only real freedom. "I have told you everything I know."

"Felscher told me about you, Hans. He decided, in the end, that you were honest about most things. But you weren't willing to speak against Rainer. That was the one thing you would lie about. But you see, that is your downfall in the end. This silly loyalty will be the end of you and all your hope."

Hans stared back at Feist, but he didn't say anything.

Feist continued to study Hans for quite some time. "I'm going to let you think about all this," he said. "You will hear from me again." Then he looked around at Meier. "For now, Hans will remain on his new status. But I doubt it will matter very much. Before long, if he persists this way, he will be returning to prison. And I must say, this is not the best for you, Meier. You've supported him more than you should have, perhaps. It will not be good for you if I report how easily deceived you are. It might be wise for you to have a good talk with this young man."

Meier didn't say a word. He looked as though his breath had been knocked out of him.

Feist stood. He shook hands with Meier, who stood abruptly, stiffly.

Then Feist walked to Hans. "I see why people like you. You're an artist, in your way. But you met the wrong agent in me. I'm not a romantic. I'm not emotional. I deal with realities. Your testimony makes no rational sense. I am willing, however, to grant you a little time to see what you must do. Just tell *Herr* Meier when you want to clear this matter. He'll let me know."

Feist didn't shake Hans's hand. He walked by him, opened the door, stepped out, and shut it, leaving Hans with Meier—no doubt, on purpose.

"Hans, you can't do this," Meier was saying, almost before the door had shut. "You could ruin my entire career."

Hans didn't bother to say anything. He was still trying to make sense of what had just happened to him. The thought of returning to prison was horrifying, but it wouldn't have been so bad had he known for sure that Rainer wasn't working with the *Stasi*.

Chapter 14

Gene was on an airplane on his way to Honolulu. His leg was healing well, and his doctor hadn't felt that it was necessary to send him home. Gene did, however, have an R&R—"rest and recreation" leave—coming, and he had decided to take it now. He had always thought he would wait until later in his tour to use the leave, so that he would be fairly "short" when he returned to 'Nam, but he hated lying around a hospital, and he decided this was a good time to be with Emily. He had been out of the jungle for a while and had reverted to feeling something like a human being. He thought maybe it was a good time to be with someone who remembered him that way.

When the airplane landed, Gene checked the schedule of Emily's flight from Salt Lake. She was coming in a couple of hours after him, and the flight was on schedule, so he decided to wait for her at the airport. But he was tired after his long flight, and he was nervous. His leg hadn't bothered him on the airplane as much as he thought it might, but it was aching now, and he didn't feel like walking, but when he tried to read a copy of *Time* magazine, he couldn't really concentrate. What he knew about himself was that he was frightened to see Emily, and yet he wasn't sure why. This, after all, was his trip to paradise. And he did love the mild air that blew through the open airport and all the tropical plants and flowers. More than that, he would actually be able to hold his wife in his arms. But as the time for her arrival approached, he felt his tension mount. He had bought a lei for her, made of purple orchids, but he kept fumbling with it. He was afraid he would have it ruined before he could put it around her neck.

When he finally saw her, he felt something like a jolt in his chest. Emily was wearing a red shirt, bright against her dark hair, and she was looking around excitedly, her eyes full of animation. He wanted to cry, she was so beautiful; he wanted to let go and feel what he was supposed to feel. But his chest was tight, and he felt a reticence he didn't know how to shake. He almost wished that he hadn't come here—not now, not until his tour in Vietnam was completed.

But he stepped forward and waved to her, and she ran to him. He grabbed her in his arms and was filled up with the smell of her, the sound of her voice in his ear, the touch that he had thought about so many nights out on patrol. He wanted the full joy of this, but he felt a kind of panic setting in. He pulled back and looked at her. Then he put the lei around her neck. "You look great," he said, and was surprised by the stiffness in his voice.

She gave him a quick, concerned look, and then she took hold of him again and kissed him. "Gene," she said, "just hold me."

So he did. And he felt vibrations run through him. But his fear was growing. His hands were shaking; his vision didn't seem clear. He was the one to pull away again.

"Are you okay? How's your leg? I'll bet you're really tired, aren't you?"

"Yeah, I am tired. But my leg's not too bad."

"Does it hurt?"

"Some. Not as much as you'd think."

"Why won't they let you come home, Gene?"

She was looking at him with those beautiful blue eyes, and everything about her was so shockingly familiar. He wanted to be the same for her. He wanted to be Gene. "The doc said it was a wound that would heal up okay. He said if they sent everyone home who got a wound like this one, they wouldn't have anyone left."

"That's what they need to do, just bring everyone home."

But she had hold of him again, and he kissed her. He remembered the touch of her lips, felt the shape of her body—such powerful memories—and yet none of this seemed quite real. He was shaking worse now, and he didn't want her to know. "Let's get your luggage and catch a taxi. I want to get to our hotel." But he was worried about that, too.

The next couple of days went better than Gene had feared they might. He found himself relaxing a little more all the time, talking more naturally with Emily. She was so much herself, lively and funny and intense, and so wonderfully affectionate. She was clearly worried about him and happy to be close to him again. They talked about home, about the family, and spent literally hours talking about Danny, who sounded like a little boy now, not a baby. What they didn't talk much about was Vietnam or his reconnaissance missions.

On Sunday, their third day together, Gene and Emily went to sacrament meeting in Honolulu. It was the first day Gene felt that time was going too fast, that all this would be over too soon. During the sacrament he felt the emotion getting to him, and he prayed that he could reach Emily, return her love more completely. It was as though she were doing all the work, encouraging him, strengthening him, building him up, and he was giving so little back to her. She was going through a hard time too, and she needed some strength from him. That night they walked on the beach at Waikiki, and he tried to assure her that he would be home in a few months, and even though he wouldn't be entirely finished with his service, he would be nearing the end, and then things could get back to normal. He could work with his Uncle Wally in one of the family businesses and start back to school. He told her he still thought about law school, or maybe graduate school in business, but the fact was, he didn't think about those things at all. He had forgotten how to think about the world. He didn't know whether it really existed anymore. Emily seemed an angel to him now, and it was difficult to believe he would ever be allowed to return to the realms she lived in.

Still, Emily needed to hear him talk about the future. "We'll be okay," she told him. "Everything will get back to normal, and Danny won't even remember this time, once he's older."

"I'll have GI Bill money, too. That'll make it easier to go back to school."

It all sounded like it meant something. But he wondered, did she know that he was only acting? The fact was, Gene's confidence was gone. What he really believed now was that his chances were not good. He had seen what had happened out there on that ridge. Dearden was dead; so was Saunders. And Kovach and Melnick were messed up. That's what could happen to men who kept going back out on reconnaissance patrols. Emily was going to go home to their son, to the world, and do the best she could. She would wait for him, and trust, and think the way people in the world thought, and Gene was going back to the jungle, over and over, and the odds were against him. He had known that from the beginning, but he hadn't believed it. Now a bullet had passed through his flesh, and Dearden was dead. There was no bubble around him. He could die, the same as the next guy, and he had joined a unit where death and maiming were the ordinary course of things. Lurps loved to say they had a better chance of getting home because they were so good at what they did. Maybe there was something to that. He didn't know what the actual stats were. But his inner reality told him the claim was a blatant lie. Dearden's broken face was the evidence he kept seeing in his mind.

Gene had awakened the previous night, alarmed by a voice in the hallway outside his and Emily's hotel room. Once his fear had passed, he had lain there a long time trying to drink in the pleasure of knowing that he was safe, that Emily's body was next to his, that everything was clean and cool and comfortable. It was then that the fear had hit him full force—the horror of going back to the jungle—and he understood the nervousness that had been plaguing him since he had arrived here. He was afraid to enjoy this time, afraid to feel too much for Emily, afraid to be soft, to be normal. Next week he would be back at Camp Eagle, and soon after that he would be back in the jungle, and he would long for the clean sheets, the nice meals, the gentle air, the touch of his wife. If he enjoyed all this too much, he would hurt more for the loss of it. And if he promised too much, Emily would hurt all the more when he didn't come home.

On Tuesday morning, with their week mostly gone, Gene rented a car, and he and Emily drove to Laie. The drive was beautiful, but sitting in a driving position caused a good deal of pain in Gene's leg. But he didn't tell Emily that. He wanted to drive and feel free, to feel the way he had when he and Emily had dated and gone for long rides, had talked and laughed and listened to the radio. So he played the radio now, and when the Carpenters sang "Close to You," Emily leaned toward him and sang "just like me, they long to be, close to you."

At the temple, Gene and Emily learned there was no set schedule for sessions, that one would be started when enough people had gathered. Emily found that charming. Gene was a little nervous about it at first, but the long wait turned out to be good for him. Gradually, as they sat in the chapel, dressed in white, he felt a growing sense of peace—a calm he hadn't known since the day he had landed in Vietnam. He felt consoled, comforted. There was something so pure about this place, and the purity seemed to pass into him. War was vulgar, crude by nature, and Gene knew he had been corrupted by it, but what he felt here was that there was something else. There were places and emotions that were in every way opposite to war. At times, on patrol, it had seemed difficult to believe that such a place still existed, but now he was sitting in God's house. People spoke in hushed tones, moved about quietly in white slippers, smiled gently as they spoke. It was as hard to imagine the sound of weapons here as it had been to imagine peace there.

Gene found himself praying in his mind, not asking to live, but asking that he could take some of this peace back with him. And he felt, eventually, something fill him up, an assurance that God was with him. Mortality was *intended* to be difficult, he found himself realizing, as though he had never known it before. No matter how vile war was, God didn't stop caring about his children—didn't stop caring about Gene.

Gene almost cried, but he fought his emotions. He still sensed that if he let himself go, felt all that normal humans felt, he would have a harder time going back. The time away from the war was, in his own mind, a kind of illusion, and if he trusted it too much, it would only hurt him later. God was *not* an illusion—he was tangible here—and yet the Spirit would not be so easy to feel once he returned. He needed to ration out his emotions, keep them under control, and then, if he did manage to come home, allow himself only then to indulge himself.

The temple ceremony was better to him than it had ever been before. The ideas seemed simpler, clearer, than he had understood them in the past, and he felt throughout that the grand perspective of the eternities made the struggles of mortality less to worry about. It was not that he found much comfort in the idea of leaving Emily this early in his second estate, but he felt the compensation as never before: that there was another life after this one. The idea had always been an abstraction to him before, a basic trust, but now he was looking at a very real alternative in his future—one of the possible outcomes of his return to the war—and it made all the difference to believe that he wouldn't lose Emily, not permanently.

When Gene and Emily walked outside after the session, they sat down by the reflecting pools out front. It was one of the prettiest places Gene had ever seen. He held Emily's hand, and the two were quiet for a long time. He finally told her, "Em, this has been good for me. I'm glad we came out here."

"I want to talk to you about some things," Emily said.

"I know. We need to say some things."

"Everyone told me, before I came over here, that I needed to be prepared, that you were coming right out of battle, that you had been shot, that you wouldn't be the same guy. I've felt some of that, Gene, but you're okay, aren't you? Things will get back to normal, won't they?"

Gene wanted to reassure her, but he didn't want to lie. He had the feeling that she would see through him if he tried to do that. "Things change us, Em. That's just how life is. Right now, I know I'm not . . ." But he didn't know what to tell her.

"You've been fine, Gene. You seem nervous, and I know you don't want to talk about certain things, but you're still you. And after you've been home for a while, I think everything will be okay."

"Sure it will. My wound won't be a problem at all, and some of the stuff you experience in war seems, I don't know . . . almost more than you can stand. But I'm sure it goes away. My dad's okay, and he was in on a lot of really heavy stuff."

"Gene, you don't have to give me details, but I just need to know, is it really terrible what you're going through?"

Gene had fought back tears all week. He had never once given way. But this was too much, now, after the time in the temple. He leaned forward and cupped his hands around his face, and he sobbed. She clung to him and told him that she was sorry she had asked, and he tried desperately to get control quickly, but the tears kept coming. In time he sat up straight, and he tried to think what he could tell her. "When I go out on patrols, I go with four or five other guys. We keep each other alive. I'm not really close friends with all of them—you know, when we're back at the camp. But out on patrol, you only have each other." Gene had wanted to tell her more than that, but now he thought maybe that was as far as he could go. He didn't want to fall apart again.

"When you were shot, someone else was too. I know that."

"How do you know?"

"The report that the army sent said that you helped someone back to your helicopter after you'd been shot. That's why they gave you the medal."

"They told you I got a medal?"

"Yes. You got a Bronze Star. Didn't anyone tell you?"

"I didn't get a medal. That was a mistake."

"Gene, they sent the letter. It was official."

"No, it wasn't." He didn't want to tell her the rest.

"It's okay, Gene. I know you promised that you wouldn't try to be a hero, but you had to help your friend."

"That's right. I did have to help him. He would have helped me. There was nothing heroic about that. I told them that, but they left the medal by my bed. I don't want it. Did you tell my parents about that?"

"Of course I did. They know."

"Emily, I promised my dad. I promised you. I'm not taking chances." Now the tears were coming again. He swallowed and then held his breath, willed himself not to cry, then said what he needed to get off his chest. "They killed Dearden, Em. And they killed a guy named Saunders. And they shot up Melnick and Kovach. Now Pop is about to go home. I'm the only one going back; I don't have anyone from my team."

"Dearden was the one you liked so much, wasn't he? You wrote to me about him."

"Yeah, we were friends. We just . . . I don't know how to tell you. We helped each other get through. But after they shot him, I rolled him over, and his face was nothing but blood. His whole forehead was blown off."

Gene couldn't do any more of this. He had wanted to tell her, but he had also known that he shouldn't. He had no idea why he was indulging himself this way. She would only worry more, and maybe she would see the blood in her own mind, all the images that he had in his head. When Gene shut his eyes sometimes, Dearden's face would suddenly be there, covered with blood and dirt and brain. He woke up at night in a panic because he kept hearing automatic weapons, grenades, the slash of helicopter blades.

"Oh, Gene," Emily was saying, "I didn't know it was that bad." Now she was crying, and Gene wanted to take the words back. Now she would always know, and he hadn't wanted to put that burden on her. "How can you go back?"

And that, of course, was the question he had been asking himself all along. He had thought of asking for a transfer back to some unit away from the action. He had thought of telling someone that he couldn't go back, that he was traumatized, that he wasn't well inside his head. But how could he do that when the other guys in his unit were still inserting into the jungle?

"My dad did it," he said. "He got wounded in the leg, and his wound was worse than mine, and then he still fought the rest of the war in Europe."

"Why do you do that, Gene? You're not your dad. He told you that wasn't something you had to try to live up to."

"I know. I'm not. I'm not trying to be a hero."

"Then why did you join a reconnaissance company? I found out you had to volunteer to get put in a group like that."

Gene had always hoped she wouldn't know that. "I didn't volunteer exactly. They asked for me, and then, when I got there, they gave me the chance to leave. But I don't know . . . it didn't seem right to walk away from it. Every unit faces danger. A guy can get shot, no matter where he serves."

"Tell the truth, Gene. Your dad dropped behind enemy lines. You had to do it, too."

"No. That's not true."

"I think it is. But you don't have to go back. You could say something. You deserve a desk job now. You've been wounded."

There was no way she could understand. He never thought of being a hero, or about proving anything to anyone, but he also knew he couldn't back out on the guys in his company. Plenty of men had been wounded and then gone back.

"Gene, I want you to make it home. Please. Think about that more than anything. I think you get over there and start thinking you're playing football or something. You think you have to be the one to show how tough you are."

"No. That's not true." Or at least it wasn't exactly true. But Emily could never understand. No one could. For everyone else, war seemed to be about killing, but there was a finer impulse, too. A soldier—at least a decent one—could think about more than himself. Gene would never take a chance for a medal, but he knew he would take a chance to keep another man from dying out there. That's the only beauty that existed in war, and it was a higher beauty than almost anything he knew.

"Gene, promise me. Promise you'll do everything you can to keep yourself safe."

It was what he had promised before, but he hadn't known anything then. And so he said he would, but he meant it the way she thought about it—the way people from the world thought of it. He knew he would be going back on reconnaissance with a new team, and he would owe them something, and they, if they were the kind of soldiers they ought to be, would owe him something too.

❧

On Wednesday night Gene flew through the night, back to Vietnam, and then caught a helicopter that was heading back to Camp Eagle. He reported to his company commander. Captain Shreeve invited him to sit down, and then he asked, "How's the leg, Corporal Thomas?"

"It's okay."

"Is it still weak, or are you ready to go back out?"

Gene had known the question was coming, and he had planned what he would say. "The doc said I need to work out a little, to rebuild my conditioning and get that muscle used to some work. But I'll be ready soon."

Captain Shreeve leaned back, as though he needed to think. He was a young guy, probably younger than Gene. His uniform was ironed and creased, his hair cut close. Gene knew he was a West Point grad. "I can maybe give you a few days, Thomas, but we're in a world of hurt around here. Since that team of yours got wiped out, we've lost another man. And the trouble is, no one wants this kind of duty now. A lot of men figure they don't want to stick their neck out for a war that's supposed to be winding down."

"Imagine that."

Captain Shreeve moved forward suddenly, almost came out of his seat. "What's that, Corporal?"

Gene hadn't had much experience with Captain Shreeve, but he knew something now. Gene chose his words carefully as he said, "I think it's hard for guys to come over here when they know the government is trying to get out of the war, not win it."

"But that's not a soldier's job to question, is it?"

"No, sir."

"All right. I hope *you* understand that. Because you still have a job to do, and you're now one of our most experienced men. I've put in the papers to have you promoted to Sergeant, E-5. I'm making you the team leader of a new team I've put together. We usually only use staff sergeants as team leaders, but we just don't have enough right now. It's a light team we're calling "Rifle," just you and four others, but we'll try to get you another man as soon as we can. These are not green guys, Thomas, but they haven't been in the situations you've been in. I expect you to do some training with them for a week or so, and do some hard work on that leg, and then you'll be going back to your assignment."

"Yes, sir."

"I know what hospital time can do to a man, plus R and R in Hawaii.

You get soft, very fast. The best thing in the world is to get back to your duty, so you stay sharp."

"Yes, sir," Gene said, but he wondered whether Captain Shreeve actually knew anything at all. He hadn't even hinted that he had regrets about what had happened to the Spartan team.

"So what about it? Are you going to give me what I need? I need leadership, and I need it now."

"Yes, sir. I'll be ready to go."

"All right. That's what I want to hear. You're a decorated hero, Thomas. You've proved yourself in the heat of battle. But your best days are ahead of you. You're ready to teach others what some fine soldiers have taught you. I know you won't let me down."

"No, sir."

Captain Shreeve stood, and so did Gene. Gene saluted and then left. But a number was in Gene's mind when he walked out the door of the hooch. One hundred twenty-six. That's how many days he had left on his tour. That's how many days he had to survive. When he had arrived, almost eight months before, he would have thought a number like that sounded wonderful, but right now it could have been a thousand and not sounded any worse. A team leader's job was to bring his men back alive. That's what Pop had always tried to do. Gene didn't know how to keep promises to his wife and keep promises to the army at the same time. There was no way Emily could understand that.

He tried to remember the assurance he had felt that day at the temple. He wanted the comfort, the calm he had experienced. But all that was hard to remember now.

Nine days passed, not seven, before Gene received his first mission as team leader. By then he had worked with his light team and liked what he saw. They were young guys, and cocky, but they understood the jungle, and they had all been out there at least a few times. His ATL was a tightly built little corporal from Oklahoma named Cutler. He was hard talking, profane, and something of a braggart, but he moved like a panther, and he didn't miss anything that was going on around him. There was only one real radio man on the team, a big fellow named Becker, but an eighteen-year-old boy named Estrada would handle a backup radio, and he was catching on fast. The other man—who looked more like a Boy Scout than a soldier—was named Echols. He was actually older than the others, although only twenty, but he was as simple as his appearance—just a nice young man who didn't seem cut out for the army, let alone the Lurps.

Gene and his men inserted in the humid but tolerable air of morning and then worked themselves into position as the heat became suffocating. They were supposed to start at the bottom of a valley along the Song Bo River and work their way to the top. Enemy movement had been detected in the area, and Gene's team, Rifle, was to locate any NVA who might still be around.

All day Gene let Cutler walk point, and Gene walked the rear security spot. Cutler moved the men slowly as Gene had instructed him to do, and he kept quiet for long stops as he and the others listened and watched. By late afternoon, the heat was breaking the men down. They had sweat through their jungle utilities and lost so much water that occasional drinks from a canteen could not possibly have kept up with the loss. Gene gave them a chance to refill their canteens at a river, and they moved again, kept going for quite some time, but they set up their night perimeter early, in a spot where they could observe a trail below them.

The team waited in silence, and Gene could see in the men's faces that they had all reached that state of exhaustion and tension that seemed to take away a man's sense of meaning. They kept their silence, but Gene knew they were in no mood to talk anyway, no mood to do anything. The night would pass slowly, and then another day of hiking up this valley in rough terrain and oppressive heat would follow. It would take three days to reach the ridge where their extraction would take place. But contact could come at any time, and that could change everything.

Gene scheduled and assigned the night watches, his own to come deep in the night. His leg was throbbing, and the insects were bad in spite of the repellent he was wearing. But worst was what he had feared. He told himself not to think about Emily, not to think about Hawaii, not even to think about the peace he had felt in the temple. It was better to keep his mind on the present, to keep his ears alive to the sounds. He needed to stay sharp, think about his men, guide them wisely, and keep them out of trouble. But he didn't have to think in words; he felt the pressure of the hard ground, and he felt the contrast to the mattress in his hotel room at Waikiki. He longed for the air of Hawaii, the trade winds. He longed for smells of tropical flowers instead of the stench of this rotting jungle. But of course, more than anything, he wanted to lie down next to Emily and hear her breathing next to him. Did he have 117 days to go, or was it 116? He never lost track back at camp, but sometimes, out here, the days blended.

Everyone had warned him—he shouldn't let himself get uptight about being short. Men got paranoid toward the end of their tours. They became increasingly aware of the irony. What if they survived all those miserable days only to die at the end? But that kind of thinking would only create bigger problems. So he lay on his side and didn't try to sleep. He listened to the night sounds and told himself that right now only today counted. He needed to take care of these men, and he had to handle things one day at a time.

CHAPTER 15

Kathy had always wanted to see more of Luzon, and she knew the school vacation period might be her best chance. Before Martha finished her service in the Peace Corps and left for home, she and Kathy wanted to see Baguio, the mountain resort, and the famous rice terraces at Banaue. Martha's friend Jeff Levenger was also about to end his service and wanted to make the same trip, so he and his roommate, William Griggs, rented a car, and the four traveled together. They had all heard the mountain terraces called the "eighth wonder of the world." Ancient tribes had miraculously dug them by hand. As it turned out, the terraces were as impressive as advertised—and beautiful—but Kathy and her friends joked that the ninth wonder of the world was the fact that they got up the mountain and back. The car was too small, too crowded, and certainly overmatched by the incline. But the worst thing was dealing with the rains that started almost every afternoon and continued all night. The mountain was muddy, and the road treacherous at times. Then, soon after the four returned from their trip, a typhoon blew in, and the winds tore some of the metal roofing off Kathy and Martha's house. The two spent one long night with rain pouring into their house, but at least they got help in repairing the roof the next day. They were just thankful they hadn't been traveling when the storm hit.

Kathy had another trip she needed to make, but Martha was running out of time and couldn't go, so Kathy traveled the only way she could afford. She took a bus down the Bataan Peninsula, all the way to Mariveles, and then followed the road back along the western shoreline and north to San Fernando. This was the route of the famous Bataan "death march." All her life Kathy had heard her father called a "survivor" of the march, and he had sometimes related some of the agony of that ordeal. She had even seen pictures of him when he was rail thin, after returning home, and yet, according to him, the picture had been taken after he had already put some weight back on. The story was part of her childhood, part of her family's history, but it had never seemed exactly real to her. Since coming to the Philippines, she had heard much more about the death march and the ghastly experiences of the POWs in the Luzon camps. She needed only mention that her father had been part of that experience to receive instant respect from Filipinos—especially for her father, of course, but even for her. Over the past year she had realized it was important for her to see the road her father had walked. She needed to understand this part of who he was.

But Kathy wasn't quite prepared for what she experienced. The old bus she traveled on was tediously slow, packed as always with people and animals. In Balanga, it broke down, and she had to wait three miserable hours until she could find another bus with room for her. Her father had marched in April, before the rainy season, in the worst of the Philippine heat. She knew that heat, and as she bounced along in the tired bus, she imagined all his steps and all those days without food or water. She had always thought of the march as a long hike, and she had understood that her dad had been hungry, but she hadn't known until she had come to the Philippines what the sapping, humid heat could do to a person. By the time she reached San Fernando, she was exhausted—in some ways sorry she had ever set out on the trip—but she was also thankful. Since school had been out she had read a couple of books about the march, and she knew much more about it than her father had ever told her. But she had remembered his account of riding in a crowded, closed boxcar after the march itself had finally ended. Men had died, standing up, unable to drop to the floor in the packed space. She now knew, from the books she had read, that her father had boarded that train here in San Fernando, so she walked to the railroad tracks and found a freight train with a row of dilapidated boxcars. She tried to imagine the father she knew now, reduced to nothing, and then put through one more torture. As she stood there, trying to picture it all, she thought she understood some of what her dad was made of. It wasn't just that he was a survivor; the real miracle was that he was so kind and caring after all he had gone through. He had taken on the worst of man's inhumanity and not been destroyed; in fact, he was superior to most anyone she knew. He was decent and good and committed to the Lord.

Kathy thought, too, that she was her father's daughter much more than she had ever admitted to herself. She wasn't as good as he was, but she had some of his tenacity. Her father's astonishing act of will in surviving couldn't help but pass to the next generation in some way, but his act of forgiveness was greater, and she had never known that until now. Grandpa Thomas always talked about living up to the tradition of the Thomas forebears who had crossed the plains in the early days of the Church, but her dad was as courageous as any of those early Saints. Kathy wanted to live up to his example.

Kathy returned to San Juan changed, she thought, and softened. Her attitude had been adjusting for quite some time, but she felt that in imagining her father's trek, she had gotten a look at herself: where she had been going—or not going. She was trying to see her future, and she knew she wanted to change the way she had looked at her Peace Corps service so far. While she had been gone, nothing had happened with the public toilet project, but she found herself more willing to accept that. Building *was* tough during the rainy season. Maybe the mayor had not just been making excuses.

Before Kathy had begun her travels, Bill Goldman had heard about Kathy's tirade against the mayor, and he had talked to her again, this time without his usual good humor. She had been unable to say anything except "I know. I know." She had thought of telling him that she hadn't meant to say such things, that she had lost her temper, but she had been using that excuse all her life, and she was weary of it—weary of herself, actually. Now, after this pilgrimage to Bataan, she wanted to believe she could handle things better than she had in the past. Maybe controlling her temper wouldn't be such a battle. True, she had made those kinds of vows before, and maybe the feelings her trip had created would gradually leave her, but she wanted to believe that wouldn't be the case.

A new Peace Corps volunteer would replace Martha soon, but she hadn't arrived yet. Kathy worried about who the new person might be. She liked most of the volunteers, but she wasn't close to them. At parties, they drank, and even though she had been more of a radical than almost any of them, she found herself less drawn these days to the sort of "knee-jerk liberalism" she had supported for such a long time. She still believed in the things she had fought for—civil rights, women's rights, the end of the war—but she was tired of the clichés. Hatred of government had become a sort of mantra to most of the volunteers, and they all seemed to know the standard beliefs that were "on the list." She was trying to think things through for herself now. She kept wondering what could really help the people of these islands. Some of the volunteers seemed to care more about feeling good about themselves than they did about actually making something happen for the people. As she looked back, she feared that her own motivation had also been too wrapped up in a need for self-satisfaction.

Kathy had plenty of work to do to get ready for the beginning of school, but she was aware that beginnings in the barrio were mostly theoretical and that a number of weeks would go by before classes were operating in earnest. Still, she wanted to be a good teacher, and she really thought she could be. That was her goal this year: to fuss with the mayor less, stop advocating changes, and merely make a difference in the lives of her students. That's not what she had expected to do in the Peace Corps, but it was the situation that had been handed her. She would make the best of it, then go back to the States and think about what she wanted to do next. She was considering graduate school, or even law school, but what she found difficult was that her zealousness was dying a slow death, and it was that very trait that had defined her for such a long time. What did she want to do with her life now? She sometimes laughed at herself when she realized she had left high school intent on solving all the world's problems. Since that hadn't quite worked out, she wondered what her next project should be.

Sometimes Kathy thought about Marshall. The two were clearly not right for each other, and there was no reason to think that could change, but she had loved some things about him. And his kiss had been the only meaningful kiss of her life. The fact was, she had begun to fear her future. She had no relationship, not even a friendship with a man, and there was a good chance she never would. She had taken herself "out of the running" during the time most young women were getting married, and she would not be back in the game for another year. There were Peace Corps volunteers who had shown some interest, but these were young men in the height of their youthful "ardor," and she suspected that marriage was not what they had been thinking about when they had paid her some attention.

All that was nothing new, but something else had been surprisingly difficult for Kathy. She had recently received a letter from her Grandma Bea. Grandma had bumped into Marshall, whose family was still in her ward. She had reported on Marshall from time to time over the years, and Kathy had known about his mission and his continued studies at the University of Utah. But this time Grandma had written, "Marshall is going with a girl he met at the U. They're planning to get married." Then she added, "He told me that he won't graduate for another year because he has changed his major too many times."

This last sounded like Marshall, but Kathy wondered, Would he wait until he graduated? Probably not. And yet, what difference did it make to her? When she had written to him, she had held out hope that he would hint at some interest in seeing her again when she returned from the Peace Corps, but he had said nothing of that sort, and so she had not written again. She certainly didn't want to appear desperate—even if she was feeling a little that way.

For the first time in her life, Kathy was fighting something that felt like depression. No one could have much energy in this almost constant rain, and living alone was not easy for her—with the sounds of rodents and lizards running about at night. She had even caught a man looking through her bedroom window early one morning when she was dressing. She had been shaken by the experience and much more nervous about being alone. It bothered her too that she felt so lazy lately. She spent too much time reading escape novels and lounging around in cut-off jeans and ratty old T-shirts.

That's what she was wearing when someone knocked on her door. She thought of not answering, but decided, as hot as it was, whoever was out there would understand her choice of clothing. But when she opened the door, she wished she had ignored the knock. She knew in an instant who this must be. An American-looking couple was standing in front of her: a tall man in a white shirt and tie, handsome, well groomed, smiling; and a woman in a dress, her hair permed, smiling even more brightly. They were surely missionaries.

"Oh, hello," she said. She glanced down at herself. "I'm sorry I look like this."

"You look beautiful, sweetheart," the woman said. "I can spot a Mormon girl a mile away."

"I'm President Finlinson," the man said. "I'm president of the Philippine Mission. This is Sister Finlinson."

Kathy shook their hands. "Come in," she said. "How did you know I lived here?"

"We have our ways," President Finlinson said, and he laughed.

Kathy led them to the little living room and asked them to sit down on her rattan chairs. The heat was horrible in the room, and she didn't know what to do about it. The windows were open, but no air was moving today. Rain would probably come again in the afternoon, but that wouldn't cool the house; it would turn it into a steam room.

As the president and his wife sat down, he said, "We knew you were here, and we just wanted to pay a call. How is everything going for you?"

"All right. My roommate went home and I don't have a new one yet, so it's been a little lonely lately, but school starts soon, and that will keep me busy."

"Do you like the Peace Corps?" Sister Finlinson asked.

"I guess so. It's not quite what I expected, but I've had some interesting experiences. I'm not sorry I volunteered."

There was something so familiar in the Finlinsons' pleasant manners, the slightly rural twang in their voices. Kathy felt as though she were being home taught—and taken home in the process. "What is it you've found disappointing?" the president asked.

Kathy had already learned that missionaries were less than impressed with the Peace Corps, and she was a little suspicious that President Finlinson would enjoy her answer if she complained too much, so she was careful. "In the Philippines, so far, most of the volunteers have been assigned to be teachers, or teacher aides. I guess I was hoping to make more of a difference in people's lives. The schools already have enough qualified teachers, so it's hard to feel useful. At the same time, there are some basic changes needed in the barrio—ones that seem obvious—but we don't get much chance to do anything about that."

President Finlinson nodded, and Kathy could tell he was thinking about something. There was some reason he was here, and she was sure he was getting ready to let her know what that was. "Do you know where you *could* be a big help, and where you *could* make a difference?" he asked.

Kathy smiled. "In the branch in Manila, I think you're going to say."

"I must be predictable." The president smiled.

"I've gone to church a couple of times, but it's fairly involved for me to get over there by bus and jeepney," Kathy said. "I have to change jeepneys three or four times. And . . . well . . . I just don't know whether it will work."

"What will work?"

"I think the approach the Church takes and the one we take are almost opposite. I talked to one of your missionaries, and he told me he didn't think much of the Peace Corps. I almost felt like I wouldn't be welcome at church—I guess because of the image the Peace Corps has for a lot of people."

"I think the Peace Corps does wonderful work," Sister Finlinson said. She had more light in her eyes than seemed quite normal, but Kathy liked her. She didn't seem to be faking.

"We do see things among some of the Peace Corps people that make us a little embarrassed as Americans," President Finlinson said, "but I don't doubt the sincerity of what they're trying to do. As my wife says, they do some really good things. I do think, however, that we change people more fundamentally with our approach."

"But that's just it, President. We're not here to change people. I don't think we should try to turn Filipinos into Americans. We have a tendency to come here with our own set of values, and we tend to push those off on people who have cultural norms of their own. There's something really arrogant about trying to 'fix' them. It's exactly why Americans are hated in a lot of countries. We act so superior."

President Finlinson looked serious, and he nodded a couple of times. "Yes. I understand that, and I agree. But the Church isn't here to make Americans of anyone. We want the people to stay the wonderful people they are. We love them. We want to bring them the one thing they are lacking: the restored gospel of Jesus Christ. They need the added perspective. They need to know what life means."

Kathy was surprised at her own reaction. She had been half ready to argue with him, to claim that Americans couldn't help bringing their American ways, whether they were Mormons or not. But his last words struck her with some power. She thought of the people in San Juan. They were kind and generous, but they did need the perspective she had grown up with—something that would give them an incentive to grow and become better.

"Kathy," Sister Finlinson said, "we've seen what the gospel does for the people here. You need to be around the members and see what happens to people once they join the Church."

Kathy wondered about that. It was what Mormons always said—that the gospel changes lives—but she wondered whether it wasn't actually the other change they had been talking about: maybe the people just started to seem "more like us." But she didn't say that. She didn't want to argue with these nice people. In fact, she really wanted to believe they were right.

"We need you, Kathy," President Finlinson said. "You've grown up in the Church. You have that basis to work from. You could be such a great example to the young women in the branch. To all the women. And President Luna tells me you play the piano. Just that alone would help a great deal."

"Why don't you come to church again?" Sister Finlinson said. "I think it will make you happier to be around the Saints once a week. I really do."

Kathy nodded, and she thought about it, but she didn't answer. "Where are you from?" she asked.

"West Jordan," Sister Finlinson said.

"Do you know my parents, by any chance?"

"I've met your father," the president said. "We were stake presidents at the same time."

"Did he write you recently?"

President Finlinson smiled. "Of course."

Kathy smiled too. She wasn't bothered, actually, not the way she might have been a few years before.

"Okay," she said. "I'll come this week. And I'll try to come more this year."

"Good."

"It's home, Kathy," Sister Finlinson said. "It's where you belong."

Kathy laughed. She had thought so for a time, when she had gone before, but Sister Finlinson had no idea how far from home she had been. And Kathy wasn't at all sure she still had a home.

~

That Sunday Kathy did make the trip into the city for sacrament meeting. It took longer than she liked, and she got caught in a downpour, walking from the last jeepney to the church, but she had taken her umbrella. Her shoes and the bottom third of her skirt were soaked when she reached the building, but no one seemed to pay attention. They were wet, too. She was surprised when she entered the chapel how many people remembered her and were pleased to see her. President Luna made a point of coming to talk to her. "May I speak to you after the meeting?" he asked.

"Yes. Of course." But Kathy was nervous about that. She thought he would ask her to play the piano, maybe in Sunday School, since they already had a woman who played the organ in sacrament meeting. But Kathy hadn't played a piano in a long time, and she wasn't sure where she could practice. Even more, she knew that if she came into Manila, she would have to stay all day if she also attended sacrament meeting. She wondered whether that was fair for her new roommate, who would be arriving soon, to be left alone so long on Sundays. Several people had told Kathy when she had come to church before that she could come to their homes in the afternoon while she waited, but she was a little uncomfortable about doing that. Maybe she would only come for Sunday School if that's what the branch president wanted her to do. But still, she told herself she would accept the calling, whatever it was. There was no question that's what her father would do, and her mother, too. And what the Finlinsons had said sounded right—she needed to be around the Saints and see what came of that.

Kathy liked the meeting. A young couple named Roces spoke. They were new members of the Church, having been baptized only a few months before. They were both sort of childlike in their joy at having found the gospel. Brother Roces said, "We get up in the morning, and we thank the Lord for the new life we have, and before we go to bed at night, we thank the Lord again. Our friends ask us what happened to us. Why are we so happy? At work, one man told me, 'Carlos, you are not the same as you were. You don't look the same.' I told him that I have answers now to questions I always ask. Then I ask him to meet with the missionaries. He won't do it—not yet—but I will try again." He laughed. "I know many in the Philippines will join this church. It's what we need here."

The words struck Kathy. It was what President Finlinson had said. She thought of the barrio, where so many of the men sat and drank beer or tuba and ignored their families. So many people in San Juan were caught in a rut, living out their days the way their parents and grandparents had, and finding little that inspired them to do anything better. She wondered what would happen if the missionaries came to her barrio. Could they give the people more than Kathy was giving them? She had felt for a long time that Church members exaggerated their own influence for change, but the Roces were remarkable. She honestly knew no one like them in San Juan. Sister Roces wasn't exactly pretty, but she was beautiful. She smiled, and her eyes were alive with emotion. She told the congregation, "I don't know I can love so many people. I love my family, but I have you now, too, and you very close to me. You are my family, my brothers and sisters. I wait for Relief Society all week, and when I walk into the church here, it's hard not to cry, I'm so happy. I have so many sisters here." And then she did begin to cry.

Kathy tried to compare her experiences at home. She had grown up in a nice ward, and she had been close to some of the kids, but they were also her neighbors and school friends. She had never thought of the Church as her main connection to those neighbors. She had liked some of the nice older people in the ward and had always felt that she knew lots of people who cared about her, but that had been as annoying as pleasing at times, since most of them had obviously questioned some of her choices. Back then, though, it had never really occurred to her that most young people didn't grow up with such an extensive connection to so many adults. The bishops she had known, growing up, were kindly, good men, and she'd also had many teachers and Mutual leaders who still sought her out when she returned to her ward, who still cared what happened to her. For so many years she had been seeing that as simply dutiful, as though their only interest was to bring her back to their way of doing things, and she had found their simplicity, their patterned expressions of testimony amusing at best and disturbing at worst. But as she thought about the barrio again, she wondered what that kind of family feeling would do for the young people as they were growing up. The people in San Juan had a marvelous feel for cooperation and support, but they hardly noticed that they weren't growing, weren't taking each other to a better place. She tried to tell herself that was all right. They weren't driven like Americans; they were satisfied. But there were too many things that shouldn't be satisfying, too many ways their lives really did need to change. Maybe it was the Church, more than anything, that could bring that to them.

The closing hymn was "Choose the Right." Kathy had, for years, liked to joke that the Church needed to think about choosing "the left" once in a while, but today she listened to the words: "Choose the right! There is peace in righteous doing. Choose the right! There's safety for the soul."

She had cared so little about safety for such a long time, and she wondered now, was she getting old? Was "safety for the soul" merely the easy way out? But "peace in righteous doing" had a lovely ring to it. She really did long for peace.

After the meeting, she talked to some of the members. Half the families invited her to come home with them for dinner, but she told everyone she had to get back to her barrio. She still felt uncomfortable about the idea of being pulled in too close. She was afraid, for one thing, that if people started seeing her more often, they would then expect her never to miss.

She found President Luna's office in the hallway, and she waited there until he arrived, smiling, apologizing for taking so long. "Sister Manglapus wanted to see me," he said. "Her husband is very ill right now. He's not expected to live much longer. The dear soul, she clings to him, but she knows that she must let go." He used his key to open the door, and then, as he held it open for Kathy, he added, "She joined the Church years ago, when missionary work first started here, but her husband never joined. That hasn't been easy for her. Those of you who have grown up in the Church, you're very fortunate."

Kathy nodded, but she wondered. Wasn't that another of the Church's clichés? Mormon families had problems, the same as other people. It bothered her when people made it sound as though Church membership made everything perfect. And yet, she did feel a sense of satisfaction as she thought of her own home: remarkable parents, really. She had tested their patience, but they had never given up on her. She thought of her house, itself—the feeling there—and her love for her brothers and sisters. It really had been a wonderful place to grow up.

"Sit down, Sister Thomas. I'm so happy I can talk to you." He walked behind his desk and took a seat. The office was small, and Kathy was sitting directly in front of the president's desk. He was taller than most

Filipinos but shorter than Kathy. She was glad to sit down and not feel that she was towering over him.

"Sister Thomas, I spoke to President Finlinson. He told me that you hope to come to our branch more often now."

"Yes. As much as I can. There will be some weeks when I just can't make it."

"I see."

Kathy hoped that would cause him to have second thoughts about a weekly assignment. She did want to come, but she was uneasy about the idea of having to come every single Sunday.

"He told me that you sang in choirs when you were in school."

"Well, yes." But this was surprising. Kathy hadn't told him about her singing. Her dad must have written to the president about that. But why?

"We have no branch choir, and it's something we would like very much to begin."

"I'd love to sing in the choir—when I can be here."

"Yes. That would be nice. But we need someone to *lead* the choir."

"Be the director?"

"Yes."

"Oh, President Luna, I don't know. I've never directed a choir in my life."

He smiled. "You say that as though you have lived for such a long time."

"No. I just mean that I've sung with choirs, but I don't know anything about directing them."

"You know more than anyone else in our branch. We don't need a choir like the one at the Tabernacle. We just need someone who can help our brothers and sisters learn some nice hymns, so they can sing them in our meetings."

"Would we practice every week?"

"As much as possible. You could practice with them just before sacrament meeting."

"But what if I had to miss some weeks?"

"We would understand that. If you could let us know the week before, that would help us."

Kathy nodded. She wasn't sure she could do that all the time, but she was surprised at her own emotion. She wanted to do it. She wasn't at all sure she could do the job very well, but it was something she could do without teaching, without speaking. She didn't want anyone to share in her confusion and skepticism. She could simply express the positive feelings she did have—toward God, and toward the Church—through hymns she loved. "President Luna, I would like to try. I might not be very good at it, but I do want to try."

"That's wonderful. It will make our meetings so much nicer."

"When would we start?"

"We could ask our members—the ones who want to sing—to stay after sacrament meeting next week, just to get started, and then tell them to come early the week after. How soon do you think they could sing in sacrament meeting?"

"I don't know. You'd better give us plenty of time."

He smiled. "But not too long."

"All right."

"Sister Thomas, you know what it means to grow up in the Church, to have members all around you, to have a father who loves the Lord and holds the priesthood. It's what our members need to feel from you. You can teach them to sing our hymns, but you can do more than that. You can help them feel what it means to be true members. Our people are mostly new in the Church, and they need to understand what they are part of."

"President Luna, I've struggled with my testimony. I haven't attended church very much the last few years."

"I know this. But there are things you have learned that are inside you. The people in the choir will know this. You don't have to say too much. They will know it in your music."

Kathy wondered. Maybe they would only feel her doubt and sense her hypocrisy. But she wanted to try this. It seemed the right calling for her.

Chapter 16

Diane was sitting on the family room floor in her parents' house. Jennifer was playing with some wooden blocks that had been in the family forever. Diane would occasionally help her build a little tower, which Jennifer would knock down, then laugh, but most of the time Diane was merely leaning back against the couch and letting her mind wander. It was a hot August day, but she thought she might take Jennifer out, maybe drive over to Mt. Ogden Park where there were some swings Jennifer liked—just something to get out of the house for a little while. The truth was, Diane had been hiding out most of the summer. She didn't like to see people she knew—especially people she had grown up with. She made excuses and didn't go to church very often, or she showed up a little late for sacrament meeting and sat on the back row. Then she carried Jenny out early, as though she were fussing too much or needed a diaper change, and she drove home. She just didn't like all the questions people asked, or the ones they didn't ask. She knew that Mom had told ward members, and word had gotten around, that Diane was separated from her husband, planning a divorce, and she knew what people always said: "If you ask me, it always takes two to make a marriage go bad."

The last thing she wanted to do was tell anyone that Greg had hit her. For some reason she didn't really understand, she was ashamed of that. There were other things she often asked herself. Why was it that everyone she knew, including her mother, had had doubts about Greg and yet she hadn't seen through him? But that only led to the worst question. Was it, in some ways, really her fault? She had never satisfied Greg—not as someone to talk to and share his ideas with, and not in the way he wanted most. Maybe there was something wrong with her. Everyone had always said how pretty she was, but over the past couple of years she had come to wonder whether she had anything to offer other than that. And now, when she looked in the mirror, she didn't see much she liked anymore. She had lost the weight that Greg had worried about, but that was because she didn't care about eating. She hadn't had any appetite all summer. If anything, she was too thin, and she looked old to herself. Sometimes she tried to smile into her bathroom mirror, just to see whether she looked all right, but she couldn't generate a smile that was convincing. There was just nothing to smile about now.

Diane tried to take each day as it came, but she had nothing to look forward to. She told herself that Jenny needed her, but she also knew how little she was able to give. She felt no enthusiasm about anything, and Jennifer had to sense that. Diane tried not to cry in front of the baby. She didn't want to show her how much she was hurting. But the two lived together in the basement most of the time. They ate upstairs with her parents and Maggie and Rickie, and Grandma and Grandpa and the kids were great about playing with Jennifer, but Diane usually returned to the family room, downstairs, fairly soon after dinner. She and Jenny had a bedroom down there—the old "guest bedroom"—and had their own bathroom. They even had the TV downstairs. The kids came down to watch sometimes, but it was summer, and they were outside a lot, or Maggie was off with her friends. So most days were quiet and lonely, and most evenings Diane watched summer reruns of *Ironsides* or *Bewitched* and played with Jenny on the floor and then stayed up late. She told herself she wanted some time to herself, but she also knew that she hated going to bed and not sleeping. And that's what often happened. She had never had trouble sleeping in her life, but now she found herself lying awake and pursuing her possible alternatives. But every road seemed a dead end, no matter how hard she tried to tell herself otherwise.

Greg called her about once a week. He claimed that he was working on the divorce proceedings, but she knew he was delaying in every way he could. And she was getting no money for child support. If it hadn't been for that, she might have listened to him when he tried to convince her that he wanted her back. He would always ask about Jennifer and discuss practical matters, but then, more often than not, he would begin, in his sweetest voice, to tell Diane how much he missed her. If she didn't cut him off, he would talk to her about getting counseling. He would admit that all the problem was his and say that he wanted to change. He would tell her how much he wanted to take her back to Seattle that fall and give their marriage another chance. They were, after all, married for time and all eternity.

Diane always told him that he had ruined any chance for them to be together forever, but the truth was, she sometimes felt that maybe she should go back to him. Maybe he knew how serious this was now. Maybe he would never hurt her again, knowing that she really would leave him if he did. Life would be so much easier that way, and she wouldn't have to face the world every day—all the people who seemed to say with their eyes, "Oh, you're the little beauty queen who couldn't even build a successful marriage."

Diane had the feeling, whether grounded in any fact at all, that all her old neighborhood friends took delight in her failure. After all, they had been jealous of her growing up. Wasn't it only natural for them to say to themselves, "Maybe she's pretty, but what did it get her?" And maybe they were right.

What held Diane back from capitulating to Greg was the realization that he was still trying to manipulate her. He had come to Ogden twice to see Jennifer, but he hadn't stayed long and hadn't really seemed to find much joy in seeing her. On both occasions Diane had let him have some time alone with Jennifer in the living room, but from downstairs Diane could hear him trying, rather unnaturally, to talk and play with her. Both times, Jennifer had cried for her mom before long, and Greg had given up.

But even worse were Greg's controlling instincts, even though she was not with him. If he had wanted to impress her that he was willing to be fair and was ready to try again, why didn't he just send her a check every month? He kept explaining the various legal reasons that child support hadn't been established yet, and she would say, "Greg, are you going to help me take care of our daughter or not?"

"Of course I am. That's the whole problem with divorce, though. Everything gets in a legal tangle. I want to support her by having us together."

Did he think that his failure to provide for his baby would somehow blackmail Diane into coming back? Or did he just like the revenge he could get this way? In any case, his failure to send her anything was proof enough to Diane that he hadn't really changed. He had always controlled their money, and he wasn't about to give her any that she could use at her own discretion—not even to feed their baby.

Diane was lost in her own thoughts when she realized that her mom had come down the stairs and was standing not far off. Bobbi had taught a couple of classes at Weber State that summer, but the term had ended now, and she was around the house more. Diane found herself avoiding her mother, though, if for no other reason than the fact that she was always trying to be so upbeat—as if that would somehow raise Diane's spirits.

"What are you two up to today?" she asked.

Diane found the question annoying. She knew what was behind it. Her mom thought she ought to be doing more, "getting on with her life," as she liked to call it. The fact that Diane was merely sitting on the floor was clearly something her mother didn't approve of.

"I think I'll take Jenny to Mt. Ogden Park before it gets any warmer. We need to get outside."

"Yes, you do." Another accusation. Mom always said that Jenny didn't run and play enough, that she was spending too much time cooped up in the basement. "I'd get going now, though. It's going to be hot as blazes today."

"We will." But Diane didn't move. She didn't have to jump up and do whatever her mother thought was right. Diane would do this on her own schedule.

Mom sat down in the overstuffed chair across from Diane and the baby. "Diane, you sound like you're really down in the dumps."

Diane looked up. She didn't want to have this conversation again. "I'm fine," she said. "I just want to give Jenny a minute to finish what she's doing." There actually was some logic to that. Jennifer was involved with her blocks for now, and that wouldn't last long. But Diane knew that she would fuss if Diane pulled her away when she had found something that was engaging her interest.

"Honey, you're not fine. We need to start figuring this whole thing out. You need to decide what you're going to do."

"Do?"

"Yes. You've got a life to live. You can't hide away and lick your wounds forever."

"Jenny, let's go," Diane said. "Should we go swing?" Diane stood and tried to pick the baby up, but Jennifer started to squeal.

"Honey, I'm sorry," Mom said. "I know it makes you mad when I say things like that. But talk to me for just a minute."

It was easier to let Jennifer do what she wanted to do than drag her off, so Diane set the baby down again, but she didn't want to talk. She sat on the couch, and then she said, "Mom, this isn't your problem. It's mine. As soon as I start getting child support, I'll move out, and we won't be here in your hair all the time."

"Do you think that's what my concern is, Di?"

"No, Mom, I don't think it is. But I do have to figure this out for myself."

"But are you doing that? Are you even thinking about your future?"

Diane looked at Bobbi. Her hair had started to turn gray in the past few years, so she had begun putting some kind of rinse on it. Diane didn't like the way it made her look. Her hair was darker than it had ever been, and she was having it cut shorter. "It's just so I don't have to fuss with it," she said. But it made her look old. And she was beginning to talk as though she were old. She had even started to sound like Grandpa Thomas at times, and that's something Diane never would have expected from her.

"I've got it figured out, Mom. I'm going to dress up really pretty and put on my makeup, and then I'll try to find me a new man, over at the park. A lot of cute guys hang out at the park and watch for single women who have babies."

"Is that your answer—to find another husband?"

Diane rolled her eyes. "No, Mom. That *isn't* the answer. I would probably just find another Greg."

But that was the problem. Diane had always thought in terms of finding a good husband and raising a nice family. She didn't have any other answers. It would be difficult to find someone else now. Men wanted to find someone young and pretty, not a divorcée with a baby. She kept telling herself that she needed to set her own goals and do something interesting with her life—not depend on finding another husband—but she had no idea what she wanted do, or what goals she ought to have. She had never imagined herself as having a career.

"Why don't you go back to school this fall?"

"I don't see how I could do that."

"But that's what you need to think about."

"How could I leave Jenny all the time?"

"Here's what I've been thinking." Bobbi leaned forward, and her face took on that "I've thought this all through" look that Diane knew all too well. "I'm getting tired of reading freshman comp papers. I think I'd like to take a year or two off. You could stay here with us, and I could watch the baby—which I would love, actually. And you could go back to school full-time. You could even carry a pretty heavy load and go year round. I don't know how many credits you need, but if you really went after it, you could finish pretty fast."

"Mom, think about it. My grades weren't that good before, and I never took a huge load. I'm not a good student."

"Maybe you will be this time. You *are* smart, Diane, and for the first time, you really have something to work for."

"What?"

"Isn't it obvious?"

"You mean for Jenny?"

"Well, yes. But also for you, Diane. If your life is going to be happy, you have to make something happen. You have to know what you want and go after it."

"But I don't know."

"Maybe not. But you aren't going to find it down here. You need to take some classes, find the major you really want, and start moving ahead with life."

"I know what you're really thinking, Mom. If I get back on campus, some fine young man will fall in love with me, and all my problems will be solved."

"No, Diane. No." Bobbi waited until Diane looked at her. She pointed her finger at Diane and sounded just a little angry when she said, "That's how you did college before. You weren't trying to learn. You were just trying to catch the right guy. This time, go for yourself. If you find someone along the way, fine. He'll know who you are, because *you* will know. It's time to stop looking for your identity in the reflection you get from some man's eyes."

Diane shook her head and laughed. She hunched down on the couch with her legs stretched out in front of her. "Mom, you try to sound like the Mormon Gloria Steinem, but I think you're really Grandpa Thomas.

It's my sitting around that bothers you. I have to be up and doing something or I don't have any worth in your eyes."

"That's not the point, Diane. It doesn't matter what I think. You've got to feel good about yourself, and you're not going to do that until you start growing in some way. That's why we're put on this earth—to learn and grow—and I don't think we can be happy if we're not doing that. You can spend the rest of your years feeling sorry for yourself, or you can learn from your new challenge. And Jenny's going to know the difference. If she sees a mom who believes in herself and does good things with her life, she'll respect you, and she'll model you. If you vegetate here, or get yourself some job you don't care about—just get by any old way you can—she'll learn that from you."

Diane stood up. She picked up Jennifer. "Mom," she said, "for as long as I can remember, you've been giving me speeches like this. If there's anyone in this world who expects the worst from me, it's you. You always—"

"That's not true."

"Don't give me that. I'm tired of hearing it. As soon as I get my first child-support check, I'll move out. Then you won't have to see me sitting around feeling sorry for myself."

"Diane, don't put this on me. Just ask yourself, wouldn't college be the best option right now?"

"I don't know, Mom. But I know I have to go because I want to—and not so you won't be ashamed of your daughter who didn't get a degree."

"That has nothing to do with it." Bobbi stood up. "I'm not talking about college. I'm talking about the opportunity to find work you'll like or to do interesting things with your life."

"Maybe raising my baby isn't such a bad thing to do."

"Then do it! Don't sit down here on the floor all day and watch her while she plays. Show her what life is supposed to be."

Diane stared at Bobbi: her mom, who always had the answers, who always found life so *interesting;* Mom, who would never be happy until Diane was more like her.

"I'm going to the park," Diane said. "I'll see you later." She picked up Jenny and ignored the baby's protests this time.

Bobbi was still talking, but Diane ignored her. She took Jennifer to their bedroom and dressed her in a little sunsuit, with a bonnet, and she took her to the park, but Jenny lost interest in the swings rather quickly, and Diane didn't like the look of some of the teenaged guys hanging around, eyeing her, baby and all. So she put Jennifer back in the car—Mom's car—and drove up Ogden Canyon. She thought of all the drives she had taken with Scott, her first boyfriend, all the dreams she had envisioned for her future back then. She took Jenny to South Fork, beyond Pineview Reservoir, where the campgrounds were, and she walked to the bridge where she and Scott had liked to look down at the river and feel the strange sensation, as though the river were standing still and the bridge were flying backwards at breakneck speed. But it was not Scott she thought of. It was Kent, whom she had also brought here once. He had loved her so much, and he was such a sweet boy, but she had turned him down for Greg. And Kent had found someone else to marry. Diane held Jennifer, looked at the river, and sobbed. Jennifer clung to her, obviously worried, and Diane knew it was only Jennifer who kept her from wishing herself in the water.

Diane drove home and slipped downstairs quickly so her mother wouldn't start another conversation. But Mom had heard her, and she followed her down. "Diane, you had a call while you were gone. It was Margaret Lyman. She and John want to come up and see the baby."

"It's about time. They've only waited three months."

"Diane, she was nice. She said that things had been awkward, and they didn't want to get in the middle of the situation, but they do want to be part of Jennifer's life, no matter what happens."

"What does she mean by that? What's happening is that we're getting divorced. Don't they know that?"

"I suppose. But anyway, you need to call her." She reached out with a slip of paper, with the number on it.

"I know their number," she said. "I'll call her." But Diane waited a few hours before she worked up the courage. Then she spoke to Margaret politely and correctly, but with none of the familiarity the woman clearly wanted. They agreed that she and John could come visit the following evening.

Diane was nervous all the next day, but she knew what she would do. She would greet the Lymans politely again, but she wouldn't hug them, would call them Margaret and John, not Mom and Dad—as they had always liked her to do—and then she would let Jennifer get used to being around them. But once Jennifer seemed all right, Diane would leave the room. She didn't want to talk to the Lymans any more than she had to.

The day was long, and then Greg's mother called and said they would be a little late, since John had been held up at the office. What else was new in that family? When they finally arrived, it was seven-thirty, and Diane was glad. At eight she could tell them it was Jennifer's bedtime. She wanted them to see that she was a good mother, that Jenny was clean and well dressed, and that Diane had rules for her behavior—including bedtime.

What surprised Diane, however, was that even though Greg's mom wanted to be friendly, his father was very correct. He was obviously feeling the awkwardness of the situation, but he also seemed resentful, perhaps, to have to visit his grandchild this way. At least there were no attempts at embraces. At first Jennifer refused to go to them, but Margaret knelt by her and talked, and Jennifer began to smile. After a time, Jenny did let her grandmother pick her up, but she soon wanted to get down.

Diane had brought some toys upstairs, thinking that Jenny might want that. "Do you want to play with the blocks, honey?" she asked.

Jennifer crawled to the blocks and started pulling them out of an old box. Richard and Bobbi and Ricky had gone downstairs after greeting the Lymans, and Maggie was gone with friends for the evening.

Once Jenny seemed comfortable with everything, Diane said, "I think I'll go downstairs for a while and let you have some time with Jenny." She stood up.

"Oh, please stay," Margaret said. "She'll be more comfortable. She doesn't even know us now."

Diane wanted to say, "Who's fault is that?" but she decided not to make things any worse. The truth was, Jennifer might fuss if Diane left. So Diane sat down on the couch. The Lymans were sitting in the two chairs across from her, John still seeming formal and tense in his dark suit and tie.

"Diane, are you doing all right?" Margaret asked.

"Sure," Diane said, but her voice didn't sound convincing, and she knew it. All the same, she wasn't going to tell them she was struggling.

"This is so awful, honey. We're just sick at heart about what's happened. We've wanted to see you and the baby all summer, but Greg kept saying, 'Maybe we can work things out.' I know, more than anything, that's what he wants."

"I'm sorry, Margaret, but that's not going to happen."

Greg's dad had said next to nothing since arriving, but he spoke up now. "Why not, Diane?"

Diane hardly knew what to say to the man. She wondered what he knew. "It just can't. You ought to know that."

"No. We don't know that. We don't understand what happened. We watch our son, and he looks like the world has fallen out from under him. He's miserable, and he's unhappy with himself. He keeps telling us that he wasn't a good husband. But he also says that he wishes he could have one more chance."

"I don't think it's good for us to talk about this, Brother Lyman." She didn't know what to call him. She had tried to call him John when he came in, but she had never called him that before.

"Help us understand," Margaret said. "What would be wrong with trying one more time? Wouldn't it be worth the effort? This situation is terrible for both of you, and especially for Jennifer. Wouldn't it be worth it for her?"

Diane looked at Jenny, not at Margaret, when she said, "I *am* doing this for her. I didn't want her to grow up with something like that."

"Something like what?" John asked. "I know he was way too wrapped up with school—the way he always is. And I know he can be cranky when he gets tired, but—"

"Is that what you think? That I want a divorce because he was cranky?" She took a breath and tried to calm herself. Then she asked with less heat in her voice, "What has he told you about us?"

Margaret looked afraid of what she might hear. "Honey," she said, "he tells us, more than anything, how much he loves you. He did tell me once that you two realized, after a while, that you didn't have as much in common as you thought you did, that you were very different in a lot of ways, but he felt that you were both trying to work some of those things out. He admitted that it was his bad temper that had caused most of the serious troubles, and I know he can get upset—and caustic. We're not saying he was an easy man to live with. We just think he's learned his lesson and would try harder next time, if he had another chance."

Diane couldn't believe all this. But she didn't want to tell them the truth about their own son. It seemed cruel to do that. She waited for a time, hated the silence, and then said, "Jenny says 'Mama' sometimes, and she—"

"Oh, Diane, it breaks my heart," Margaret said. "I want her to have a daddy. It isn't right for a child not to have a daddy."

"I'm sure it isn't. But a bad marriage can't be good for a child, either. Those were the only two choices I had."

"Here's what I don't understand," John said. "We admit that our son's got some problems, and no doubt you must have made some mistakes yourself. I don't see why you two can't get back together, get some counseling, and not give up so easily. It seems like young people these days bail out the first time things get tough. Margaret and I could have gone our separate ways lots of times, but we didn't think a little spat had to end a marriage. If you would—"

"Is that what you think we had? A little spat?"

"Well, no. I'm sure you had some serious arguments, but I still say a couple can work through those things."

"Brother Lyman, you need to go back and ask your son what the real problem was—because he hasn't told you. Don't come up here and tell me I haven't done my part. I put up with some things I shouldn't have, and I gave him some extra chances. But he doesn't deserve another one."

"What are you talking about, Diane?"

"Ask him. And then ask yourself why he hasn't told you before. It's not just shame. Among his other faults, your son is a liar. I'd think you would know that by now."

"Diane, don't start that way," John said. "Maybe I'm seeing some of why he had problems with you. It sounds like you have a temper of your own."

"John, don't," Margaret said. "Let's not—"

"I want to know what she's saying." He looked back at Diane. "Don't just hint around at things, tell us what you're talking about, Diane."

But Diane looked at Margaret and didn't want to hurt her. Jennifer did need grandparents. "It doesn't matter," she said. "But there's no way to work this out."

"No, there isn't," John said. "Not when you won't try. I have a feeling your lawyer has been talking to you—preparing you to lie about Greg so you can get what you want out of this."

Diane was stunned. She looked at John and she saw Greg. They looked alike, but it was more than that. She heard it in his voice, the tone, the coldness, the sense of superiority. Diane had had enough. She said, calmly, "Brother Lyman, your son hit me. He threw me down once and I forgave him. He slapped me with the back of his hand, and I left, but my bishop talked me into trying *one more time*. I went back, and that time he hit me with his fist. I have the pictures of my face, if you want to see them, so don't talk to me about false accusations."

Margaret was crying now, muttering, "I just can't believe he would do that."

"I *don't* believe it," John said.

"Then let me tell you why he hit me. I found a note from another woman—a woman he may have been involved with at the law school. I don't know whether they committed adultery, but I do know they were together a lot, and they were much too close. The note was way too familiar. It was after I asked him about the note that he lost his temper and hit me in the face—while I had Jenny in my arms. If you want to see the pictures, I'll go get them right now." Diane stood up.

"We didn't know," Margaret said. "Honestly, we didn't know."

"That's because Greg still doesn't know he has a problem. But I want you to know, your granddaughter is going to be fine. I'm going back to college this fall. I'm going to get a degree, and I'm going to show Jenny that we're all right. We don't have to accept that kind of treatment from a 'daddy.' It scared Jenny to death when Greg would lose his temper and shout at me, and then start hitting me, but at least she's young enough that she won't remember. She'll remember a mom who did what she had to do to make a good life for her."

"Diane, we'll help," Margaret said.

"That's nice of you to offer, but it's not what I want. I only want what's fair, and your son is not helping. I haven't had any child support yet."

She saw the look of surprise in John's face, but he was finished. He didn't speak.

"I'm going downstairs now. I'll give you a few minutes with Jenny. But it's almost her bedtime." Diane looked straight at John. "You were late getting here even though you had a chance to see your granddaughter tonight. It's exactly what Greg would have done. He never did put his family first." As she started for the stairs, she heard Margaret crying. Diane stopped and turned back. "I'm sorry, Margaret. I don't want bad feelings between us. I want Jenny to love you."

Margaret couldn't talk. John had stood up. He looked angry, but he didn't say anything. Diane continued to the doorway that led to the steps. As she opened the door she saw her mother, halfway down the stairs. Diane shut the door and then hurried down to her. She grabbed Bobbi and then finally let her emotion release. She cried so hard she knew that the Lymans had to be hearing her.

"I heard what you told them. It was the right thing," Bobbi said. "Are you going to do it?"

Diane hadn't known she was going back to school until the words were out of her mouth, but she had known for some time it was what she had to do. Now the idea not only sounded right; she also felt good about it, and about herself. It was a feeling she hardly remembered, but she liked it. "Yes," she said. "I'm going to start this fall if I can. And this time I'm going to study."

"That's good, Diane. That's good. And I'll watch the baby. You're going to be okay."

Diane wasn't entirely sure of that, but for the first time since she had walked out the door of her apartment, back in Seattle, she felt that was actually possible.

Chapter 17

Gene was down to sixty-two days and a wake-up. It now seemed conceivable that he could survive his tour—no matter how often he had doubted the possibility during the past couple of months. But he had noticed lately that the very fact that he was getting short—a "double-digit midget"—was working on him more and more. He didn't want to make a mistake now, with the end in sight.

It was early on a September morning, and he and his team were waiting on the helipad at Camp Eagle. It was still dark, but the dawn would be breaking soon, and a slick was on its way from a nearby firebase to pick up him and his men and insert them into the nearby mountains. What worried Gene was that he was repeating a mission, leading his men up the Song Bo River Valley, inserting low and extracting from a high ridge. Last time they had discovered no sign of enemy activity, but new reports said NVA troops might be moving that way. What he didn't like was following a pattern, walking the same path, using the same landing zones. The North Vietnamese were sharp observers, and even though the team hadn't made contact last time, that didn't mean that they hadn't been observed—or that their tracks hadn't been noticed.

Gene was standing in the cool air, liking the feel of it, but remembering the air in Utah this time of year. It was the beginning of football season back in the world—warm days, cool nights. He thought about the smell of mown grass, the nervousness he would feel before a game. It seemed funny now. There had been so little to be afraid of, really. Just a game. He had never thought of his being in a situation like this back then: going out to face an enemy, sneaking through a jungle, always knowing that snipers could be out there, that a trail might be booby-trapped.

"So what do you think, Echols?" Corporal Cutler asked. "Is today the day we die?"

The men were standing together, more or less in a line. Gene was still leading a light team, four men besides himself. Cutler, who was standing next to Gene, never seemed to stop talking, and he loved to bait Echols, who was actually older than Cutler—bigger, too—but seemed such a kid.

"Shut up, Cutler." Echols cursed. "Don't get started again today, all right?"

"Hey, I ain't gonna die. I got my good-luck penny in my pocket."

In the dark, Gene didn't see what happened, but Cutler had apparently pulled out the penny, then dropped it. He let out a string of vulgarisms and dropped to his knees. "Hey, don't anybody walk around. I gotta find it."

Now the other guys were laughing, and Cutler swore at them. It was obvious that he found nothing funny in this. Gene had noticed from the beginning that guys got superstitious when they went into the green. Almost all of them carried something in their pockets, or had a favorite bandana. They had their various religious symbols, too, and even though their talk was often obscene, most of them prayed when things got scary.

"Come on, Cutler," Gene said. "Keep the noise down." It had been clear from the beginning that Cutler was less than impressed with Gene. Gene was only a buck sergeant and had little time even at that grade. All the other team leaders were staff sergeants. But then, Cutler seemed to suspect himself of being just a little better than anyone, regardless of rank.

"No problem. I just found my penny. We're okay, boys. We're going to live. I'm lucky enough now for everyone. This penny was minted in 1950, the year I was born. It's brought me this far, and it's going to get me home."

"Just keep your head down and your mouth shut," Becker said in his big, slow voice. "That's what'll keep you alive."

But Cutler seemed full of nervous energy this morning. "Hey, Sarge," he said to Gene, "what do you carry for luck?"

"Nothing."

"Are you kidding me?"

"No. And keep your voice down."

"Don't matter. That slick will be here in a minute, and it'll wake up the whole camp." He hesitated and then asked, "You pray, though, don't you, Sarge?"

"Yes."

"Did you pray this morning that God would get you home from this patrol?"

"No, Corporal. But I prayed for you."

"You're kidding me, aren't you?" Cutler asked, although he used a cruder expression. "You prayed for me and not for you?"

"I prayed that my team would make it back safe."

"But you didn't include yourself?"

"Not in those words."

"Why?"

Gene didn't really want to talk about this. He was jittery this morning, the same as he always was before a patrol, but his nerves seemed worse today, maybe just knowing that he had piled up three hundred days.

"Don't you ever pray for yourself?"

"Sure, I do. But I worry most about doing my job—which is getting you guys home. I let the Lord decide what he has in mind for me." This was true, but Gene had never expressed the idea to himself. Since he had been shot in the leg and his last team had been wiped out, he found himself feeling that he didn't have the right to ask anything for himself. He didn't know why he had lived and Dearden and Saunders had died, but it was hard not to feel guilty about that. It almost seemed that if he asked God to save him, he was asking for someone else to take his bullet. There was no real rationality in that, but he was still having dreams since that bad mission. In it, he always saw his friends on the ground, with blood flowing, thick and red. He would wake up in a panic, and he would lie awake, afraid to sleep. But always, the same thought occurred to him: Why them and not me?

Gene wanted to believe that there were things he was supposed to do in this life and that he hadn't had his chance yet to complete them all. He even feared that if he died now, he hadn't done enough, hadn't been as big a man, as good, as he wanted to become. All the same, he had seen other men die who also wanted to live. And most of them had prayed.

Gene picked up the first sound of the helicopter—a low hum—at about the same time a red line was beginning to rim the eastern horizon. All this was much too familiar.

"Did you pray for Echols, Sarge? He's the one who needs your prayers. This could be his day. There might be a bullet out there with his name on it."

"Shut your mouth, Cutler," Echols said, with force.

"Hey, Sarge, someone told me you were named after a guy who died in World War II."

Gene was surprised to hear Cutler say that. Some of the guys on his old team knew that, but he didn't realize that any of the other men in the platoon had heard the story. "Just quiet down now. That slick is only a couple minutes out."

"Is it true, though?"

"I was named after my uncle, who was a Marine. He died before I was born. He hit the beach on Saipan—his very first landing—and was shot immediately."

"So a guy *could* think of that as a bad omen, to be named after someone like that."

"I don't believe in omens."

"I do. But I'd say it's a good one. Maybe your uncle looks out for you. Maybe he hangs around you like a angel, and bats bullets away."

"He missed one then," Estrada said. "Sarge already got hit once."

Cutler laughed. "Now *that's* a bad omen. You don't want a angel looking out for you who swings and misses. In this league, you don't usually get three strikes."

"Okay, everyone. That's enough," Gene said. "Saddle up. Our ride is here."

"There ain't no gooks where we're going," Becker said. "This is another cakewalk."

"Don't assume *anything*," Gene said. "I don't care how many lucky pennies Cutler has in his pocket. If we start making assumptions, we can all get wasted."

The Huey was getting louder, and Gene could see it now, like a big night bird, the sound of it taking on a pounding rhythm. It was working its way downward, and the image brought back the reaction Gene always felt as a mission began: fear so thick it was choking; his heart sounding in his ears; his breath hard to catch. And this time, thanks to Cutler, he had his Uncle Gene on his mind. He had seen his uncle's pictures and heard so many stories that he had a false memory, one that had apparently built up in his imagination since it couldn't have actually happened. Still, it seemed as though he remembered Uncle Gene coming into Grandma and Grandpa's house one day—just walking in, wearing his uniform. He had picked Gene up and ruffled his hair. "You're a good boy," he had said. "I'm glad you got my name."

Gene had never told himself that he had to live up to that name, that he was doing something for the family that way, but some vague idea of that sort had come to him indirectly. Family members would say, "Your Uncle Gene would be proud of you," or "You remind me of your uncle out there on the basketball court. You even move the same way."

But U ncle Gene had lasted five minutes in war, and Gene had lasted three hundred days. Maybe that *was* a good omen. Maybe Uncle Gene *was* looking out for him. Gene didn't know whether things worked that way, whether God sent spirits from the other side to do such things. If he did, didn't he love his sons who fought for North Vietnam just as much? What seemed more likely was that God shed tears when he watched what was going on and kept his angels for better purposes.

The team inserted as before, taking up a tight perimeter just downhill. Then they waited and listened. Eventually Gene could see Cutler watching him, waiting for a signal, but Gene had thought he had heard something not long after the slick had departed, so he took his time. He checked his watch a couple of times and decided to stay put for half an hour instead of the usual fifteen or twenty minutes. Before he moved the team out, he crawled over to Cutler and whispered, "If you move out too fast, I'll take over the point. We can't go crashing down this hillside. Take about twenty meters at a time, and then stop to listen."

"What's wrong, Sarge?"

"You heard the report. The enemy is supposed to be here now. And I think I heard something, right after we hunkered down."

Cutler nodded. He wasn't laughing now. Gene saw in his eyes that he didn't like the idea that someone was around. No doubt, he would take this first move carefully.

So the men moved out, Cutler first and Gene last, and they did walk in short, slow moves. Gene's whole body seemed on alert during the stops. He heard every bird, every move of a twig in the still morning air. Colors seemed a little more intense than usual as the sun angled into the jungle, and the odor of rotten vegetation seemed more potent. Gene didn't know whether he was getting a warning, or whether he was just indulging himself in unwarranted fear. Some Lurps said that guys who were short were dangerous. It was always good to be cautious, but not too cautious; decisions should never be made from fear. A man had to rely on the sharp instincts that developed after a long time in the jungle.

Gene didn't understand what was going on inside him now, but he wanted this mission to be quiet, and he wanted to get back to camp. He had promised Emily that he would be careful, that he would get home, that they could have their lives together, as planned. He had to make that happen.

It took three exhausting hours to reach the trail—not because it was a long hike, but because Cutler had followed orders and taken his time. But the heat was intense now, and the men had lost a lot of water. Dehydration could set in fast in this kind of heat, so Gene ordered the men into cover for the third time now, just above the trail, and let them rest and drink from their canteens. Cutler moved over to Gene after a time and said, "If we're going to make it all the way up this trail in three days, we gotta move faster. We've still got a long way to go today, if we're going to get as far as last time."

"I know. But don't get careless."

"I don't want to be out here an extra night, Sarge. Three is enough."

"I know. But better an extra night than to walk into a booby trap. Watch the trail and watch for sign. Let's go now, but don't be thinking about how much ground we've got to cover. Let's keep these men alive."

Cutler nodded, and he moved out, with Estrada at slack, Echols in the middle, and Becker in front of Gene. Gene didn't like the idea of walking a high-speed trail. It was too easy for a sniper to watch, too easy to get a clean shot, and it was a natural place to set up an ambush. But this was a long valley, filled with thick, triple-canopy jungle. There was no getting to the top, walking through heavy cover. Gene hoped, in a way, that they could get some sign of enemy presence today, maybe observe movement or an indication of recent camps. Then they could report that and maybe fall back to the original LZ and get out early.

But the day turned out to be uneventful. The team discovered no evidence of recent movement on the trail, found no trace of camps, picked up no smell of fires or bodies. Cutler started moving faster as the day progressed and the heat got worse and worse, but Gene signaled him to take it easy, and once he sneaked up and whispered to him that he was getting sloppy; he needed to watch the trail more closely. Cutler knew as well as anyone that wires could be hidden in the vegetation on the trail, or that booby-trap holes could be covered over with sod. Snipers could also be watching from the taller trees. But fatigue could make a man apathetic, and such intense heat could interfere with a man's concentration.

Gene let the men drink often, and they stopped at the stream that ran close to the trail and refilled their canteens. He made sure they used their water purification pills, but he knew they had to keep themselves hydrated. Late in the afternoon he called off the march, earlier than usual, and moved the team into good cover, well off the trail. Cutler was mad about that. Gene could see it in his face, but for now he didn't say anything. Once the claymores were set and everyone was pulled in tight, Cutler whispered to Gene, "We've got to stay at it longer tomorrow or we have no chance of getting out in three days."

Gene nodded. "We'll do that, but don't move any faster. If you do, I'll take over."

"Come on, Sarge, something's going on. You're acting like—"

"Don't break silence again. Get some rest."

Gene gave out the assignments for the night watches, but there were still many hours before dark. It was a relief not to be hiking uphill in the heat, but the hours ahead would be long and slow. The men used their Lurp rations to make cookless dinners; then they lay back on their poncho liners in the soft loam. Some went to sleep, but Gene was too antsy for that. He was always nervous on patrol, but since he had taken over as team leader, he worried even more, and he had an especially bad feeling about this mission. He had learned from Pop and all the old-timers that it was a mistake to ignore those kinds of instincts.

Gene had sweat through his fatigues, so he was soaked from head to foot. He had been fighting ringworm lately, a big patch on his upper leg and backside. He was chafed besides, and itching in his groin. On top of that, too many of his recent patrols had put him through streams that soaked his boots. He could tell he was starting to develop immersion foot. He took off his boots, one at a time, even though he hated the vulnerable feeling that gave him. If an enemy found the team now, the idea of making a run without a boot on was anything but inviting. But he powdered his feet and let each foot dry for a time.

When night finally came, Gene didn't sleep. He was focused on every sound and smell. He never heard anything he could interpret as suspicious, but he didn't miss a thing. The jungle was like a circus at night, the insects and lizards and frogs going crazy. Gene always hated the idea that snakes were moving around at night too. He had seen a good many in the jungle, without ever having had trouble with one, but tonight he seemed more conscious than usual of that possibility and found himself imagining that something was touching his arm or leg. He tried not to move around much, but with the itching, the eventual cold on his wet body, and his mind at work the whole time, no night of his life had ever seemed so long.

But the men were ready early in the morning. They added water to their rations and ate them, and then they "saddled up"—got their equipment ready—and moved back to the trail. The day was much the same, and Cutler was trying more all the time to push the pace. Not long before noon, Gene moved past the other men and stopped Cutler. "We're getting into a dangerous area up here—perfect for an ambush. I've let you move ahead pretty fast all morning, but we gotta be careful now."

"Sarge, come on. There's no reason to think this is any worse than what we've been through. I haven't seen so much as an old footprint, all day."

"Cutler, listen to me. Quit worrying about spending an extra night out here. It doesn't make that much difference. We've got adequate food and a source of water. There's no reason to push the pace."

"That's not what this is about. You're getting short and you're losing your nerve. If you can't take it anymore, you'd better let the CO know."

"Corporal, you say something like that to me again and I'll have you up on charges. Lay off and do as I say."

Cutler rolled his eyes, but he didn't say anything. He did slow down, however, and he began to stop more often to listen. Around 1400 hours the men took a fairly long rest and filled their canteens. But while they were sitting and drinking, Gene was almost sure he heard movement—a little snap, maybe someone stepping on a twig. Becker had picked up on it, too. They signaled to the others to listen. But there was nothing else.

Gene waited much longer than Cutler was pleased with. Gene could see that in his face. Finally Gene gave the signal to move out, but he was even more worried now. He wondered whether it wasn't time to abandon the trail. But doing so was noisier and not necessarily better.

The third time Cutler stopped to listen, Gene picked up another sound. It was subtle, just a little movement, a rub, in the cover above the trail, but Gene sensed that it was not an animal, not the wind. He was almost sure something was about to break loose. He signaled for his men to move off the trail and into cover downhill, close to the stream. Cutler was giving him angry looks, and Gene was sure everyone thought he was going crazy, but he knew what he had heard, and he had been in these jungles many more times than any of the rest of them.

But an hour went by and nothing happened. The team either had to keep moving up the trail, or Gene had to claim they had made contact and retreat back to the bottom of the valley. But he had no proof of contact, and there was nothing to say it was safer to move down the valley than up. So he signaled for Cutler to move ahead.

Cutler moved stealthily this time, maybe alarmed by Gene's concern, or maybe just following orders. He was watching, stopping often. Gene walked backward most of the time, watching the trail behind. Slowly, they edged upward, hearing nothing, seeing nothing, and Gene began to breathe a little better.

Then, suddenly, Cutler's weapon was ripping bullets up the trail.

Gene saw a muzzle flash ahead, and then Cutler yelled, "I got him. But he's not alone up there. Fall back." He was already moving, walking backward, his rifle still aimed up the trail. He fell back behind Estrada and grabbed in his pocket for a new magazine of ammo so he could reload. Estrada covered what was now the back of the line as the men began falling back.

"Not too fast," Gene told the men. "This could be an ambush." He was leading now, heading down the trail, watching, walking hard but not running. The NVA liked to put one or two of their soldiers up front to stop a team and send them running backward. Then, when the team wasn't being careful enough, they would attack from the side of the trail with automatic fire or grenades.

Gene was watching both sides of the trail, but he was picking up speed when he heard fire from behind again. He spun around and saw that Estrada was down. "Keep going," he yelled to his men. He let all but Cutler go by him, and then he hurried back to Estrada, who was lying on his back, his eyes wide, seeming to feel more fear than pain. Cutler was firing again. "We still got a gook up there," he shouted. "I didn't get him."

Estrada was grasping his shoulder. Blood was running through his fingers. But his wound was certainly not life-threatening. Gene helped him to his feet. "Fall back. You'll be okay," Gene told him. Then Gene stepped up next to Cutler and looked up the trail. Just as he did, there was a flash inside his head. His thought was that something inside him had blown up, all on its own. His muscles were collapsing. He crashed to the earth, face down, but felt no pain, felt nothing.

He heard words. "I got him, Sarge. I got him."

But he didn't know where the words came from or what they meant. His head was full of strange buzzing sounds and light. Then hands were on him, and he was rolling over onto his back. A face was over him.

"You'll be okay, Sarge. Don't worry. We'll get you out of here."

What he knew was that the face was lying. Men always said that. But it didn't matter, either. Nothing mattered. He was rising, floating.

More faces were appearing. Hands wanted to probe at him, wanted to make his body hurt. There was pain finally, from them, working its way from their hands into his gut. "Leave me alone," he said, or maybe the words were only in his mind.

"We'll get a medevac in here fast, Sarge, but we've got to move you to an extraction site. We're going to carry you down the trail to where we stopped a while back. There's a clearing by the river."

It was Cutler. Gene knew him. But he wondered what his words meant. Didn't Cutler know what Gene knew? Echols knew. Gene could see it in his face. He was cursing, looking sick.

"I'm sorry, Emily," Gene said.

"No, no! Don't start any of that. We'll get you out of here."

Everything was going black. But then light flashed through his head again. He could see Cutler again. Cutler was slapping him. "Stay with us, Sarge. Stay with us. We're getting you out. You are not going to die. Do you hear me? You are *not* going to die!"

The light was going out again. Gene couldn't see the faces. Everything was melting away.

It was September, 1970, and Hans had finally received his first full week of vacation time. He had taken a train to Schwerin, and he had spent some lovely days with his family. They had talked for many hours, and he had slept in his old room. So many times, in prison, he had dreamed of such a thing: to spend whole days with his family, to feel the comfort and relaxation, to eat good food and sleep in his own bed. Now, after having been out of prison for most of a year, and having gotten used to a certain level of freedom, the experience was not quite so magnificent as he had thought it would be, but he had to keep reminding himself that he was fortunate to have come this far. Of course, constantly on his mind was the possibility that he could be going back to prison. Every day now, since he had been visited by Agent Feist, he wondered when his day of reckoning might come. He had expected it long before now. He had not admitted what he had known about Rainer, and the *Stasi* might well be aware of what he actually knew. So what were they waiting for?

But today he was walking with his sister, Inga, and that helped him forget such matters. She was sixteen now, and Hans was having to adjust his thinking about her. Since coming home, he had realized that she really wasn't a little girl anymore. He had always known that she was unusually intelligent, but he saw now that she was thoughtful, too, and she was going through a difficult time. Hans and Inga were spending Saturday afternoon together, hiking the shores of Lake Schwerin. Hans had lots of memories of this place and loved the beauty, but he thought too of the time he had helped Greta back to the shore, after she had cramped in the water. She had held him in her arms that day, and he had believed that she cared for him. He really had expected to marry her someday, and now she was happily married to someone else. He had heard good reports of her and her husband, that they were busy in the Church and were expecting a baby, but remembering her only brought back the disappointment. She had once given him a little kiss, but only to say good-bye.

Still, today it was his sister he needed to think about. Hans and Inga had stopped to sit on a grassy spot near the lake. Hans was watching the reflection of several rounded, swelling clouds as they drifted over the hills beyond the water. "I've never doubted the Lord," Inga was telling him. "You were always such a doubter, and maybe I'm simpleminded, but I trust the Lord, and I say my prayers, and I believe. But I don't see why things have to be so hard for us. Papa tells me that people have always suffered for the Lord, from the first apostles on down—and I know that's true—but I also hear people say that we will be rewarded for our faithfulness, and that never seems to happen in our family."

"There are all kinds of rewards, Inga," Hans told her.

"That's also what Papa says. But why can't we have the things we want—the righteous things we pray for? It always says in the Bible that if we ask, in faith, the Lord won't turn us down. It just seems like we ask for bread and he gives us rocks—even though he says he won't do that."

Hans stretched out on his back and put his hands behind his head. All this was what he had often thought about over the past few years. He had found his answers, but he knew better than to say something facile to Inga. She would have seen the obvious answers already, or she would have heard them from Papa. So he asked a question instead. "What are the rocks we've received, Inga?"

"Papa never has a chance to move ahead in his work. Everyone else is given promotions and raises, and he stays in the same position—at the same salary. You know that's because he's a member of the Church."

"Yes. But what does he say about that?" When Inga didn't answer,

Hans looked over at her. She was watching the water, looking distant. She had been such a cute little girl, and now she had come into those in-between years when her face was breaking out a little, and her skin had lost its childhood sheen. She was going to be as pretty as her mother someday, with the same huge eyes, but the worry Hans saw in her face wasn't helping now. She looked best when she smiled. He asked again, "What does he say, Inga?"

"You know what he says. Everything with him is a blessing. He finds his joy in serving in the branch presidency. He finds his joy in his family."

"What's wrong with that?"

"Do you see him when he comes home at night? He goes to work every day, knowing he will do the same thing as the day before. He finds no pleasure in it. He tells us he's happy, but I don't think it's entirely true. He tolerates his days so he can enjoy the Sabbath, and so he can provide for us. But I think, when he was young, he was like you. And me. We want to do something that's exciting, that gives us satisfaction. That probably won't happen for me, and almost certainly won't for you. You're the one who's being punished the most, and you're the one who is closest to the Lord."

Hans spent his life trying to avoid that very thought. He did feel that he had worked hard to improve his faith and seek the Spirit. And he wondered at times why he couldn't be released from the trap he found himself in. But that was self-pity speaking. "Inga, I made a choice. I helped Berndt when I knew that if I was caught I would go to prison. I also knew there was a good chance I *could* be caught."

Inga shook her head. "That's only because of this country we live in, where people have to be walled in or they leave. I wish so much that we had made it out, Hans. We talked so much back then about going to Salt Lake City and how happy we would all be there. I was just little then, and it was all like a dream of living in a castle and being surrounded by handsome princes. That dream has made my whole life difficult, Hans. I had all those pretty visions before my eyes when I was so innocent about what I expected, and then we came back here and everything went back to how it had always been."

"Papa feels that we were supposed to stay—so we can help keep the Church alive here."

"I know. I hear that from him almost every day. And I know that's why you stayed when you could have gotten away. But since you told us that, I've cried a hundred times, Hans. I feel so bad for you—and what you gave up. And it's selfish, but I keep wondering, if you had gotten out, maybe someday you could have helped me get out too. Can you think how lovely it would be to live in Salt Lake City and have so many friends who believe in God and in the prophet? Every day at school someone makes me feel stupid for being religious."

Hans remembered those days so well. He had been weaker than Inga. He had wanted to run from the Church so he could have a future in his career. Inga never seemed to think of turning her back on the Church; she only wanted a chance at a little peace, a little more satisfaction in life. Hans wished so much he could give her better hope for that, but he wasn't going to lie. "All those things make us strong, Inga. It's why we can—"

"Hans, don't say it. I'm tired of all that talk. Papa tells me until I'm sick of it. Why don't the people in Utah have to be as strong as us? Why do we get all these so-called blessings? I would like to have just one day when my friends at school didn't treat me as some sort of *oddity*. They're not my friends, really. I don't have any friends."

"I know, Inga. I know exactly what you're talking about. It was the same for me. But in prison, when I could read the scriptures for so many hours, what I started to see was that life is short. The harder our lives are, the more we learn, and then we take that with us to the next life."

"Life doesn't look short to me, Hans. I can't think of it that way. I don't know whether I can ever find a husband in the Church. And if I do, maybe he'll have the same life as Papa, always being held back for his religion. What will that do to him?"

"Some do much better than others, Inga. There are Mormons who have risen a good deal in their careers. So much depends on the job you have—and how much your skill is needed. And remember, things might get better. Papa says they're better now than they used to be. He did get a raise last year, even if it wasn't much."

"That's what we always say. Things might get better. And then the government hands out a crumb and we grab it and say, '*Danke Schön.*' Other countries aren't like that. Our leaders don't want us to know it, but we're the only country that has to wall its people in. It's insane, and we accept it like a bunch of cowards. If people had any courage, there would be a revolution. And I would fight for it."

"That's because you're big and strong, and very, very *fierce*. The government is scared to death of people like you."

"They should be," she said, still trying to sound serious, but then she smiled, looked better, and told him, "I can beat up on you, you know." She doubled up her fist and socked him on the shoulder.

She caught him on the front of the shoulder, and the blow hurt more than Hans wanted to admit. So he laughed and said, "Look out, or I'll have to show you who the big brother is around here."

She leaned over and kissed Hans's shoulder, then gave it a rub. "Hans, I love you," she said. "And I'm sorry to complain so much. You've had so many things happen to you, and you have such a good philosophy on life. But that's half of what makes me angry. You're the one who deserves better."

"Things will work out, Inga. I don't know how, but they will. There will come a time when we will thank the Lord for having lived here."

"When, Hans? In the next life?"

Hans thought about that. "Maybe," he finally said. "I've been telling myself for quite some time that I may not have a lot of happiness in this life. I may have to wait. But I got out of prison, and the Lord told me to stay in the GDR, when I might have left. I have the feeling that he's going to give me more opportunities—and I think that will happen for you, too. I think all the Saints will be blessed for staying strong. And not just in the next life. I just have to believe that something better is coming for us in this one."

"In time."

"Yes. In time."

"I'm not patient, Hans."

"Who is, at sixteen?"

She slugged him again. "I'm not a little girl. Don't treat me like that."

"You're not a little girl. That's true. But you're young, and so am I. And young people have trouble with patience."

"I know," she said more softly. She sat and looked out across the water for quite some time before she added, "Thank you, Hans, for your strength. You make me angry sometimes, you're so humble and good. But it gives me strength to watch how well you accept all the things you've had to live with."

Hans didn't respond to that. But Inga couldn't have known what he was fearing now. He had loved his days of freedom, however limited they were, but he could lose everything he had gained, and it could happen at almost any moment. The *Stasi* could show up one of these days, and he could be taken away. If Rainer had set him up, then Hans might have already been betrayed by a man he considered a friend. Loyalty was punished in this country—all loyalty except submission to the state. Even though Hans told himself the Lord was going to bless the Saints, and him along with them, in the short-term he might have a lot more misery to look forward to. "Inga," he said, "my troubles may not be over. The *Stasi* still watches my every step. If they do something to me again, you can't give up your hope. You'll have to be patient, and I will too, no matter how hard it seems."

"Don't say that, Hans. I trust in the Lord, but there are some things that are just too unfair. I can't believe the Lord would let them hurt you any more."

"Lots of people have gone through worse than I have, Inga—better people than I."

"There are no better people than you, Hans. I can't even think of anyone better."

Hans laughed, and then he got up. He pulled Inga up too. "Let's walk some more," he said. But before they walked, he hugged her. He loved this little sister, and he feared for his safety more for her sake than his own. He hoped that, somehow, better opportunities would open up for her.

Hans left the next day, on Sunday morning. He wanted to stay for church, but he had to be back at work on Monday morning, and he had one other thing in mind. His train would pass through Magdeburg, so he bought a ticket for only that far, and he made up his mind to stop there long enough to visit the Dürdens, or that is to say, Elli. He knew that he was only exacerbating a problem by doing so, but he still wanted to see her. He knew a dozen reasons why he shouldn't see her, but when he had stepped to the ticket window, he had said the words all the same: "A ticket for Magdeburg, please."

It was early afternoon when he arrived, and he knew that the Dürdens would probably be home from church. They very well might be away, perhaps taking a walk or visiting with other members. It was silly to stop when he didn't even know whether they would be at home, but he took a streetcar and then walked to her house, a couple of streets beyond the end of the streetcar line. When he rang the doorbell at her apartment building, he realized that he was actually shaking.

After a moment he heard a woman's voice on the speaker. "*Hallo.* Who's there?"

"It's Hans Stoltz."

There was just a moment of hesitation, and then he heard, "Hans, please come up. Push the door."

He heard the buzzer and only then realized that it was Elli herself who had answered. She sounded so much like her mother.

He walked up two flights of stairs, and then there she was, standing at the head of the stairs, smiling, showing her dimples. He was surprised all over again at how pretty she was, as though she kept improving, month by month. "Hans, why didn't you tell us? I look so terrible."

"Yes, you do. It's very difficult just to have to look at you."

She was smiling all the more, putting out her hand. She was wearing a pretty tan dress, one she had worn to church, he was certain, and he couldn't imagine what it was that she could have done to improve herself. But she was smoothing out her hair; maybe that was her concern. "Why are you in Magdeburg?" she asked.

"I'm on my way back to Leipzig. I've been home to see my family all week."

"They let you take so much time away from your work?"

"I'm a salaried employee now. I make next to nothing, of course—and have to pay my rent and buy my food—but at least I get a little vacation time.

"But this is a step forward, Hans. It's an improvement for you."

He saw how much she had brightened with the idea. "Yes. A small one."

"I knew it would happen. You didn't expect this much freedom, Hans—not nearly so soon. I know things will keep getting better for you."

He nodded. "Perhaps," he said. And he couldn't resist smiling back at her.

"Come in, please. My family will be so happy to see you."

So Hans walked in, and he talked to everyone, spent half an hour of his precious time, before he got up the nerve to say, "It's nice weather out. Maybe we could take a little walk."

Elli's little sister laughed at that and said, "Oh, yes, I think Elli would like to do that."

But Sister Dürden was quick to say, "It is lovely outside. You two should go out."

And so they were soon gone, and they walked where they had when Elli was just a kid and Hans was her Sunday School teacher—along the river. The swans and ducks were still there, the pretty willow trees and the shaded walkways, but to Hans everything was different. Elli walked close to him, brushed his shoulder at times, and he was happier than he could remember, but he also knew he was toying with his own heart, and with hers. However much he wanted to see her, it was something he should have resisted. As they chatted, it was what he kept telling himself, that he shouldn't have come.

But there were some things that Hans really did want to know, and he had to admit to himself it was part of the reason he had made the stop here. "Elli," he finally got up the nerve to ask, "have you heard anything from Rainer?"

"Yes, he was here two weeks ago. He came down on the train in time for sacrament meeting, and then he walked back to our apartment with me."

Hans was astounded. How could that be? Hadn't Rainer been arrested? He was also confused by Elli's tone of voice. She sounded quite neutral, as though she wasn't embarrassed to admit his continued attentions. Did that mean she was taking more interest in him again? After all, Hans had ruled himself out.

"Was everything all right with him?"

"I don't know. He isn't happy, I know that. And he's not happy with me. I told him I couldn't imagine us ever getting married. He told me not to say that, to give him time to join the Church, but I don't think he'll do that."

"He would make a fine husband, don't you think, if he *would* embrace the Church?"

"I don't know, Hans. I'm not sure I trust him. If he joined, and I married him, I'm not sure he would be true to his commitments. He likes his beer, you know, and I don't think he has given it up."

"Does he say that he has?"

"He did at one time, but now he avoids the topic."

"Did he say anything about any trouble in his life?"

"What do you mean?"

Hans was trying to put everything together. If Rainer really had been arrested, had the *Stasi* released him? What seemed most likely was that Agent Feist had been lying. Hans thought it all the more likely that Rainer was working with the *Stasi*, trying to catch him in a lie. But if that was the case, why hadn't Hans heard any more from Feist? Even more important, had Rainer said anything to Elli about getting out of the country? Maybe at one time she had been planning to leave with him, and had had to hide that. But it was hard to believe that Elli could be that deceptive. There was something so innocent in her tone.

Hans felt, more than ever, that he was walking on thin ice, that any moment he could go crashing through. He had no idea whom to trust, but he suspected that it was Elli he could rely on more than Rainer or Feist. "I'm just wondering what's going on with him now. Does he have any plans?"

For the first time Elli did seem a little less comfortable with the conversation. "Oh, you know Rainer. He always talks about things he wants to do."

"Elli, maybe I shouldn't ask this, but did he ask you to join him in any of his plans?"

Elli stopped. Then she turned and walked toward the edge of the walkway. She faced a little rock wall and looked down at the river. "He still wants to get married," she said. "I told you that."

"Elli, Rainer came to see me, and he talked about plans he has—ones that could be very dangerous to you."

Elli nodded. "I know what you mean. I didn't think he would say anything to anyone else about that."

"He wanted my help. He thought I knew about such things."

"He's going to end up in very big trouble, Hans."

"I heard that he had been arrested, Elli. Didn't he say anything about that?"

"No. After I told him I couldn't see us ever being married, he told me good-bye. I asked him whether he still wanted to leave the country, but he only said, 'If you don't know anything, you have nothing to deny.'"

Hans nodded. That made a few things more clear. At least Hans felt sure he could trust Elli.

"You shouldn't have anything to do with Rainer, Hans. The *Stasi* is surely watching you. And if he tries to escape, or even manages to do it, that can't look good for you—not if they know he has come to see you."

"I know all this." But Hans decided not to tell her about the visit from Feist. He didn't want to worry her any more than he had to. He did say, "Elli, the *Stasi* will always watch me. I can't hope for anything less."

"But they've given you a salary now. Doesn't that prove they have confidence in you?"

"Perhaps. It came a little sooner than I expected. But it's not income to *live* on—only one to survive with, and just barely that. I actually have a little less than I had before, now that I'm forced to pay my own rent."

Elli turned toward Hans. "You worry too much about that. People can get by on very little."

He knew what she meant, but he also knew how easy it was to be idealistic about money when a person hadn't had to grind out a day-to-day existence, watching every *Pfennig*. "Elli, my situation is always precarious. If I slipped and said one thing that someone at work—or anywhere—didn't like the sound of, I could be reported, and then who knows what might happen to me?"

"I think you'll find the opposite. You'll be so good at your work, you'll continue to receive more opportunities than you expected, just like the freedom to travel home you have now."

Elli's face was so simple and pretty, and her voice so honest, Hans felt terrible not to tell her about the complications that Rainer had caused him. He felt guilty that he had come here, too. All he had done, by coming, was deny what he had told her before—that they had no future with each other.

It was obviously what she was thinking, too. "Hans, why did you stop to see me?"

"I just . . . like to see you. And I was worried about you. I don't want Rainer to lead you into trouble."

"Tell me this: Are you in love with me? Does that have anything to do with your visit?" She wasn't laughing, wasn't even smiling. In fact, she seemed more likely to cry.

"Elli, I told you before, I—"

"Don't start that again. Just answer my question. I need to know the answer."

He looked at her a long time before he said, "I think about you all the time, Elli. I wish I could be interested in you, but I can't. It's impossible. So what purpose does it serve to talk about love?"

"I'm not talking about a purpose. I'm not even saying we would ever marry. Those are other questions. I just need to know whether you love me." She waited, and then added, "Hans, I've been in love with you since I was sixteen years old. It's always hurt me that you didn't feel the same way about me. But now, it seems that maybe you do feel something for me. So tell me if I'm wrong."

Tears had come into her eyes, and Hans felt his own eyes fill. "Yes, Elli, I do. But I'm sorry. I shouldn't have come here."

She was stepping toward him, and then she put her hand behind his neck and pulled him forward. It was he who kissed her, however, and he felt a pleasure in the touch of her lips that was warmer and better than anything he had ever experienced. He held her for a moment, there on the walk, where others were not far away, and then he stepped back. He had the feeling that the rest of his life was going to hurt all the more for having allowed this kiss, and at the same time, he didn't regret it at all, and some inherent optimism inside him was telling him this all had to work out somehow.

"Thank you," she was saying. "I can wait now, no matter how long. But I'll be true to you forever."

"Oh, Elli, no. Don't say that. You might have other opportunities, much better ones. We can't promise anything to each other. I'll just have to see what's going to happen to me."

"I don't care about that."

"Elli, Rainer came to my apartment. He told me that he wanted to escape. The *Stasi* knows that. An agent has questioned me. What I'm afraid of is that Rainer might be working with them, helping them build a case against me. Why else would he be free and able to come here? The agent told me that Rainer had been arrested."

Hans saw the worry come into those lovely blue eyes, and he was immediately sorry to have burdened her. But she needed to understand why he was hesitating.

"What did you tell the agent?"

"I denied that he had said anything about leaving the country. I told them Rainer merely made a friendly visit."

"It's good that you said that, Hans. You were true to your friend."

"But he may not be a friend. He may be working against me."

"It doesn't matter. You did what was right. And the Lord is going to protect you. Somehow, everything is going to be all right. I'm going to marry you, Hans, whether you like the idea or not."

"Elli, I do like the idea. I've tried and tried not to think about it, but it's in my head all the time. I just don't want to ruin your life. And I could."

"It will be all right. I asked the Lord whether I should love you, and I felt calm and good. You're the best person I know, and it's right to love you. Now it's the Lord's problem, how to make things right for us."

It was such an innocent thing to say. Elli was still very young, and she didn't seem to recognize what tragedies could come to people. God didn't make any guarantees that a good life meant protection from all the hard things there were to face in life. All the same, looking into her eyes, he found himself believing she was right. He knew he shouldn't, but he kissed her again.

Chapter 19

Gene was hearing voices; either that or he was dreaming. He didn't know. He only knew that he was cold, and something was buzzing in his head. He kept sliding back into darkness, but the voice was persistent, telling him to open his eyes. He tried to do it, over and over, but the thought didn't seem to reach his muscles. Then his eyelids finally fluttered, and light filled his head. He closed his eyes again.

"Come on. That's it. I want you to look at me."

It was a woman's voice, a voice he knew from somewhere. But he didn't know where he was. Still, he managed to open his eyes fully for a moment, and he saw a face he seemed to recognize—a young woman with glasses, with freckles, her face close to his.

"Can you see me, Sergeant? Tell me if you can see me."

He could see her, all right, but he couldn't say it. He tried to nod, but he didn't know whether it happened. He wondered what was wrong with him. Why wasn't his body working right?

"Sergeant, tell me. Open your eyes again and tell me if you see me."

His eyes opened more easily this time, and he could see her. "Yeah," he managed to say.

"That's very good. Now tell me your name."

But Gene was tired, and this all seemed silly. He wanted to sleep again.

"Sergeant, listen to me. I want you to tell me your name."

"Gene Thomas," he said in a whisper. He was getting angry. What was wrong with this woman? She ought to leave him alone. "Don't," he said, but that was all he could think to tell her.

"Don't what? Tell me."

"Don't talk to me."

She laughed. "I have to talk to you. You need to wake up. Do you know where you are? Do you know what's happened to you?"

He opened his eyes again and tried to see past her face. She was dressed in white. There was a tube running into his arm. Somewhere in his mind was a sense of what was happening, but the whole thing was hard to think about.

"Tell me where you are, Thomas. I won't leave you alone until you tell me."

"Hospital," he said.

"That's right. You had surgery, didn't you? And I talked to you after that. Do you remember?"

He remembered that much. Everything had been like this before.

"But you had to go back in. The doctors did some more work on you. Do you understand that?"

"Yes."

"It's okay now. You're going to be all right. You were shot in the abdomen, two bullets, but we operated, and now you're going to be all right. Do you understand that?"

"I need to sleep."

"Not right now. You need to wake up. Where are you from, Sergeant Thomas? Tell me that."

"Not now."

But she was laughing again. "Yes, now. Tell me this. Are you married? You're sure cute."

His eyes opened again. She was pretty, he thought. Brown eyes. "Yes."

"Yes, what? Yes, you're married?"

"Yes."

"I was afraid of that. What's your wife's name?"

"Emily."

But now everything was coming clear to him. He had run up the trail to help Estrada, and then something had happened. An explosion in his head. He hadn't known about the bullets. Or maybe he had. Cutler had said things. He took a deep breath. He tried to think. Emily—what about Emily? He had told her he wouldn't take chances. Had he taken a chance? He wasn't sure. He had merely gone back to get Estrada. And then his brain had flashed, and Cutler had said he shouldn't die. "What happened?" he asked.

"You were shot in the stomach."

"No. What happened to my team?"

"That I don't know. But you don't need to worry about any of that for now. We're going to take good care of you. As soon as you can travel, you're going to get a nice trip back to the States. You're going to see Emily. Do you have any kids?"

"Yes."

"How many?"

"One."

"Boy or girl?"

"Boy."

"What's his name?"

Gene didn't want to talk anymore. He was going home. He would see Emily. And Danny. But he was messed up, bad. It was what the guys all talked about—going home messed up, not able to work maybe, not the same man anymore.

"What's going to happen to me?" he asked, and now he felt awake, and scared. A dull, deep pain was in his body, almost everywhere.

"I don't know all the details, Sergeant. Captain Warren will talk to you a little later. I don't know whether you'll need more surgeries. For now, I'll let you rest again, but I want you to let me know if you're in pain. We're going to take very good care of you. Okay?"

"Okay."

But Gene was scared. He didn't want to eat his food through a straw the rest of his life. That's what men said, that some guys went home messed up and had to eat their meals through a straw from then on. That was the worst, to go home messed up, with legs or arms gone, or eating through a straw. Gene had his arms and legs, he thought. He could feel them, he was pretty sure. But maybe he would never be himself again. Maybe he would always be messed up now. What would Emily think of him?

He needed to think more clearly about this, what this was all going to mean, but he was slipping again, and it was easier to let go.

Gene knew that time had passed, quite a bit of time, when he woke up again. And this time a man was in the room, a doctor with a mask hanging loosely from his neck. He was talking to the woman with the freckles. He looked away from her, at Gene, and he asked, in a tired voice, "How are you feeling, Thomas?"

Gene didn't know. It was a difficult question. So he didn't answer.

The doctor stepped closer to the bed. "I think we did a pretty good job on you," he said. "You were shredded up pretty bad inside. We had to take out part of your liver, but that's not a major problem. Back in the States, I'm sure they'll go back in and maybe take some more of your intestines out. Your bowel was pierced, but we did our best to patch it up, and we tried to save everything we could. We did a lot of stitching and repairing, but a belly wound is tough, and you had two bullets tearing things up in there. So it's going to take some time. You've got a rough time ahead—maybe a year or so, depending on how things go. But you're out of danger. When you got here, I wasn't sure we could keep you alive."

Gene felt the fear again. What did the doc mean, a rough year? What would he have to go through? Would he ever be himself again?

"You might have a certain amount of trouble all your life," the doctor said with virtually no emotion, "and you might be looking at several more surgeries before you're finished, but the day will come, you'll feel pretty much back to normal. The good news is, you're getting out of here. It's not exactly the million-dollar wound the men talk about, but you're alive, and you're going home. That's more than some guys end up with."

The nurse had been standing back, but she came to the bed now. "Captain Warren's been cutting all day. He's tired. You have to forgive his bedside manner."

"He might as well have it straight," the doctor said. "If I tell him it's an easy path from this point on, he's going to hate me later."

"But you don't have to worry," the nurse said, touching Gene's shoulder. "You're going to get good care, and we'll control the pain. You'll be good as new someday. Emily's going to get you back, all in one piece."

"I'm going to get some sleep," Captain Warren said, and he walked away.

"We'll keep you around here in post-op for a while, Sergeant," the nurse said. "My name's Gerri. Call for me if you need anything."

"My name's Gene."

"Yes, I know."

"Just call me that, okay?"

"Well, that's the other good thing. They'll keep you in the army until they get you up and running—and then you'll get out. Your soldiering days are over."

It was the first time Gene had thought of that. He would never have to go back to the jungle again, never lead another reconnaissance mission. He liked that idea until he thought again of his team. How bad was Estrada, he wondered? And had the other guys gotten out alive? If they had, they would all be going back to the jungle, and he wouldn't be there to look out for them. That worried him. Cutler wasn't ready to lead anyone anywhere. Gene wanted to go home, but it worried him to think that he was finished and those guys had to keep going back.

Gene slept a lot the next few days. But he spent more hours awake each day. He hated the pain medication and what it did to him—the hazy confusion in his head—so he tried to go without the stuff as long as he could. He needed to think, to figure out was going to happen to him now, and what his life would be like. But when the confusion began to clear, the pain would set in, and that, too, could keep him from thinking straight. What he felt, in either state, was a nagging sense that he had no control over anything, that these wounds were going to change his life in ways he didn't know yet. Were all his choices still open to him, or would he have to make decisions on the basis that his body was limited now, unable to do certain things? Would everything be the same between him and Emily? How long before he could get on with his career, with school maybe? He had been down to sixty days. If he could have held out that long, he could have gone back whole, normal; he could have picked up his life. Now, everything was unknown.

On his third day after surgery, Captain Shreeve showed up. Gene was in a ward by then with a roomful of men, but he hadn't said much to anyone. He didn't feel like talking, and not many of the other men did either, it appeared. Captain Shreeve walked to Gene's bed, looking a little too "spit and shine," and said, "Thomas, how are you holding up?"

Gene was surprised by his own anger. He had the compulsion to swing his arm at the guy and knock him away. He decided not to answer.

"They sure got a lot of tubes running in and out of you, don't they?"

What was Gene supposed to say to that?

"The doc tells me he's going to fly you out of 'Nam in the morning."

"No one told *me*," Gene said, and his voice sounded almost as hostile as he felt.

"Yeah, well, I guess that's the story. I just wanted to wish you well. You put in almost a year, and you did everything you were asked to do—and more. You're the kind of man who makes me proud to serve our country."

Gene could never look at Shreeve without thinking that it was he who had killed Dearden and Saunders. Gene didn't want to hear any of this lifer's blather, and he didn't want to be told that his belly wound was glorious and heroic. But he held his tongue, merely stared at Shreeve, and hoped the man felt his disgust.

"They tell me you'll be good as new in time. I was happy to hear that."

"Good as new?"

"Well, you know—more or less, I guess."

Gene looked away from the guy. He wasn't going to talk to him.

"Well, anyway, I know this is a hard time right now, but thanks for all you did. Cutler tells me you went back to help Estrada, and he tells me you could smell an ambush before it even happened. He thought you were being too careful, but now he says you knew all along, something was going down. That's the kind of instincts our best men acquire. There's no way I can replace a man like you."

Replace? What did that mean? Buy another slab of meat? Gene had played hide-and-seek with the North Vietnamese for ten months, and no one had gained an inch of ground; no one had changed anything.

"Well, anyway, I'm sure you're in a lot of pain, and I don't want to bother you anymore. But I salute you, Thomas. You've paid a heavy price for your country, but you can always be proud of the way you fought. I know that your father, the congressman, is proud of you. I wrote to him myself and told him what an outstanding job you did."

Gene rolled his head back toward Captain Shreeve and stared at him. "Get out of here," he said.

Captain Shreeve's head jerked back a little, as though he had been struck in the forehead. "Oh . . . sure. I guess you . . . I mean . . ."

"Get out of here."

"Look, Thomas, I know how you feel right now. I don't blame you. But I still—"

"I said, get out of here," Gene told him, in a voice that had begun to shake.

Captain Shreeve nodded, and then he turned quickly and walked away. The man in the next bed was laughing. He swore, and then he told Gene, "I've always wanted to tell an officer what I thought of him. That was good."

But Gene was breathing hard, and he was struggling with pain in his middle, all the way to his neck and deep into his groin. What he wished now was that he had grabbed Captain Shreeve by the shirt, pulled him down, and shouted into his face how much he hated this stupid war and what it had now done to him.

Gene received heavy medication for the flight, and he had lots of attention, nurses and doctors checking him all the time, but the long trip was still a horror. His pain had been getting worse, not better, and the tubes were becoming more cumbersome to him, more annoying. But worst was the bumpiness of the flight, which shook his insides and sent them into spasms of pain. He would wretch at times, a taste of blood in his mouth afterward, but there was nothing else to come up. He was hot, too, miserably hot, and then a few minutes later he was shivering and needing more blankets. A nice nurse, Asian with a Texas accent, was very concerned for him and stayed with him most of the time, which was something of a comfort, but he wondered at times whether the flight would ever end. And then, when the airplane finally landed, he was told they were in Alaska, at Elmendorf Air Force Base, just to refuel, but they would be flying on to Washington, D.C., and the Walter Reed Army Hospital.

He slept a little better during the final part of the trip, but the vibration and bumps kept his stomach in turmoil. Then he had to be carried out to an ambulance and bumped along streets and around corners until he felt he couldn't stand any more. The nurse—Donna was her name—stayed with him, and finally, after a ride up an elevator and down a long hallway, he was in a quiet room by himself, with no movement. He slept then for a long time. He awoke now and then and drifted away again, but he felt full of medicine and distant—and he no longer cared. He just wanted to sleep and feel nothing. He had tried to think, and everything he found to think about scared him, so it was easier to float and hope that the pain would start to go away.

But somewhere in the long day or night, he realized that someone was stroking his head and talking to him. "Gene, I'm here," the voice was saying. He opened his eyes in the dimly lit room, but he didn't have to see. It was her voice—Emily's.

Gene cried then. He tried to reach for her, but his arms were strapped down. "Oh, Em," he said. "I'm sorry."

"Sorry? Sorry for what?"

He didn't know how to tell her. But he was sorry for everything—sorry he hadn't found some way to stay home and not put her through all this, sorry he had let himself get pulled into the Lurps, sorry he was messed up. He had let her down. He had given himself to her, strong and young, and now what did she have left of him?

"We're okay now, Gene. You're out of the war. And you're going to be all right. They're going to operate again in the morning, but I'll be here when you wake up, so don't worry about anything. I'll make sure they do things right. Just sleep if you want to, and I'll sit right here by you."

She was still touching his face, his hair, and tears were on her cheeks. Gene could feel his own tears running down the sides of his head. She wiped his tears away, and she kept saying, "It's okay now. Everything's okay now. The doctor said you're going to be fine. It's just going to take time."

Time. Gene didn't want time to cure him. He just wanted someone to do something, take away all this confusion in his head, take away all the pressure in his chest, all the tubes and the pain in his arms. Everything. He didn't want to pass through all this.

But he slept, and when he awoke, it was like before, with a nurse talking to him, and then Emily, telling him to wake up, and then more sleep and night and day that were the same, and somewhere in the middle of all that Emily telling him that he needed another surgery. He tried to tell her that he couldn't do that, that he felt he was dying, that the medication was stealing his breath away and his strength, that he couldn't think, that the stuff was eating up his brain. But he couldn't get any words out, and she kept stroking his head and saying it was okay when he knew it wasn't. She was there, after all this time without her, and he couldn't touch her, couldn't hold her in his arms. But she had kissed him; he knew that. During those hours, when he was rising and falling, in and out of light, she had kissed his head and his lips. He knew her lips and her smell and her voice. He just couldn't hang on to consciousness, and when he started to get there, it frightened him anyway.

But a morning came when she was there again, and she was saying, "That's good, Gene. You need to be awake for a while."

He opened his eyes and saw her clearly for the first time, and close. There was light in the room, and she was real, her face not a memory, but with those little lines in her lips that he had forgotten about and her eyes way too blue, as always. "Did they operate?" he asked, even though he knew the answer.

"Yes. Twice. After a few weeks, they'll have to do more. But for now, they're just going to let you heal. You'll have a colostomy bag on your side for a while, but eventually everything will be hooked up normally. It's going to take time to get back to normal—maybe a long time."

"How long?"

"Maybe a few years."

"*Years?*"

"Yes. I know that's hard to think about, but Gene, you almost died. You lost so much blood inside. The doctors back in Vietnam said if you had gone another minute or two without a blood transfusion, you never would have made it. They said the helicopter pilot took a big chance, going in after you, but he did, and your men carried you to the helicopter.

It's a miracle you made it, honey, with two bullets going through your intestines like that, but you did make it, and the very worst is over."

Gene didn't think that was true. He knew that for him the worst was surely ahead, but he did want to believe all this: that he would be okay in time, and life could go on. "Where's Danny?"

"He flew out here with me, but he's with your mom right now. Your parents have been here a couple of times. Do you remember?"

He didn't. But he remembered now that he was not too far from where they lived. "I think so," he said, and he had begun to think that he did remember.

"You're going to have to be here for a while, but the doctor said, before long, we can get you to the VA hospital in Salt Lake. Danny and I are going to stay as long as you're here. I'll bring him over to see you as soon as the doctor says it's all right."

Gene was trying to picture it all: what his life would be now. "Will I be able to eat like a normal person?" he asked.

"Not for quite a while, honey. But yes. The doctor said you might always have to watch what you eat, because some things are hard to digest, but you will be able to eat."

Gene looked past Emily's face. He stared at the ceiling tiles. The pain was getting worse again, but he didn't want to sleep. He wanted Emily. But he didn't want to talk about all this. He tried to think of something else to say, but there wasn't anything. Everything he knew anymore had to do with the jungle—the stench and itch and wet of the jungle. He knew about silence and about applying cammo to his face. He knew about immersion foot and heat rash and insect bites. He knew about hunting down human beings—people he had begun to call "gooks," even though he had promised himself he never would. So what was he supposed to say to a nice girl who had lived her childhood in a place called "Bountiful" and then moved from there, ten miles, to Salt Lake? He had thought he would come home and talk to her the way he had before, but to do that, he first had to think of something to say.

"Is everyone okay?" he asked. But he had her letters. She had told him those things.

"Everyone's worried about you, of course. Your dad understands about these things more than most of us do, and he's worried about you. He's out in Utah campaigning right now, but he's flying back in a couple of days. He wants to talk to you, when you're ready. Your Grandpa Thomas is still having some trouble with his heart—with water building up around it—but he's pretty good. And he's really proud of you."

"Proud? Why proud?"

"Proud that you served your country. He's not so happy with the way the war has turned out, but he's proud that you did your duty."

Gene was staring at her now. Didn't anyone know what he had done over there? Didn't they know what the war had turned into? Gene wanted more pain medication now. He needed to call for a nurse.

"Your dad and I both got letters from your captain. He told us what you did. He's put you in for a Silver Star."

"What?"

"Yes. He said you ran back into fire to save a man's life."

Gene was horrified. How could Shreeve pull something like that? "That's not how it was, Emily. That's not at all how it was. A guy went down, and I went back to cover for him so we could get him out. That's what you do. *That's just what you do*. Anyone on the team would do that."

"Gene, don't get excited. Just calm down."

"I promised you, I wouldn't try to be a hero. And I didn't. It's just what you do in a circumstance like that. It's what we all do."

"Okay. I understand. Just rest now."

"It's just what we do, Emily."

"I know. But Captain Shreeve said that—"

"He's a liar, Emily. He came to the hospital and I told him to leave me alone. He wants one of his men to get a medal because it makes *him* look good. And he knows my dad is a congressman."

"Okay. Please, honey, you have to calm down."

Gene hadn't known he was being so loud. He was just trying to tell her. But two nurses were suddenly next to him, saying the same thing Emily had been saying. "Calm down. Calm down."

Gene was out of breath, panting and crying, frantic. But he didn't want a medal. They had to understand that. He had led his men into an ambush. Estrada was wounded. Nothing good had happened, nothing good of any kind.

But Emily was leaning over him now, and she had worked her arm around his shoulders. It wasn't an embrace—that wasn't possible—but her face was touching his, and her tears were running onto his cheek. "I'm sorry, Gene. I'm sorry for all this. But you'll be okay. I'll take care of you, and you'll be okay. Your dad told me some things—how you might feel—but I'm sure I don't understand."

"I don't want a medal," Gene said.

"Okay. We'll talk about all that. We'll get over this together. But you rest now."

He saw the nurse, with a hypodermic needle, and felt the pang of pain in his hip. It's what he wanted. He felt the other pain subside, faster than seemed possible, and he let himself drift away again. But he wanted Emily next to him, and he whispered, "Stay with me, okay?"

"I'm right here. Don't worry," she said.

But he did worry. He worried that he had made her cry, that he had scared her. He worried that she still thought he had tried to be a hero.

Chapter 20

High school in San Juan was finally settling into its regular schedule. Kathy had returned to school with a better attitude this year, but sustaining those feelings was not easy for her. She tried hard to be a good teacher, but she felt confined by the limitations Mrs. Sanchez and Dr. Retanda had placed on her. She loved the kids, but she never knew whether that mattered very much. Maybe kids learned just as much, or more, from teachers who kept their distance. Kathy occasionally injected a little something new into her curriculum, but she drilled hard on grammar, as expected, and hoped that when Mrs. Sanchez returned the following year, she would have no complaints. But grammar wasn't fun to teach, and it was discouraging to watch the students write down the correct answers, only to return to the dialect they normally spoke—unaffected by the grammar lessons. The youngest of her students were the age of seventh graders in the United States, but they seemed even younger. Even the older students had an innocence about them. She found charm in that, but at the same time, they didn't have opinions about much of anything and didn't seem to recognize that there were things to care about, to stand up for. She would try to bait them sometimes by asking challenging questions, then take one side of the argument, only to reverse herself. But *everything* sounded true to them, and they could nod at one opinion and then at the opposite one with equal willingness.

Still, Kathy had found a level of comfort with the people in the barrio that she hadn't expected. Local folks, for one thing, had stopped making so many comments about her being tall. She had become a fixture in the town, no longer a curiosity, and everyone waved to her and shouted her name. "Hello, Miss Thomas," they would say, blending the syllables into a single word, so it all sounded like "hellomestomoss." Kathy's Tagalog was coming along better all the time too. She could converse with people, especially the older people, well enough to feel closer to them than she had when they had been forced to try their English.

What amazed her more than anything was that one day in September some men had begun to dig in the spot where she had suggested the community might want to build public toilets. She feared that a house might be planned for the spot, but the workers assured her they were preparing to set footings for a public toilet. She had allowed herself to hope that her efforts had actually paid off after all, but then nothing more happened. The ditches, after that one day of digging, sat idle, and subsequent rains washed them mostly away. She saw the mayor now and again, but she didn't ask him about the work, and he said nothing. She decided that like a lot of good ideas in the Philippines, this one would get lost in a sea of good intentions.

Kathy continued to visit homes and teach hygiene lessons, now with her new roommate, Tamra Farrell. She was never certain that people remembered what they were taught, or put anything into practice, but she had begun to have more fun with the townspeople, to relax and chat with them, and certainly the women she visited made her feel welcome.

On an October day she was sitting at her desk as the students in her last class filed out. She was assembling the papers she planned to take home to read that night, placing them in folders, when she realized that a young woman had approached her desk. She looked up to see Carmen Bernas. "Yes, Carmen," Kathy said. "What can I do for you?"

"I am not taking the test," she said.

Kathy was confused for a moment, but then she realized what Carmen meant. "You mean that you missed the test when you were absent yesterday?"

"Yes."

"Did you bring an excuse for your absence?"

Carmen looked at Kathy blankly, as though the words didn't mean anything to her.

"Did your mother write a note to say why you weren't here?"

"I help my mother. My brother is sick."

"Did you ask her to write a note for you?"

Again, no response, and Kathy knew why. The mother probably couldn't read or write, but it wasn't something Carmen was likely to admit.

"Do you want to take the test, Carmen?" Kathy asked.

"Yes." She was gripping her arms around her waist, pulling her blue jumper tight against her thin waist. She seemed nervous, or maybe upset.

"All right. But not now. I'll let you take it tomorrow, during class."

"Thank you." But she didn't leave.

"That's fine then. I'll see you tomorrow."

"Yes." Still she stood, as though waiting for Kathy to release her with a specific command. But just when Kathy was about to tell her to go, she said, "My brother is *very* sick. He has fever." Tears were suddenly in her eyes.

Carmen was not a beautiful girl, but she had those dark, lovely eyes that almost all Filipinos had, and she had a childlike shyness that seemed to border on fear. Kathy wasn't sure what to do. "He'll be all right, won't he?"

But Carmen didn't answer that question. She stood for a time, silent, and then tears began to drop onto her cheeks. "I did not wash my hands," she said. She tried to wipe her tears away, but they were coming faster now.

"Oh, Carmen," Kathy said. She got up, stepped around the desk, and took Carmen into her arms. "You can't blame yourself. There are so many ways a child can get sick."

"I helped Mama cook, and I did not wash my hands," Carmen said, and now she was sobbing. Kathy felt the girl's hands move tentatively, then grip Kathy tightly around her back. "I'm sorry. I'm scared Roberto will die."

"Did your mother take him to a doctor?"

Carmen didn't answer again, but she didn't have to. The only doctor was in another barrio. Most of the people in the barrio relied on *albularyos*—healers. It was not common for families to get real medical help.

"Carmen, do you want me to come to your house? Is there anything I can do?"

"I don't know." The tears were still coming, and she was clinging to Kathy. She would be embarrassed soon, afraid to look Kathy in the eye. Kathy knew that, but she also knew that Carmen needed some time, so she held the girl and patted her back, and she told her, "Sickness comes to every family. Washing hands is good, but sometimes we get sick anyway."

In time, Carmen's crying slowed, and Kathy said, "Come on, now, let's get Miss Farrell, and we'll walk to your house. I'll talk to your mother. Maybe there's some way I can help."

So Carmen stepped back, and she wiped her eyes and her nose on the sleeve of her white uniform blouse. Kathy wasn't about to tell her not to do that, but she did get some tissue from a box on her desk, and she gave it to Carmen. Then she put her arm around Carmen's shoulders as they walked from the classroom and down the hallway to Tamra's room. Tamra was an aide this year, with no classes of her own, and that was difficult for her. She had been a teacher in the United States, with four years of experience. She was also a confident young woman, almost brash at times, and she had already had a few run-ins with the principal. She wasn't as tall as Kathy, but she was built strong, and she had a big voice. She must have seemed masculine to Filipinos, and overbearing. The teacher she worked with, Mrs. Barbosa, didn't like the "criticism" she had received from Tamra, even though Tamra thought she had done nothing more than give "suggestions." Kathy and Tamra had spent some late nights talking about the role they were playing in the school, and more than once Kathy had talked Tamra out of quitting and going home. It was a strange role for Kathy, telling someone to tone down her assertiveness, to be patient with the people and understanding of their culture. It was, of course, what Martha had tried to teach Kathy the year before, but it was also what Kathy really had come to believe. To her, Tamra seemed much too sure of herself, too quick to decide what was wrong at the school, and far too blunt in the things she said to other faculty members. "You have to understand how people think and feel here," Kathy had told Tamra more than once. "After you've said something like that to Mrs. Barbosa, she won't listen to you. All she remembers is that you were rude to her."

"But I wasn't rude. I was very nice about it," Tamra would say, and Kathy would hear herself, hear the same frustration she had expressed the year before.

But Tamra saw that something difficult was going on with Carmen, and without asking a lot of questions, she grabbed her umbrella and set out with Kathy for Carmen's house. It wasn't raining at the moment, but it would again—that was certain—and the streets were deep in mud. The rainy season was supposed to be ending soon, but Kathy saw no sign of any change so far. She had bought herself a pair of shoes that looked like hiking boots, and she now trudged through the mud with little concern—the way Martha had always done—but Tamra tried to pick her way along, avoiding the wettest spots. Kathy had also learned not to give much thought to the humidity. It was always there. Her clothes were damp when she put them on and wet when she took them off. She couldn't wash her things as often as she wanted to—not by hand and without a dryer. In the rainy season she could only hang things up in the house, and they never really dried. She had lost the capacity to notice the smell of mildew, but poor Tamra hadn't. She was still in that initial state of disbelief that she could actually live this way.

Carmen's house was actually a nipa hut, on stilts, but the lower level had been closed in with bamboo walls. Kathy had to bend low to step through the door. Inside, she could stand up straight, but the ceiling was close enough to make her feel claustrophobic. The only light was sunlight through the cracks in the bamboo and from the open door. The room was divided with a bamboo partition. Carmen entered the little back room and came back in a couple of minutes. "He's not so bad now," she said, and Kathy saw the relief in her face.

In a moment the mother stepped from the back room. She was a neat little woman, but she looked tired. Her hair had been pulled back tight at one time, but strands were loose now, and little red lines were spread through the whites of her eyes. "Hello, Miss Thomas," she said, and she nodded.

"This is Miss Farrell," Kathy said. She decided to speak English, for Tamra's sake.

Mrs. Bernas gave her the same respectful nod. "Happy to meet you," she said.

"How is your little son doing?"

"He better now. He no hot."

"Do you think he should see the doctor anyway? We could go get him."

"No. Ka Sepa make him better."

"Was Ka Sepa here already?"

"Yes. Roberto get better."

"But maybe a doctor could give him medicine."

"Ka Sepa give him. Roberto get better."

Kathy knew better than to argue, but the idea worried her. Sepa was one of the barrio healers. Kathy had heard stories of how he would drop hot candle wax into a glass of water and use the shape that formed to diagnose the illness. He then used mixtures of herbs for treatment, or burned various concoctions for the patient to breathe. Kathy, of course, was skeptical about all that, but her students told stories about the healings the *albularyos* had brought about in their families. She had the feeling that faith had something to do with that.

Still, Kathy would have been much more comfortable with a doctor. "Carmen, did you touch Roberto's head?" she asked.

"Yes. It is not hot. He will be better."

Kathy saw the change in Carmen. She really was confident. But Kathy told Mrs. Bernas, "It's important to give him lots of water to drink. Do you have clean water in your house?"

"Yes. Good water."

Most of the houses had water that was relatively clean. Peace Corps workers boiled it, just because it probably had organisms that locals were used to and Americans weren't, but Kathy had learned that the water wasn't the real problem. "Is there anything we can do to help, Mrs. Bernas?"

"Prayform."

For a moment Kathy hadn't understood, but then she realized that Mrs. Bernas had said, "Pray for him." "Yes, of course. I pray every day, Mrs. Bernas. Tonight I'll pray for Roberto." Kathy knew that Tamra was a skeptic about religion and wasn't likely to make any such promise, so she left her out of the conversation.

"Pray now?"

Kathy wasn't sure what to do. She was representing the Peace Corps, not only herself, and she wasn't sure that she should participate in religious matters with the people, but her doubt lasted only a second, and then she knew that it was actually the one thing she could do. And so she said, "Yes. I'll pray."

Kathy didn't mind when Mrs. Bernas turned toward the crucifix on the wall and crossed herself. She put her arm around Carmen's shoulders and pulled her close, and then she bowed her head. "Father in Heaven," she said, "please, bless this house. Please bless these good people who live here. Bless Mrs. Bernas and Carmen with peace in their hearts, and bless little Roberto. Grant him thy healing power. Restore him to full health." Then she closed her prayer in the name of Jesus Christ.

By the time Kathy finished the little prayer, she couldn't talk. She had never felt such power enter her, had never felt so sure in her life that something truly spiritual had happened. She had spent much of her life thinking that when people bore testimony of such experiences, they were expressing what they wanted to believe more than what really was. But something had happened inside her, had filled her chest and calmed her concern. She was still gripping Carmen, and she began to cry. Carmen seemed to know what had happened. She cried too, and she reached around Kathy's waist and held onto her as she had before.

Mrs. Bernas came to them. She touched Kathy's arm. "Thank you," she said. "Thank you."

Kathy still couldn't talk. She had the feeling that everything she ever did in her life, from this moment, would be colored by what she knew now—what she had always wanted to know.

"Roberto get better," Mrs. Bernas said.

"Yes," Kathy managed to say. And then she let go of Carmen and took Mrs. Bernas into her arms. "You must rest," she said. "You can sleep now, and Carmen can watch Roberto."

"Yes. Carmen help me."

Kathy had seen how deeply tired Mrs. Bernas was. She was a good woman, doing her best. Kathy wondered why she hadn't always been able to see that in these people. As Kathy moved toward the door, she realized there was something else she needed to say. Tamra was stepping outside when Kathy turned back. "Mrs. Bernas, Carmen was worried that Roberto got sick because she didn't wash her hands. I told her there are lots of ways for children to get sick. She shouldn't blame herself."

"Yes. I understand."

"But it is important to wash first, before cooking, isn't it?"

"Yes, Miss Thomas."

"I know Carmen will do that now. And I know you will."

"Yes, Miss Thomas."

Kathy looked at Carmen. "But even when you wash your hands, people can get sick. Do you understand? It wasn't your fault."

Carmen nodded. She still had that look of relief in her eyes. Kathy wondered what a burden the poor girl had carried for a day or two, thinking that her little brother was dying and she was to blame. Kathy walked on out. A drizzle had begun to fall, and Tamra already had her umbrella open. Kathy didn't bother, not for that bit of rain, but she looked back at Carmen again. "Everything will be all right now," she said.

"Thank you."

"Good-bye, my dear. Sleep well tonight. Don't worry about the test for a few days. You can take it when you feel ready."

"Thank you," Carmen said again, but then she stepped to Kathy one more time and hugged her. "You are the best teacher," she said.

"Oh, thank you," Kathy said, and she gave Carmen a last squeeze, but as she walked away, she was embarrassed that Tamra had heard this.

But it wasn't those final words that were on Tamra's mind. She sounded rather upset when she asked, "Are we supposed to do that?"

"What?"

"Pray for them?"

"Oh. That wasn't us. I mean, that wasn't the Peace Corps. That was just me."

"But what if someone asks me to pray? I don't do that."

"Don't worry. I've never seen it happen before."

"So how did she know you would do it?"

"I don't know. I'm not sure she did know." But that wasn't what Kathy felt. She felt satisfied that somehow, to Mrs. Bernas, it had seemed like the right thing to ask. And Kathy was still basking in what she had felt. After all she had tried to do in this community, with so little effect, that prayer seemed important—maybe the best thing she had done in the barrio. She couldn't have made that case to Tamra, but it was what she felt. She wasn't going to go around from house to house saying prayers, but she was going to treat people with the same love she had felt in Carmen's home.

On Sunday Kathy went to church. Since accepting the position as choir director, she actually hadn't missed a week. Sometimes she spent most of the day in Manila, attended Sunday School in the morning, had dinner with a member family, and then stayed for choir practice and sacrament meeting later on. There were times when she felt it wasn't fair to leave Tamra alone all day, and so she went to the city only for choir practice and sacrament meeting, but she actually missed those full days with the families she was coming to like so much. She loved the choir, but even more, she enjoyed the way all the members competed for her, asking her two and three weeks ahead to come to their homes.

Kathy had grown especially close to President Luna's family, and that's where she was today, in his home. The president had had to stay at the church after the morning meetings were finished, but that reminded Kathy of her own home on Sunday afternoons. Her dad had usually been gone on Sunday, attending church meetings, doing interviews, or making visits to the members. On those days, Kathy had often helped her mother prepare dinner, or looked after her brothers and sisters, especially Douglas, who had loved to have Kathy's attention. Now, she played with the children, and she chatted with Sister Luna. And she thought of her mother. Kathy had never really found much to talk to her own mother about, not after she was fourteen or so. She had begun by then to spout her opinions about almost everything, and her mom had shown more patience than interest. But Sister Luna, half a world away from Salt Lake, was more like Kathy's mother than almost anyone else she knew. She had a similar serenity and graciousness. She cared about Kathy, wanted to know all about her, and when Kathy talked about her rebellious history, she found no reason for alarm or censure. She merely listened, asked questions, and tried to understand.

When Kathy expressed her frustration over the war in Vietnam, Sister Luna said, "We know war in the Philippines. We remember. We have no love of war here."

She didn't express her political feelings about Vietnam, or anything else, but her understanding of the realities of war meant something to Kathy. So often, in the United States, people seemed to talk about Vietnam as though it were an abstraction, a question of politics, with no sense of the tragedy in all the loss of life. But Sister Luna had seen the destruction of Manila herself when she was only a child.

"Did you ever see any of the prisoners of war?" Kathy asked. She had told Sister Luna previously that her father had been one of those prisoners.

"I saw them sometimes in Manila. They worked in the city sometimes, with guards watching them. And I saw them march to the ships that took them away to Japan. My heart was sore for them. They were so thin, and their clothes were worn to nothing. We would stand by the street and watch, and when no Japanese guards were looking, we would hold up our fingers like this." She made the "V for Victory" symbol. "But the prisoners didn't dare do it themselves. It was taking too much chance."

"My father told me that. He said it gave them strength to know that Filipinos still supported them. The people sneaked food to him sometimes, too. He saw a Filipino shot down and killed because he tried to feed the men who were in the death march."

"Yes. So many died. It was such a terrible time."

Kathy had been denouncing war for a long time, describing the devastation and loss of life, but she saw in Sister Luna's eyes that she understood much more than Kathy did.

Later that afternoon, Kathy took a taxi to the church in time for choir practice. The choir had practiced several weeks, but this would be their first performance. The truth was, this choir would have been considered weak in most wards she had been in. Some of the people had to travel rather long distances to get to the church, and they didn't always show up. Or they arrived very late. Kathy usually had only a handful of people, mostly women, when the practice started, and maybe twelve or fifteen by the end.

All the same, she had worked hard to get them singing parts as well as possible, with some pretty good help in the bass section but woefully little in tenor or alto. Still, she had a couple of lovely soprano singers, and she chose hymns that were not terribly challenging. She had felt at the last practice that things were going fairly well, but today, even though she had pleaded for everyone to come on time, her pianist was half an hour late. The woman, Sister Taruc, came in apologizing, and Kathy understood—the jeepneys were so unpredictable, and traffic had been bad that day. Kathy had done what she could with those who had arrived on time, but she was gradually realizing that two of her best voices were not going to be there, and one of them had a solo part.

Kathy had a decent voice, but she didn't have great range, and the part was high, so she was hesitant to take the solo, but she had no other choice if the choir was going to perform as rehearsed. So she practiced the part and pleaded with everyone to come in at the right moment, even if she was turned around at the time. Sometimes, in practice, the singers seemed to come in as several voices instead of one, so disaster, under pressure, seemed a definite possibility.

But as it turned out, the members of the choir responded to the moment. They sang out as Kathy had been begging them to do, and they paid careful attention to her direction. They sang a special arrangement of

"Lord, Accept Our True Devotion" that Kathy had received from her mother, with a packet of other music.

The choir was nearing the end of the song, and Kathy was feeling relieved, even elated, that things had gone as well as they had. And then she looked at Sister Robles, an older woman with a voice that probably did as much harm as good. It was scratchy at best, and it squeaked on the high notes, but as the choir was singing "Ever praising, ever praising, Thruout all eternity," Kathy saw that tears were rolling down Sister Robles's cheeks. As the line repeated, Kathy's own eyes filled, and she saw the effect that had on the other choir members. When the last note ended, she could see the emotion in all the faces. They looked satisfied with themselves, but more, they seemed to have felt the meaning of the words.

President Luna praised the choir before the congregation, and after the meeting the members came up to tell Kathy how wonderful the music had been. The choir members also came to her one at a time to thank her and to embrace her, and it was their emotion that moved her the most. She had expected a degree of satisfaction if they pulled the song off all right, maybe even some praise; what she hadn't expected was the outpouring of love from her little choir. She had always wondered how her mother found so much joy in "church service"; much of it to Kathy had seemed perfunctory and routine. She had served in minor ways, but she had never felt so connected to a whole congregation. Her dad used to say that was what the Church was for, to bring people together so they could serve each other. But Kathy had only heard that as a platitude. But then, she hadn't realized, back when she had known everything, that there were questions she had never thought to ask—answers she needed but had never thought to seek.

Chapter 21

Gene was lying in his hospital bed, watching Emily. She had brought in a little Christmas tree, which she had set on a table near the door to his room. She was carefully stringing lights on it. "This is going to be so nice," she was saying. "Danny is going to be *so* excited. He always likes to look at the picture of the three of us. He points at you and says, 'Daddy, Daddy.'"

Gene was looking forward to seeing Danny. Alex and Anna were bringing him over. It would be his first visit to the hospital.

"You won't believe how big he is."

It was something she had said many times, and Gene was sure it was true, but he couldn't think of anything to say in response. He wasn't using as much pain medication as he had at first, but there was enough in him—or maybe something going on inside his body as it healed—that he always felt as though he were seeing through a kind of filminess, always hearing voices as though from a distance. He heard the words and then the meaning seeped into his brain afterward. It was the Sunday before Christmas now, and Mom and Dad were coming over to see him before they flew to Utah for the holidays. Gene wanted to be happy, wanted to feel some of what this first Christmas back in the States was supposed to mean to him, but he actually felt very little. He wasn't depressed; he just couldn't get himself to care or even to focus clearly on what was happening around him.

"Danny doesn't know what *hospital* means, but I told him you had to stay in bed. I don't think he'll really get the idea until he's here. But we'll have to keep him from grabbing at your tubes. He's just at that age where he has to look at everything, and for him 'look' means 'touch.' He'll soon be a two-year-old, and you know what that means."

Gene had heard about the "terrible twos," and he remembered his own little brothers and sisters being into everything at that age, but he didn't know what any of that would mean to him now. It was hard to believe that he would ever again have the energy to move around normally, let alone play with Danny. He had always wanted to teach him to play sports, to wrestle with him on the floor, carry him on his shoulders—all those things a dad did. Everyone said he would do those things in time, but it tired him merely to think about them now. And worse, it didn't seem to matter, though he fought against his own impulse. He didn't want this torpor, this sense of detachment, to rob him of the self he had always known.

"Are you okay, sweetie?"

"Sure."

"Can you see the tree?"

"Yeah. It looks nice."

Emily laughed. "Well, not really. It's a pitiful little thing, but it was the only small tree I could find."

In truth, it did seem too small to carry the burden of a string of lights and the glass balls she was hanging on it now. But he didn't say that. "It looks fine," he said.

"You don't feel great today, do you?"

"I don't know. Not too bad."

"Gene, we'll have lots of better Christmases—a whole lifetime of them. But let's make the best of this one. We'll always remember it. I know that all this is hard for you—and it's hard for me, too—but I just keep thinking that Danny and I could have been on our own now. You came so close to dying, but the Lord must have wanted you to live." She walked over to the side of his bed. "I prayed so much that you could come home, and I know you were praying for it too. Now, we have to be thankful that you made it, and not feel sorry for ourselves that we have some hard times to pass through."

Emily had begun to cry. She wiped the tears off her cheeks with the flat of her hand, and she tried to smile. "Yeah, I know," Gene said. But he didn't mean it. He didn't mean anything. He was just saying words. He wished that he could cry and be thankful, like Emily, or smile and say something encouraging, but he didn't feel thankful, didn't feel hopeful, didn't even feel discouraged. He felt more like a lump of matter, barely sentient.

She touched his hair and then the side of his face. "I know you don't feel well. I can see it in your eyes. But you're going to be okay. I'll make you okay. More than anything, I look forward to the day when you can come home to me, and I can sleep next to you. I've missed that for such a long time."

Gene made an effort to think about that, to respond the way he knew he should, and then he said, "I love you, Em. It will be nice when I can come home. I'll get myself going again, eventually; I promise you that."

"You make it sound like you're doing something wrong, but you shouldn't think about it that way. You fought to stay alive, and you're fighting now, just to deal with the pain and to keep your spirits up."

But it wasn't true. He didn't remember fighting for life. He didn't remember much of anything. And he wasn't fighting now; he was merely lying there, wishing he were human.

Emily went back to the tree and finished putting on the decorations; then she strung tinsel over everything. She talked all the while, and Gene did the best he could to respond. And then, in the hallway, Gene heard a little voice saying, "Daddy. Daddy."

"Oh, here they are," Emily said, and she hurried out the door.

In a moment Alex came in, carrying Danny, with Anna and Emily right behind. Alex walked to the bed. "It's Daddy," Emily was telling Danny. "It's your daddy."

But Danny looked confused, or scared. He reached around his grandpa's neck, gripped him tight, and turned his head away. Emily hurried over and took Danny from Alex. "Honey, it's your daddy. I told you he would be in bed. Remember?"

But Danny was now grasping Emily. He wouldn't look at Gene.

"This is all a bit of a surprise to him, I'm sure," Anna said. "He's been saying, 'Daddy, Daddy' all the way over here in the car."

"It's okay," Gene said. "I'm not much to look at, that's for sure."

"It's the tubes and everything," Emily said. "Just give him a few minutes."

"Sure."

But Gene *did* feel this. He felt the one emotion that sometimes erupted in him, unexpectedly. He was suddenly angry—fiercely angry. He hated the war, the things he had experienced in Vietnam. All his noble ideas about defending America, protecting democracy, seemed, as never before, an enormous lie. It had all come finally to this: lying in a hospital, impotent and worthless, a fearful sight to his own son. What a merry Christmas.

"Look at the Christmas tree, Danny," Anna was saying. She took Danny from Emily and walked to the little tree. "See the pretty decorations?" Danny looked, and then reached for the tree, and Anna had to step back a little. She told Gene, "He doesn't really understand all this Christmas stuff. We took him to a mall and tried to have him sit on Santa's lap for a picture, but he wouldn't have anything to do with that. Santa scared him to death."

"At least I'm not the only one who scares him," Gene said, and he tried to laugh. But it was the anger that had come through in his voice, and now the room was silent. He had done it again, made everyone uncomfortable.

But he kept still after that, and gradually the mood improved. His mom and dad had brought some presents. They left them under the tree, or at least in the corner, not far away, and they told Gene and Emily to open them on Christmas, but they let Danny open his now. It was a big, red fire truck, which he liked. He played on the floor with it, making little squeals that were clearly intended as siren noises, and little growls for engine noises. Gene couldn't see him, but he liked hearing him play. He was sorry he had seemed so harsh before. He tried to talk more, to sound as normal as he could.

When Alex and Anna finally got ready to leave, Alex said, "Son, we need to talk one of these days."

"Sure," Gene said.

"When we get back, after the holidays, I think you'll be feeling a little more like your old self."

"Yeah, I guess. I'm sorry I can't do any better now."

"You're doing fine," Mom said. "You've come so far already. When we first saw you, it seemed hard to believe that you would ever come back to us at all."

Gene wanted to believe that he was improving, that he would keep getting better. He tried to think of himself that way.

"I understand some things that only a guy who's been to war can know," Alex said. He put his hand on Gene's shoulder. "There's no hurry, but I think I can help you as you start to feel better physically. A lot of what you have to deal with is mental—as I'm sure you realize already."

"I'm fine, Dad. I just need to get my strength back."

Alex didn't disagree, but Gene could see that he thought otherwise. All the same, Gene didn't want to talk to him about war or about "mental problems." He just wanted to get back on his feet, to get his strength built back up, and then he wanted to forget everything that was behind him. He was still thinking way too much about the jungle, about Dearden and the other guys, about the sounds and smells of the war. It was best to get all that behind him, not to talk about it and make things worse.

After Alex and Anna left, Emily picked Danny up again and said, "This is your daddy. He's been sick, but he's getting better."

Danny stared at Gene this time. Clearly, he saw nothing he recognized, nothing from the picture he had known so long. But Gene tried to smile at him, and Danny was at least curious now, more than afraid. "Can you give Daddy a kiss?" Emily asked. But that was too much. Danny pulled back, and then he squirmed to get free and back to his fire truck.

"It's okay," Gene said. "All this is frightening to such a little guy."

"He'll get used to it, and he'll get to know you. While your parents are gone, I won't be able to stay so many hours with you—unless I can get a baby-sitter some days—but I'll bring him with me most of the time, and he'll get so he knows you're okay. You'll have to talk to him a little more all the time, once he'll let you." But Emily was fighting not to cry, and Gene could hear it in her voice. "He really does look at that picture all the time. He loves to point to his daddy."

Gene didn't like the thought. The picture was the real daddy and Gene was a sad shadow of what the photograph showed. But Gene's anger was gone, and now, his struggle, once again, was to care. The fact was, Danny was making a lot of noise again, the sounds tedious, and Emily's pep talks were tiring. He wanted to sleep.

"If we go now, will you be okay for the evening?"

"Sure."

"I'll bring Danny over tomorrow, later in the day, and on Christmas Eve we'll have a nice little family night together. Then we'll come back on Christmas morning. Maybe we can phone Grandma and Grandpa Thomas's house and talk to everyone. We'll make the day as nice as we can."

"Okay, that'll be great." But he didn't want to make the phone call. He didn't want to talk to his grandpa, and in truth, he wished Emily wouldn't take so long to say good-bye. He wanted to sleep.

Kathy's choir sang three carols in church on the Sunday before Christmas. Christmas was on Friday this year, so Sunday seemed to Kathy a little too removed from the actual day, but Filipinos loved Christmas and celebrated all through the month. In San Juan, for more than a week now, she had heard the church bells ringing at four o'clock every morning, calling the people to early mass. Those loud bells had made Tamra furious, but Kathy had been going to bed early, and most mornings she got up and went to mass with the people. They loved seeing her there and greeted her with joy. She hated getting up that early, but she had enjoyed the experience once she got herself up and going.

The choir members had worked hard, but on the day of their performance, they seemed to revert a little more to their enthusiasm than to the training Kathy had given them. She found herself frustrated until she once again looked at their faces as they sang, seeing their happiness. The members of the branch were equally pleased. Everyone had heard angels sing—even if not always on key—and Kathy realized she had too. She really did need to listen more with her heart and not worry about the precision her high school choir director had always sought.

Out in the hallway, after the meeting, Sister Robles was waiting. She had a little package wrapped in brown paper and tied with string. "This is only a little gift," she said. "I wish to give you a big one, if I can. The singing makes me so happy."

It was Sister Robles who had led the choir astray—she, as much as anyone—and yet she was also the one who had seemed to hear accompaniment from heaven. Her eyes had been distant and serene, and as usual when she sang, full of tears. "Thank you, Sister Robles," Kathy told her. "It's so kind of you." Kathy had learned not to say that she "shouldn't have done it." Filipinos loved to give, and nothing hurt them more than to have their gifts turned down.

"Is it possible you could come home with me for a little dinner before you leave the city?"

Kathy had so many reasons to say no. She had been in the city all day, and she had left Tamra alone. She had also eaten a wonderful, big meal with the Lunas family not long before sacrament meeting. More than anything, Kathy wanted to get home before dark and have a little of the day left for herself. But she couldn't possibly say that to Sister Robles. A year earlier she could have done it without a second thought, but looking at Sister Robles's dear old face now, she knew it would disappoint her much too much.

"Yes, of course," she said. "I can't stay very long, but I would love to visit with you. I've wanted to get to know you better."

Sister Robles was weathered beyond her years. She was probably not seventy, but she looked much older, with deep wrinkles in her face and neck, and filmy eyes that obviously didn't see very well. But those eyes were wide with joy now. She smiled and thanked Kathy, as though Kathy were doing her a great honor, merely to go with her to her home.

The two walked to a street corner nearby where they caught a bus to Sister Robles's neighborhood. Sister Robles insisted on paying the bus fare, and Kathy really was pressed not to turn down this second act of generosity, but she was certain that Sister Robles had counted the *centavos* and knew what all this would cost: the gift, the travel, the meal. She couldn't have invited Kathy without considering the cost, but still, for today it was Kathy's kindness to accept. On another day she would do something as nice in return. She already looked forward to doing that.

Sister Robles had prepared *arroz caldo*, a special soup made of chicken and rice, and a noodle dish called *pancit* to go with the fish and rice main dish. And for dessert she had baked banana bread. The meal was simple and lovely, but it took much longer than Kathy might have liked. Still, the two talked quietly about the Church and what it meant to Sister

Robles, about the good members of the branch and the branch president she loved so much, and they talked about Kathy's home and family.

Sister Robles wouldn't let Kathy help with the dishes, but she asked her to sit with her for "only a few more minutes" after they had finished eating. So they moved from the kitchen table to the tiny living room, which was clearly the room where Sister Robles slept. The mat was rolled up now and placed in a corner, not on the floor, but Kathy no longer thought of this manner of sleeping as somehow inferior to her own bed at home. Sister Robles would have found such a bed uncomfortable.

The two sat next to each other on wicker chairs, and Sister Robles continued to ask questions about Salt Lake City, about President Joseph Fielding Smith, about the Tabernacle and its choir, and so many things she wanted to know.

Kathy answered for some time—now *much* longer than she had intended—and then she said, "But Sister Robles, tell me more about you. Have you always lived in Manila?"

"Oh, no. My husband and me, we come from a little barrio, north from here. It was a good place, but my husband thought we could have a better life if we came here. He drove a taxi here, or did other jobs, but I always wished we had stayed at home. He wished it, too, I think, but he never said it. He wanted his children to have an education. He wanted them to do better than they could do in the barrio. That's why he worked so hard even if he didn't like the work so much as the farming he did in the barrio."

"And how are your children doing?"

"Not so well as he wanted, but they do all right. They live here in Manila too, and they work as hard as my husband did. I guess it's not so bad."

"Are any of them in the Church?"

"No. But I talk to them. Maybe someday they will listen to me. Right now, they don't think enough about God."

"And your husband? Did he join the Church?"

"No. He listened to the lessons when the missionaries came to us, but he knew his mother would never forgive him if he left the Catholic Church. He did love the people, though, and he went with me to church, many days, when he wasn't driving his taxi."

"How long ago did he die, Sister Robles?"

"It's been almost four years now, and every day I miss him. The last Christmas he was with me, he was very sick. He was tired from so much work. And he was a little sorry, I think, that our three sons had not been able to go to the university. It was what he had dreamed of. But he loved them, and he loved me, and he wore out his body working for all of us. He told me, the last day that he could talk, that he believed he would see me again, the way the Church taught him. He liked the way we teach it."

"It must be a wonderful thing to love someone so much and to know you will see him again."

"Yes. And now it's what you must do. When you go home, you must find a good man. It's the next thing for you. The important thing."

Kathy laughed. "You sound like my mother."

"Yes. I hope I do." She smiled, and then she waved her crooked finger, as if to give Kathy a little lecture. "There is nothing better in this world than to love someone and to be loved. The other things don't matter so much."

Kathy had been taught that basic concept all her life, she supposed, but on the jeepney, as she began her trip home, she kept thinking about the idea. What were all the "other things," she wondered? What were the things that had seemed so important to do "before she got married"? And why had she considered so often the possibility that she wouldn't marry? The sad thing now was that she might have missed her chance. But she kept thinking of dear Sister Robles—who used her scratchy little voice to sing with angels—and what she had said: there was nothing better than loving and being loved. It seemed so obviously true that Kathy wondered how she hadn't known it all along. She thought of Marshall, the only boyfriend she had ever had. She remembered how she had felt when she had been with him, how much she loved the way he had treated her. It really had been the happiest time of her life, and yet, it had been over in a matter of weeks.

It was Christmas afternoon, and as so often in the past, Diane was at Grandma and Grandpa Thomas's house. She had avoided her family for quite some time after she had first returned to Utah, but she had begun to feel better about herself and her life this fall. She was back in college, for one thing. She had taken a full load of classes fall quarter and had done well. Her grades were the best she had ever received. She had started out a little shaky, even scared, but it hadn't taken her long to realize that if she kept up on her assigned reading and took good notes in class, she did well on tests. It was a surprising realization. Always before, she had been haphazard about doing her reading and then would try to catch up the last night. But now, with a baby, she had to plan her schedule carefully and study part of every day. She had also surprised herself by entering into class discussions. It had taken her a while to try that, since she had never said much in years past, but she was nearing twenty-three and was older than most of the students, the majority of whom had come straight to college from high school. The younger kids were worried about parties and club socials and who was dating whom. She sensed that a lot of them hadn't read the assignments, at least not thoroughly. That made competing with them rather easy. Besides, she had begun to think about life and issues more than she ever had before, and she had some things to say.

Still, it was strange to be at Grandma's house with her cousins, most of whom still weren't married. They surely must have wondered what had gone wrong in her brief marriage. She hardly knew where she fit. She had been one of the married adults for a couple of years, and now she was single, yet one of the mothers. She spent a little time with her cousin Joey and his wife, Janette, and with Wayne and Dixie, who had gotten married that summer. Even Sharon had a boyfriend with her—a talkative, rather nervous young man named Joel. Diane had already gotten the word from two aunts today: "This time Sharon seems to be getting serious." But all the students were talking about life after college, their hopes and plans, and none of it sounded much like anything Diane could expect. She had the feeling that her cousins felt awkward around her, too, as though they didn't know what was okay to say and what wasn't. She was, after all, the first divorcée in the family.

Diane spent some time talking to dear old Brother Stoltz, Anna's father, whose wife had died a couple of years earlier. He was a pleasant man with a stout German accent to go with his stout German body. But he was more honest than most everyone else. "I know you are going through a difficult time," he said. "It's too bad for you. I'm sorry."

"But I'm doing all right, Brother Stoltz," she said. "I'm going to college, and I'm enjoying that."

"Yes. This is one thing about America. People can do what they want. My grandson in East Germany has no opportunity now to study at the university. You know his story, I suppose."

"I know he was put in prison for trying to help someone escape. But didn't he turn down a chance to come over here?"

"Yes, this is true. He didn't want to leave his family. Or the Church. He's a very good young man. But his father, my son, passed through the darkest days any man can know—much like your Uncle Wally did—and he's stronger for it. This prison has not been such a bad thing for my grandson. Here in this country too many people have things easy. This difficulty you are going through, it will make you better and stronger. I can promise you that."

Diane rather liked that idea. She had been a pampered American kid, and she had gotten everything too easily. She didn't mind this new image of herself: someone who was making her way through life by hard work, not "taken care of" because she was pretty.

In fact, it was her grandfather, later in the day, telling her how beautiful she "still" was that caused her to speak to him in a way she never had before. "Grandpa, say that to me if you want to, but please don't ever say that to Jenny. I don't want her to think she's pretty and that's enough."

Grandpa was sitting in "his" chair, although it had been reupholstered recently. He was looking down at Diane, who was sitting cross-legged on the floor. Jennifer had finally gone down for a nap, and Diane was glad for the peace. Jennifer had been a little too excited by all the adults paying attention to her and by all the older kids who wanted to play with her. Diane was glad she was getting some sleep before the ritual opening of presents would begin.

Grandpa smiled. "You sound like Kathy," he said.

"I wish I had been a lot more like Kathy before I met Greg. I wouldn't be in the situation I'm in."

Grandpa looked at her curiously, but he seemed to decide to let the statement pass. Instead, he said, "All I meant to say was, you're still young, and you're a wonderful young woman. You'll find another husband one of these days."

"Before, you said 'beautiful.'"

"Well, I meant inside and out."

"No, you meant I'm pretty. But I don't want some guy to marry me just because he likes my looks."

"Well, sure. I don't disagree with that." He looked at her for a time, as though wary about what he could say. But finally he asked, "Honey, is there just no chance at all that you could work something out with Greg? Your mother tells me he would come back to you in a minute if you would take him back."

"Did she say I ought to do it?"

"No. But I'm just saying—"

"That it was my fault as much as his, and we could work things out if I weren't so stubborn? That's what his parents told me."

"Diane, I don't know what happened. In any marriage, there are some difficult days. But I don't think we should give up easily on a temple marriage. I've told you how I feel about that."

He had told her far too often, in fact, but she had never told him her side of the story. She still didn't want to. "Grandpa, there are lots of things you don't know."

"Of course not. But there are arguments in every marriage. You can't just walk out the first time things don't go the way you expected."

But Diane was sick of hearing that. It was what John Lyman had told her. Her anger surged, and without thinking, she said, "What about the first time he beats up on you, Grandpa?"

Suddenly the room was silent. People were all around, in the dining room and living room that adjoined, and everyone had been talking and laughing. But Diane's voice had suddenly taken on an intensity she had rarely shown in her life, and everyone had heard.

Grandpa was as silent as the rest.

"He did, Grandpa. He knocked me around twice and I stayed with him, but the third time he slugged me with his fist. I packed up Jennifer and left."

"Well . . . good for you," Grandpa said. And then, after a long pause, he added, "And I hope I never see that young man again. If I do, I just might knock him on his back."

No one laughed. Grandpa meant it. He was frail now, but he was a big man, and Diane had a feeling that he could call up enough wrath to do just what he claimed. She hardly thought it was a good idea, but she was moved that he would feel so defensive for her.

Diane looked around the room and saw that everyone was still looking at her and that they were finally looking her in the eye. It was Aunt LaRue who said, "You did the right thing, Diane. I'm proud of you." She walked over, kneeled on the floor next to Diane, and whispered, "Why didn't you say anything? No one knew about this."

The talk in the room picked up again, and Diane was glad in a way not to have everyone looking at her, but she was relieved to have them know. "I'm not sure, Aunt LaRue. I just didn't want to say anything."

"Be careful, Diane. Women who get beaten by their husbands sometimes find ways to blame themselves. And wife-beaters are masters at making their wives feel they're getting what they deserve."

"I guess. But what makes me mad at myself is that I married him. Everyone else seemed to see through him. I feel so stupid that I didn't. It bothers me to have people know what a stupid choice I made. But I prayed and prayed about what I should do, and I thought I was making a good choice."

"If there's one thing I've learned in my life, Diane, it's that getting answers is not like making a phone call. We let the things we want get mixed up in the process. Greg seemed like a nice enough boy."

"But did you like him?"

"Actually, no."

"I didn't either," Grandpa said, "and I like him a whole lot less now."

"So why couldn't I see it? That's what bothers me."

"Look, Diane," LaRue said, "I made some choices when I was young that I regret now. And I can't go back and correct them. But if we never make mistakes, we never learn anything. And after all is said and done, that's what we're here for."

"I know what you mean, Aunt LaRue. I've learned some things too, and I'm not sure I could have learned them any other way."

LaRue put her arm around Diane's shoulders, then pressed her cheek against the side of Diane's head. "Well . . . you're growing up, Di. I'll have to admit, I wasn't sure you were ever going to do that."

Diane thought maybe that was true, and she liked the idea. But she still wished she had found another way.

Hans was home in Schwerin, and he had Elli with him. His parents were already in love with her. It had taken them about five minutes, it seemed, to get to know her, accept her, and make her feel at home with them. It had been natural, and part of that was because of Elli and who she was, and the rest was because of Mom and Dad and Inga, and who they were. They were all listening to the same spirit, Hans was sure, and the spirit in the little apartment had been powerful as they had taken turns embracing Elli and wishing her well.

On Christmas Eve, in the morning, Hans had gone to see Berndt's parents. He had seen them before when he had come home last time, but he felt the need to talk to them again. There were things that were still on his mind. So he sat with them in their apartment, at the kitchen table, and he told them, "I know you miss Berndt now, more than any time of the year."

"Yes, of course," Brother Kerner said. "But we also worry about you. You don't have to feel responsible."

"I know. I understand that better now. But I still wonder what I might have done to convince him not to try to escape. Maybe if I hadn't helped drive him there, no one else would have helped, and the plan would have been called off."

"He would have found a way. It was all he ever wanted to do."

But that was not exactly what Hans wanted to say. "What I mean is, I had a responsibility to him. I should have tried harder. We all have a responsibility to each other. That's the thing our government doesn't want us to believe. They want us to report on each other, all for the cause of socialism, but socialism is supposed to bring us together to share a common purpose. What it leaves out is love. We all have to love one another, and then our common purposes are obvious."

Hans could see in the Kerners' faces that he had said too much. Criticism of the government always set off an alarm. It wasn't that the

Kerners disagreed, or that they suspected Hans of some sort of betrayal. It was simply a habit of mind to avoid such conversations.

"Berndt and I weren't close friends, really," Hans said. He was older than I, and we didn't spend much time together, especially after we tried to escape that first—"

"We know nothing of any other escapes. Please don't talk of such matters."

But they did know. They simply chose not to take responsibility for that knowledge. It was too dangerous for them. After all, they had raised a disloyal child, and that would reflect upon them forever as far as the Party was concerned.

Hans nodded, and he only added, "He did escape, in the end, and we will, too. This country makes life difficult for us, but it can't take away what we know. And we know that we'll see him again."

They were silent again, both looking down at the table, but then Sister Kerner stood, and she reached out to Hans. She took him in her arms and thanked him. "Thank you for coming," she said. "What you say is true. We will see him again. Have a wonderful Christmas."

Brother Kerner was more reticent. He stood and shook Hans's hand. "Your parents tell me that you are engaged to be married to the Dürden girl."

"Not formally. But yes, we do hope to marry. We can't afford it for quite some time, however. My salary is very limited."

"Yes. We understand. It's part of our sorrow for you."

"Elli believes that miracles will happen. I try to trust in her faith when my own isn't strong enough. But for now, I don't have much to offer her."

"You have *everything* to offer her," Sister Kerner said. "You are a righteous young man who holds the priesthood. You have been tested, and you have held firm. What more could a young woman want?" Then she smiled. "And you're a nice-looking boy. Your Elli probably noticed that, too."

Hans thanked her, and he liked to think that Sister Kerner was right about him, but on the streetcar, as he returned to his family's apartment, he thought as he often did, about Elli's future. Eternity looked very promising; that was true. But life didn't appear to hold out much hope. And now he had made things worse. He had brought Elli to his family, and they loved her as he did, and she loved them. It was all the more to give up, if things could never be worked out.

Chapter 22

Winter quarter had started now, and Diane had taken a job at the Weber State Union Building. She worked only ten or twelve hours a week, mostly in the afternoons, and at $1.60 an hour she didn't bring home much of a paycheck. Her divorce wasn't final yet, with all the delays Greg had created, but at least he had started paying child support, although not a generous amount. The money she earned didn't add all that much, but that was not really the point. Diane wanted to start taking over her own life. Maybe working in the kitchen at the Union Building, at minimum wage, was only symbolic, but she knew she had to start doing something for herself and for Jennifer. Bobbi watched the baby—which helped a great deal—but Diane had rented an apartment, and she and Jennifer spent evenings and nights by themselves. The apartment was not far from the college, which meant it wasn't far from her parents' house—but it was in another ward. It wasn't easy for Diane to relate to her ward members as a divorcée and a single mom, but at least she wasn't quite the "tragic figure" she had felt herself to be in her home ward.

Diane was trying hard not to feel sorry for herself, and she loved the surge of confidence that was driving her, but that didn't mean she wasn't lonely. Her life was taken up by school, study, work, and care of Jennifer. That fall she had finally gone with her mother to see *Anne of a Thousand Days*—in second run—and she had seen a couple of other movies, but she had no close friends, and she certainly wasn't part of the social scene at Weber State. The popular students were usually in the social clubs. Diane knew girls a little younger than herself who were in LaDianaeda and

Otyokwa, and were always dating the guys in Excelsior, Sigma, or a returned-missionary group called Delta Phi. There was also a crowd that liked to hang around the Institute of Religion much of the time. But Diane had no time for any of that, and she wouldn't have fit in anyway. Her divorce wouldn't be final for a couple more months, and even when it was, she couldn't see how that was going to change anything.

Diane had decided that if she eventually met someone, she wasn't going to rule out marriage, but that wasn't her first priority. She wanted to get her degree and find a way to make a living, and she wanted Jenny to feel confident that she had a mom who could manage for them. Greg had come to see Jennifer just before he returned to Seattle for his final year of law school, but he hadn't returned, not even when he was home for Christmas. When he had visited, Diane had stayed out of the room and let Bobbi handle the situation, but Jennifer had shown little sign of knowing Greg, and Diane doubted that he would ever be much a part of her life. In some ways that was better, since Diane feared that he would find ways to manipulate Jenny's loyalties and imply that it was Diane's fault that she didn't have a daddy. But all this was sad to Diane, and she felt best when she worked hard, stayed busy, and tried not to think very far into the future.

One January afternoon Diane was out in the big open dining area of the Union Building. It was long after lunch, and the room was deserted except for a few scattered students who were either gathered in small groups, chatting over snacks and drinks, or making an attempt to study. Diane was wiping off tables and picking up paper cups and wrappings left behind. She actually preferred to stay in the kitchen, where no one but her fellow workers saw her, but she didn't mind cleaning the tables. She liked to think of herself as someone who was working her way up from the bottom, paying her dues. She saw herself as finally creating her own future, and that idea appealed to her.

But on this afternoon she was wiping off a table when a young man spoke to her. "It's nice to see the sun for a change," he said.

Diane had been busy and not paying much attention to anything else. She looked around to see a guy at a table by himself. She was almost certain that he was a returned missionary. Weber State was not all that different from BYU in a lot of ways. The majority of the students were LDS, and if a guy was a little older and dressed neatly, he was almost sure to be an RM. What she also noticed, however, was that he was good looking. He had light hair, almost blond, that was rather nicely disheveled, and the tan cheeks of a skier. Diane hadn't skied for the past couple of years, but she still associated skiing with the cute boys she liked in high school.

Diane glanced at the windows. Snow had been falling off and on for a couple of days, but now the sun was out and bright. "Yeah," she said. "It's a pretty day." She decided to finish the table she was cleaning and then move away.

"Do I know you? It seems like I do," the guy was asking. "Which high school did you go to?"

At BYU, students had come from everywhere, but at Weber most everyone was from somewhere around Ogden. Still, the question sounded funny to Diane. High school seemed distant now. "I went to Ogden High," she said.

"Really? So did I."

"Well, I'm sure I was there before you."

"Oh, come on. That can't be. When did you graduate?"

Diane could see in his confident eyes and the casual way he was flipping his hair back that he knew he was good looking, that he also thought she was, and that this conversation was only going to get more awkward. "It was a long time ago," she said, and she moved to another table, farther away from him.

He raised his voice a little and asked, "Don't give me that. I think you're a freshman."

Diane didn't answer.

"Just tell me. What year did you graduate?"

"Sixty-six," she said. She looked up and smiled. She saw his surprise, and that made her laugh. What bothered her was that she liked this attention, liked the guy's looks, and found herself having to resist the temptation to flirt with him. But that wouldn't work. She wiped off the table quickly and moved to one that was farther away.

But he had gotten up from his table by then and was walking toward her. She decided to answer his question, settle the matter, and then leave. "After I graduated," she said, in a businesslike voice, "I went down to the Y. This is the first year I've been back here." She considered telling him that she had been married and was getting a divorce, but she hated saying that to anyone. "I need to go get some clean water."

She picked up her little bucket and was about to make her escape when he said, "You're Diane Hammond, aren't you? I knew I knew you. I just haven't seen you since high school, and I was thinking you were younger."

She nodded. "Well, anyway . . ." She told herself to leave, but she didn't.

"Every guy at Ogden High had a crush on you. But us younger guys knew we didn't have a chance. You were the *unattainable*—the Holy Grail."

"Not quite." Diane thought about her hair. She had cut it short this fall, and now she had a net over it. No wonder he hadn't been sure he knew her. She looked horrible with the thing on.

"No, really. I used to watch for you in the halls, just to get a look at you. Every one of my buddies was the same way."

Diane smiled, but she wasn't going to comment on that. "So have you been on a mission?" she asked.

"Yeah. I was in New Zealand. I got back last summer."

"Was that a good place to go?"

"The best. Really. I had a great experience down there."

"What are you majoring in?"

He grinned. "Business, I think. Something like that."

"And skiing?"

"I manage to get to the slopes once in a while."

"Once in a while each week?"

"Well . . . yeah. I might skip a class now and then, but I missed two ski seasons. I have to get my legs back."

Diane was starting to get the picture. "You don't have the slightest idea what you're going to do with your life, do you?" she said.

He colored a little, and he laughed. Then he ran his fingers through his hair the way Troy Donahue had always done in the movies Diane loved when she was a teenager. "I have some things in mind," he said. "I just haven't decided on a major."

"Well, I have to get back to work."

"Hey, my name's Dave Doxey."

"I knew Lois Doxey in high school. Is she your big sister?"

"Yeah, she is. So uh . . ."

Diane knew what was coming. "I'll see you, Dave. It was nice to talk to you."

"Hey, wait a sec. I was just thinking. We've got Snow Carnival coming up. Would you maybe think about going to the Snow Ball with me? Maybe you're going out with someone already, but—"

"Could I bring my daughter along?"

"What?"

Diane knew she had no reason to be angry with the poor guy, but she found him irritating, and she couldn't resist saying, "I have a little girl. She's a year old. But that doesn't bother you, does it?"

"Really? You have a baby?"

"I was married for a while, Dave. Now I'm not. Some guys don't like to date divorced women, but I'm sure that makes no difference to you. After all, I'm the Holy Grail."

"Hey, I was just . . . you know . . . talking about high school."

"But you're thinking this whole thing over now, aren't you? You're not so sure you want to take me to the big dance after all."

"It's not that. I just . . ."

"It's just what?"

"I don't get what's going on. I didn't say anything, and now you're all over me."

She stepped closer to him and put her hand on his shoulder. She exaggerated the cute, flirty voice she had once known how to use. "I'm sorry, Dave. I didn't mean to hurt your feelings. So what do you think? Do you still want to take me to the dance?"

But he couldn't come up with an answer. He stammered a couple of times but nothing resembling a word came out of his mouth.

"I didn't think so. Well, that's all right. My divorce isn't final. So that would be a problem anyway. But I'm sure you'll call me, once you know I'm really free. Check back with me, okay?"

He still didn't speak, so she simply turned and walked away. She went to the kitchen and got some clean water, then stalled for a time before she walked back out. By then, he was gone. Diane told herself to feel triumphant. She had put the guy in his place. He was a superficial *boy* who had no idea what he wanted out of life—except to ski—and he was scared of a divorcée. The only trouble was, she didn't feel triumphant. She felt as though he had put *her* down.

When Diane stopped by her mother's house to pick up Jennifer, she was still feeling subdued by what had happened. But she didn't want to feel that way, so she told her mother, "Guess what? A guy tried to ask me out today."

Diane was holding Jenny, who was clinging to her, obviously happy to have her home after being gone all day. Bobbi had gathered together bottles and pacifiers and toys, and she was standing by the kitchen table, placing them in Jennifer's diaper bag. "Did you tell him your divorce wasn't final?"

"Well, yeah. But I told him a few other things first." And then she rehearsed the story of what she had said to him.

Bobbi laughed, and she changed the subject for a time. She talked about Jennifer not taking much of a nap and what she had done about the diaper rash Jennifer was getting, but after a time, she said, "Diane, I hope you won't scare off every guy who shows some interest in you. Sooner or later, it would be nice to find someone. I've told you, the most important thing is to get your own life going for now, but I still think it would be nice for Jenny to have a father, and for you to have someone in your life."

"Mom, these college guys are checking out the freshman girls. They don't want *used property*. This guy today lost all the color in his face the instant I mentioned I'd been married."

"Maybe that happens sometimes. But if he had gotten to know you—before you ran him off—maybe he would like Jenny and could handle a situation like that."

"Not this guy. He's making up for his lost skiing time. His major is 'business, or something like that.'"

"Okay. Maybe he's not what you're looking for. I'm just saying, you can't assume that every man you meet is opposed to marrying someone who's been married."

"I know. But the young guys are like that. They're my age, more or less, but they don't want to marry someone who's already got a child, and I know they don't like the idea that I've been married to someone else. I don't blame them, really. When I meet a guy who's divorced, the first thing I ask myself is why his marriage didn't work out. Maybe it was his fault."

Bobbi motioned toward the table. "Sit down for a minute. Do you want something to drink?"

"Mom, I've got to go. I'm all right. Really. I've known for a long time what I'm up against. I can deal with it."

Bobbi smiled at Diane. "So once the divorce is final, you won't scare all the guys away like that?"

But Diane found herself a little annoyed. For all her mom's "modern thinking," she resorted to the values she had grown up with when she dealt with real life. "Mom, there are a few things I know that you don't."

"Like what?"

Diane did sit down. Jennifer squirmed to get off her lap, so Diane let her go. Jennifer walked into the living room where some of the toys that stayed at Grandma's were still on the floor. "There's something far worse than being single, and that's having a bad marriage. I think it's hard for you to imagine what my life was like."

"I'm sure that's true, Diane."

"I'm not going to throw myself at guys this time—and hunt down anyone who will have me. If I meet someone who loves me for who I am—and someone who can accept Jenny—that might work, but I'm going to get to know him very well before I take a chance. I have the feeling that there are lots more like Greg out there, and maybe not so many like Dad."

"I'm not sure about that, Di, but I don't think it works to turn into a man-hater, either. There's so much of that going on these days. I listen to what the women's liberation movement is saying, and I agree with some of it, but sometimes they make men sound like the enemy."

"I don't feel that way. But I want a guy who has some substance to him—who can think about something besides what clothes he wears or what kind of car he'd like to drive."

"This is my Diane talking—the girl who used to spend three hours getting ready for a date?"

"Yes. The same Diane." But she was surprised at herself. When had the change taken place? Surely, while she was pregnant, and then a new mother, she was busy and had to learn to get ready quickly when she went to church or attended a function at the law school. But it was more than that. In some ways it was the extreme value Greg had placed on her looks that had made her wish she were nothing special in that way. She had longed to feel loved for other reasons, and she never had.

This fall, as she had begun to find some of her classes interesting, she had started to think about things she had never worried about before. She had asked herself whom she would vote for in the '72 elections. What did she think of Nixon? What did she think about the war and the student protests? What was her opinion of Gloria Steinem, the Black Panthers, labor unions, air pollution, busing kids across town to school—and a thousand other things? She didn't have Greg around to announce to her how she should think about politics and world events. She didn't feel tied to her parents' conclusions either. It was almost as though she were inventing herself, finding her root assumptions, her genuine beliefs and concerns. She also thought a great deal about the kind of world she wanted for Jennifer. A boy who was home from his mission and trying, more than anything, to get his ski legs back was not just unimpressive; he was a kind of joke. Did he even understand what he had done on his mission, what he had taught? Diane had always been religious in the sense that she went to church and tried to do what she was taught. But religion had been expanding for her since those dark days last summer when she had asked herself why the world was being so unfair. She had prayed in a new way lately, had sought answers she had never had to ask before. Now, she prayed with Jennifer each night, and then she prayed carefully, thoughtfully, after Jenny was asleep. She didn't read the scriptures as much as she thought she should—with her life so busy—but she thought about her beliefs a great deal. The questions that came up in her college classes related not just to the meaning of "life" but also *her* life. She hadn't expected to have to start over on herself, from scratch; she would have been content to let a man guide her through most of the decisions and questions she now faced. But given her reality, she found some real satisfaction in thinking for herself, and she didn't want to marry anyone who would try to take that back.

Diane didn't say all that to Bobbi; she didn't have time. But she did say, "Mom, a lot of men can't be happy unless they can think for their wives. You've never had to face that. I don't ever want to again. And I also don't want to be married to some guy who *can't* think. And those guys are everywhere."

Bobbi was grinning. "So this is my daughter—the girl who once asked me what the point was of taking history classes. It was all just stuff that happened a long time ago."

"Hey, come on. I was in junior high."

"High school."

"Okay, but what teenager cares about history?"

"I did. Your cousin Kathy was a nut about history by the time she started high school."

"Okay. So there are aberrations, and you were one. But *normal* teenagers don't care."

"I admit that, but what about Jennifer? Do you want her to care about history and social issues and . . . everything else?"

Diane thought for a few seconds. "I guess I don't want her to be so terribly concerned about things as Kathy was, but I do want her to read, and I want her to find out that it's fun to learn."

"That's what I wanted, Di. And I probably tried way too hard to push things like that at you. That may have been why you rejected those things for such a long time. So what are you going to do, so you get it right?"

"I don't know. I'm not going to tell her how pretty she is all the time—like that's the most important thing in the world. But other people are already telling her. I guess the only other thing I can try to do is talk to her a lot about the ideas I have, tell her about things I read—stuff like that."

"That's what Richard and I did, and you told us those things were boring."

"I know." Diane tried to think of those days, when school had seemed nothing more than a place to meet boys. It worried her that Jennifer would feel the same way. She looked up at her mother and smiled. "At least I learned some values from you two, and they're finally kicking in. It's not like you were wasting your time."

"Wow. That's nice to hear." Bobbi reached across the table and took hold of Diane's hand.

"I was in my biology class yesterday," Diane said. "We were talking about the process that goes on as cells divide and create a life, and I was just amazed by the idea of it. I looked over, and some of the students were all blurry-eyed, and I know they were thinking, 'I wonder what will be on the test,' but I was thinking, 'This is the miracle that happened inside me when God made Jennifer in *my* body.' I had tears in my eyes."

Suddenly Mom had tears in hers. "Strange the way life works," she said. "I know this divorce is tough, but I sure like what's happening to you."

"Yeah. Me too."

"But honey, I still think the happiest thing in life is to share those thoughts and experiences—and miracles—with a partner you love."

"Mom, you don't have to convince me of that. I've watched you and Dad all my life. I know what you mean to each other. But I can't spend my life saying, 'I'll find another man, and then my life can go on.'"

"I believe I told you that last summer."

"You did. But I'm just saying, I know better than you, I think, that I might not find anyone else. But I've got to think about Jennifer, and I've got to find ways to be happy. I won't run every guy off, but I'm not going to encourage anyone who wouldn't be a really great father to my little girl."

"Yeah. I agree."

Jennifer had come back now, and she was pulling at Diane's finger. She wanted to go home. And that's what Diane wanted to do. She needed to spend some time with Jennifer, read to her, and play, and fix her something to eat. And then she had to get Jenny down for the night so she could study. Diane knew already that she would be up late. It was hard, living this kind of schedule, and it was late at night that she felt her loneliness the most, but at least she liked what she was learning, and that was a joy she had only found slowly in her life.

Diane did put in a long night, staying up until past midnight, and then she got up early to get Jennifer ready to go to her mom's house. And it was hard when Jennifer cried. She loved her grandma, but she didn't like to have Diane gone so long each day. That hurt, but Diane knew that Jenny would be fine after a few minutes, and she didn't have a lot of options. She was carrying a heavy load this quarter so she could get finished as soon as possible. She was thinking now that she wanted to get her degree in elementary education so she could teach and be gone from home the same hours that Jenny would be in school. Diane's problem was, she felt as though she had never learned enough of what she had supposedly been taught, and she wouldn't be much of a teacher until she built her knowledge in lots of subjects she had neglected earlier. So she was taking geography and biology and music appreciation—and wasn't yet taking some of the education classes she would need. That might put off her graduation, but she was worried she would look like a fool, even to little kids, if she didn't learn some basics in a lot of areas.

Her geography class was at eight o'clock, every morning. That was one thing she didn't like about the quarter system, that so many classes met daily. But the professor was excellent. The only problem was, he was requiring more papers than she had expected, and he had promised to hand back the first one this morning. That worried her.

Professor Murphy lectured the whole hour and then handed back the papers at the end of the period. By then, Diane had built up a case in her mind that she had done a lousy job. She had never been much of a writer, so she had always hated getting papers back. She waited as he called out names and walked around with the papers, and then she tucked hers into her folder and decided not to look at it until she was alone. But as she was walking from the classroom, Professor Murphy said, "Diane, that was a very thoughtful paper. You're a good writer."

It crossed her mind that he was being sarcastic. No one had ever said that to her—not once in her life. But she thanked him and walked into the hall. Then she stood by the wall, next to the door, and opened the back page of the paper. The grade was an "A," and he had written next to the grade that the paper was well researched and clearly expressed. It was true that she had had her mom read the first draft, and Bobbi had made some suggestions about her organization, but still, there weren't a lot of red marks. She knew what she had done that was different, too. She had written the paper early and then revised it a couple of times. She had read it over, found some spelling mistakes, changed some of the punctuation, and fixed some sentences that didn't make sense, and then she had decided to retype the whole thing. That was something she had never done in the past. But she was standing in the hallway with an A on her paper and a professor had just said that she was a good writer. She wondered why no one was staring at her. Brain cells seemed to be dividing, blossoming inside her head right then and there. Some kind of miracle was happening. She thought of finding a phone and calling her mother, but she realized she didn't have to. It was good enough to hold this for now, just for herself.

Chapter 23

Hans felt as though he had always been waiting. He had feared the *Stasi* long before he had been arrested, and then he had waited such a long time to get out of prison. Now he was waiting for the *Stasi* to pounce again. There was no question in his mind that at certain times he was being followed, and that awareness caused him to believe that he was always being watched. Some agents or informants were simply better than others, he suspected. But he didn't dare employ the tricks he knew to shake an agent loose. That would only imply that he had something to hide. So he got on his streetcar after work, watching, looking around to see who was with him that day, and then, at the bakery, he glanced out the window while he bought bread. And most often he went straight home. He had stopped talking to *Herr* Hartmann at the dairy store; the man's chatter seemed much more dangerous now. He had also stopped taking walks. The pleasure was lost when he felt he was being spied upon the whole time, whether he actually was or not.

But why didn't the *Stasi* strike? What else did the agents want to know? If Rainer was working for them, surely they knew enough to put Hans back in prison. And as far as that went, if that's what they wanted to do, they didn't need a good reason.

Hans had only a few pleasures that gave his life meaning now. His income was meager enough, but since he always hoped to spare some money to take an occasional trip home—or to Magdeburg—he could afford nothing but food and shelter, and the truth was, he spent too little on food. He had learned in prison to get by with little to eat, and he found that a big meal only made him sick, but he also knew that he didn't have enough variety in his diet, simply because fruit was so expensive and he relied too much on bread to fill him up. Still, what could he do if he wanted to see his family once in a while—and Elli?

Hans did have his scriptures, and he had his Sunday School calling in the Church. He had his friends at church, too, and without those families he hardly knew what would keep him going. But his best pleasure—and greatest pain—came from Elli's letters. She wrote him two or three times a week, and he wrote her just as often, but he never read one of her letters or wrote one back to her without feeling that he was doing the wrong thing. He knew they had pledged themselves to one another, but she was too young to make such a promise. The circumstances of their lives might cause her to regret these years she was giving to him. She should be meeting other young men in the Church all across the GDR, and finding someone who was a better prospect for her. All the same, he loved the letters, loved the affection she expressed, and in spite of himself, expressed his own feelings for her.

And he imagined. He pictured a day when he and Elli would be together all the time. He dreamed that he could somehow manage to make a better living, provide for her, and they would have children and be able to give them the things they needed. As a boy, he had hoped for prestige and importance, but now he hoped only for basic pleasures: a family, a chance to serve in the Church, the opening of a few more opportunities. And he wanted to be left alone, not watched and suspected all his life. Fantasies slipped into his mind at times. He pictured a day when there would be no wall, no fences, and people in his country could travel as other people did. He imagined a day when Latter-day Saints would be allowed to go to a temple for their endowments. He even pictured himself being sealed to Elli. But those were things better not to dwell upon. He felt sure the Lord would bless his people for their hard work and loyalty to the Church, but such doors were not likely to open for a long time, probably not in his lifetime.

Still, Hans tried to trust that things would work out for him someday. He knew that hope was a principle of the gospel, part of faith, and that it was right to hope for good things, to trust that the Lord would look after him. But he had gone through too many years of disappointment, when his hope was always dashed and proved a kind of enemy. He told himself to pray to learn the things he needed to learn and to use his challenges for growth, but he never promised himself a quick answer to his problems or even a major change in this life. God would have to decide what was best. Hans knew how proud he had been as a young man. Maybe it was better not to have too many things go well. Maybe that same pride was still in him and would come back if his conditions changed. He told himself to settle for this routine, to find joy where he could: in his Sunday meetings, in his love of the members, and in his minor accomplishments. He was just thankful that Elli was now in his life and was willing to put her trust in him.

Then one night in February Hans came home from work to find Rainer standing outside his apartment door. This was the last thing Hans wanted. He could only get himself in bigger trouble, talking to Rainer again.

"Oh, Hans, God be thanked you have come home," Rainer said, speaking almost in a whisper. "I've been freezing in this hallway."

"Rainer, you shouldn't come here. I've been followed lately. Someone probably knows you're here—or will see you leave."

"I had nowhere else to go, Hans. I'm hiding out. The *Stasi* is looking for me."

Hans felt his hope drain away. He was caught, either way. If Rainer was telling the truth, Hans should have nothing to do with him. If he was lying, and was actually here to seduce him into a mistake—to please some *Stasi* agent—that was even worse.

"Hans, could I come in, at least for a few minutes? I need to get warm." Hans couldn't send him away so cold, no matter what was going on. So he unlocked the door and let Rainer in. But once inside, Rainer said, "Hans, if you could let me stay here only a few nights, maybe just two or three, I could make some contacts, and then I would leave you alone."

"I don't understand, Rainer. What hope do you have to hide from the *Stasi?*" He walked toward the stove in his little room. "Come over here. I'll stoke up the fire and put in a little coal."

"Oh, thanks, Hans. You're the only friend I still have. I appreciate that you would let me in." He walked over and stood close to the little cookstove while Hans stirred the embers, added some kindling, then put in the coal—two lumps for the evening.

"I know it's not possible to hide for long," Rainer said. "My only hope is to get out of the country. But I'm working on that. I'm just stalling while I get some papers made, and then I'll be heading into Poland. I have a plan. People have gotten out that way, and I'm going to do it too. I'm working with people who know what they're doing."

"I don't understand what's going on, Rainer. Why did the *Stasi* let you go, and why are they chasing you again?"

"They suspected me before, but they didn't have any proof."

Hans wasn't at all sure he believed that. He doubted that the *Stasi* cared much about "proof." "So what's happened now?" he asked.

"I had to make many contacts, trying to find someone who could make papers for me. You know how it is in this country. Everyone is a potential informant. I came home one day and saw an agent waiting down the street, watching my apartment. They're such fools. They think we don't recognize them, but they all look alike."

"Actually, they don't. The smart ones are very hard to detect."

"What's been going on, Hans? Are you sure they're trailing you?"

"Yes. And I think half the reason is that you came here before. If they're chasing you, they're watching me. I can assure you of that."

"I'm sorry, Hans. You're the only person I could turn to. I could have gone to Elli's family, but I didn't want to cause trouble for them, either."

Hans sat down at the table. He knew that any minute a knock could come at the door and agents would not only arrest Rainer but take in Hans, too. This was clearly a conspiracy from the *Stasi's* point of view. Rainer was trying to get papers, and the two had seen each other twice lately. What more evidence would they need? Hans could see already that he would be going back to prison. "Rainer, listen to me," Hans said. "It may be too late, but if you care anything at all about me, please leave now. You would be better off in a hotel or in some back alley than here. This is the last place in the GDR you should have come to."

"I know that, Hans, but I've saved enough money to make my escape, with nothing to spare. I spent some money getting here, and I'll need everything I have to get to my contact in Poland—and to pay him. I can't stay in an alley, not in this cold."

But Hans's suspicions were only deepening. Too many things about this story didn't make sense.

"If I can stay just one night, I'll figure things out tomorrow. But I don't know what to do tonight."

Hans was almost sure what was going on. He stood, and he looked at Rainer, stared him down for a time before he said, "When will the agent knock on my door? I would think you have given him enough time by now. All he has to do is say you were here. It shouldn't be necessary to prove that you stayed the night."

"What are you saying, Hans?"

"You know very well what I'm saying."

"But how can you? I wouldn't do that to you."

Hans sat down again. He placed his elbows on the table and leaned over. He saw what was coming, and it broke his heart. Prison life would be terrible again, and any hope for a life with Elli would be gone, but the thought that Rainer would do this to him was what pained him the most, at least for the moment. "Rainer, no one runs from the *Stasi*. It doesn't work, and you know it. And you aren't stupid enough to ask *many* people—as you claim—about identification papers. Added to that, why would you come here? You know this is the place they would watch. Why would you spend your sparse money to go in the wrong direction and then return? I don't believe that or anything else you've told me."

Rainer approached, placed his hands on the table, and then leaned forward. "I admit, Hans, I've been sloppy. I'm not as smart as you are. I always think I can manage things, but I make mistakes when I try to deceive anyone. I've always been open and honest with people, and I don't know how to behave any other way. I don't know what else to tell you. I'm your friend, and I'm asking you to trust me."

Hans tried to measure the words. Was there any chance they were true? Rainer certainly sounded sincere. But the facts came back at Hans far too powerfully. "Rainer, when I was in prison, *Herr* Felscher, my interrogator, wanted me to report on you—to tell him I had admitted my part in Berndt's escape to you. He claimed you had already admitted to knowing about my involvement, and I suspected that might be true. But you and I had made a promise, so I kept it. I said I had told you nothing. Felscher didn't believe me, but he never could break me down and get me to say anything against you. Then, after you came here last time, an agent came to the office where I work. He accused me of being involved in a conspiracy to help you and Elli escape the country. I told him that you had only come to pay a visit as a friend." Hans waited until Rainer finally looked him in the eye. "Rainer, I've lied for you many times, and I did it because of our promise. Now I suspect that you were working against me from the beginning: when we were roommates, when you were visiting Elli while I was in prison, and since I've been in Leipzig."

Hans saw the change in Rainer, saw how ashamed he looked. He straightened up and walked back to the stove. He stood with his back to the fire, his hands behind him, and he didn't speak for a long time, as though he were considering what he should do. Finally, he said, "Hans, I've lied to you this time—today—but not before that. I always told them when you were in prison that you hadn't said a word to me."

"You saved yourself by saying that. If you admitted to anything, they would want to know why you hadn't said something sooner."

"Yes. But it was also our promise. They worked very hard on me, and gave me promises, but—"

"You're not stupid enough to accept their promises."

"*Ja,* that's true—in part. I admit I'm not as good a person as you. But when I came here last time, they followed me, and they told me they knew I was trying to leave the country. They were certain you were involved, at least in helping me. I denied that, too."

"What else could you do?"

"Nothing, perhaps, but they promised to help me, to let the suspicions against me drop if I told them anything that could put you back in prison. All they wanted to know was something you had said against the government, or to claim that you said something about your time in prison, perhaps denouncing your treatment. I told them you were a loyal citizen and there was no reason to mistrust you." Rainer stepped to the table and set his hand on the Bible Hans kept there. "That is the truth, Hans. I swear it."

"Don't do this, Rainer. You don't believe in the Bible. That's only more of your deception."

"But I do. I'm not a Communist now, Hans. I'm going to join your church."

"You could have done that long ago."

"I know. And I was frightened to take the step. But now I would do it—if I could."

"What does that mean?"

"Hans, an agent *is* waiting outside. But he isn't coming in. He wants me to stay at least a night. That way you are protecting a fugitive of the government."

"So you're saying that you kept your promise until now?"

"Yes."

"Why should I believe that?"

"It doesn't matter whether you do or not. I'll leave now, and I'll tell the agent that you wouldn't let me stay overnight. I'll tell him that you told me to give myself up, that it's wrong to hide out, and it's wrong to try to escape the country."

Hans stared at Rainer. Maybe he shouldn't believe any of this, but he did. "What will happen to you, Rainer?"

"You know what will happen. I'm going to prison. The first time I was arrested, the *Stasi* only questioned me—mostly about you. They knew I had tried to buy false papers, but I'm sure they wanted to prove you were part of my plan. That's why they let me go—so they could track both of us and see whether we met somewhere. When they picked me up again, they told me that if I helped them make a case against you, that would prove my loyalty, and they would give me a lighter sentence." Rainer wouldn't look at Hans now. He stared across the room. "I was scared about prison, so I said I would help them. I'm a weak person, Hans. I'm humiliated to admit what I was trying to do to you. I told myself that you probably informed on me, and that was why they let you out, but I didn't really believe it. It's just my weakness."

"Don't you see what they've done?" Hans said. "They've used us against each other, and we've both lost. It's the way it always works. This government cares nothing about the loyalty of one citizen to another—but only to the state itself."

"Don't say things like that. They'll do everything to get me to say that you talked that way. I'm going to leave now, and I only hope I won't weaken again and say things they want to hear."

"You won't do that."

"You don't know that, Hans. I'm not a good person—not the way you are."

"But look what you're doing for me. You could have turned me in and improved your situation."

"Or so they told me. The truth is, they might have used the information against you but then done nothing for me. It's exactly what I would expect of the *Stasi*."

"Maybe. But I don't believe you're a bad man, Rainer. If they put you in prison, use the time to grow. I read my scriptures constantly, when they let me have them, and that changed me more than anything else could have. I'll do what I can for you, Rainer—always. Maybe we'll end up serving in the Church together."

"I don't know, Hans. I doubt I have the strength to do what you did." He reached and placed his hand on Hans's shoulder. "But it's time for me to go."

"What can I do?" Hans asked.

"Pray for me. I'm going to try to be strong. But don't write to me. It would look bad for you if you kept contact with me—even if they were to read your letters and you were careful what you said."

"I don't care. I will write to you. But don't expect all the letters to reach you. They'll try to break you, Rainer. And they have lots of methods. The important thing is to know who you are. Stay true to that."

Rainer smiled. "If I ever find out who I am, I will."

"This might be the time, Rainer. It's harder than anything you've done before—much harder—but you'll learn to pray, and learn to live on your own, with only God to get you through."

Rainer walked to the door, but he stopped there and turned back. "Elli never would have married me," he said. "She was always in love with you. You need to know that."

"Thank you." Hans walked to him, and the two embraced. "I feel like

I'm turning you over to them, Rainer. I wish there was something I could do."

"You shouldn't worry. I got myself in trouble. I never should have brought you into this. I'll tell them that you were upset with me for coming here, that you are trying to prove yourself a good citizen, and my visit only makes you look bad."

"They won't believe it. They'll stay after me."

"Maybe. But they won't have anything to use against you."

Rainer patted Hans on the shoulder again, and then Rainer opened the door and stepped out. "Tell Elli that I love her. And tell her she was right—she should be with you." He shut the door.

Hans felt horrible. He went back to his table, sat down again, and waited. He still wasn't sure. No matter what Rainer told the *Stasi*, someone still might come after him. Agents could easily build something out of the connection between him and Rainer. They could assume a conspiracy even though Rainer hadn't stayed long. And of course, it was always possible that Rainer was still lying. Hans had made a statement against the government; maybe that had given Rainer what he needed.

For the better part of an hour, Hans didn't eat, hardly moved. He was listening for a sound on the stairs, but the sound didn't come. So finally he ate, and then he tried to spend some time preparing his lesson for Sunday, but he had a terrible time concentrating. When he went to bed, he didn't sleep well. He thought of Rainer and what he would have to face now. Rainer wasn't as weak as he thought he was, but it was hard to imagine that he would hold up well in prison. Hans also thought of the possibility that an agent would be at his door in the morning. He sometimes thought now that he couldn't start over in prison, that he would break emotionally if he had to pass through such hard days again. What he longed for was some assurance that the possibility wouldn't hang over his head forever.

But in the morning no one appeared, so Hans ate a bit of breakfast and took his usual streetcar to work. The morning passed as usual, with a large load of work to do—but nothing that he found interesting. Shortly after lunch, however, *Herr* Meier called Hans to his office. Hans worried that a *Stasi* agent, perhaps Feist, had come in without his noticing. But Meier was in his office alone, and he seemed pleased about something. He told Hans to sit down. "How is your work going?" Meier asked.

"Not bad. I may need to stay a little late tonight to complete the project I'm working on, but it's almost finished."

"You do more work than anyone else in this office, Hans. I depend on you too much. I hope you don't feel overworked."

There were times when Hans did feel that, but it was not a thing to say. "I'm doing fine," he said instead.

"I wonder how things are for you. You work very hard, but you have little to show for it. That must be discouraging to you."

"Yes, of course. But I'm not in prison. And I was able to visit my family at Christmas. These are things that mean much to me."

"You are involved in your church, too, I understand."

"Yes." Hans had actually never discussed his church affiliation with *Herr* Meier. But he often noticed that Meier knew more about him than the two had ever discussed. Hans knew that Meier had been briefed by *Stasi* agents, probably told what to watch for.

"Is this a help to you, the church you attend?"

Hans had no idea what this was all about, but *Herr* Meier still seemed in a pleasant mood, as though he were about to announce something Hans would like. "I have good friends at my church," he said. "They are a support to me."

"And what is the attitude of these church friends about our government? They don't discourage your loyalty, do they?"

"No. We are taught to honor the law and to be good citizens."

"Don't they tell you that our government is godless—an enemy to religious people?"

"We don't talk about political matters at church. We talk about living a good life and serving others."

"Hans, I have no respect for religion. I think it is superstition and nonsense. But I must say, there is something about you that is right. I don't know what you actually think of our government, but I watch you day after day do your work and do it with excellence, and never once have I heard you say anything or seen you do anything that isn't exemplary. You treat people well, and you accept my assignments with goodwill, even though I know you are capable of much more sophisticated work."

"Thank you, *Herr* Meier."

"I have the feeling that you're trying to prove yourself and show your government that you're worthy of trust."

"Yes. That's true."

Herr Meier laced his fingers together and set both hands on the desk in front of him. He had begun to smile. "Some months ago, I requested that you be given an expanded opportunity. I asked Party officials to let me move you to another office, one where you would be able to use your ability more fully. I received no answer from them, even though I renewed my request last month. Then this morning I received a telephone call. Your promotion has been approved."

Hans thought of Rainer. He must have done what he had promised. The *Stasi* must have felt that Hans had passed some sort of test. But at what cost? Hans wondered what was happening to Rainer now. Those early days in prison had been so frightening to Hans.

"You will have much more responsibility, Hans, and more challenging work. But I think you will like that."

"Yes, I will."

"You don't seem very happy about this."

"I am, *Herr* Meier. I am." But he was still thinking about Rainer.

"Aren't you going to ask me the other question?"

"What question?"

"About your salary."

"Will it change?"

"Yes, of course. You'll be raised by almost fifty percent. I know that isn't much, considering the work you'll be doing, but it opens a door. There might be other raises—modest ones, but each one can help."

"That's wonderful news, *Herr* Meier," Hans said, but he still wasn't feeling it. He was remembering the cell in *Hohenschönhausen* prison, where he had first sat alone and wondered how he could last a night, let alone months or years. He was remembering the strain of having to sit on a stiff chair, with nothing to do. And he was thinking of the food, of the cold, of the frightening interrogations.

"I'm sorry to lose you in my office, Hans. I won't find anyone as good to replace you. But I am happy for you. You deserve this opportunity. Finish the project you are working on today and then rest for a day. Just stay home. Monday you will start your work in *Herr* Köhler's office upstairs. I'll take you up later today to make his acquaintance."

Hans thanked Meier again, and then he went back to his work. This was what he had wanted for so long—not just the raise and the better work but the hope that further raises could come, that he might be able to think about marriage. His status hadn't actually improved all that much. He would still be making far less than his father, and his father, with Mother working too, only managed a humble life. But this was hope, and on any other day it would have excited him. But it felt as though he had moved ahead at Rainer's expense, and that was not easy to live with.

He worked hard that day and finished his project. He used the next day to sleep a little extra and to prepare the Sunday School lesson he hadn't finished the night before. He also wrote a letter to Elli. He didn't mention Rainer. Hans didn't know whether the *Stasi* intercepted his letters to Elli. He had never noticed any sign that they did, but he wasn't about to say something damaging in writing. Elli's house could be searched for some reason—or for no reason—and he could incriminate himself. What he did tell Elli was that a glimmer of hope had appeared in his life. He didn't want to make too much of his good news since Elli would do that on her own, but he knew this would be, in her mind, an answer to her prayers, a confirmation of her trust that the Lord was going to open a way for them. What he would tell her about Rainer, when he saw her, would hurt her, however. Maybe she would have never married Rainer, but she had at least considered the possibility at one time, and Rainer had certainly been a close friend.

Hans hoped for the future too, but he hated what he'd had to do to move ahead. What he had told Meier was not untrue. Mormons *were* careful about what they said about the government, especially at church. They *did* honor the law, and they *did* try to be good citizens. But what Hans had held back was his belief that his government was deeply evil. Rainer was a good young man; all he had wanted was the freedom to make his own choices. A government that didn't respect that right didn't deserve his allegiance, and yet he'd had to imply his loyalty to Meier, and he felt compromised—guilty—for having done it.

CHAPTER 24

Gene was on an airplane, this time with his wife next to him, holding his hand. But the trip wasn't easy. It was April now, 1971, and he had spent almost six months in the Walter Reed Army Hospital. Since Christmas he had gone through two more surgeries. He now had a colostomy bag on the side of his lower abdomen—which he hated—and was able to eat some foods, but he had lost so much weight he hardly recognized himself when he looked in a mirror, and his muscles were so weak, it tired him to walk very far. He had been pushed to the airplane gate in a wheelchair, but with Emily holding one of his arms, he had managed to walk across the tarmac, up the stairs into the airplane and down the aisle. Anna was right behind, carrying Danny. Gene was self-conscious about all this. He knew he looked like the pictures he had seen of Uncle Wally when he had first come home from the war—thin and pale and hollow-eyed.

Emily moved into a row of three seats and then tried to help Gene into the aisle seat. But Gene glanced at the young man sitting by the window, a fellow with hair down to his shoulders and wire-rimmed glasses. He reminded Gene of John Lennon, the way he was looking lately. "I can do it," Gene said, and he used his arm strength, which had remained in decent shape, to lower himself into the seat. He was breathing hard but trying not to be heard. He just wanted to blend in and not be noticed again now that he had made it that far.

Anna had the seat across the aisle, with Danny next to her. Emily looked across at Anna and said, "I'll trade off with you after a while, Mom. I know Danny's going to get restless."

"He'll be fine," Anna said. "He almost fell asleep in the car, and I kept him awake. I think he'll drop off pretty fast now." Danny had had his second birthday just the week before. He was talking more all the time, but he was a busy little boy, and sometimes it was difficult for Gene to be around him. At least he knew his daddy now, and during the better times in the hospital, Gene had been able to play with him a little.

Gene was glad to be going home. He had longed all winter for the day that would happen. Emily had stayed the whole time with Gene's parents and had come to the hospital almost daily. She had been a boost to him, but he knew he hadn't always treated her well. All too often he had taken his frustrations out on her, and she had occasionally responded with some harsh words of her own, but overall she had been remarkably patient with him, and he did appreciate that. What Gene hoped now was that life could gradually get back to normal, even though he still had a long way to go. He shut his eyes and tried to rest. His last surgery had been five weeks before, and except for the final one, in which his intestines would be reattached so he would have a normal digestive track—more or less—that was supposed to be the last. That all sounded hopeful, but he felt so battered down that it was hard to think he would ever feel truly healthy again. "Do you need a pain pill?" he heard Emily ask.

"Not yet." Gene had come to feel that pain was merely part of him now, as normal as the touch of air on his skin. He could handle lots of it. What he still hated was the blurry, unfocused feeling in his brain when he took pain medication, so he took as little as possible and told himself the pain wasn't all that bad. But he was grouchy much of the time. He knew he had said things that hurt Emily, and that was not like him, but he often felt a sense that no one understood what he was experiencing, and even more, a simmering anger that he didn't know how to direct. It seemed, especially in the logic that extended from his pain, that someone should be to blame for all this. He didn't know why he deserved to pass through so much, and he wanted to tell someone it wasn't fair. But there was no one to tell. He prayed almost constantly for help and mercy; he couldn't blame God. He had vented his feelings about the war many times, but that was like screaming into the wind. Very few people seemed to believe in the war anymore, so what he got mostly, even from army doctors, was agreement.

But he was going home. He would live in his family home again, and he would try to spend more time with Danny. The doctors were saying he could go for walks and start to rebuild his strength. Then, in another few months, he would have the final operation, and a few more months after that he would begin to feel somewhat normal. Gene told himself the worst was behind him. Maybe by fall he could return to college and get his life going again. The problem was, he didn't know how to think about normal life. He hadn't seen it for almost two years. He tried to think about grad school or law school. He asked himself what he wanted to do, but the options didn't seem real to him. He couldn't imagine that he would ever feel strong and clear enough again to sit at a desk and study, hour after hour. It was hard to believe that his powers of concentration would return, that he could ever feel healthy enough to move about the way he once had. He would sometimes lie in bed and try to remember what it was like to feel strong and whole—the way he had felt when he played football and basketball back in high school. He could remember games—plays, scores—and he could remember some of the pleasures. What he couldn't remember was how his body had felt. He hadn't been conscious then of his own power and mobility. He hadn't known it was something special to burst ahead, suddenly, effortlessly, and drive his shoulder into a player, or make a fake and cut away from a tackler. It was all quite miraculous now to imagine and at the same time painful to think that he would never again have a body that could react that way. Doctors assured him that he would get much of that back, that he could play basketball again someday, but his body was telling him he would always be something of an invalid.

"Do you live in Salt Lake?" Gene heard Emily ask the young man by the window. Gene didn't open his eyes.

The man laughed for some reason. "Oh, no. I'm just changing airplanes there. I'm going on to Los Angeles. I go to UCLA."

"What are you studying?"

"I'm a grad student in anthropology. I've spent a couple of months in South America working on a research project for my dissertation. I was way up in the Andes living with the people in little villages most of the time."

"Oh, wow. That must have been interesting."

"Yeah. It was. I hated to come back. Now I have to start the writing, and that's not the fun part."

He laughed easily, sounded comfortable. But it was strangely jarring to Gene to remember that people were free to travel around, do research, work on their degrees. Gene wondered how the guy had avoided Vietnam. Maybe he had gotten into grad school before the deferments were dropped. Or maybe he faked some problems on his physical. A doctor at Walter Reed had told Gene about guys who had asked doctors who were friends of the family to write letters that said they had allergies or bad backs. Or guys would purposely lose or gain a whole lot of weight so they didn't fit the requirements. The doctor claimed that some guys would even injure themselves—break a bone or stare at the sun and ruin their vision. Or they would breathe a lot of dust and bring on an asthma attack. Something like five million men had been rejected by the military during the war, and a lot of them had actually found ways to make sure they failed.

Gene didn't know how to feel about that. Maybe they were right. Maybe it was what he should have done. But he couldn't have done it back then, and he couldn't do it now, even knowing what he knew about the war. All he could think was that soldiers were still over there, and every day they were going down, getting themselves killed or mutilated, and this UCLA guy was flying off to South America to hang out in mountain villages.

"So do you live in Salt Lake City?" the student asked.

"Yes. We're going home."

"My name's Jeff, by the way."

This guy was obviously more than happy to chat with such a pretty woman. Hadn't he even noticed that Gene was there?

"My name's Emily, and this is my husband, Gene."

Gene opened his eyes and lifted his head enough to look at the guy. He tried to tell himself that it didn't matter how long his hair was, but Gene still hated that look. Jeff hadn't shaved, either, but he couldn't produce much of anything that could be called a beard. He was reaching out his hand, so Gene did too, but crossing his body that way, twisting to reach, was painful. He tried not to show that. He was wearing slacks and a shirt, and a jacket. The colostomy bag didn't show, but he was always conscious of moving with the thing on his side. Sometimes gas from his body passed into the bag and put out a smell. There was nothing Gene could do to stop that. "Nice to meet you," he said, and then he let his head drop back to the seat.

"I took an anthropology class at the University of Utah," Emily said. "I found it really interesting."

Gene understood what she was doing. She wanted to keep this Jeff guy from asking Gene a lot of questions. She was protecting him, and she was right that Gene didn't want to talk to the man, but he was bothered that she would be so willing to converse with someone like that. Gene wished she would pick up a magazine and say nothing more.

But she was telling Jeff, "I was a sociology major, so I'm interested in some of the same things you probably studied."

"What are you doing with your sociology degree?" Jeff asked, and he laughed.

"Actually, I haven't finished my degree yet. I have a few hours left.

But right now I'm being a mom. That's my little boy over there. He's with his grandma." Gene glanced over and saw that Danny was looking at a book with Anna.

"So aren't you going to finish?"

"Oh, yes. I plan to. In fact, I'd like to do graduate work. There's not much I can do with an undergrad degree in sociology."

"Hey, there's not much you can do with a doctorate these days. At least while I'm a grad student I can work as a teaching assistant and bring in a little money. I don't know whether I'll even find a job when I'm finished."

Poor guy, Gene was thinking. Maybe he could sign up with the army. There should be some openings there.

"What do you do?" Jeff was asking, and it took a moment for Gene to realize that Jeff was speaking to him.

Gene opened his eyes again. He tried to decide on an answer. Emily took the chance to say, "He graduated in business, but he wants to go back to school. He's considering law school."

"Sometimes I think that's what I should have done," Jeff said. "I was at Berkeley when the free-speech movement was all ablaze. We considered lawyers the lowest form of scum. But all us revolutionaries are trying to find a way to make a living now. Reality has set in." He laughed, his voice rising girlishly.

Gene was still looking at Jeff, trying to think whether he should say anything.

"Are you okay?" Jeff asked. "You look really tired."

Emily began to answer, but Gene cut her off. "I've been in a hospital for almost half a year. I've had a whole series of operations. But I'm going home now. I'm glad for that."

Gene was surprised at himself. He wanted to be normal, sound normal, make this guy think that nothing too serious was going on.

"What happened to you?"

"He was shot in the abdomen. He was in Vietnam."

"Oh."

And now a silence set in. Gene watched Jeff, saw how he let his eyes disengage. He clearly didn't know what to say.

"It's been a terrible time for him—for both of us—but he's going to be all right."

"Good. I'm glad to hear that." Jeff reached under the seat in front of him. He pulled out a briefcase and looked into it. Then he pulled out a book. He settled back into his seat. But he seemed to feel the need to end the conversation. "Well, I'm sorry you had to go through something like that."

"Vietnam or getting shot?" Gene asked. He didn't know why he was doing this, but he wanted to make the guy nervous. The truth was, Gene's view of Vietnam was probably not so different from Jeff's, at this point, but he knew what "movement" guys thought of men who had been willing to serve.

"Both, I guess. I'm sure it was hard for the soldiers."

"I didn't kill any babies, in case you're wondering."

Jeff had brought the book up, but now he dropped it to his lap. "Look, I'm opposed to the war, and I was lucky enough that I didn't have to get involved, but I don't blame the war on the guys who did have to go. A lot of my friends would say you should have gone to Canada, or gone to jail, rather than go over there, but that's a hard question, and everyone has to answer it for himself."

"What would you have done?"

Jeff thought for a time. "I don't know. I didn't get drafted, so I didn't have to decide. But I guess I would have sought conscientious objector status, and I tell myself sometimes that if I hadn't been granted a CO, I would have refused and gone to jail. But I don't know. You had to decide and I didn't."

"I went willingly. I went because I believed in the war."

Gene watched Jeff's face harden. "Well, then," he said, "maybe you got what you deserved."

Gene had an impulse to reach across and grab Jeff, then pound his face until it was bloody. How could the guy think such a thing, let alone say it? What human being *deserved* what Gene had been through? He thought of the nightmare called war, and what he had had to do. Had he deserved that, too? But Gene held back everything he wanted to scream at the guy and only said, "You don't know what you're talking about. You can't."

Gene rolled his head back and shut his eyes. He felt the tears forcing their way out through his lids, and he heard Emily say, "At the time, he just felt that he was being loyal to his country."

"Yeah, well, I never did buy into that. Kill for Nixon. Wave the flag while you drop the napalm."

"You don't know my husband, Jeff. You don't know what the war cost him. It's not fair to say that."

Gene was trying with all his strength not to cry. But all he could think was that he *had* killed. He *had* killed. He had been trying all winter to get those images out of his head, but they didn't go away. So maybe Jeff, the grad student, was right.

But Jeff was saying, "Look, you're right. I don't know him. And I'm sorry about that crack about him deserving what he got. No one deserves a bullet in the gut. But I wish all of us would think a lot more carefully before we jump on the bandwagon for these wars our government thinks up. Sooner or later, we've got to find some other answer, better than war."

Gene had thought that a thousand times in the past few months. He had tried to think whether the world would ever come to that point. But he still knew that Jeff was talking about a world he didn't know and people he would never understand. It was all an abstract question to him. For a lot of men, it was the formative experience of their lives, and whatever Jeff thought, they had gone to Vietnam because they thought it was their duty.

Gene didn't speak again to Jeff, and Emily didn't say much. The plane stopped in Chicago, but Gene and Emily didn't get off. Gene finally took a pain pill, and it knocked him out. He slept most of the way home and woke up groggy. But he made a special effort, on landing, to walk from the airplane under his own strength. The problem was, he was tired beyond belief, and his dream of coming home, the one he had imagined so long, offered him little joy. He just wanted to get to a bed.

He was glad that only his dad, who'd had to fly to Utah a few days earlier, had come to the airport. Gene greeted Alex without saying a lot. He was mostly happy to see that he had arranged for another wheelchair. What worried Gene was that people would recognize "the Congressman" and collect around him. Then there would only be more questions. But Alex helped Gene into the wheelchair and then crouched in front of him. "How are you holding up?" he asked.

"I just want to get home," Gene said.

"Okay. We'll get you there as fast as we can. We've told the family to wait a couple of days before they come to visit. I know this flight has been tough on you."

"I'm okay, Dad. I'm just tired." But his voice said more than his words, and he knew it. He *was* tired, and pain was filling his head, but he was feeling lots of other things. Home had been a picture in his mind, but his arrival, when he had imagined it, had always happened after he was starting to feel like himself again, but he was far from getting to that point. He had felt depressed all winter, but he suddenly felt overwhelmed with discouragement.

Just as the airline representative was about to push Gene forward, Jeff came by. He stopped and bent over, and he placed his arm on Gene's shoulder. "Hey, I just want to say again, I'm sorry. I've been pretty negative about the soldiers who went over there, but I've had a stereotype in my head—and that isn't fair. I can see what you've been through, and I wouldn't wish that on anyone."

Gene didn't know what to say. He was too tired. So he just nodded, and then he felt a surge of pain through his body at the sudden movement of the wheelchair. But the guy pushing him couldn't have known.

The little group moved through the airport, Alex now carrying Danny and greeting a few people along the way but never stopping. Gene refused to make eye contact with anyone, but he knew that people were staring at him. He was the Congressman's wounded son. There had been stories in the local newspapers.

In the next few days Gene saw his grandparents and most of his uncles and aunts. They all showed up at the house to welcome him home and wish him well. He hadn't yet seen Uncle Richard and Aunt Bobbi, from Ogden, or his cousin Diane, who was home now, divorced, but she did call him. "We've both been through a few things, cuz," she said. "None of it is exactly what we had in mind for ourselves." She laughed, and he was glad she could do that. He found himself wanting to talk to her longer.

One of the big difficulties for Gene was that Danny still didn't feel comfortable around him. Gene couldn't get down on the floor and play the way he wanted to, and holding Danny didn't work very well, the way Danny would usually squirm. But Gene had been able to read him some stories, and he came out to the family room sometimes and sat with Danny while he watched *Sesame Street* or some of the other late-afternoon children's shows. Danny would babble about his toys or what was on television, but half the time Gene didn't understand him. Still, it felt good to be with him, and he really was a good-tempered little boy.

Alex and Anna stayed for a few days, but they had to get back to Washington. On the night before they left, Alex found Gene in the family room. Gene was sitting in his dad's chair; it reclined, and that felt better than anything that forced him to sit up straight. "Son," Alex said, "I want to talk to you about a couple of things before we leave."

"Sure," Gene said. "Turn the TV off. I wasn't really watching it."

"Are you catching up a little on your rest now?" his dad asked.

"I guess. I'm not as tired as I was when we got here. But I'm not sleeping very well."

"Are you having bad dreams?" Alex had sat down on the couch across from Gene; he didn't look relaxed. Gene could tell that something more than a casual conversation was coming, but he didn't want to be probed. He knew about his dad's dreams after the war, and doctors had talked to Gene about the effects of the medications. He was trying to deal with all that, but he didn't want to describe to his father what he saw in his dreams. He had the feeling that saying too much about that would only solidify the pictures in his mind. "It's not so much that. I just feel tired, and yet, my mind won't shut off. I'm trying not to take as much medication; I think maybe I'm addicted to some degree. I've just got to live without the stuff a little more all the time."

"Is that what your doctors tell you?"

"They say there's no reward for having pain. They want me to take what I have to."

"That sounds right to me."

"Maybe. But I don't feel human when I take that stuff. I've got to get off it."

"Well . . . I guess that's a good sign. Some guys keep gobbling more and more pills, and then they can't get off."

"That's right. I'm not going to do that."

But that wasn't what Alex wanted to talk about. Gene could see that by the way he was still sitting up straight, looking nervous. "Gene, Emily told me what that guy said to you on the airplane. I hope you're not thinking about that."

"No. I'm fine. He apologized. You heard him."

"I know. But maybe you've had some of those thoughts youreself."

"I don't know. I think a lot of things. With the medicine and everything, all kinds of thoughts come into my head. But I try not to dwell on that kind of stuff."

"Tell me if this sounds right." Alex did finally sit back, and he rested his ankle over his knee. He looked at his own hand on his ankle, not at Gene. "You say to yourself, if I just don't think about it, it will go away. I'm not going to end up a psycho case, so if I feel like I'm going nuts sometimes, the best thing is just to quit thinking."

"Well, yeah. Something like that. I think a lot of guys have come home from 'Nam and started feeling sorry for themselves. They complain about everything, and the next thing they know, they've talked themselves right into a psych ward. I'm just trying to move on with my life."

"It's not working, is it?"

"What do you mean?" But Gene knew what his dad meant.

"Do things flash into your head? Pictures? Things you saw in the war?"

"Sure. That's happened. But from what I hear, that's pretty normal."

"Normal, yes. But it's still scary."

Gene nodded, but he didn't want to talk about this. He was never going to talk about some of the things he had seen. His dad should understand that. He had experienced some of those things himself. But it did no good to talk about it. The best thing was to stay away from that stuff and just think about the future. A guy at the hospital, a shrink, had told him that wouldn't work, that it was better to get into a group and talk, but Gene had seen the groups at the hospital. They were full of guys who had gone off the deep end. Gene had his wounds to deal with, and he would do that, but he wouldn't give in to all the anxiety and fear that some guys talked about.

"Dad, I've got enough trouble with a torn-up gut. If I can get that taken care of, I'll figure I'm home free. In your war, guys came home and dealt with their problems themselves, and then they moved on. Vietnam vets don't want to do that."

"Gene, I had problems—for quite a while. I still have some problems. I've been having certain dreams over and over, my whole life. I was thinking that you and I have some things we could talk out together. Not tonight, maybe. But you know, gradually. I'll be back and forth, and I'll be here for quite a while next summer. Maybe we could open up about some of that stuff. It might help both of us."

"I don't see how." Gene didn't like what was happening to him. He felt himself breathing faster. He didn't want to get cranky with his father, but he didn't want to carry on this conversation any longer either.

"I don't know all the psychological theory on any of that stuff," Alex said. "But I think our minds store up a lot of emotions and fears and regrets, and those kind of powerful feelings have to get to our consciousness somehow. They come out in dreams and in flashes, and they show up in the way a guy loses his temper for no good reason. When I got home, a guy said something I didn't like, and I grabbed him. I had hold of him, and I think I would have cut his throat if I'd had a knife in my hand. And then it was over, just that fast. But it scared me."

"I know what you're talking about. But what good does it do to talk about it?"

"Psychologists have guys get together and open up. It does help, they say. It just gets it out in the open, and you find out other guys feel the same way."

"I guess. But Dad, I haven't grabbed anybody. I don't think I'd do that."

"Gene, I feel it in you. I can see it in your eyes. It's like stored-up resentment. When Grandpa was talking the other night, I saw how furious you were."

Gene raised the recliner. He didn't want to sit back any longer. He wanted to tell his dad that he was fine and then go to bed, whether he could sleep or not. "I love Grandpa, Dad, but he thinks he's got the answer to every question. You know what he was saying." Gene tried to imitate his grandpa's big, deep voice. "'If the politicians had let the military men run the war, it would have been over in a year.' That's garbage, Dad. We dropped *everything* on Vietnam. We would drop thousands of tons of bombs to try to kill off a platoon of VC or NVA. After the bombardment, our troops would go in and find five or six bodies, at best. The rest would just slip back into the jungle. We never did take any land and hold it. We hunted for gooks, but for every one we killed, two more just took his place. Nixon thought he could bomb Hanoi and that would bring the North to its knees. He found out that didn't work either."

Gene's voice was getting more and more intense. He had found himself wanting to stare into Grandpa Thomas's face and tell him that he knew nothing about the war—no more than the hippies who thought it could all end with flower power. That was what drove him crazy about the world—everyone had an opinion about Vietnam, and not even the guys on television understood the first thing about it.

"So why didn't you say that to Grandpa? Maybe he needs to hear it."

"What good would it do, Dad? People just believe what they want to believe. It's what I did before I went over there. Until you've seen your friend on the ground, with blood running from his chest—or out his ears and eyes—the war is just something to talk about." But now Gene had crossed a line. His voice had begun to shake. He was going to stop, *now*. "Look, Dad, I'm tired. I'm going to go in and stretch out. I don't know if I can sleep, but I can rest better that way."

"Okay. I don't want to force this, Gene. But if you hear people saying things that don't make sense, and you don't say anything, it's just going to build up in you. I think you and Grandpa ought to talk sometime."

"Maybe, if I'm going to tell him what I think, I ought to tell *you*."

"That's right. We need to—"

"I don't mean that. I want to know why you didn't do something. I understand about President Johnson. He had such a big ego, he didn't know how to pull the plug on the war. And Nixon is trying to finesse the thing so he won't look bad. But why didn't Congress do something? Why are we still sending guys over there? We're not fighting a war anymore; we're sacrificing men's lives so we can claim we're leaving *with honor*."

"But if you pull out suddenly, it could—"

"It could save a lot of lives," Gene shouted, but he had hurt himself with the effort, the pain grabbing in his insides. He held his breath for a moment, but he had started to cry. "We did it all for nothing, Dad. I've got this pain in my gut, and it's never going to go away. But I can't give you one reason why we should have been there. We accomplished *nothing*. And Dearden is dead. No matter what we say, Dearden is still dead, and a lot of my friends are messed up, just like me. The problem is, I can't tell you that we whipped Hitler and made the world a better place. There's not one thing I can say that makes me feel any better about what we tried to do over there. We didn't stop Communism; we gave it a boost."

Dad got up and came toward Gene. He reached to touch him, but Gene wanted to slam his father in the face. He wanted to hit something or someone—a whole generation who had thought up the stupid war. He stood up too quickly, hurt himself again, and then saw his mother standing in the doorway. He didn't want to push her, but she wouldn't move, so he screamed at her. "Get out of my way!" He hurried to his bedroom, but Emily was there, sitting in a chair. She had been reading, but now she was staring at him. She was about to say something, but Gene couldn't take that. "Just don't talk," he screamed. "Don't talk to me. Everybody! Just leave me alone."

Chapter 25

Kathy was not sure how she had ended up in charge of the party in the Manila Branch, and yet the role seemed rather natural to her now. She had become very much a part of the branch in the past few months. Besides, the party had been her idea. Of course, Filipinos didn't require a lot of encouragement when it came to finding a reason to enjoy themselves. Kathy suggested that the party could give everyone a lift after such a long rainy season, but she had the feeling the months of rain bothered her much more than any of them. The fact was, the rains were letting up, and the April heat was already coming on. But all that didn't matter. It was a good time to have a party, and everyone met at the branch house on a Saturday afternoon.

Kathy had organized games for the kids, but everyone enjoyed playing—perhaps the parents more than the children. And what followed was a wonderful meal. Kathy had learned to eat a lot of things she had never expected to like. She still wasn't ready to eat dog meat—but she loved *dinuguan*, a spicy pork dish, and she liked the rich variety of stir-fried vegetables. What she enjoyed even more was seeing the men in their embroidered *barong* shirts and the women dressed in bright colors. She found Filipinos beautiful, the children especially, and she admired their gift for loving one another. One of the members played with a little band, and he had brought his friends to play with him. After the dinner, everyone danced, and no one was left out. Old fellows danced with little girls, mothers with sons, and plenty of kids with other kids. Filipinos could be shy at times, especially when called on at school, but they were uninhibited about enjoying one another. Kathy thought Americans could learn a lot from them about having fun.

Kathy danced with everyone—the men, young and old, and the children, both girls and boys. No one seemed to mind any longer that she was so much taller than they were. What she felt from everyone was an amazing degree of love. She didn't know how it had happened, but she had become central to the branch, perhaps a symbol of Church headquarters, but even more, someone everyone wanted to be close to. It had become a competition to have her in the various families' homes, and along with conducting the choir, recently she had been called upon to speak in sacrament meeting. It was something she hadn't wanted to do, but she had chosen to speak about the love of Christ, and the talk had surely meant more to her than to the congregation. Kathy had been trying so hard, so long, to figure the world out, to "correct" the things that were wrong, but she told the members that more than anything, the world needed people who loved as Christ loved: without reservation, without prejudice, without selfishness. She told the story of Grandpa Thomas, who had received the inspiration to find her when she had lost her faith and was about to separate herself from the Church, how he loved her no matter how many times she had insulted him with her own prideful behavior. Since then, she said, she had been trying to learn that truth was important, but it meant nothing until it was turned into action, and the actions that brought truth to life were acts of love.

She worried that the talk had been a little too philosophical, and in that way had perhaps run counter to the very thing she was trying to say. But the people understood, and afterward they embraced *her*, not just the things she had said. Still, the talk would have meant nothing had it not come in the context of what she was doing in the branch. She knew that the music she was helping create with the members had touched the people, especially the choir members, and she knew that it was that music that was bringing something out in her that was new. She had always been reticent to hug people, to make connections that went beyond the verbal. But these people understood that love wasn't an abstract idea; they knew that without her telling them so. The fact was, her sermon was to herself.

At the end of the party, when many of the members had left and Kathy was helping with the final work of cleaning up, sweeping the floor, President Luna said to her, "Let me do that. You need to go home now."

"It's all right. I'm in no hurry," Kathy said.

"Sister Thomas, give me the broom." He was pretending to be firm, but he was smiling. "You have done enough for one day. Rest a little."

She smiled at him and handed him the broom. "I hardly want to leave," she said. "I love being here so much."

"It was a wonderful party—the best we've ever had. You know how to do these things."

"It wasn't me. I just invited people to come. It was the branch members who made it wonderful."

President Luna held the broom with both hands and used it to lean on. "I don't think you know what you've done for us, Sister Thomas. We love the missionaries, but they come and go too fast. You've stayed longer, and you've brought such a spirit to us that our whole branch has changed."

"I don't see it that way, President. I'm the one who's learned from all of you. I'm hardly the same person I was half a year ago."

"Yes. I think that's true. I've watched you change. But you brought us along with you. I've watched your happiness grow, and the entire branch caught the same spirit. Everyone tells me how much they love you—and how sad it makes them feel to know that you must leave in a few months."

Kathy had begun to feel that regret too, but never so much as she did this instant. Never in her life had she been loved this way, and she was struck with the feeling that her loss would be the greater. She worried that when she went home, she would revert to the old Kathy. She didn't want to argue with people. She wouldn't give up on things she believed and cared about, but she wanted to find a better way to move those causes forward.

Kathy turned to see Sister Almeyda, an older woman in the branch, and Sister Luna, as they walked from the kitchen. "Everything is clean," Sister Almeyda said. "We go home." She walked to Kathy, smiling. "It was a happy day."

Kathy knew that Sister Almeyda had passed through a hard time lately. She was a widow who had been alone for a long time, and her health was not good. A few months back her beloved three-year-old granddaughter had taken sick with a bad fever and died in just a few days. At the time, Sister Almeyda had told Kathy that she had lost her desire to live. She had prayed to the Lord that she would not have to linger on the earth much longer, that she would rather be with her husband anyway. "But the Lord tell me," she had said, shaking her finger—as though she had seen the Lord, not just heard him—"'You be with me soon. You take care of family now, and no complaining so much. Some of my children have bigger problems than you.'" She had laughed and then added, "So that's what I remember. I do the Lord's work, and I no complaining. Our baby, she in arms of Heavenly Father, and I don't worry for her. I tell my daughter, too, and she no complaining too."

Sister Almeyda had also told Kathy how she had joined the Church when she was in her fifties, and then had brought all her family to the gospel. All of her children and grandchildren were members, some in the Manila Branch. There were so many stories like that in the branch. Kathy had heard such accounts week after week as she had shared her Sabbath days with the members.

"Thank you so much for your help, Sister Almeyda," Kathy said. "President Luna has been thanking me for the party, but you did most of the work."

"You the light, Sister Thomas. The light. When you in room, everyone looks. You make us happy."

Kathy could hardly imagine such a thing. She had never been a light to anyone. She took Sister Almeyda in her arms and hugged her, and then she did the same to Sister and President Luna. But she couldn't say a thing.

That week, back in San Juan, Kathy was walking home from the high school when she saw four men working at the spot where the trenches for the septic lines had been dug once before. The trenches had long since eroded away in the heavy rains. Kathy walked over to see what was happening. The men were digging with considerable zeal, producing the same trenches that had been washed out. "What are you digging, my friends?" she called out in Tagalog. "A grave?"

The men looked up, grinning. "Yes, for José here. He's getting old."

"I think he's a little too fat for such a narrow grave."

The man was certainly not fat. Almost no one in the Philippines was. But the men liked the joke. The man who had spoken first, a little man in muddy pants and wearing a battered white hat, poked at the man he had called José and then called back to Kathy, "Maybe it's not such a good place to be buried anyway, not with a toilet overhead."

"So you're really going to build the toilet?"

"Oh, yes. We started last year, but the rains came. Now we're going to finish the job. It will be a beautiful toilet, just for you."

Everyone in town knew that the toilets were her idea. She had heard people make jokes about that. It sometimes bothered her that no one seemed to understand the reason that public toilets were needed. All the same, she laughed. "Thank you. And José, don't work too hard. Live to work another day."

José was not really old—maybe fifty or so—but he laughed and smiled, showing a missing tooth in front. "I'm not ready to die yet," he said.

"Of course he isn't," one of the men said. "He needs to repent for all his sins first."

Kathy laughed and waved good-bye. She thought it likely that the work would continue another day or two and then end again, but it was nice to think the project hadn't been entirely forgotten. But a week went by, and every day after school she saw the same men at work. They were digging by hand, and the progress was slow, but it was steady. And every day she joked with the men. They seemed proud that she liked the progress they were making.

One day when she came by, the mayor himself was talking to the men, and when he saw Kathy, he walked over to say hello. "So what you think?" he asked. "We have us a toilet soon." Then he switched to Tagalog and added, "It's all been planned. The lumber and the blocks are purchased. They will arrive any day now."

Kathy knew how long it could take to get anything "ordered" in the Philippines. But she was pleased with the mayor's good intentions. "That's wonderful, Mayor," she said. "I think it will be good for everyone."

"Yes. It's a good thing."

"We're still visiting the families, Mayor. We're teaching the children about washing hands. If you could mention something about this when you visit the school, that would be very helpful. The children pay more attention to someone like you, so important in the barrio."

The mayor liked that. He smiled. "I will say something. Yes. And all the teachers should teach about the little germs. That's very important. It's science."

It was hard for Kathy not to smile. He was actually trying to please her, and she wasn't sure why. A year ago, he would gladly have sent her away. The only thing she had done since then was give up. Maybe that had made the project seem more *his* idea, but still, he had become increasingly friendly all year.

"We want to finish the toilets before you leave, Miss Thomas. We'll have a nice celebration."

"To celebrate that I'm leaving?" she asked, and she laughed.

"No, no. To celebrate the new toilet. And to wish you well."

Maybe one of the male leaders from the Peace Corps had finally helped her push the toilet idea, as she had often asked them to do. There was something going on that Kathy didn't really understand.

"Everyone will miss you, Miss Thomas."

"Me? Thank you, Mayor. But I don't think so."

The mayor was wearing a tall hat woven from some kind of leaf or palm frond. He took it off and wiped his forehead with a handkerchief he pulled from his back pocket. "You were only asked to be a teacher, Miss Thomas. And you are a good one. The young people love you very much. You might have come and gone and only done that. But you have visited the people in their homes. They love you for that."

"We just wanted to teach them about hand washing."

"Yes, yes. They understand that. But you know them now. You listened to them talk. Everyone in the barrio knows you."

"They can't help that. I'm so tall."

"Yes, yes. Bery tall. But you smile at them. You talk to eberyone. Last year I thought you didn't like us. But now you do."

"Last year, I didn't understand very much, Mayor. Now I love San Juan, and I love the people. They have been very kind to me."

He was nodding, looking more solemn. "Too many with the Peace Corps, they come here and they tell us things. But they don't care about us, not really."

"Miss Sommers did. She taught me."

"Yes, yes. Miss Sommers was bery good to us. But you smile more. You laugh with the people. They like this. They like how you like us."

Kathy was amazed that the mayor would say such a thing. She had felt the change in herself over the past year, but it had come almost by default. Once she had given up on her big goals to change the community, she had resolved to make the best of her remaining time, to teach some hand washing and hope that served a purpose, but not expect a whole lot to change. What had happened differently along the way was that she had tried to visit no more than one family when she went out in the evening, and not push too hard when she was there. She had found herself taking more time in the homes, mainly because she found it fun to talk to the people, meet the younger kids she didn't know at the school, and enjoy herself. She had eaten with families, laughed with them, and found out a good deal about them. As a result, she knew almost everyone, and she could ask them about specific events and children in their families. Still, it had all been rather natural, not anything she had calculated, and while she noticed that people had become increasingly friendly to her, it had seemed that was only the result of her being around so long. She had noticed that children would meet her in the street and hold up their hands to show her they had washed, and she had told them how happy she was about that, but she wondered whether that wasn't almost more a joke than a reality.

"I do like everyone, Mayor. It won't be easy for me to leave."

He smiled brighter than she had ever seen him smile. And then he reached out, rather formally, and shook her hand. She wanted to hug him but decided that might be going too far.

Kathy walked on home and found Tamra already there ahead of her. Kathy could see immediately that she was discouraged, or at least tired, so Kathy didn't say anything about the toilet or her talk with the mayor. "Rough day?" she asked.

Tamra was sitting in one of the rattan chairs in the living room. She had taken off her school clothes and put on white shorts and a yellow halter top. She had a stack of papers in her hands and a red pencil, but there were no marks on the top paper. Either she had just sat down or she had been sitting there awhile, without the heart to start on one more set of papers. "I thought I hated the rain, but this heat is worse than anything."

It was strange, but Kathy hadn't thought much about it. Feeling sticky just seemed part of life now. "This isn't the real heat yet," she said. "In another couple of weeks, you'll think this was a nice day."

"I know. I remember when I first got here last year."

"No. April and May are worse."

"Thanks. That's what I needed to hear." Tamra looked down at the papers as though resolving to get started.

Kathy feared that her words had seemed less than sensitive now that she thought about them, so she added, "But it is hot. And this house is terrible."

"The school was hot too."

"Have you got a lot of papers to read?"

"No. Not really. Just this one set. Mrs. Barbosa took the rest of them this time. I don't think she trusts me. She keeps saying I grade too high."

"That's what Mrs. Sanchez always told me. But maybe it's better, the way they grade over here. When a student gets an A, it means something. American kids get so they expect A's just for turning their work in."

Tamra grabbed her hair in back and pulled it up off her neck. She looked disgusted. "Kathy, if you want to know the truth, I get tired of your little speeches. Everything about the Philippines is better, according to you. I'm sorry, but I don't see it that way. I think these teachers are way too harsh. They intimidate the students so badly, the kids don't dare say anything."

Kathy sat down on the old couch, across from Tamra. "I'm sorry," she said. "I know I do that. Martha used to do that to me, and it really made me mad. I think what happens is that the longer you're here, the more you accept the way things are."

But that seemed to anger Tamra. "That's just the problem," she said.

"They send us over here to help the people, but after a while the volunteers all give up. They stop trying to accomplish anything and just put in their time until they can get out."

"I know it seems that way, but—"

"I'm thinking about going home. This is really pointless as far as I'm concerned. I'm not doing anything. I watch Mrs. Barbosa teach the class, and then she calls me up in front to read something, aloud, so they can hear my English—but the kids pay no attention. One of the boys told me the other day that he couldn't understand me. It never occurred to him that he was the one speaking some sort of hybrid language that no one outside the Philippines would ever recognize."

"Look, I know exactly what you're talking about. I put in a year as an aide, the same as you. This time last year I was thinking about going home myself."

"So when did you settle for just riding out your time?"

Kathy smiled. She could feel that Tamra was in such a state of frustration and boredom that she wanted a good fight. Kathy had tried to take on Martha the same way, and Martha had seemed annoyingly sweet at such moments. Kathy didn't want to be like that, but she did think it would be a terrible mistake for Tamra to go home at this point. "Have you seen the men digging the septic lines for my toilet?" she asked.

"Oh, yes. They're working every day on it now. That's going to be your heritage—your monument. A toilet in the barrio. I can't think of a better symbol."

Kathy wasn't sure whether to take offense, but she knew Tamra was still looking for a reaction, and Kathy decided not to oblige her. She laughed. "Actually, I can't either," she said.

"Come on, Kathy, they'll never finish the thing. They'll lose interest any day now, just the way they did before. And it doesn't matter anyway, because if they ever did get it finished, the people wouldn't use it."

"Maybe. But a lot of the kids are washing their hands now, and once the toilet is finished, you can teach them about using it."

Tamra dropped her pile of papers on the floor. She leaned back and folded her arms, but then, as though reacting to the stickiness of her arms against her bare skin, she dropped her arms. "Kathy, that's not the point. Nothing is really going to change here. I hope the hand washing helps a little—if it really is happening—and toilets might help stop a few people from getting sick, but this place is going to go on just the same long after we're gone. If I'm going to stay, I want to know what it is we're trying to do."

"The mayor told me I like the people now—he can see the change in me—and because of that, the people like me."

"Hey, I like the people just fine. So what? You can get a stray dog to provide that service. When I was in college, I couldn't wait to get out in the world and make a difference—build some bridges, help third-world people to a better life. I don't see anything like that going on here."

"I need to get this dress off," Kathy said. "Hold that thought. I'll be right back."

"Kathy, don't bother. I've heard every one of your pep talks. But the closer you get to going home, the happier you are. I'm just going to cut out that second year of capitulation and catch a plane. I'll finish out this school year, but that's all."

Kathy stood. "Okay. I'm not saying you shouldn't do that. But I do have a couple of things I want to say." Kathy walked to her room and took off her dress. Then she slid on a pair of cutoff jeans she wore around the house a lot, and she found a loose-fitting cotton shirt. She had known what she wanted to say next when she left the room, but she realized the words amounted to an argument, and nothing of that sort was going to make much difference to Tamra today. Still, Kathy did need to say—or do—something that would help. She was scared for Tamra. If she gave up now and went home, she would keep a bad memory with her forever. So

Kathy knelt by her bed and prayed that she could think of the right thing to say. She got up, however, not knowing, and walked back to the living room, unsure of herself, waiting for the words to come into her head.

It was Tamra who had clearly been thinking and knew what she wanted to say. "I don't think you get your pleasure from your Peace Corps work at all," she said. "What you love is the choir you direct and the people in your church. That's what's made you happy this year."

"That's true," Kathy said. "But that's only because I love those people so much, and they love me. That *is* what happiness is all about, Tamra."

"Kathy, I'm not going to talk religion with you. I respect your right to believe anything you want. But when you go into Manila, it's like going home. That's what you love about it."

Kathy thought about that. "Actually, that's partly true. It does make me feel at home." Kathy stopped. She was falling into her old pattern, about to start building a logical case for what she wanted to say. So she stopped herself. "But mostly, I just love the people I meet there and they love me—not for any reason. When I started bringing that love back to the barrio, that's when I started to feel happy."

"That, *exactly*, is my point. When you started loving the people and quit trying to change things, *you* were happier. And the people liked you better. You quit trying to make a difference, felt all good inside, and now you're going home. So what? That's nice for you, but it isn't what the Peace Corps sent us here to do."

Kathy had to talk to herself. She had arguments running through her head, and she could feel the anger coming. So she said something that wasn't really developed in her own mind, just something she wanted Tamra to hear. "There's a woman in my church who's a widow. She helped me organize that party I was working on last week. When I first met her, she was alone and not well, and her little granddaughter had just died. She told me she wanted to die too. But God spoke to her and told her she had work to do with her family—and the woman was willing to accept that. She had been feeling sorry for herself, and she knew she had to stop. Now she's as happy as any person I know."

"Kathy, don't start with me. I've been waiting all year for you to start witnessing to me. I know how Mormons are."

Kathy laughed. "That's not what I'm saying. I'm just saying that we can't change people; they have to change themselves. If you think we're going to make the Philippines better somehow, and do it in two years, you really should go home. The only change comes in people, and it happens one at a time, not en masse."

"Kathy, I'm not talking about 'finding Jesus.' I'm talking about reducing disease, helping people escape from poverty, eat better, live longer. I'm talking about bringing better teaching methods—which the principal resists with all his strength. I'm talking about putting in some sidewalks so people don't walk around in the mud, or teaching some of these men that they have no right to lord over their wives."

Kathy had answers she wanted to give, a point to make, but once again she told herself not to make it. "I know how hard this is for you, Tamra," she said. "I pray for you every night."

"Kathy, I don't know what you're trying to do, but I don't like it. And you can leave me out of your prayers. I don't buy into any of that stuff. I grew up with religion—and found out that the most hypocritical, nasty little people I met were always the ones who thumped their Bibles the hardest."

"I wish you'd come into Manila with me, just once. I'd like you to meet the people in my church. They're good. They have problems, but they're good, and you can see in their eyes how happy they are. We work and work over here, but I don't see the same light in people's eyes. I know you don't believe in religion, but I really believe it's God who can change people. Not us. Once people get that light inside them, they start hoping for better things, making themselves and their communities better. It really works. I've seen it."

Tamra was shaking her head, obviously annoyed.

"Tamra, I've seen changes in some of the people in this barrio. I think it's the beginning of some good things. And it's come only after I started to love them. That's really the only thing that has ever made a difference."

"Okay. To some degree, I buy that. If we act superior and don't show respect, they won't accept what we tell them. But—"

"It's not just respect. It's love. A year ago, I would never have said such a thing. I sound like a flower child with all their 'all you need is love' stuff. But I'm telling you . . ." She grinned. "I'm *witnessing*. Love works. And it's the only thing that does. But it has to be real. If you try to fake it, it doesn't have any effect."

"I'm sure you've done an empirical study on that assumption. You're the Smith girl, trained to *think*."

"Hey, I am. And I don't like platitudes and flabby thought. I really have done a kind of study. Everything changed when I started loving these people. And I'm going to *witness* one more thing. My church is having more effect in the Philippines than the Peace Corps ever will. There's going to be a day when a lot of people are going to find the Lord through our missionaries, and people are going to change. The missionaries won't do it, and the Church won't do it—not the organization—but God will. I can see it happening. These are good people in these islands. God loves them, and they want the Lord."

Tamra was staring at Kathy, certainly surprised, and maybe still angry to some degree. But she wasn't saying anything.

"Tamra, all I'm saying is that nothing happens when you come here and tell people what they ought to do. If you tell the children they ought to wash their hands, that's only information. It doesn't mean anything to the kids if we give that information without love. Once they feel our love, they understand we're trying to give them a gift. It takes a long time to accept the people fully, not to judge their culture against our own. It's probably in the second year that you come to accept them—if you ever do—and they start to feel that acceptance. But once you love them and they love you, toilets and sidewalks start to appear. Cultures only change slowly, and to tell you the truth, I think I've learned much more from these people than I can teach them. But if we want them to change so that *we* can feel good about ourselves and go home thinking we're great people, they sense that. Last year I wanted the kids to wash their hands because it was the right thing to do. It was my cause. It was going to be my legacy to leave the people with a public toilet and cleaner habits. I now want those kids to wash their hands because I fear for their lives. I'll worry about them after I leave. It's only when I started to feel that way that they started to listen."

Tamra nodded. Something had softened in her face.

"Tamra, I know what you've been going through. You're right where I was last year, and I can feel your pain."

"When I first met you, you weren't like this, Kathy. You seemed frustrated to me, and unhappy. I've seen you come to life since then."

"I could tell you what made the difference, but you would say that I'm witnessing again."

"You mean your church, of course. But you grew up a Mormon—and it hasn't always made you happy."

"I know. Sometimes when you're looking for an answer, you search everywhere else before you take a look at what's right in front of you."

Chapter 26

Hans was in sacrament meeting on a pretty May evening. The windows were open, and the air from outside was full of lilac. It was also a special day since President Pfeifer, the district president, was visiting and would be the speaker. He was a powerful man who could speak for a long time once he got going, but no one seemed to mind. He knew how to present his gospel insights and admonitions with humor, with stories, and above all, with reminiscences. He talked about the days before World War II, when many of the older members in Leipzig had joined the Church, and he talked about the hard days during the war. He described the difficulties of keeping in touch with leaders of the Church in Salt Lake City, both during the war and since then.

What Hans knew was that leaders did manage, from time to time, to make the trip into the GDR. Because of the Leipzig Industrial Fair, some leaders had been able to gain admission to attend, and then to visit with President Pfeifer and other leaders.

Today President Pfeifer talked about the need for young people to know the rich heritage of courage and faith in Church history. He talked about Joseph Smith and the early days of the Restoration, and then of the early missionaries who had come to Europe to begin the work in England and Wales and who eventually reached out to the continent. Hans could tell that President Pfeifer was choosing his words carefully. One never knew whether a member of the branch, even someone who seemed completely in harmony with the Church, might not be an informant for the government. Proselytizing was not allowed, but through personal contacts, occasionally there were new converts. But the members knew that the *Stasi* would try to infiltrate any organization it found suspect, and the Church would surely qualify. So members often worried about converts, whether their motivations were pure, or whether they might be government agents. That meant members had to think through the things they said, especially about the Church's connection to America. Hans knew that the members longed for more material from Church headquarters, for Church magazines, and especially for visits from leaders, but such desires were not wise to state in sacrament meeting.

But toward the end of President Pfeifer's talk, he became more forthright, even bold, when he told the young people, "There is no chapter in the history of our Church that is quite like ours. We carry the responsibility of keeping the gospel alive in this part of the world without the support that other members, in other places, are blessed to have. You young people are taught not to believe in God, and I know that you are sometimes ridiculed because you do. And yet, it will be up to you to carry the load, to teach the gospel where you can, to hold the truths in your hearts and pass those truths to another generation. The darkness of disbelief presses on us from all directions, and as we cling to the iron rod, those who jeer at us from the great and spacious building outnumber us dramatically, so we must hold to the rod with all our strength."

Hans was moved by that thought. He remembered the temptations he had passed through during his school days. There were so many reasons not to believe and so many dangers in doing so. He knew what his sister was going through now, feeling ostracized merely because she believed in religion. It was that way for every young Church member. What he had to wonder about was the next generation. Could the Saints continue to hold out, decade after decade, if the schools continued to teach atheism and the government continued to limit the career possibilities for religious people? As so often happened, when he thought about such things, he wondered whether he hadn't made a mistake in staying in the GDR when he'd had his chance to leave. He could have been in Salt

Lake City now, with his grandfather and with Aunt Anna and the Thomas family she had married into. He knew that he loved Elli, but he also knew that his love for her—and hers for him—might turn out to be the worst thing that could happen to her. If he had left the country, he could have found someone else, and Elli could perhaps have found a young man in the Church who hadn't created such problems for himself.

Still, this call to serve from President Pfeifer was inspiring. Strong young people were required to keep the Church going, and Hans wanted to be one of them. He wanted to hold to the truths, strengthen other young members, and teach the gospel to people outside the Church when the opportunity presented itself. He had passed through trials, but he had learned some things. It was important that he share what he knew.

When the meeting was over, he decided to wait and have a chance to shake hands with President Pfeifer. But many others wanted to do the same thing, so he waited at a distance. He was chatting with some friends when President Schräder, his branch president, tapped him on the shoulder and then called him aside. "Hans, President Pfeifer would like to talk to you if you could wait just a few minutes."

"Yes, of course," Hans said, but he was amazed. What could President Pfeifer possibly want to talk about? Hans's instincts had taught him to worry about anything out of the ordinary. He wondered whether *Stasi* agents had passed along some warning through Church officials. He still wondered whether Rainer had been completely truthful. Hans was always waiting for the *Stasi* to appear again, to drag him off to prison. Three months had passed since the day he had last seen Rainer, and the passing of so much time seemed to belie his fears, but the idea was never very far from Hans's consciousness.

So Hans was rather nervous as he waited, and yet he was excited, too. President Pfeifer was a hero to Hans. He liked to think of sitting down with him. Maybe he would receive a new calling. Hans had heard of people being called as missionaries even though usual methods were not available.

When President Pfeifer was finally able to finish chatting with the last of the waiting members, he came to Hans and President Schräder, shook hands with Hans, and said, "*Bruder* Stoltz, thank you for waiting," and then he walked with him to President Schräder's office. President Pfeifer motioned for President Schräder to take his own chair, behind the desk, and he turned a couple of folding chairs so they were facing one another. He asked Hans to take one seat and then sat in the other. "Hans," he said, "I've known you since you were just a little boy. Your father and mother are good people—a strength to the Church in Schwerin. How old are you now?"

"I'll soon be twenty-three."

"You seem older to me. But then, you've survived some great challenges."

Hans nodded. "I feel older myself," he said, and smiled.

"President Schräder has told me that your time in prison was a refiner's fire for you. He says you're wise beyond your years, and you know the scriptures better than almost anyone in the branch."

"I don't know if that's true, but there was period of time, in prison, when I was allowed to have a Bible, and I spent most of my time reading it—trying very hard to understand."

"What did that do for you, Hans?"

"It changed me, President—not just the Bible but the circumstance I was in. I was all alone, day and night, and I filled up my days reading and thinking about the words of the prophets and the teachings of Christ. When I felt the Holy Ghost with me, I wasn't alone. So I did everything I knew to invite the Spirit into my cell. It wasn't just reading the scriptures; it was pleading with the Lord for help and spending many hours thinking about the things I read."

"President Schräder tells me that you wrote sermons—wonderful sermons."

"I didn't write them. I had no paper. I rehearsed them in my mind, and I memorized them. I would stand in my cell sometimes and preach, as though someone were listening." Hans smiled at himself. "I spoke in church a while back, and I was able to use one of those sermons. I also use some of the ideas I developed then in my Sunday School class."

"Yes. I'm told you are a fine speaker and teacher."

Hans was not prepared for the emotion he would feel, receiving such a compliment from President Pfeifer. He couldn't stop the tears that filled his eyes. "Thank you. I do my best," he said. "In a way, I'm thankful for prison. I doubt I would have made the effort to study so much, had I not been there."

President Pfeifer was nodding, looking solemn. He seemed to see the irony and yet the truth in the statement. He was a tall man, with plastic-rimmed glasses and a receding hairline. He looked like the sort of man who might work in a government office, shuffling papers all day, and yet, there was an intensity in the way he looked at people. He seemed to focus all his attention on Hans, at this moment, to have no other thought in his mind. It was an honor for Hans to have this great man take time with him, to question him with such interest. And yet, Hans was still wondering, what was all this leading toward?

"Tell me exactly why you were sent to prison."

"Berndt Kerner, from my branch in Schwerin, wanted to escape through a tunnel, under the Berlin Wall. He asked me to cover up the entrance once he and the others were gone. I should have known better. I should have protected Berndt and talked him out of going. Maybe I could have saved his life if I had tried harder—but I thought I was being a friend."

"And how did the government find out you were involved?"

"I don't know. Perhaps someone else who was involved in the escape knew my name, or simply knew that a friend of Berndt's was the one who had helped. I told one man—a roommate at the university—and he might have reported on me, but I don't think he did. He's in prison himself now."

"Helping Berndt *was* a mistake," President Pfeifer said, "but I know you meant well."

"I'll always regret that I did it."

"And yet, I'm happy that you didn't let your prison term destroy you—that you used the time to grow. But what now? Is your life in order? Are you living as you should?"

"Yes. I'm trying. But I give way to discouragement at times. I'm still watched. I'll always be suspected. My work situation has improved, but I'll never be paid very well. I may not be able to afford to marry or to have a family."

President Pfeifer looked for a time into Hans's eyes, and then he said, "President Schräder would like to have you for his counselor. I told him this morning that I thought you were too young, but he convinced me that I should talk to you. Now, after meeting with you, I have no question in my mind that President Schräder is right. The Lord wants you to serve in the branch presidency."

Hans could hardly believe what he had just heard. It was unimaginable.

"Will you accept the call?"

"Yes. Certainly, but—"

"I know what you want to say. But don't worry about it. The members respect who you are. It doesn't matter about your age." Then he smiled. "You're lucky. You have some good sermons already prepared."

"Is it all right that I'm not a married man?"

"Of course not. There are sisters who need a husband. You must do something about that."

"But I have no money."

"You will manage. Find yourself a young woman in the Church, and the Lord will open a way."

"There is someone, but she's still young herself—only twenty."

He smiled again, looking delighted. "And who is this young woman?"

"Elli Dürden, in Magdeburg."

"*Ach*, you must act quickly. I'm sure plenty of other young men in the Church have their eyes on her." He reached out and slapped Hans on the knee. "Are you sure she'll have you?"

Hans felt heat come into his face. "She's expressed her willingness," he said. "But we've thought of all this as something in the future—a few years from now, at best."

"No. I don't believe so. You might have to wait a little. And that's all right. But don't wait too long. In this country, we have to manage as we can. Still, I've seen it many times: those who are faithful to the Church find a way to get by with very little and still remain happy. I promise you, Hans, the Lord will open a way for you."

"It's good, then. Thank you so much, President Pfeifer."

"We'll present your name to the members next week, and providing they don't vote no, we'll set you apart then."

"They just *might* vote against me," Hans said.

But President Pfeifer's smile passed slowly away, and he said, "This is only the beginning, Hans. You will do great things in your life. I know that for certain."

"President, I could have left the GDR. The government had arranged to let me go, and I could have gone to Salt Lake City, where I have family. But I heard a voice in my head. It told me I was needed here."

"Yes. It was a revelation to you, Hans. There's no doubt in my mind. And I've had one today. You are the right man to serve in the presidency of your branch."

"Thank you. I'm going to work very hard to do the job as well as I can."

By then, President Schräder was coming around the desk. He grabbed Hans and embraced him. "You'll be a strength to me," he said.

~

Two weeks later Hans was on his way to Schwerin and was scheduled to stop along the way in Magdeburg. Or perhaps he was on his way to Magdeburg, with a side trip added on to see his parents in Schwerin. However he looked at it, he was stopping in Magdeburg first, and he was excited. He had written to Elli, told her they had things they needed to talk about, and she had written back that she would meet him at the train station.

But when he got off the train and saw her waiting for him, he immediately sensed that something was wrong. As he approached her, she seemed hesitant. He wasn't one to do much hugging, or certainly not kissing in a public place, but he expected some sign of warmth from Elli. She stood, rather stiffly, he thought, and made no gesture, not even a touch of his arm. He wondered whether something had happened. Maybe she was having second thoughts about a future with him. Maybe she had met someone else. Wasn't it true that girls changed their minds? President Pfeifer had said himself that other young men would be interested in her.

"There are some things I want to talk to you about, Elli," he said. "I thought we might take our walk along the river before we go back to your house."

"Yes. That's fine."

"Is something wrong?"

"I don't know. Is there?"

He walked on into the main hall of the train station, with its high ceiling. Then he turned toward her. "What do you mean?"

"You said you wanted to talk to me. And I know you. You always have second thoughts about me, and you're pessimistic. I think you've come here to tell me that we can't be married."

"Pessimistic? I? I'm not pessimistic."

"You know what you've told me a hundred times. You're always going to be poor. Nothing will ever get better."

"That's not what I said last time I was here."

"I know. But have you changed your mind already?"

There were lots of people moving by them or waiting on benches not far away. Hans didn't want to talk here, but he was relieved. She was worried that he had changed *his* mind. She had apparently not changed hers. "I could never change my mind when I'm looking at you, Elli, and when I'm away from you, I see you in my mind every minute. So I can't change my mind either way."

She had begun to smile, and now her dimples appeared. "Am I as pretty as that?" she asked, in a teasing voice.

"No."

She looked surprised, but she was still smiling.

"If you were only pretty, I wouldn't care about you. You're much more than that."

"Why didn't you kiss me when you got off the train?"

He laughed. "I was too embarrassed."

"Embarrassed? Why?"

"There are too many people here. And I didn't know. Maybe you didn't want me to kiss you."

She stepped to him, very close, and waited, but he didn't kiss her until she stretched her neck a little toward him. He didn't kiss her very long, either, but his chest filled up and seemed ready to lift him off the ground. "We need to talk," he said as he stepped away from her.

"Yes. And maybe kiss once or twice more."

"That's a good suggestion. Even three times might not be a bad idea."

"I was so worried, Hans. I thought you were coming to tell me that we shouldn't see each other anymore."

"No. Just the opposite. That's what we need to talk about."

"Oh, yes. Oh, yes," she said. "Just ask me. You have your answer."

"Wait. Not so fast." But he felt the same way. Fast was not fast enough.

They walked on outside, Elli clinging to his arm, and then they walked toward the river. They talked of her family and his job in Leipzig, and even the weather, but Hans waited until they had reached his favorite stretch of the river before he stopped. They stood by a little wall and looked at the swans on the water. He was reminded of the swans all those years ago that had swum so easily against the current and told him that, in time, he would be able to do the same. It was a story he had once told Elli, and she had never forgotten it. "I come here at least once a week, just to look at your swans," she said. "They always remind me that we can get by somehow. My parents tell me I can't be too romantic and then find life disappointing when we have to struggle—and I'm sure they're right—but I see how calm and quiet the swans are, and I tell myself that's how I'll have to be. I can't worry myself about the flow of the river. I can only control myself."

"It won't be easy, Elli, but I have more reason to hope now. I wanted to come here and tell you in person what's happened to me."

"What is it?" She pulled at his arm and turned him so he was looking at her.

"Two weeks ago President Pfeifer visited our branch, and he called me to serve as a counselor in the branch presidency. I was set apart last Sunday."

Her eyes widened, and yet she said, "I'm not surprised at all. It's exactly what I would expect. I keep telling you, you're the best man in this entire world. You *should* be in the presidency. You'll always be a leader in the Church."

"Elli, don't build me up so much. You'll be disappointed when we're together all the time. I'm not half as good as you think I am."

"That's not what President Pfeifer thinks, is it?"

"I still can't believe he called me, Elli, but listen to this. He told me that I should get married, and not to wait too long."

Hans expected Elli to squeal, or to say something funny, but instead her eyes filled with tears. "He's right, Hans," she said. "It's what God is telling me, too."

"I told him we couldn't. Not right now, anyway. And he said that was all right. But we shouldn't wait too long. He said the Lord would open a way for us. In fact, he promised that he would."

Elli was crying now. She reached around Hans's waist, and he took her in his arms. "It's what I told you before," she said. "It's exactly what I told you."

"I know it is. You say I'm good, Elli, but you have much more faith than I do."

"I know." She pulled her head back enough to look him in the eye. "I'm glad there's something I can teach you."

He pulled her back to him and held her close, conscious that they were standing on a walkway where others might walk by, but lost all the same in her lovely touch.

Hans and Elli eventually made their way to Elli's house, and the family rejoiced to hear about Hans's new calling and the promise President Pfeifer had made. Hans stayed overnight and then traveled on to Schwerin. He didn't have much time. This was only to be a three-day trip, and he had promised Elli he would spend some more hours with her in Magdeburg during his return trip.

When Hans reached Schwerin, he was surprised at how changed he felt. He always loved coming home, but this was the first time in years that he felt himself. Maybe it was President Pfeifer's promise, or maybe Elli was teaching him to have faith, but he was actually feeling that things would be all right, that his situation would get better. He had told himself for years now never to expect happiness in this life, never even to wish for marriage. He still didn't see how it could happen. But he found himself trusting that it would.

When he arrived home, he kept his secret for a time, wishing to tell everyone together, and to say it in the right way. He knew he was tempted to feel pride in his calling, and he had to be careful about that. He had learned a hard lesson about pride—a trait that seemed to come so naturally to him—and he knew how destructive it could be to his spirit.

So he waited until after dinner, and then he asked everyone to sit with him in the living room. He told his parents and Inga, "I know it's a little strange for me to make a trip home when I can only stay a day, but I had a special reason for coming. I wanted Papa to give me a father's blessing."

Peter didn't say anything, but he nodded. Hans thought he looked concerned.

"Is something wrong?" Katrina asked.

"No. Not at all. But something's happened, and I need Papa's strength."

No one asked, but everyone was looking at him curiously. Inga was smiling, and Hans realized he was smiling himself, probably giving away at least half his secret. "I've been called to serve in the branch presidency in Leipzig," he said. "I was set apart on Sunday. But I'm rather frightened, I guess, and I wanted Papa's blessing, too."

He watched the look in his father's eyes. There was surprise for a moment, but then his face changed, and Hans saw the awe, the satisfaction. Mama got up and came to him, and Hans stood to embrace her. Then Inga and Papa came, too.

"I know I'm only twenty-two," Hans said. "But President Pfeifer said he's certain I should be the one. I can't imagine why. There are other men in our branch who are better qualified."

"There are always other men," Papa said. "And some of them might be better qualified. But the Lord has his reasons. You'll grow into this.

You'll understand why the Lord wanted you to stay in this country when you might have left."

"I think I already understand that," Hans said. "There's something else I need to tell you. Sit down. Please."

So everyone went back to their seats, but before Hans could speak, Inga said, "I think this next one is about Elli."

Hans felt himself blush. "Well, yes," he said. "President Pfeifer said I shouldn't wait too long to marry. He said a way would be opened for us."

"You stopped in Magdeburg on the way here, didn't you?" Mama asked. "Are you engaged?"

"No, no. Nothing like that. We haven't made any certain plans."

"But you did stop in Magdeburg, and you did talk about all this?"

"Yes." He grinned.

"We love Elli," Papa said. "And we know what a good family she comes from. You couldn't make a better choice." He hesitated and smiled. "But can she cook?"

Hans laughed. "We won't have enough money to buy groceries. What will it matter whether she can cook?"

Inga was up again, and now the hugging started all over. But then Papa brought a chair from the kitchen and had Hans sit down. He asked Katrina to say a prayer, to invite the Spirit, and then he took his time as he approached Hans from behind. He placed his good hands on Hans's head, and Hans felt that familiar joy, the love that seemed to pass from his father's hands and on into his own spirit.

Peter blessed Hans with wisdom beyond his years to serve in the presidency, with the insight and inspiration to help President Schräder and guidance to know the needs of the members. He also blessed Hans, as President Pfeifer had done, that the Lord would open a way for the marriage to take place. Then he said, "There was a time in my life, during the war, when I thought all hope was lost, a time when I thought I wanted to die. But after I had given way to that hopelessness, the Lord picked me up and carried me, and he guided my feet to your mother's house. It was a blessing I hadn't earned; it was a gift from the Lord, and I have been thankful for it all the days of my life. In the same way, after a time of hopelessness, the Lord is lifting you, carrying you, guiding your steps. The day will truly come when you will thank him for every experience, both good and bad, and you will thank him for Elli—another gift to you from heaven." And then he said something that left Hans astounded and weak. "I promise you, Hans, in the name of the Lord, that this marriage for mortality will become a marriage for all eternity, that the way will be opened for you and Elli to be sealed in a temple of the Lord."

So many things didn't seem possible, but hope and trust were part of faith, and Hans told himself he must trust, simply trust, and his life would take a better turn.

Chapter 27

Spring quarter would soon be over, and Diane was glad to know she would be out of school for the summer. She could give Jennifer more of her attention for a while. But Diane had enjoyed her year in college, and she had done surprisingly well. She had discovered a new field of study called "special education"—working with children who had difficulty learning—and she had decided that's what she wanted to pursue. During spring quarter she had been taking a psychology class, which she found fascinating. She realized that she had never really thought much about her world, but she was interested now to comprehend not only other people but also her own motivations. There were a couple of young married guys in her class who thought the professor went too far sometimes in interpreting human behavior, and a running argument had been going on for a while, with Diane often lining up against these two. Today, the professor, Dr. Baldwin, had mentioned that people had a tendency to project their own way of thinking onto others, even though that could lead to misunderstandings. The example he gave was that many people fear to commit a crime because they don't want to get caught, but not all people think that way. Punishment, even the death penalty, didn't seem to have much deterrent effect on criminals. That set off one of the guys who disagreed so often, a fellow named Chris. "Maybe we're not punishing them enough," he said. "Leave 'em in jail the rest of their lives, and that'd be a deterrent."

That got a good laugh from some of the students, but Diane raised her hand. When Dr. Baldwin called on her, she said, "All this 'law 'n order' talk these days sounds pretty good as long as it's someone you don't know who's going to jail. But if you know someone who's made a mistake—some actual person who maybe grew up in your neighborhood—you always feel like maybe *that* person deserves a chance to reform."

Some students jumped in on both sides before Dr. Baldwin pulled the discussion back to his original point, but at the end of class, Chris walked over to Diane's desk. He had been flirting around with her all term, which really bothered her since she knew he was married. "Well, Diane, aren't you the little bleeding heart today? If that guy who grew up down the street busts into *your* house, I'll bet you'll want him put away as long as possible."

Diane stood up. She picked up her textbook and then looked at Chris. "I guess a person would feel that way," she said. "But I'm just wondering, do we believe that people can be reformed or don't we?"

Chris didn't answer the question. He smiled knowingly and said, "What if he breaks in and takes a look at you, and then he decides he wants more from you than your jewelry or your TV? What do you do to him then? Wouldn't you kill him if you had a gun?"

The question might have been an interesting one, but the way Chris was looking at her, she had the uneasy feeling he had his own little fantasies. Diane didn't dress the way she had at BYU. She wore slacks and simple shirts, with almost no makeup. She was having her hair cut shorter, too, so that she didn't have to do much to take care of it. Still, she got plenty of attention on campus—not so much from the newly returned missionaries who were looking for a wife but, it seemed to her, from guys who wondered how exciting a divorcée might be. And word had certainly gotten around that she had been married. She had been asked out a few times, but she hadn't accepted any dates.

"I don't know what I'd do," she told Chris. "I know I'd defend my baby if I had to." She tried to walk away.

Chris caught up to her at the door and was saying something as she stepped into the hallway, but Diane had come to a stop. Greg was across the hall. He was standing straight, his hand at his sides, looking nervous. He had obviously been waiting for her to come out of class. She wasn't sure what to do, but he walked toward her. "Can we talk?" he asked.

Chris had stopped, too. But he seemed to sense the seriousness of the situation. "Hey, anyway, we'll see you later, Diane," he said.

Diane saw Greg take a long look at Chris, then back at her. "Could you give me just a little of your time?" he asked.

Diane was still taken by surprise. She had planned to do some research in the library before she picked up Jenny from her mom's house. She didn't want this. She could almost guess what Greg was there to say, and she didn't want to hear it. "Greg, I don't see the point," she said.

"Diane, I drove all night from Seattle. I have some things I have to say to you."

He did look tired. He was dressed well, as always, in a brown sleeveless sweater and a button-down-collar shirt, but he hadn't shaved for a day, it appeared, and his eyes were bloodshot. He and Diane were standing in a busy hallway, with people working their way around the two of them.

"All right. But really, I don't have much time." She began to walk. "Let's go to the Union Building. We can—"

"I thought maybe we could take a little drive and—"

"No. I can't be gone that long. I have work to do, and then I have to pick up Jenny."

"Could I go see her?"

"I guess you can, Greg. But that might confuse her. You haven't bothered all year, and she doesn't remember you. So don't expect her to call you Daddy."

"Diane, I can hear how angry you are at me. And I don't blame you. I just want you to know that."

The same old stuff.

Diane opened the door before he could, stepped outside, and then walked quickly across the street toward the Union Building. It was a pretty day, and lots of people were outside, hanging out on the lawns or talking on the sidewalk in little groups. Diane wondered who might recognize Greg. She hated the idea of being seen with him. She didn't want to set off any speculation; it had been hard enough this past year to establish with her old high school friends who she was now.

Diane walked through the east doors of the Union Building and then led Greg around to the right, into the eating area. She spotted an empty booth, then stopped and motioned for Greg to take a seat. She took the opposite side, sat down, and then looked at him, as if to say, "All right. Go ahead." She was surprised at how much anger she felt. Her reaction came partly just from looking at him and remembering what he had done to her, but even more, she hated that understanding voice he was using, the one he always took on when he wanted to manipulate her.

Now he was leaning forward with his elbows on the table, looking down. "Diane, this has been a really bad year for me—worse than I expected, and I knew it would be hard. I haven't studied like I should have, and my grades have gone down. School lost all its meaning for me, and so did life. There have been times this last year I didn't even want to go on living."

Diane didn't respond. She knew the hint of suicide, the talk of a tragic life, was part of his way of getting her pity. When he looked up, she glanced away, but again she waited. She just wanted to let him have his say and get it over with.

"Yesterday I was supposed to be studying for my finals, but I couldn't concentrate. The only thing I could think of was that I would be graduating in a couple of weeks, and I have no life ahead of me. There's not one thing I'm looking forward to. I've lost you and Jenny, and there's nothing else I care about. The worst thing is, everything that happened was my fault, and I know it. There's something wrong with me, Diane. Something is really messed up inside my head. I've ruined my whole life. I was thinking about that, and all of a sudden I knew I had to get in the car and drive down here. I had to find you. I had to talk to you. I had to find out whether there wasn't some hope left that we could get back what we had—because we had *everything*."

She thought of all the things she could say. She wanted, above all, to tell him that she had heard this little speech before, just before he beat up on her. She had heard him use this sorrowful, dramatic voice before, only to hear it change to ice once she didn't respond. But it was better to let him squirm. She looked down at the table and said nothing.

"Diane, I love you. In God's eyes we're still married forever. And that's what I want. Tell me what it would take for you to trust me enough to give our marriage one more try."

She finally looked him directly in the eyes. "Greg, you did everything you could to avoid paying child support, and then you fought to pay as little as possible. So don't cry to me about how much you miss me and *Jenny*."

"That wasn't me. That was the lawyer in Dad's office. That's just what those guys are trained to do. I hardly knew what was going on."

"You could have sent us a check a whole lot sooner than you did. We needed the money, and you knew it."

"Okay. That is right. But back then, my thinking was still messed up. I was mad at you, and I was trying to get back. I was telling myself, she won't even give me a second chance. She—"

"*Second* chance? I think you'd better do some recounting, Greg."

"I know. You're right. I'm just saying, that's what I had in my head back then. I was mad and I was arrogant. I was trying to show you that life was going to be tough without me to support you. What I didn't know was that I was the one who was going to have the hard time. At night I come back to our apartment, and I just stare at the walls. I thought I knew how much I loved you, but I didn't really know until you were gone."

"So what's happened to Sondra? Why doesn't she come over and keep you company?"

"I don't have anything to do with her, Diane. That's the truth."

"Who's choice was that? Yours or hers?"

"Diane, I know you think we had an affair, but we didn't. She always flirted around, and we spent too much time together. You were right about that. But I didn't ever break my temple vows."

"Greg, think about that. I don't know whether you had sex or not. I don't trust you enough to assume you're not lying. But look at the relationship you created with her. She felt all right about writing a little love note to you."

"That was a joke. I think she did have something in mind. I think she would have gone to bed with me, if that's what I had wanted, but that note you read wasn't serious. I *swear* to you that's the truth."

Diane found herself believing that much.

"Di, I do regret that I established an improper friendship with another woman, and I can see how misguided that was now. It was part of what was wrong with me then. And when I hit you, I did, in that sense, break my temple vows. I understand that. And I'm glad you left me. It was what I deserved. But it was also the only thing that would change me. It's taken me a year of being alone to finally get it through my thick skull that I was the one who was wrong—completely wrong—and now I know that I have to do something about my problem."

"Greg, you don't even know what your problem is. You think you have a bad temper and you lost it a couple of times. You think you can overcome that and everything will be all right."

"No." He placed both hands on the table, flat, and he looked into Diane's eyes. "It's a whole lot more than that. I dominated you. I didn't give you the chance to be the woman you're capable of being."

Diane was surprised by this—surprised he understood that much about himself. But she had said things like that to him. Maybe he was only saying, as usual, what he thought she wanted to hear. "Greg, you were destroying me. You never stopped finding fault with me. By the time

I left you, I felt fat and ugly and stupid—and useless as a wife. I'm still afraid to make a new relationship with anyone. All I can think is that no man would ever be happy with me. I couldn't satisfy his needs."

Greg was nodding, looking devastated. Tears were in his eyes. He had let his hair grow longer this last year, and it was disheveled, falling in his eyes in a way he had never allowed before. He really did seem distraught. But it was so hard to know with him what was real and what wasn't. "I know exactly what you're saying, Diane. You told me some things about myself that I didn't believe at the time, but I understand now. You were a kind of prize to me. I wanted to marry you because I thought you were the most beautiful girl at BYU. But in my life, everything has always been about me. I wanted what I wanted, and I went after it. What I didn't know how to do was think about anyone else's needs. But the one thing I can feel is that this last year has knocked the pride out of me. Being a star at the law school was huge to me. I wanted to make a lot of money, be a hotshot. That's all I thought about. Now those things mean nothing. What I want is my family. I want to be home in the evening, have time to take you and Jenny for a walk, or go get ice cream. I just want to be with you, be able to talk and go out to dinner on a date, take Jenny to the zoo—just all the stuff that a real father does. More than anything I want to believe that I still have some reason to live. And I want eternity with you. I always thought I was religious, but I was only going through the motions. Half this year I didn't go to church. I was too embarrassed to go to our ward, and I didn't want to go to the singles ward. But I started to realize there was no spirit in me. And that's what I needed. I had never stopped praying, but I started praying for the right things and praying more sincerely than I ever have. And I finally went back to church."

Diane hadn't expected to be moved by anything Greg said, but she was feeling some of this. He did seem to be seeing things in himself he had never admitted before, had never seemed to know. And he did seem heartbroken. She had loved Greg once, and she found herself responding to him now. But she knew she had to be careful.

"Diane, all I'm saying is that I've gone through a dark, horrible process, but it's brought me face to face with myself, and I think I'm now capable of being a good husband to you. I won't be ranked at the top of my graduating class, but I will graduate, and I can start working for my dad in a few weeks. When I move back to Salt Lake, I'm wondering whether you wouldn't give me another chance. I'm not talking about getting married again right away. I'm just talking about seeing each other—dating, if you want to call it that—and me spending some time with Jenny. We could take everything slowly, one step at a time, and see whether I couldn't prove to you that I've changed."

"You promised me over and over, before, that you would change."

"I know. But that was before all this. You do believe that people can change, don't you?"

It was an interesting question. Wasn't it the Christian attitude to believe that people could reform? She had argued that today. What she was also glimpsing was the life she had always wanted and had given up. This past year had been good for her in some ways, but it had also been hard. Life would be easier with Greg, with the income he would soon have and a new house perhaps, and it would be nice for Jennifer to have a father. Diane could go to church with a husband, fit in with the others, feel part of a ward. She wouldn't have to worry every minute about money, and lie in bed at night scared of some noise she heard outside. She wasn't good at being alone, and she grew weary sometimes of having no one to help her with Jenny, no one to talk to at the dinner table, no one to touch and laugh with and take a ride with. She had always wanted to be married, and she had met such a "good catch" in Greg. If he could change, if he *had* changed, maybe she could have everything after all.

"I don't know, Greg. I think people do change. But I think a lot of our traits run pretty deep. We get insights, and we think because we understand ourselves we can do something about our problems. But when life moves forward, it's easy to go back to where we were."

"I know. I've thought a lot about that. But I've also thought that if God wanted to wake me up, and give me a chance to change, he did the right thing. He took you away from me, and then told me, in effect, if you want her back, you'd better take a hard look at yourself."

"I'm not the same person I was a year ago, Greg. I'm not sure you would like to be married to me. I've had a year of managing on my own, and I like thinking for myself. I know you won't believe it, but I'm getting good grades, mostly A's, and I speak up in class. I've begun to think that I'm not so dumb. And I need that. I need to decide for myself how I'm going to vote, and what I think about things going on in the world. And I'll tell you one thing: I can't stand Nixon. I don't think you could tolerate a wife who voted for a Democrat."

Greg laughed. "Yes, I could. I like what's happening to you. For one thing, you would tell me if I started back into my old ways. And we would have lots more to talk about. As far as I'm concerned, you could stay in school now and finish your degree. You always wanted to do that, and now it would be your turn. I could watch Jenny at night while you studied."

But Greg was jumping ahead way too fast. "Greg, I don't think—"

"Let me just tell you one more thing. It's really important." He folded his arms across his chest and looked down for a time. Then he spoke more quietly. "I've been praying about all of this for a long time, and when I decided to come down here, it was in response to what I've been feeling lately. I just feel that God does want us together. He wants us to raise Jennifer together; he wants us to be an eternal family. I'm sure there's nothing he hates more than to see an eternal marriage broken apart, and I know he'll help me as I try to change, so we can be together again."

"Greg, I don't like it when you do this."

"Do what?"

"You told me God wanted us to get married in the first place. It was always *your* inspiration. I had some serious doubts during the time we were engaged, but you just kept telling me it was what God wanted. I wish I had listened a lot more to my own spirit—because I wasn't so sure. I told my dad, and he told me to get my own answer—but it seemed too late for that, and I was afraid to ask."

"Okay. I see what you're saying. The patriarch in the home should receive guidance for his family, but he can't just overrule his wife's inspiration. Those are things a couple has to work out together."

"But you always had to be in control, Greg. I never knew anything about our money. I couldn't spend a penny without worrying what you would think."

"I'm going to have plenty of money now. We won't be pinching pennies like we were back then."

"That's not the point, Greg. You made me throw that book away—*The Feminine Mystique*—because you didn't want me to get certain ideas in my head."

"Did I *make* you throw it away?"

"No. And yes. I knew if I didn't, you would make me pay—in all your subtle ways. You manipulate people, Greg. I'm not sure you even know when you're doing it. And the truth is, I suspect it's still what you're doing now. What am I supposed to say when you start implying that I'm the one keeping us apart, that I'm the one breaking up an eternal marriage? Suddenly, it's God who wants us together, and it's me who's defying God. I think maybe God isn't too happy with men who *beat up* on their 'eternal companions.' He just might have a special place for them in the hereafter."

"Diane, I'm not saying you have to follow my inspiration. You should pray about it too."

"I know, Greg. But you always think you know how my prayers are supposed to come out. Maybe God wants me to stay as far away from you as I can. Maybe he wants me to find someone who will treat me and Jenny the way we deserve to be treated. Maybe he hates the way you use prayer as a tool—just to get what you want."

Greg was staring at her now, and she saw a little change, just that first hint of cold that she remembered so well. "I think that's a strange thing to say, Diane. I'm looking for answers, and I'm only asking you to do the same. I just think we could start to see each other, find out how much we've changed, and we could both keep praying for the right thing to do from that point."

Diane knew this was a crucial moment. She didn't know how she would feel later. Maybe this was her chance to get her life back, and maybe she was about to lose that chance forever. But her inner voice was telling her not to trust Greg; she remembered too much, and she felt something evil in him, as though an animal of prey were trying to lure her closer. "Greg, I'm sorry," she said, "but I don't dare take a chance on you again. I just don't trust you. And I don't want Jenny to go through the same things again. She doesn't remember what you did to me, but she's getting old enough that she would remember now, and I feel my first duty in life is to protect her."

Greg sat for a long time with his head down. When he looked up his eyes were so full of pain, Diane could hardly stand to look at him. "I see what you're saying. If I were in your position, I would feel the same way. I hit you, and I did it in front of my daughter. And I did it more than once. So . . . I'm getting what I deserve. I've also never realized it about myself, but I do try to get you to bend to my will by telling you what I think God wants us to do. I'm discovering all kinds of things about myself right now, and I have to say, I don't like much of it. It's all really hard to admit."

Diane was almost sure this was an act. She had seen Greg use this very tone to manipulate her feelings before. But he did seem devastated, more than she had thought was possible. She didn't want to feel sorry for him, didn't want to be made a fool of again, but she did wonder whether he was capable of changing.

Greg tried to smile. "I've got to get back in my car and drive back to Seattle now. It was stupid of me to come down here like this."

"Aren't you going to rest up overnight?"

"No. I don't want to see my parents. They don't know I'm here, and they would think I was crazy to do something like this. If I get really tired, I'll stop at a motel somewhere."

"You've got finals coming up this next week?"

"Yeah."

"Well . . . be careful. Don't drive too long."

"It doesn't matter that much. Nothing matters to me right now."

"Come on, Greg. Don't say that. That's how I felt for a while, but I decided I had to make something of my life. That's what I'm trying to do."

Greg nodded, but she thought she knew what he was feeling: the hopelessness she had experienced last summer.

"I do want to see Jenny this summer. I'm sorry I haven't been part of her life. But I'm going to be now. You don't mind that, do you?"

"Greg, you're her father. Just don't pop in and out of her life. Be consistent. Get to know her, and let her get to know you."

"I will. And . . . could we maybe talk once in a while? You know—just keep in touch?"

"Sure. We'll have to talk if you're going to spend time with Jenny."

"What if we just got acquainted again, a little at a time—almost like we had never met before?"

"I don't know, Greg. No. I don't think so."

"I don't mean that we would go out. I'm just saying I want to be a grown-up. And I want you to know I'm making some progress."

"Sure. But I don't see any way we would ever get back together."

"Okay. But maybe you would like to meet someone new someday—so Jenny will have a father around the house. And what if I were that someone new?"

"Greg, please. Don't do this."

"Just leave a tiny corner of your heart open. Don't tell yourself there's absolutely no chance it could ever happen. That's all I ask."

Diane didn't answer even though she thought she should. But she didn't want him driving back to Seattle feeling so hopeless.

"Well, I'd better go." He reached across the table and put his hand on top of hers for a moment. "I love you. I always will," he said. And then he got up and walked away.

Diane sat at the table for a long time. She tried not to cry. She tried not to feel anything for Greg. But she was confused, and she did cry.

Chapter 28

The final weeks of Kathy's Peace Corps service rushed by quickly. She spent her evenings visiting as many of the families in town as she could, mainly just to say good-bye. The toilet building had continued to move ahead, and surprisingly, the same workers seemed to show up every day. They didn't get as much done as a crew in America would, but the trenching was slow, all done by hand, and the plumbing seemed even slower. A couple of weeks before she was to leave, the laying of the concrete blocks seemed to go rather quickly, however, and she could see that the workers were making an all-out effort to finish the job.

On the last Sunday before her departure, she made her trip into Manila on the jeepneys, and she found herself feeling painfully nostalgic. It was even fun to crowd in with the local people, laugh with them, and greet the people she had seen on the same route on previous Sunday mornings. She had gone to Sunday School that morning and then returned to her home in the barrio afterward. She normally didn't make the trip twice, but today she had wanted to spend some time with Tamra, and not leave her alone all day. Along the way, the jeepney she was riding picked up Sister Pinong and her three little children, also on their way to church. Sister Pinong was a member and her husband wasn't, but she came every week and brought her children, the oldest of whom was a little boy of six. He looked sparkling with his hair combed neatly and his white shirt clean and pressed. His four-year-old brother, who had been dressed just as carefully, now looked a little ruffled. Sister Pinong was carrying her baby, Isobel, who was looking about, seemingly fascinated by all the noise and motion. Kathy was sitting one row back when the Pinongs crowded in with others on a bench-like seat. Kathy leaned up and touched Sister Pinong's shoulder. "Good morning," she said. "Do you want me to take Isobel so you won't be so crowded?"

Sister Pinong smiled and nodded. She lifted the baby, and Kathy reached for her, then hoisted her over her mother's shoulder. Then Sister Pinong lifted her smaller son onto her lap, easing the tight fit for everyone on that seat. Kathy had sat by the Pinongs in church once and realized how difficult it was for a mother to keep three small children under control in sacrament meeting, so after that she had often sat with them and helped. The boys liked Kathy, but it was Isobel who had become Kathy's little friend. She beamed at Kathy now and touched her face with her fingers. She was more than a year old, maybe fifteen months, but tiny. She had a pale, milky complexion, with huge dark eyes. Today she was wearing a yellow dress with a yellow ribbon in her hair.

Sister Pinong turned as best she could and spoke over her shoulder. "Are you sad today about leaving?" she asked.

Kathy was a little surprised that Sister Pinong was aware that this was her last week. Kathy hadn't wanted to mention it to everyone. She knew that Filipinos loved to make something special of such leave-taking, and she hadn't wanted to call that much attention to herself. She had scheduled the choir to sing the week before, so she wouldn't have such a busy day today, and she had said good-bye to the choir at their last practice, the previous week. That hadn't been easy. Kathy had been working with a young woman in the choir, a new convert who was musical and would eventually do all right as the choir director, so Kathy was glad the choir would be okay without her. Nonetheless, she knew she was going to miss the satisfaction she had experienced when the choir performed.

"I am a little sad," she told Sister Pinong. "Everyone has been so kind to me here."

"We will always remember you, Kathy."

Kathy didn't think so. But she held Isobel tighter and found herself wishing this time of her life didn't have to end.

At church, however, no one said anything about her departure. She had not wanted the branch to make a fuss, but she had wanted to tell the members good-bye, and for some reason they seemed unwilling to talk about that. When she greeted Sister Luna, Kathy said, "I hope you know how much you've meant to me. We've spent some wonderful Sunday afternoons together. Those times were important to me."

Sister Luna hugged Kathy and thanked her, but she didn't say good-bye, didn't even express her sadness that Kathy was leaving. That hardly seemed like her, but it caused Kathy to think that she was making too much of her own departure. After all, she was rather like the missionaries who came and went. The branch certainly got used to that, and having Kathy leave was probably much the same. So she sat in church, once again with Isobel on her lap, and told herself that she would tell some of her friends good-bye after the meeting and then leave quietly.

But the truth was, Kathy was feeling disappointed. She half expected President Luna, as he conducted, to say something about her leaving, but he didn't even remember to release her from her position and sustain the new choir director. After the sacrament was passed, he announced only that one of the missionaries would speak, followed by old Brother Concepcion, who was notorious for forgetting about closing time and speaking on and on.

Kathy found herself paying little attention to the talks. She was still feeling some nostalgia, but the strength of her emotion had diminished. She thought it was rather a good lesson to learn: people came and went, and no one person was all that important to a branch. She was ashamed of herself for the things she had imagined might happen today. She was a member of the branch and had done her best, but she was also like a pebble dropped in a pond. She had made a few small ripples, but those would smooth quickly, and the pond would remain unchanged.

Brother Concepcion didn't talk nearly as long as she had expected, however, and then President Luna got up again. "I forgot something," he said. He was smiling. "All those who wish to give Sister Thomas a vote of thanks for the work she has done with the choir, please come forward."

Come forward?

But then Kathy saw what was happening. It was the choir, rising from their seats, walking forward and then moving into their positions up front. Sister Ramos, the new director, looked out across the remaining congregation. "Please join us for the final verse," she requested. And then the choir sang "God Be with You Till We Meet Again."

Kathy held little Isobel tight, and tears ran down her cheeks. And when the entire congregation began to sing the final verse, Kathy sobbed.

When the hymn was over, the president did extend a formal release, and then he said, "Sister Thomas, we needed music in our branch, and you brought it to us. But it's your love we will hold in our hearts. Our people are new in the Church, just learning how to make a branch be what it should be. You showed us how to do that. Your work in the branch was important; your love, more important."

When the meeting ended, Sister Luna came to Kathy and said, "Wait for just a moment. The members want to go out first." She laughed. "The choir had an extra practice during the week, but no one was supposed to tell you they were going to sing. It was hard for all of us."

Kathy still couldn't say anything. Sister Luna walked with her to the back doors and then, as Kathy walked out, she saw that everyone was waiting in a line. One after the other, everyone embraced her—the women and men, the children, even the teenagers. They told her over and over how much they loved her, and Kathy tried to say all she could, but she had never been so moved in her life, so talking wasn't easy.

When Kathy got home, she told Tamra about her experience. Tamra listened, said that it must have been nice, but she said little more. Kathy and Tamra had come to a kind of standoff since the day Kathy had tried to tell Tamra how important it was to love the people in the barrio. Tamra had actually seemed somewhat happier lately, but school was out and she was planning to do some traveling. So Kathy finally asked the question she had been wondering about. "Tamra, are you going to stay for your second year?"

"I don't know. I need to decide right away, but I'm not sure what I'm going to do. I hate to admit it, but I want to do some traveling, and I don't want to leave until I've done that."

"But the school needs to know."

"Why? If I don't show up, they'll just do the same things they always do. I'm just a fifth wheel anyway."

"But you'll have some of your own classes this year."

"Yeah. Classes I'm not allowed to teach the way I want to."

"Tamra, that's not true. I followed the curriculum the way they wanted me to, and I didn't do as much of the experimental stuff as I had in mind, but I really think we have an influence on the kids—especially the girls. We're such role models to them."

"I know. I've thought about all that. But any change we make is so small and so slow, I'm just not sure it's worth another year of my life."

"Well . . . you're the only one who can decide."

"That's right."

This last statement was just a little too forceful, and Kathy knew what Tamra was saying: "So don't push me."

Kathy was leaving on Thursday, so she had a lot to do. She needed to pack and send some things home that she couldn't carry with her, but she also had a number of people she wanted to visit one last time. On Monday, she received a letter from the mayor. It was an invitation to the ceremonial opening of the public toilet. She had seen the men painting lately, but she hadn't been aware that it was so close to being finished. She had no question that the mayor had made a special effort on her behalf, and she appreciated it, but she had been planning to see friends on

Wednesday evening, and this little "ceremony" was going to complicate her life. The mayor loved nothing more than to give long speeches, and he would certainly spend a good deal of time praising himself. She doubted that many people would be willing to attend, even if they knew about it, and she hadn't heard a word in town about the event. She suspected that she would be there with the mayor, maybe the principal, and probably some of the men on the barrio council. So on Wednesday evening, when she walked to the little toilet building, near the school, she was hoping, more than anything, that the mayor wouldn't talk long and she could get on to visiting her friends.

She was still well down the street when she saw the banner, and then the crowd of people. She realized, first, that most everyone in town must be there, and then she let the words on the banner sink in: "Thank You, Miss Thomas." As she walked closer, a brass band began to play. It took her some time to realize that the song was "Onward, Christian Soldiers," played with all the skill of a junior high band—at the beginning of a school year. She didn't know whether the song was in recognition of her religious background, or whether it was the only tune the band knew, but it somehow seemed right. She kept walking, grinning as she drew closer and saw the mayor, all dressed up, the town council, the teachers from her school, and nearly all the families she knew. Most of the young people she had taught were in their school uniforms even though school was out, including some who lived in other barrios.

She saw the mothers she had been visiting all year, the men standing about in clean shirts, mostly white, everyone smiling, looking very pleased with themselves. What Kathy knew was that Filipinos loved almost any excuse for a party—a festival—and other Peace Corps volunteers had been honored much the same way. So she told herself not to think this was anything very special, but so many were there, and they looked so joyous to see her arrive that all the emotion she had felt on Sunday, at church, returned. Two years ago she had hated this place, and now, these were her people. She knew virtually all of them, and she loved them, but what astounded her was the obvious truth: they loved her, maybe as much as the people in her branch did. She had always been a thorn in someone's side, always the one to make people uncomfortable. Even her parents, however much they loved her, had often seemed on edge, just to have her home. But these people genuinely loved her, and she had never thought that could happen. Behind everything she had ever thought about herself was a sense that she might be good at times, might be right at times, might even be charming at her best, but she had never suspected herself of being worthy of people's love.

The mayor stepped forward as she approached. He greeted her with a handshake and a great smile, and he announced, in Tagalog, loudly enough for everyone to hear, "We honor you today, Miss Thomas, and we thank you for all you have done for us."

That was his speech—his entire speech. The rest was all food and celebration, and dozens of hugs and kisses from the dear girls she had taught and from their mothers, and kind words from everyone. But in the end, the moment for the dedication came. The mayor called "Miss Thomas" forward, and he pronounced what must have been the second shortest speech of his life: "Miss Thomas has taught us much about our health. You children must not forget what she taught you. This fine toilet will make our barrio much better—better for everyone. You old fellows, you must use it too."

Everyone laughed.

"We now ask Miss Thomas to break this jar to declare our toilet officially completed."

Kathy took a little hammer and struck the pottery jar that was hanging from the open door. Something sprayed in all directions. It was probably something fancier than tuba she supposed, but it definitely contained alcohol, and now she had the smell all over her. She laughed, and everyone cheered.

As soon as there was some quiet, the mayor said in a loud voice, "We now invite Miss Thomas to be the first to use our new toilet."

This brought another huge cheer, and then laughter, as Kathy felt her face burn. She thought of saying, "I really don't need to right now," but it hardly seemed a possibility. So she stepped inside, was glad to close the door, but could only imagine everyone waiting outside, perhaps listening, and waiting for her to reappear. She didn't "use" the toilet; she just couldn't deal with the thought of doing that with everyone out there. But she waited for a while and made a point of washing her hands. She was glad to see that the water was running—even if there was no soap. But then she realized her problem. If she didn't flush the toilet, they might notice. They might all be waiting for the sound, as proof of her accomplishment. So even though she was mortified to do so, she flushed and heard a great gurgling sound, followed by another cheer from outside. And then she realized she'd better wash her hands again, just in case the children could hear.

She took her time, pretended to work up a big lather, and then she turned the water off, shook her hands dry as best she could, and stepped to the door. She really didn't want to face the whole town again, but she opened the door and accepted the roar of approval, her face still hot. And then the party continued, with food and drink and music.

At some point in the evening, she felt a hand on her shoulder. She turned around to see Tamra there, looking subdued and serious. "I've decided to stay another year," she said.

Kathy nodded and took Tamra into her arms.

Kathy flew home that Thursday and arrived in Los Angeles an hour before she had left. She waited for a couple of hours, so tired from the overnight flight she could hardly keep her head up, and then boarded another airplane and flew home to Salt Lake. Her parents were there, and Douglas, who would always be a child, clung to her and told her never to go away so long again.

She was still so tired she was numb, but when her dad pulled into the driveway, she came to life a little. She had left this home six years before, when she had gone east to college, and since then she had often returned, but there had come a time when it hadn't seemed home anymore. This time it did. Kathy would be staying in Wayne's old room.

Kathy didn't have her old room back, but she went there instinctively and stood for a time. Nothing was the same. Glenda had redecorated, had actually made the room more "girly" than it had been before. She also had pictures of the Osmonds on the wall. Kathy had heard the Osmonds sing barbershop on the *Andy Williams Show* before she left for the Philippines, but it appeared from the poster that they were turning into a rock group, which surprised Kathy.

What Kathy remembered, however, was the fifteen-year-old she had once been—the age Glenda was now—and how the world had appeared to her then. Kathy had already taken an interest in certain causes by then, but she had been part of this family, part of this house, part of the Church. What she felt now was that she had been very far away, but that she belonged here again, and she liked that feeling. She thought of the night she had packed for college and Marshall had been there. He was married now, but she still liked to remember the night he had kissed her. She wondered whether any other guys like Marshall were around.

However familiar everything was, Kathy felt a strangeness, too: both from the dry air outside and the cool air inside. Her parents had installed air-conditioning while she was gone. They had bought a color television set, too, and the kitchen had been remodeled, with all new cabinets. There were also new carpets and a new dining room table and chairs. Kathy had always known that her family had money, but Dad had never been one to let go of much of it. She wondered what was happening now.

Kathy took a nap that afternoon, in Wayne's room, but at dinner she told her dad, "You've been spending a lot of money, haven't you? Are you getting extravagant in your old age?"

It was her mom who answered. "I kept complaining about my old-fashioned kitchen, so he finally gave in and had it remodeled."

"I figured that was a lot cheaper than buying a new house," her dad said.

"I hinted at that, too," Lorraine said, "but I didn't really want to move. I just figured your dad would rather fix the house up than build a new one."

"Sure. He always does what's cheaper," Glenda said. "I learned a long time ago, you choose the bicycle you want, and then you find one that's more expensive, and you say, 'I like these two bikes.'"

Wally smiled at her. "You just think you had me tricked," he said. "I always knew what you were up to. If you had cried a little and said you wanted the other one, you probably would have gotten it."

"Yeah. That's what *I* learned," Shauna said, and everyone laughed.

Douglas was grinning, probably not understanding the joke quite fully. "I can ride a bike," he said. "Real good."

"I know you can, Douglas," Kathy told him, and she rested her hand on his. "I've missed you so much."

"I know. You said that in your letters. Mom read 'em to me."

But then Shauna said, "How come you're so different, Kathy?"

Kathy glanced around at everyone. She saw that old look of worry coming into her dad's face, as though he was thinking, "Oh, oh. Let's not pop the bubble already." But her mom was smiling. "You do seem different, honey. I think the Peace Corps was good for you."

"What's different?" Kathy asked.

"You seem a little softer. I felt it the minute you walked into the airport."

"I did too," Wally said.

Kathy was surprised they noticed, but she liked the idea. "There are things I didn't tell you in my letters. I didn't want to make claims and then change my mind."

"What kinds of things?" Lorraine asked.

"I went to church a lot this last year."

"Actually, you did tell us that."

"Well, yeah. And I told you that they made me the choir director, but beyond that, I didn't tell you how involved I got in the branch. I got so I loved the barrio, but the best day of the week was Sunday, when I could be with all my friends in the Church."

She saw the response from her parents: the pleasure in their faces. She knew what they had been praying for all these years, and she knew what they were hoping. But they didn't ask. Her parents knew better than to pressure Kathy.

"I saw what the Church can do for people. We tried to change lives through the Peace Corps, and we didn't get very far. But the Church changes people inside. It was amazing what happened to people when they joined."

Wally was nodding. "I've seen that," he said.

And then everyone waited, as though they wanted Kathy to say the rest. But she only said, "I took the feelings I had at church to the barrio, and everything went better there, too."

"When something is true, it works," Wally said.

"Yeah. I think that's right. It was good for me to see that."

And again everyone waited. But Kathy didn't want to make promises. Who knew how she would feel about everything after she had been away from the things she had experienced in Manila?

"What are you going to do now?" Lorraine asked.

"I don't know. I just want to stay home for a while, if that's okay."

"Of course it is." But Kathy saw tears pool in her mother's eyes. Everyone obviously knew what Kathy was trying to say.

"I'm thinking about graduate school. But I don't even know what I want to study. So until I decide, I might just look for a job, and . . . I don't know . . . see if I can find the Kathy I've been looking for. I've got a little better idea what I want her to be now." She looked at her dad. "Do you think the bishop could find a calling for me?"

"I'll talk to him about it. I think he can probably find an opening." But now it was Wally who had tears in his eyes.

So Kathy decided to give him one more surprise. "What I really wouldn't mind is to find myself a husband. Have you seen any eligible young men around the stake I can try to entice? Or maybe some not-so-young ones?"

Wally laughed, but Lorraine said. "You could give Marshall another try. He's home this summer."

"I doubt that his wife would like the idea."

"He didn't get married."

"What?"

"He broke off his engagement. His mom is really upset with him. She told Grandma that he can never make up his mind about anything. He's completed enough hours for about three different majors, but he hasn't taken enough of his required classes to graduate."

"Yeah, well, that doesn't surprise me. I don't think I'll try to get anything restarted with him. The guy would drive me crazy—and I found out a long time ago that he has no interest in me."

But later, when Kathy was back in her room, she found herself thinking about Marshall. He sounded as though he had never really grown up, but she was surprised at the little spark of pleasure she had experienced when her mom had said he wasn't married after all.

Chapter 29

Gene, we need to go over there for at least a little while. I promised your grandma we would."

"You shouldn't make promises like that for me, Emily. I don't want to be out in that heat very long."

Gene and Emily were lying in bed. They had slept a little later than usual, since the day was a holiday—the 24th of July, 1971. It had been a hot night, but the temperature had cooled toward morning, and Gene had finally gotten some sleep. He couldn't remember the last time he had slept really well, all night, at least without being full of pain medication.

"We'll stay in the shade, and we won't stay long, but Danny loves so much to be around the family. He needs to go."

Gene didn't care, not really. As it had turned out, he'd had to have another surgery after returning to Utah—one he hadn't expected—and once again, everything seemed gone from him. It was not just that he was tired or that he didn't feel well. He seemed to have nothing left. He tried to present himself to the family as normal, but he lacked the energy to do much, and above all, he lacked the patience. Danny loved to repeat things: to hear the same story, or to zoom a car around on the floor. That was all right, but after a few minutes, down on the floor, Gene would feel the discomfort of bending or reaching, and even more, the tiredness that no longer presented itself with the drama of exhaustion but only as an annoying lack of interest. Danny seemed to sense Gene's attitude, and he misbehaved in response—threw his toys around or even tore pages out of books—things he clearly knew would get a rise out of Gene. But even then, Gene didn't care, as hard as he tried to act as though he did. He usually withdrew then and went to his and Emily's bedroom to lie on the bed. Emily was tired too, and she tried to be patient, but Gene could sense how all this was wearing thin for her.

"What time are we going over there?" Gene asked.

"Grandma Thomas just said 'after the parade.' Everyone else is going downtown to the parade, where they always sit."

"At least we had an excuse to avoid that."

"Gene, come on. Don't do that. Danny would love to go."

The Thomases, since the days of Brigham Young himself, apparently, had been going to the big parade. Gene had grown up going every year, and in truth, had liked it. It was something he supposed he needed to pass along to Danny. But when he had thought about going, he had only imagined an endless procession of high school bands and amateurish floats sponsored by the stakes around Salt Lake, so he had told Emily that he just couldn't sit that long.

But Emily was clearly irritated, as she was rather often lately, and Gene knew he had to be careful. "We'll go next year," he said. "Danny's kind of little this year anyway."

"We'll do everything *next year,* won't we?"

Emily could become angry sometimes, but it wasn't like her to be sarcastic, or to sound so caustic. Gene took a breath. He didn't want to get in a fight. He even knew that his attitude was wrong. "Actually, yes," he said. "If I can get this next surgery over, and get rid of this colostomy bag, I do feel like I can start to do a lot more. And I *want to*. You know that. If I don't start getting on with my life pretty soon, I'm going to go crazy."

Emily could never seem to understand how much Gene hated having that bag attached to him. It interfered with everything in his life, including their own closeness.

The bedroom window was open, and Gene could hear the birds outside enjoying the morning. He could also hear Emily inhale, as though she were taking a calming breath before she said what was on her mind.

"Gene, you say that, but whenever I ask you what you plan to do, you say you don't know. Your uncle keeps asking you whether you want to take over the dealership eventually, and you won't even give him an answer."

Gene had worked for Uncle Wally lately, when he could. He didn't sell cars, out on the floor, but he worked in an office, processing the paperwork for sales. Wally had been paying him a salary even before he could do anything, and he was overpaying him now, since Gene couldn't really put in many hours. Gene appreciated that Wally would do that for him, but it was charity, and that bothered him. He also had no interest in automobile sales and couldn't imagine a life around the dealership. But try as he might, he couldn't think what he *was* interested in doing. He kept saying that he was going back to school, but he couldn't think what he wanted to study.

"I told you. I don't want to sell cars."

"Don't talk so loud. Everyone's still asleep."

The family was home from Washington, living again in the house with Gene and Emily, and Sharon was home from BYU for the summer. She actually should have finished, but she kept taking more classes, without filling all her requirements for graduation. Gene had the feeling she didn't want to graduate because she was still interested in Joel, the fellow she had been dating down there for the last year or so. He was behind her in school, having served a mission, and was apparently acting rather noncommittal. All the aunts were worried about that. Joey and his wife were in Salt Lake too. He was working this summer, also for Wally, but at the parts plant. Kurt was living in Salt Lake with some friends, supposedly going to school, supposedly working, but actually botching everything. Gene was sure he was still taking drugs. So it was only Kenny and Pam, both teenagers now, since Pam had recently turned thirteen, who were there with his parents, but still, the house seemed full of people, and his mom seemed to take over a little too much when she came home, leaving Emily feeling like an assistant. Gene's dad still hinted at times that he wanted to talk with Gene about Vietnam—but that was something Gene was not going to do. So it was awkward, and that was part of why Gene didn't want to go to the parade. He wanted a morning alone. He had told Emily to go with everyone else, but she had been stubborn about that. She said she didn't want to leave him by himself.

"That's fine, Gene. I can see where you might not want to stay at the dealership. But what *are* you going to do?"

"Em, I don't know. I've thought about law school and business school—you know that—but it's hard to make a decision when I'm not ready to get started. I'd have to take exams to get into law school, and I'm just not ready to do that yet. But one of these days we need to talk about my options and make up our minds."

"I do try to talk with you about all this, and you won't do it."

There was anger under all this control, and Gene hated the implied accusation. He couldn't hide his reaction when he said, "Excuse me for having surgeries, Emily. They're a bad habit of mine. That little gook who shot me actually meant to put me where I wouldn't have to bother people. I guess his aim was bad. Maybe you ought to talk to him."

"Don't do that, Gene. I hate it when you talk that way."

"I'm sorry. I should have referred to 'the nice young man from North Vietnam' I happened to meet while I was strolling in the jungle."

"I'm not talking about that. I'm talking about your self-pity. It just isn't like you to make so many excuses."

Gene hated that accusation more than any other. He felt a rage building in his head, his muscles. He wanted to scream. He wanted to curse. He wanted to do anything but lie there and listen to her. "*Self-pity?* Is that what you think this is?" His voice was fairly controlled, but anger was shaking his vocal cords. "Let them cut you next time, if you think it's so easy. Hang this bag on your side. Live for a while on *soft foods*, as the doctor calls them. I've got some other names I can think of."

Gene had learned the language of soldiers in Vietnam. He hadn't used it, or rarely had, but it always came to mind at times like this. He wanted to be vile. He wanted to let his anger release in words that would stun his wife. He wanted to go back to the hospital, where men knew how to describe what they were going through, with language as disgusting as their condition. But he didn't. He didn't swear, didn't scream. He made fists with his hands, shut his eyes tight, and felt the pain boil. Every breath seemed an act of will for the moment, but he knew enough not to say things he would regret.

"I'm sorry," Emily said. "I didn't mean it that way. I know the pain you go through. But you always had things you wanted to do. You were always so excited about life. I want you to be *you* again. I want Gene back—the one I married." She rolled onto her side and began to cry.

And that melted Gene's anger. But he was scared. He had almost lost control. He knew the words that had come into his head and how close he had come to saying them. He couldn't roll onto his side easily, but he scooted himself closer to Emily and put his arm under her. She rolled next to him and continued to cry. "I'm sorry," he whispered.

"I'm so terrible, Gene. I don't know how I could say that to you, after what you've been through. I prayed so hard that you would live, and now I'm not grateful enough that you did."

"No. You're right. We've got to start thinking about the future. We will. I promise."

But they didn't talk. They lay there and listened to the birds sing. Gene wanted to like that, wanted to relax, but he didn't.

At one o'clock Gene and Emily drove to Sugar House Park. As it had turned out, Alex and Anna had decided to take Danny to the parade, so that had given Gene and Emily some time alone. They didn't really talk much, but after their spat that morning—and the apologies—Gene felt a little closer to her. Still, he was dreading the picnic: the heat and the noise and, most of all, the questions. Everyone always wanted to know what he was going to do—the same question Emily kept asking him. Someday he hoped he would be able to think again, and then he would decide, but no one understood his absence of energy, the buzz in his head, his inability to focus and to follow a thought.

Gene carried a couple of aluminum lawn chairs to the shade by some big trees. He had spotted Grandpa and Grandma Thomas already established there, having laid claim to a nearby picnic table. Alex and Anna had brought Danny back from the parade, but Anna had had to put the final touches on a big potato salad, so Gene and Emily, with Danny, had come on ahead. "Where is everyone?" Emily asked.

"Not here yet," Grandpa said, sounding grumpy. "The parade's been over quite a while. I don't know where they are."

"They all had to stop home on the way," Grandma said, "and it's so hard to get out of town after the parade these days. We used to drive down and park right there where the parade came through. But there's getting to be too many people in Salt Lake now. Everything's too busy." Grandma was now focusing on Danny, whom Emily was carrying. She got up from her chair and reached for him. "Hi, Danny," she said, and he beamed. She took him in her arms, and he gave her a squeeze around her neck. "Do you want to go on the swings?" Grandma asked him.

"Uh huh," he said, and he turned to look for them.

"We'd better go now, before the park fills up." She set him down and took him by the hand.

"I'll go with you," Emily said, and the three walked away.

Gene unfolded the lawn chairs and then sat down next to his grandpa. "How are you feeling, Grandpa?" he asked.

"Oh, not too bad. But what I've got isn't going to go away. The only thing they can do is give me all these pills that make me go to the bathroom all the time. That's supposed to keep the fluid off my heart, but I just have to drink all the more, I'm so thirsty all the time. It doesn't make any sense to me. What about you? Are they still filling you up with pills every day?"

"Yeah. I'm taking some things."

"I'd be careful with that, Gene. You can get addicted to those pain pills, and that can ruin your life about as fast as anything. I don't know what happened to the day when a man had a little pain and just told himself, 'That's part of life; I'll learn to live with it.'"

Everything Grandpa Thomas said sounded like a criticism to Gene. He had felt a special connection to his grandpa before he had left for Vietnam, but the man seemed to become more opinionated the older he got. Now he was asking, "What do you think of these Pentagon Papers? Does the Supreme Court have the right to force the military to reveal all that stuff to the public?"

Clearly, Grandpa didn't think so. But Gene wanted the nation to know all the lies that had been told during the war in Vietnam. It was becoming increasingly clear that distorted information had kept people believing in the war long after leaders had known the cause was hopeless. Gene knew better than to say that, but still, he allowed himself to say more than he probably should have. "We live in a democracy, Grandpa. People ought to know, so they can make decisions based on the facts."

"Well, sure. I believe that—in a general way. But when we fought World War II, people had the good sense to know that a lot of things had to be handled by the president and his top advisors. There are times when the public *doesn't* have the right to know everything."

"That's probably true." Gene didn't mean it. But he didn't care. And he didn't want to talk with Grandpa about Vietnam.

Grandpa laughed. "I know what you're thinking. Ol' Grandpa Thomas, he's still got something to say about *everything*. And I guess that's right. But at least I read the paper, and I pay attention to what's happening. Now we've given these eighteen-year-olds the right to vote, and they don't even bother to do it. You ask most young people about things that are going on and they don't even know what you're talking about. Don't ever let yourself be like that, Gene. You're a smart boy. It's going to take young men like you to lead this nation. You need to think about following in your father's footsteps."

"I'll never run for office, Grandpa. I don't have any interest in politics." Gene was noticing how hot it was getting to be. He wondered how long he would have to stay—and how long he would have to talk to Grandpa. The man was from another age. He hadn't worn a tie today, but he had on a white shirt, and he was wearing suit pants, with suspenders. He had no other clothes, except for his "work clothes," which he put on when he weeded the garden. And those were bib overalls.

"Don't be so quick to count yourself out of politics, Gene. Your dad used to talk that way, but it turned out that being a war hero was very helpful to him when he ran for office. People are going to know your name—Alex Thomas's boy—and you've been decorated, the same as him. I think you should start thinking toward the day when you can take over in his district once he runs for governor or for the Senate."

"He's not going to do that. He told me. He may not even run for Congress again."

"He says that, but he will. And there are some very important people in this state who want to see him as our governor. Personally, I'd rather see him in the Senate. That's what I keep talking to him about."

Gene grew weary of the way Grandpa tried to tell everyone in the family what they ought to be doing. He had told Gene several times that he ought to learn the parts business and then look to the day when he could take over that business. It was the same business that Gene's dad had turned down many years before, and Gene had no interest in it at all.

Gene saw his parents park and get out of their car with Kenny and Pam. Beverly and her family had pulled in just before them. The two families collected together and greeted one another. Aunt Bev was carrying little Michael, the son she and Roger had had the year before. He had apparently fallen asleep in the car. Aunt Bev's two older girls, Vickie and Julia, were older than Pam but good friends. The three soon spotted Danny at the swings with Grandma and Emily, and they headed that way. Danny and his cousin Jennifer, the first two great-grandchildren, were always the stars of every family gathering.

"When can you start back to school, Gene?" Grandpa asked. "Can you get going this fall?"

"I'm not sure. I've got another surgery in a couple of weeks. It should be the last, but the recovery is supposed to be kind of rough."

"I understand that. But if you could get started in the fall, that would get you back on track. I wouldn't wait too much longer."

Gene had no idea what that meant. Was he "off track"? From Grandpa's point of view, he probably was.

Now Richard and Bobbi had parked near the others, and the gathering at the edge of the park was getting bigger. Diane was with them, and had Jenny, and everyone began passing her around to hug her. All of them would be coming this way soon. Gene was relieved, in a way, just to have Grandpa's attention pulled to the others, but he was thinking he might make an excuse soon and then walk home. It was a fairly long walk from the park, especially in the heat, but he could be alone in the house for a time, and that was something he liked. He could tell everyone he wasn't feeling well, but he feared that Emily would want to drive him home, and he didn't want that. She liked his family, and she enjoyed this break in her routine. He would have to get away without seeming all that sick and then convince Emily that he could handle the walk.

"The thing is, Gene, I've seen a lot of men come home wounded like you. Back during the war, I saw a lot of it, and—"

"What's this we've got now?"

"What?"

"You said '*the* war.' I guess that means World War II."

"Well, sure. That's what we always call it, but I'm not saying you didn't fight in a war. I'm just saying—"

"When guys came home from *the* war, people thanked them, maybe gave them a pat on the back. People treat us like we were over there napalming villages—just for the fun of it."

"I know that. But you know I don't have that attitude."

Gene did know that. But he was tired of hearing about *the* war. No one back here had any idea what Vietnam soldiers had been through. World War II had been bad—Gene didn't doubt that for a minute—but he doubted that the soldiers from that generation would have traded for the kind of war men had to fight in the jungles of Vietnam.

"What I'm saying is, most of the soldiers, back then, used their GI Bill money to get a good education. They used their time in the service to their advantage. That's the thing to do."

"I know, Grandpa. I'll start this fall if I can. But part of my problem is, I'm not sure what I want to study—or what kind of work I want to do."

"See, that's just the thing. You've got to make up your mind, and then you've got to go full bore. Some guys came home from the war and spent too much time licking their wounds. You know, they lost an arm or something, and they figured they could get a little disability check for that, and they acted like the loss of an arm was more than they could deal with. Well, fellows like that usually moped around all their lives, and they never made anything of themselves. Another guy would come home with both legs gone, or something like that, and still, he would get going, and by darn if he didn't do very well for himself. It's just a matter of making up your mind. In this country, a man gets what he works for. A lot of young people these days don't understand that."

Gene had begun to grip his chair. He could almost hear the conversations that had preceded this little speech. Maybe his dad had told Grandpa, "Gene just can't seem to get himself going. He mopes around the house all the time." It was the same thing Emily had been hinting around about that morning. Maybe it's what the whole family was saying about him.

"I'm not moping around, Grandpa. I don't think anyone has a right to say that."

"I didn't say you were. I was talking about the way some men were, back during the war. I'm just telling you to be the one who grabs hold. You've always been the grandchild I expected the most from. You're blessed with good looks, a good mind, the ability to lead people. I remember you on the basketball court, and you were the guy out there who took charge. When a game was on the line, you would find a way to win it."

"That was high school, Grandpa. Can't anyone ever forget that? That was *years* ago."

"I know that. What are you getting upset about?"

Gene didn't know. But he felt it again. He wanted more than anything to slam his fist into something. He wanted to tell Grandpa to shut up, just once in his life.

"I'm just saying you're a natural leader. That's something you were born with. You can—"

"Don't! All right? Just don't give me a speech. I don't want to hear it. I'm sick of this 'golden boy' thing you've always tried to pin on me. I'm a mess, if you want to know the truth. I feel like I'm about one breath from blowing apart. I don't want to lead anyone anywhere. I just want people to leave me alone."

Gene got up, didn't look at Grandpa, but started away. He was going to walk home. Someone would tell Emily, and she might come after him, but he couldn't get himself to think any of that through. He just had to get away from his family before the rest of them started telling him what he needed to do. His whole life they had been telling him who he was and what he had to live up to. He had to be a *Thomas*, whatever that was. He was sick of it. He just needed to have one full day when his head was clear, when he could think the way he remembered thinking, and then he would decide what he had to decide. But for now, he had to escape the questions. So he walked away, angling away from the family toward Twenty-First South.

A voice was calling to him—a man's voice—but he kept going, and then he realized that someone was hurrying toward him, trying to catch up. He glanced to his right and saw Uncle Richard, of all people, trotting toward him. "I'm going to walk home, Uncle Richard," he called. "Tell Emily to stick around." He took a breath and tried to get his voice under control. "I think the heat is bothering me a little."

"Okay. Why don't you let me walk with you."

"No. That's fine. I'm not sick or feeling weak or anything."

Richard kept coming. He stopped in front of Gene. "Did Grandpa start in on you?" he asked, and he smiled.

Gene was taken off guard. Richard was the quiet uncle, a man Gene had liked forever, and yet someone he never really felt he knew very well. But Richard knew something. "Well . . . yeah," Gene said. "You know Grandpa."

"Right now, my guess is, it feels like you may never get your breath again—and if you have to talk to everyone in the family, you'll break wide open."

Gene stared at Richard. He was the professor, the Democrat, the uncle even the younger cousins called "the handsome one." He was a set of images but not exactly a person to Gene. And there he was, standing with his hands in his pockets, smiling, somehow knowing what Gene was feeling. But Gene didn't want to let this conversation continue either. He still wanted to keep walking.

"And now you're thinking, 'I'm stuck here with my old Uncle Richard. If I'm not careful, he'll be offering *his* advice.'"

"Actually, yes. I just . . . I don't . . ."

"Is it hard to concentrate? You try to think things through and you can't seem to think at all?"

Gene stared at Richard for a time. Finally he asked, "Did you go through something like that?"

"Yes. Somewhat. But not as bad as your dad. He was in worse shape than I was."

"My dad?"

"Yes."

"The war hero?"

"Yes."

"He said it was hard, but I didn't think he ever—"

"He was in bad shape, Gene. He and Wally and I talked a lot. We got each other through that time. He was having such bad dreams he didn't want to go to bed at night. One time, at work, there was a loud noise, and before he knew what he was doing, he dropped on the floor and rolled under some equipment. He was right on the edge, Gene. But he started talking with me and Wally."

"I have dreams sometimes, but I'm okay."

"No, you're not, Gene. You're not the same person who went to Vietnam."

"I know. But they've been cutting on me ever since." Gene looked to see what his family was doing, but most had walked over to Grandpa. The others were at the swings with Danny and now Jenny. "I think I'll just stroll home, take it easy, and—"

"I was on a ship that went down in the Leyte Gulf—the first ship sunk by a kamikaze in World War II." He hesitated, and he looked carefully into Gene's eyes. "I got burned in the attack. You've seen the scars on my hands." He held his hands up, the backs toward Gene. "I hardly knew what was going on, but someone put me on a life raft. That was fine, but the trouble was, there were lots of men in the water. They wanted to get on our boat, and they started swimming to us. Everyone of us would have gone down if they had climbed on, so some of the men in our boat used paddles to keep the other guys away. They knocked their reaching arms away, or if they had to, they hit them over the head. Because of that, most of us on the life raft lived—and over half the guys in the water died."

Gene was stunned. He could see the old pain in Richard's eyes. The man did know. But Gene was beginning to feel something, beginning to cry, and it frightened him.

"Your dad killed a German with a knife. He grabbed him from behind and slit his throat, and he got blood all over his hands. He couldn't get that out of his mind. I'm sure he never has."

"Okay. I know what you're saying. But I . . . uh . . . better just . . ."

"Wally watched guys die around him every day—thousands of them. He made it through, but he saw lots of his friends starve to death or die from disease. When he got home, he just kept asking, the same as I did, why he lived when so many others died."

Now the tears were coming, and Gene didn't hold them back. "I was with a team that got all shot up. Every one of us got hit—and two died. One was a really good friend."

"And you wonder why you got home and he didn't, don't you?"

"Yeah. Of course I do. And then they tried to give me a medal. I covered one of my own men, like I was supposed to do, and they wanted to give me a medal for that."

"No one understands, do they? How do you feel about that? Have you ever seen your dad's medals?"

"Yeah. I found them in a drawer."

"But he didn't show them to you, did he?"

"No."

"And now you know why."

"Yeah. I guess. But I didn't think he felt that way about it." Gene was shaking, the pain in his gut feeling raw and his chest heaving as he tried to catch his breath.

Uncle Richard took hold of Gene's shoulders. "We were all there, Gene. Your dad and Wally and I. We know. You've got to talk to us."

"I can't. I just can't. I don't want to think about it."

"I know. But you have to. If you bottle it up forever, you'll have something a lot worse going on inside you than what those bullets did."

Gene didn't know. He couldn't think what was right. But he was feeling something. It felt so good just to feel. He was losing his strength, so he sat down on the grass, and Richard sat down next to him. "We could all get together and talk about this stuff. Your dad has tried. So has Wally. And we all understand why you resist. But it can make a difference."

"All right. *Maybe* I can do that. I can't say for sure right now."

Gene heard someone approaching, and then he heard Kathy's voice. "How come you two are hiding? I've been looking for both of you." Gene couldn't twist his body very well, but Kathy came around in front of him. She had been home for a few days, but Gene hadn't seen her. "Don't get up," she said.

Richard had already gotten up, and he gave Kathy a hug. They chatted for a minute, and then Richard slipped away. He seemed to know again what Gene needed: one person to talk to for now, and someone he did want to see.

Kathy kneeled in front of Gene, then leaned forward and pressed her cheek to his. "Gene, I've worried so much about you," she said. "Are things getting better?"

He smiled. "Not that much. But I'll be okay." She was looking into his eyes, and he was self-conscious about that. She had to know that he had been crying.

"They tell me you have to have one more operation."

"Yup. The fun never stops."

"What's it doing to you, Gene, all this surgery?"

Kathy always knew what the real questions were. "I don't know. I feel numb a lot, from the medicine. I start to feel a little better and then it starts all over every time they cut me again. I have this disgusting colostomy bag hanging on me. The waste comes out of me there. This next operation, they're going to hook me back up, and I can get rid of that thing. Maybe I can feel like a human being again after that."

Kathy kept looking into his eyes. Gene always felt as though she understood more about him than anyone else did. "Mom tells me you're not going to church," she said.

"Yes, and my mom told me you *are* going to church." They both laughed.

"Yes, I go to church, and that's exactly what you need to do."

"Not with this bag. It makes noises—and smells. It's humiliating."

"People understand about things like that."

"I wouldn't want to sit next to me—not if I wanted to get something out of church."

"Then you don't understand what church is, my young friend."

"And you do?"

"Yes. Some people learn very slowly, but once they get it, they get it."

"Oh, brother. Now you're going to turn into the family sermonizer. You'll take over for Grandpa."

"He told me that he got you upset, and he doesn't understand why."

"I know." Gene looked down at the grass. "I'll talk to him. It'll be okay. But not today. I need to get away from here."

"Gene, Grandpa saved my life. I made up my mind I was out of the Church, and he called me back. He made me agree to give it one more try."

"I know."

"So now I'm calling you back."

"I'm not *out* of the Church. I'm just *hiding out* for a while."

"But that isn't you, Gene. That's not who you are."

That sounded right. Emily had said the same thing that morning; she wanted Gene to be Gene again. That's what he wanted too, but it was hard to remember anything about the boy he had been before Vietnam. It was hard to remember anything.

"Come back over to the family, okay? I'll run interference for you."

"I just want to get away from here."

"Hey, I know all about that. I'm the family expert on the subject. But it's not the answer. Walk back over with me. Everyone loves you, and they want you to be with them."

Gene managed to get to his feet, and he looked back across the park. His mother was looking toward him, obviously worried, and Grandpa motioned for him to come back. He thought how much he had loved these picnics back when he had played softball with all his cousins and had stuffed himself with fried chicken and potato salad. Some things would never be the same again, but he did know that he needed to go back—as much as anything, so people wouldn't worry about him. So he walked back to the others, and he told Grandpa Thomas, "I'm sorry, Grandpa. It seems like everything upsets me right now."

Grandpa got up from his chair, and he did something he didn't do very often. He wrapped his big arms around Gene. "I talk too much," he said. "I always have. I know you're going through a rough time."

"I'll be all right," Gene told him.

Grandpa stepped back, and he looked into Gene's eyes. "You will, Gene," he said. "You'll be fine. And we'll all help you."

Gene hadn't thought he wanted any help—or needed it—but he found himself thinking that his Grandpa was right.

Author's Note

This is not the end. There will be one more book in the *Hearts of the Children* series, and that will complete the ten-book saga of the Thomas family.

Of all my challenges in attempting to write good history in these books, nothing has taxed me more than portraying the Vietnam War in a way that is balanced and fair. Gene's attitude toward the war is only one of many possible responses, and I know that some veterans of Vietnam will feel that his response does not represent their own. That, of course, is the limitation of historical fiction. It can present personal experiences in a way that history books rarely do, but it can never tell the "whole story." This is also recent history, and opinions about the war still run deep. In some cases, those feelings remain bitter. I always risk the danger of stepping on the toes of people who feel very strongly—one way or the other—about the value of the war, the way it was run, and the politics that lay behind it. I can only say that I have read widely, including many firsthand accounts, and I have talked to many vets. I have tried to understand the complex feelings of those who fought there.

It's often said of Vietnam that American forces and their allies won all the battles and lost the war. Or in other words, they fought bravely and effectively in a war they could not win, given the set of strictures and political realities they had to deal with. The men and women who served in Vietnam did what they were asked to do, and yet they were often criticized or even insulted. My hope, as always, is to honor the soldiers but never to honor war. In the case of Vietnam, perhaps all the more honor should go to the soldiers because they fought under miserable conditions in a war that made so little sense.

My attempt is not to give the final answer about Vietnam or, for that matter, anything else in the sixties. What I hope to do is offer a picture of the contending forces that were at work at that time. I have placed my characters in those complex, angry times in order to probe the dynamics of living the Christian life—the "Mormon" life—amid the realities of our complicated world. My characters are people trying to do the right thing in a world that pulls them in conflicting directions. I hope to provoke readers into thinking about similar forces at work in their own lives—and to discover the spiritual resources that are available to meet the demands.

I have read many more books this time around, especially on Vietnam. Additional books on "Lurp" teams and Ranger reconnaissance teams are: *Charlie Rangers*, by Don Ericson and John L. Rotundo (Ballantine, 1989); *Covert Ops*, by James E. Parker, Jr. (St. Martin's, 1995); *Inside Force Recon: Recon Marines in Vietnam*, by Michael Lee Lanning and Ray William Stubbe (Ballantine, 1989); *Blood on the Risers*, by John Leppelman (Ballantine, 1991). Other books I consulted on the soldier's life in Vietnam are: *. . . and a hard rain fell: A GI's True Story of the War in Vietnam*, by John Ketwig (Macmillan, 1985; Sourcebooks, 2002); *Acceptable Loss*, by Kregg P. J. Jorgenson (Ballantine, 1991); *Company Commander Vietnam*, by James Estep (Simon & Schuster, 1991); *Gone Native*, by Alan G. Cornett (Ballantine, 2000); and *Green Knight, Red Mourning*, by Richard E. Ogden (Kensington, 1985). Two excellent but chilling accounts of Vietnam written by war correspondents are *Dispatches*, by Michael Herr (Random House, 1968) and *The Cat from Hué*, by John Laurence (Public Affairs, 2002). An excellent history of the 1968–69 period in Vietnam is *After Tet*, by Ronald H. Spector (Random House, 1993). One of the best books that explains the way America became entangled in the Vietnam War is *A Bright Shining Lie*, by Neil Sheehan (Random House, 1989). And finally, the most stunning book I have read about war lately has the simple title *What Every Person Should Know About War* (Free Press, 2003). It's a book by Chris Hedges, who has written philosophically about war, but in this book he presents only the facts—simple facts that might leave you shaken, as they did me.

On the Philippines and the Peace Corps, additional books I read this time were: *All You Need Is Love: The Peace Corps and the Spirit of the 1960s*, by Elizabeth Cobbs Hoffman (Harvard, 1998); *Serving in the Peace Corps: True Stories of Three Girls in Africa and the Philippines*, by Carli Laklan (Doubleday, 1970); *Inside the Peace Corps: A Thirty-Year History*, by Karen Schwarz (Doubleday, 1993); and *From the Center of the Earth: Stories out of the Peace Corps*, by Geraldine Kennedy (Clover Park, 1991).

I worked in Public Affairs in Provo for a few years and was asked to represent the LDS Church on the Domestic Violence Coalition. I had my eyes opened about problems of family abuse. It was partly from that experience that I learned some patterns of behavior that appear in my plot about Diane and Greg. I have also talked to victims of domestic violence and found similarities in the patterns of behavior in those who abuse. I don't mean to say that every case is the same, but I think victims of abuse will recognize traits in my characters that will ring true.

I feel the need to make one correction, or apology, or excuse, or . . . I don't know what to call it. People often compliment me on my research and call it "meticulous." Well, I wasn't so meticulous about keeping track of my plot at one point in volume 3 of this series. As I was finishing up the book, I realized that I hadn't accounted for what was happening to Anna's parents, the Stoltzes. I put in a couple of details about them but didn't go back and check my outline. What I had forgotten was that I had allowed poor Sister Stoltz to die in a previous volume. Admittedly, authors sometimes enjoy their seemingly supernatural powers in creating plots and people, but I never intended to kill a character and then bring her back to life. So in the second printing of *How Many Roads?* dear Sister Stoltz is laid safely back to rest, and she remains at rest (where I promise she will stay) in this volume. I received only two letters about my mistake, but others must have noticed. I'm forced to admit that my meticulousness appears to have limits. Maybe I'm getting old, or tired, or both.

My son Tom thought he had caught me in another error. When Kathy attends church in Manila, I describe some young men preparing the sacrament. Tom wrote on my manuscript, "But this is Sunday School." Tom is thirty-six, so I understand his confusion. He doesn't remember—and perhaps no one under forty will remember—when the sacrament was passed twice on Sunday: at Sunday School in the morning and again at sacrament meeting in the evening. That was before the three-hour block changed a lot of things. Those were the days of two-and-a-half minute talks and practice time for learning less-familiar hymns, all of which took place during "opening exercises" for Sunday School. I don't know all that because I'm meticulous but *only* because I'm old.

One other little matter: I have occasionally used real people in my novels as minor characters, as I did with the mission presidents in Germany. When I have done that, I have called attention to that fact in these notes. Let me just point out here that there was no President Finlinson in the Philippines, and no President Luna in Manila. They are fictional characters.

I have many people to thank, as usual. My friend Major Richard N. Jeppesen, USMC (Ret), advised me on my military chapters once again, this time along with his friend and Vietnam vet, LTC Jeffrey C. Berry, U.S. Army (Ret). I asked Mary Ellen Edmunds, Sandra Rogers, and Regina Anderson questions about the Philippines in the late sixties and early seventies, and I appreciated their information. The following friends and relatives read my manuscript and did everything from catching my typos to advising me on my plot and characters. Those include: my wife, Kathy; Tom and Kristen Hughes; Amy and Brad Russell; Pam Russell; Rob and Stacy Hughes; and Shauna and David Weight. My good friends Emily Watts and Jack Lyon have been my editors again on this book. I doubt that most readers comprehend the crucial role editors play in the process of turning a manuscript into a book. I'm indebted to both of them.

I have dedicated this book to Sheri Dew. Most LDS Church members know her as a former member of the general Relief Society presidency and current president and CEO of Deseret Book. But to me she is a friend who believed in this project from the beginning. When I first thought of writing historical fiction about the World War II era, Sheri was vice president of publishing at Deseret Book, and she got excited about the idea. She helped me develop the concept, and she, along with Ronald Millett, then president of Deseret Book, gave me a contract on the basis of an outline and some sample chapters. At that time I had written many children's and young-adult books, but Sheri believed that I could not only write for "grown-ups" but also portray the vast saga of a Mormon family surviving World War II. After I completed that series, Sheri suggested I write about the sixties, and when I proposed continuing with the Thomas family, she liked the concept. I jumped into another huge project.

A publisher/editor serves a writer in delicate, important ways. Sheri read a draft of *Rumors of War,* the first volume of *Children of the Promise*, and told me, "You need to cut about fifty pages out of the middle hundred and fifty." That was not so delicate. The delicate part was the trust she gave me. She believed I could write such challenging books when I was not entirely certain about that myself. For that, I owe her a great deal. *Children of the Promise* and *Hearts of the Children* have turned out to be a kind of "life's work," but I never would have started the project without Sheri's encouragement.